HENRY TREECE was born in the West Midlands in December 1911. Educated at Wednesbury High School he won a scholarship to Birmingham University where he graduated in 1933. War-time service as an intelligence officer with R.A.F. Bomber Command interrupted a very fine teaching career. His literary career began as a poet; Messrs Faber published four volumes. Contact with George Orwell helped him enter the world of radio broadcasting of verse plays, short stories and schools programmes. In 1952 came Treece's first historical novel, *The Dark Island*, and during the years until his death in June 1966 he wrote a succession of Celtic novels for adults, including *The Great Captains*, *The Golden Strangers* and *Red Queen, White Queen*, as well as the Greek novels *Electra*, *Jason* and *Oedipus*. *The Green Man* in 1966 was the last adult work. His work also included criticism and a number of co-edited anthologies *War-Time Harvest*, *Transformation* and others. Among the many historical novels for children are the Roman books *Legions of the Eagle* and *The Eagles Have Flown;* the trilogy *Viking's Dawn, The Road to Miklagard* and *Viking's Sunset;* *Man with a Sword* (Hereward the Wake); and the much praised posthumously published *The Dream Time*. Mary Treece, his widow, lives in Abingdon, in Oxfordshire.

Henry Treece

THE
DARK ISLAND

Introduced by Michael Moorcock
Illustrated by James Cawthorn

SAVOY BOOKS
In association with
NEW ENGLISH LIBRARY
TIMES MIRROR

First paperback edition
Savoy Books Ltd, 1980

First published by
Gollancz, 1952

Published by
John Lane The Bodley Head 1958

Copyright Henry Treece 1952

Cover Artwork: Michael Heslop

Published by Savoy Books Ltd,
279 Deansgate, Manchester M3 4EW, England.

Typesetting: Arena Typesetting, Manchester.

Reproduced, printed and bound in Great Britain by
Hazell Watson & Viney Ltd, Aylesbury, Bucks

ISBN 0 86130 021 1

Introduction

By making living men of his historical characters Treece joined
the small group of novelists who used the historical romance
for moral and literary purposes of their own. His contemporaries
included Graves and Duggan. In my view Treece outshines them
by virtue of a deeper understanding of the pre-Christian mind
and a less self-conscious style which allowed him to express a
greater intensity of emotion — and a greater range, too. He was
a committed Romantic, like Mervyn Peake (whom he knew) or
Dylan Thomas (who was his friend) and refused to let any
fashionable considerations distort his vision.

Since Treece, a number of writers — Garner is the best known
I suppose — have dealt with the Celtic spirit to the point where
the 'dark mind' is almost a cliché and, as I've said elsewhere,
Herne the Hunter seems to have become an obligatory function-
ary in at least one scene in each book. But none of these newer
writers — good though Garner, Sutcliffe and Cooper, say, can
be — has been able to capture the sense of raw passion of adult
men and women who are not always mystically inclined yet
dwell in a world of mysticism; who are as practical in their
daily desires and ambitions as any twentieth century people, yet
who acknowledge a reality of symbols and supernatural forces
which does not so much shape their lives as amplify and define
them. There is little overt 'magic' in these tales, yet the magic —
the mystery — permeates them. In a cruder sort of story (even
one drawing on *The Golden Bough* as Treece's surely does) the
sorcery would be isolated — an event. In Treece it is as much
part of life as the wild landscapes of Dark Age Britain, as the
stones and hills, the forests and the seas, the fortified townships
and isolated villages dwarfed by the great grey skies.

Treece was an aggressive and dedicated Romantic; a chief
spokesman for the Apocalyptic Movement of the late 30s and
the 40s, very much out of tempo with what might be called the
Austerity Movement which found its voices in the work of
social realists, reductionists of the belted-raincoat-and-cup-of-tea
-in-a-Lyons-tea-shop brigade who derived their inspiration from

the well-bred populism of Auden or Day Lewis. These Angry Younger Men mocked the creative imagination because, perhaps, they equated it with their limited experience of degenerate romanticism (Nazism and so on) and the threat of chaos represented by the A-Bomb, because they failed to understand that the real Romantic does not posture, he *inhabits* (as do Treece's characters) a world which to them would be a world of madness, and he has to bring terrible disciplines to bear on himself and his work in order to control and shape his visions and communicate them:

> In my definition, the writer who senses the chaos, the turbulence, the laughter and the tears, the order and the peace of the world in its entirety, is an Apocalyptic writer. His utterance will be prophetic, for he is observing things which less sensitive men have not yet come to notice; and his words are prophetic, they will tend to be incantatory, and so musical. At times, even, that music may take control and lead the writer from recording his vision almost to creating another vision . . . Throughout this book, my attempt has been to approach life and art (with particular reference to poetry) from as many angles as possible, attacking chaos on all sides in an effort to attain something like a unified vision. The impulse behind that attempt is a Romantic one. . . I attempt to prove some correlation between that Romanticism and the form of Anarchism laid down by Herbert Read. . .

(Foreword to *How I See Apocalypse,* 1946)

Those who know Treece's historical novels — or possibly only his juvenile historical novels — often do not know that Treece was an important publicist, critic and anthologist for the Romantic movement which existed around the time of the second world war and with which Mervyn Peake was sometimes associated. It was a movement which tended to place a high value on being Celtic and produced, as a consequence, a legacy of sentimentalism tending later to discredit the original spirits of that movement, just as for a while the work of Yeats and Synge came to be similarly discredited in Ireland (unfortunately maudlin drunkards are much attracted to the more obvious aspects of such a movement). This Apocalyptic Movement found its first real expression in the anthology *The White Horseman* (1941) whose introduction (by G. S. Fraser) Treece quotes in his own collection of essays *How I See Apocalypse:*

The New Apocalypse, in a sense, derives from Surrealism, and one might even call it a dialectical development of it; the next stage forward. It embodies what is positive in Surrealism, 'the effort,' in Herbert Read's phrase, 'to realize some of the dimensions and characteristics of man's submerged being'. It denies what is negative — Surrealism's own denial of man's right to exercise conscious control, either of his political and social destinies, or of the material offered to him, as an artist, by his subconscious mind. It recognises, that is, that the intellect and its activity in willed action is part of the living completeness of man, just as the formal element is part of the living completeness of art.

I think it is important to an appreciation of Treece's work for the reader to understand how much of a conscious artist he was, how much he sought to achieve in his novels. Because a Romantic tends to shun classical forms of criticism or self-expression, people are inclined to believe that he is somehow an inspired naif. Mervyn Peake has suffered critically because of this view, often propagated by people who should know better. Nobody who knew Treece or read his criticism or his poetry could underestimate either his intellect, his talent or his powers of control. And perhaps it is this control, this ability to shape a genuinely mythic tragedy from his material, that makes Treece one of the greatest of all historical novelists. He chose characters who like him existed in a world teeming with images charged with meaning, naive only in that they could not 'read the signs' in a sophisticated modern way (as Treece did). Mervyn Peake wrote in one of his poems 'I am too rich already, for my eyes mint gold. . .' Only those who have experienced this wealth can have any understanding of what energies are involved in the ordering and spending of it. Most writers — even those working in a romantic idiom — grasp desperately for images and ideas, nurse them and make the absolute maximum use of them. Treece, like Peake, merely sought to describe and make coherent the wild, colourful and sensuously textured world in which, day to day, he lived. And that is why he chose, in the main, to write in the form of the historical novel, where his imagination would be allowed, as he saw it, a fuller stretch. In his day, it could be argued, it was one of the few 'admissable' forms in which the romantic imagination was allowed to flourish. One can only regret that he is not still alive and writing in a climate so much better suited to his temperament, for an audience so much better able to appreciate his virtues. As it is we are left with a large body of work (prose, poetry, criticism) which thoroughly deserves republication and I applaud with all my heart these new editions of his great Celtic tetralogy.

Michael Moorcock
Ladbroke Grove
August 1978

PLACES IN THE STORY

Abus	The River Humber
Armorica	Brittany
Brigantia	The lands north of the Humber
Camulodun(um)	Colchester
Dubra	Dover
Eburac(um)	York
Evrauc	An invented name, near York
Gesoriacum	Boulogne
Lindum	Lincoln
Londinium	London
Lyonesse	The drowned land of the West
Mai Dun	Maiden Castle
Mona	Anglesey
Segedun(um)	Wallsend in Northumberland
Siluria	South Wales
Sorbiodun(um)	Old Sarum
Tamesa	The River Thames
Verulum	Verulamium, or St. Albans
Viroconium	Wroxeter in Shropshire

Other proper names

Caradoc	Caratacus
Cunobelin	Cunobelinus, or Cymbeline

THE DARK ISLAND

Britain is a dark island of mists and woods. It lies farther north than any other known land, so that the sun is seldom seen there. The people of this island are brave in battle but fearful of their gods and priests.

Their chief god is Lugh, who is the sun; he is so powerful that his name may not even be mentioned by believers. He lives in the mistletoe and his shrine is the oak. His priests are the Tree-men, or Druids, who cut the sacred mistletoe at full moon with their golden knives. They are the law-makers and the teachers, the poets and the physicians. They speak Lugh's words for him, and then even the kings, of whom there are many in Britain, are afraid.

The animals of this island are like those of other countries west of Rome, but with this difference that they are all hairy creatures; the dog, the wild-cat, the long-horned cattle and the badger. Some of them, such as the hen and the hare, are sacred and may not easily be killed. All these animals, together with such birds as the eagle, the owl and the hawk, give their names to the Brotherhoods which are so loved by these Britons.

The men of this island are not of one sort; some are dark, others yellow, and then there are the red ones. They have all come to the island in boats at different times; but once there, they all fall under the spell of the great stones. In this, as in the blue rank marks which they make upon their foreheads, they resemble the people of the East; the men of the rising sun and the men of the setting sun.

Arminius Agricola, Ambassador to Camulodunum
A.D. 25—A.D. 30

PROLOGUE
A.D. 30

THE MILITARY ATTACHE'S voice cut, harsh and un-
friendly, across the great thatched and timbered hall. "By
Jupiter and his seven-headed dog, but I can show you a sort of
magic to beat that!"

Heavy with the native mead, he clattered and stumbled
through the peat-smoke towards the log-fire in the centre of the
hall, the silver bracelets at his wrists making gleaming arcs in the
firelight as he swung his long arms about drunkenly. He was a
short man, almost as broad as he was high, bull-necked, and
bow-legged from much riding, swarthy as an African, with
curling black hair and bright Spanish eyes, an ex-centurian, risen
from the ranks, whose coloured ribbons, hanging from the
shoulders of his body-armour, proclaimed the service as a soldier
in India, Scythia and Germany that lay behind him.

"Damn me, but I've seen a one-eyed Russian who could show
a thing or two to your wizards! This stuff is only fit to trick
you blue-faced, sheep-eating mist dwellers! By God, but it
wouldn't do for Rome! We like real entertainment there, I can
tell you!"

He laughed loudly and stupidly as he swayed on his feet by
the fire. His grotesque, dwarfish shadow leapt and pirouetted
against the heavy skin hangings on the walls, and for a moment
there was cold silence in the hall.

The tribal leaders, magnificent in their long tartan cloaks and
gold gorgets, suddenly stopped talking and laughing and drinking.
They stared in amazement at their Roman guest, smiling just a
little ironically. Two slaves, lying shackled with iron chains by
the wall, put down their harp and flute and listened, mouths
wide open in wonder, for they came from a far western tribe
that had no contact with Rome and did not understand its
language; yet, from the sudden tense atmosphere around them,
among their Belgic conquerors, they knew that something
strange and perhaps dangerous was happening. They guessed
that the black foreigner was about to do something unusual.
Even the treasured war-horses, standing knee-deep in straw at
the dark end of the hall, ceased pawing the ground and were
still, snuffling the thick air; and the three great woolly-haired
sheepdogs that lolled in a privileged position close to the fire

turned their white heads towards the man who had dared to shout in the King's presence.

Then another voice called out from the long tables. "Silence, Lepidus; remember that you are a guest in Britain. Remember that you are at the King's table. Come back here and sit down!" It was the Ambassador to Camulodun himself, Arminius Agricola, an old German who had in his time broken more Roman heads than most until they made him a citizen of the Empire. He was a moderate man, the warrior turned diplomat, and always anxious not to provoke the tribes among whom he was stationed. One could not afford to upset the tribes just now. Now while they were so amenable, taking on Roman ways and paying their tributes with no complaints. It wasn't as though Rome had any real right to tributes, or any real reason for keeping an ambassador among the Catuvellauni, except that, after Caesar the "Hairy One", the Senate had thought it might be advisable not to relinquish the Empire's moral hold, fragile as it was, on these Britons of the south-east. And here was this idiot, Lepidus, letting himself get drunk on the native wine and acting like any soft-headed barbarian! But what could one expect, sending a Spaniard out to act as military attache! The Spaniards weren't even fit yet to be citizens. They were too headstrong, altogether too fiery. There was too much African in them. What was needed were more Germans or more Gauls. They could keep their heads among these Britons. They knew how to drink. They knew more about the British gods. In fact, Arminius speculated, the British gods weren't so very different from the German gods. Just a name or two, here and there, but the sacrifices were the same, as near as made no matter. Yet here was a Spaniard making fun of the British magic, and that involved gods. Arminius glanced down the long room and saw that the chief druid, Bydd, the King's brother, had got up from the table and was making his way outside, muttering and waving his arms about. He saw him kick out at one of the slaves as he passed. That was a bad sign. One might laugh at the druids in their white shirts, and their savage wreaths of mistletoe hanging round their ears, but they were a power not to be despised.

Arminius looked along the table. The chiefs were restive, and their glances becoming more and more hostile. They were a strange unpredictable people, the Britons, never the same two minutes together. Arminius stood up, pulling his tartan cloak about him, toga-fashion. "Sit down, Lepidus, I order it," he began, but a rough, woad-streaked hand took the ambassador by the arm and pulled him back onto the bench. "Let the lord speak! If he is happy, let him amuse himself! No doubt he will amuse us too!" There was a certain menacing sarcasm in the voice, and Arminius suddenly became sensitive of the respect due to Rome. He turned sharply towards the tribesman who had spoken to him. He was a tall, red-haired man, whose blue-lined face was made even more sinister by the old sword-cut which had broken his nose and laid open both of his cheeks nearly to the ears.

"But he will bring discredit to the Empire, my friend," began Arminius, a little too pompously. The broken-nosed tribesman scuffled and spat on the floor and then drank another noisy draught from his silver-rimmed mead-horn. "To hell with the Empire! To hell with Rome!" he mumbled. He began to turn towards Arminius, pulling angrily at his long moustaches, remembering his wounds. Then suddenly he coughed and slid down from his seat under the table, already asleep.

Lepidus began to shout again, turning from side to side, annoyed now by the sneering faces that showed wherever the fire gleamed. "Bring me a sword, one of you! I'll show you magic!" Here and there along the room hands slid down to sword-belts and steel glistened in the light of the torches. "Bring me a sword! You, with the eagle's feathers in your hair, where's your sword?" He stared across the hall, and a tall, dark-skinned chieftain out of the hills rose from the table. He inclined his head towards the end of the room, then turned and spat in the direction of the fire. There was a hush as he flung his long cloak over his shoulders and stalked from the hall.

Then, for the first time, the King spoke. Cunobelin, King of the Belgic Catuvellauni, whose dominion stretched from Belgium to the Welsh border; a massive man with a nose like the beak of a hawk and a red beard that hung in two great spikes from his chin, whose woollen tartan cloak was decorated with innumerable small silver acorns, so that wherever he turned he was followed by flashes of white light, whose great arms were bound from wrist to elbow with coral and amber bracelets, and whose deep vibrant voice filled the great hall, bringing down silence on all the tumbled mass of men and animals that clustered under his roof. When he spoke it seemed that the fire stopped crackling and the black cattle outside stayed in their bellowing. "Let the slaves play 'The red bulls of Cader'," he said, "or else give the Roman a sword and let him amuse himself."

A serving-girl whispered to the two slaves, who shrank in the shadows as the King spoke, but they shook their tousled heads from side to side, with eyes wide with fear. A young courtier leaned towards the King. "The slaves do not know that music, sir," he said. The King's mood changed in a flash. "Then, by God, let the soldier have his sword. And mind that you give him a long one; I see that he needs support!"

Lepidus heard the King's words and bowed arrogantly towards him. It was too dark now for him to see the King's face as he spoke but the Roman sensed that Cunobelin was making a fool of him.

"Your honour!" shouted Arminius, rising to his feet again. But before he could go on, hands took him by the shoulders and forced him down into his seat. Then one of the clansmen slid a sword along the floor towards the Roman, and the tribesmen sat back to watch the fun.

It was a long sword they gave him, almost as long as the Roman himself, a slim, Moorish blade, set in a golden hilt, bartered for sheepskins and tin from some Gallic mercenary who must have served in an African campaign. Lepidus took the weapon and ran his eye along its edge. He bent the thin blade back and forth between his strong fingers, then into an arc above his head. He seemed very satisfied with his toy. Then he stepped away from the fire and, setting his feet firm in the rushes, made the bright steel whistle in silver circles round his shoulders. For some moments nothing could be heard in the hall but the hiss of the sword and the crackling of wood from the fire. The talk at the tables was still, and the tribesmen looked at the squat figure with interest, for he was undoubtedly a swordsman. Even the kept-men, the men-at-arms, rough undisciplined fighters who carried a sword or a javelin for the chief who was able to offer the most pay and loot, leaning against the skin-draped walls, drinking their fill or playing at love with the serving-maids, even they paused in their games to watch the Roman.

At last Lepidus rested on his sword, a fantastic hunched figure in his great cloak and steel breastplate. He looked round the hall, conscious that all eyes were on him, appraising his skill, wondering what he would do next. "Throw me an apple!" he called to the tables. And a young clansman, less drunk or proud than the rest, tossed an apple through the air towards the Roman with a laugh. Lepidus watched the fruit as it swung through the smoke. The long sword swept out and the apple fell, neatly halved, at his feet.

There was some murmur of approval, though this was hardly the magic they had all expected. Most able fighting-men could do as much without attributing their skill to the spirits. Then the young Briton who had flung the apple turned and touched his forehead with the back of his hand towards the King's shadowy figure at the head of the table. He vaulted easily over the table and stood beside the Roman. "Lend me the sword," he said. And he stood and faced the fire, his back towards the watching tribesmen.

"Glyn, my friend," he called, "do you throw me an apple as I threw one to the Roman."

Once more an apple was thrown, and, as it reached its mid-point across the room, the young man turned and ran towards it. His long sword moved so swiftly that it was hardly possible for the eyes of the watchers to follow its full course. But it moved across, and then down, and the apple fell, this time cut into four parts.

Now the hall was filled with the noises of shouting and the banging of horn-cups on the solid tables. The young man bowed gravely and insultingly towards Lepidus and handed back the weapon. "It is your turn again," he said roguishly. The Roman's eyes flashed, and he made a wry face. Then he bowed, as insultingly as his opponent, and, swaggering across to the nearest table, plunged his hand into a dish and took from it a handful of plump round olives. In the firelight he selected seven of the largest and flung the others at the sleeping dogs.

"Now, my friends," he said, "I want you to watch this very closely, for this is not the child's play you are used to. This is the real magic." But as Lepidus flung the olives into the air the young tribesman laughed out in amusement. The Roman stood still, glaring at him, while the olives fell back onto the straw-covered floor. For a moment Lepidus did not move, but continued to stare at his young rival. The clansmen at the tables rocked with laughter and beat their drinking-horns against their plates. So the Roman was a fool, after all! At first it looked as though he was going to turn out to be a swordsman! But he must be a droll, that one! The way he stared at the olives as they fell about his feet! Only Arminius was still serious and aloof. "Lepidus," he ordered, "sit down at once, I command you!" The Roman's face was dark with anger as he turned towards the ambassador. It was uncertain, in the guttering light of the torches, whether or not he made a gesture of contempt towards his superior, then, with an abrupt movement, he turned towards the young Briton. "Have the goodness to take the ambassador's advice and sit down, sir," he said evenly. "Your turn will come again, in a moment. I shall not be long in finishing the game."

At first the young man bridled, and he made a fumbling movement inside his cloak, but a voice from the tables quietened him and he sat down to wait on a heap of skins by the fire. Then once more the sturdy little soldier selected himself seven olives, and once more he cast them above his head, this time, it seemed, with an utter negligence. His head moved rapidly as he watched their motion, then his sword sprang again, flying in and out like a silver humming-bird. And when the half-stupefied tribesmen could see again, the olives lay scattered all about the fire, each one cut in two.

This time there was no shouting, but only an awe-stricken silence in the hall. Then Cunobelin spoke again, wonder showing even in his proud voice. "Come here, Lepidus," he said. "Such handiwork deserves an appropriate reward." The King slipped off one of his coral bracelets and held it out, but Lepidus did not move. Looking above the King's head he said gravely, "Thank you, King Cunobelinus, but I am a Roman soldier and my only reward comes from serving Rome." His bright eyes stared arrogantly towards the King, and his thick lips curled almost contemptuously as he spoke. Arminius left his seat and went to the King. "Forgive him, sir," he said, almost in tears, "but he is the worse for drink." For a moment it seemed that the thunder would surely break out and the lightning strike down this too-daring soldier. Then, when the tension was at its greatest, a wizened old man, dressed in coloured rags, ran out into the circle of light and began to intone in a nasal, high-pitched voice, swaying from side to side, his eyes shut tight and his thin hands held high above his head.

From table to table a murmur spread. "Roddhu! It is Roddhu himself back again!" Men nudged each other and forgot even to drink. "They said he was dead!" . . . "My brother saw the sword pass through his throat!"' . . . "Quiet, this one has died many times. He always comes again." And all men stared towards the little moaning figure, half-aghast.

At first the smoke swirled out of the fire and completely hid him from view. Then the flames burnt blue and yellow and at last green, and Roddhu seemed to be standing in the midst of them. And as he swayed and sang it seemed to all men there that a great wolf ran the length of the hall, howling, and disappeared through the far door. Then a pack of hounds following him and baying. The air was full of dust and straw for a moment. Then men saw that the door was still closed and that the fire was burning clear again. And no one dared to speak for a time. Then Lepidus stepped from out of the shadows behind the fire again and touched the ragged creature on the shoulder. "Little master, you are clever, very clever. But can you do this?"

And he took two sharp knives from a table and, flinging them into the air, caught them both and balanced them on the thumbnail of each hand. As the firelight played on them, it seemed that they were solid limbs, so steadily did they stand from the Roman's hand. Then, as the men round the hall hissed in approval of this feat, Lepidus tossed the knives above his head, only a little way, and bowed towards the King. All eyes in the hall followed the bright tracks the blades made, until, a yard above the Roman's head, they disappeared, and no knives fell to the floor.

Only the little old man grinned, and nodded towards Lepidus, his eyes twinkling. "Yes," he said, in his child's voice, "you have learnt something. A little, perhaps; and you would have made a good pupil if I could have caught you before you learned pride. But it is too late now." The old man turned to move away, but Lepidus was on him like a tiger. "Stay, old bungler," he roared. "Let us play together, so that I can show your people a few gipsy tricks. You will not have seen their like, I promise you."

The old man turned in his tracks, and as his face came round into the firelight the warriors at the tables gasped at what they saw. It was the face of an ape, and not the man they had seen intoning by the fire. And the voice was changed too; it was a deep voice that spoke words they did not understand. But they saw the Roman raise his long sword and thrust viciously at the wizard, and they saw the old creature leap back with a surprising agility, so that Lepidus had his work cut out to keep his balance. Then they saw that Roddhu had picked up a willow wand from the floor and was using it like a sword, and that each time the Roman thrust, the frail stick turned his bright blade away as though it did not exist. And suddenly they saw Roddhu touch the Roman lightly on the shoulder with his wand, and they whistled in amazement, for the Romans stopped dead in the midst of a thrust and stood quite still, like a frozen man or a statue.

Then Roddhu flung his stick into the fire, and when it had

done twisting like a snake and had fallen to ashes, Lepidus moved again, like a man who has just awakened from a long sleep. At first he seemed puzzled, then hurt, and as the onlookers stared, they saw him shake himself, like a dog that has just come from the water, and plunge his sword as far as the hilt through the crackling bundle of rags that was Roddhu.

At this stroke of treachery, tumult broke out round the tables, and half the men in the hall were on their feet, bright blades flashing in their hands, their hearts turned towards the Roman. But before they could move clear of the benches they saw the old man, standing bolt upright with the long sword through him, pass his hands before the Roman's face. For a moment the air was full of strange twangling sounds, and a smell like burning flesh came from the fire. Then they heard the long sword fall to the ground, and they saw it lying in the straw, with never a trace of blood on its blade. Roddhu was standing still, smiling with his old face again, waiting and gently rubbing his hands as he looked at Lepidus. And where the Roman had been standing they now saw a tottering skeleton, hung about with rusted armour. Then a strong and sickening stench of decay swept through the hall, and they saw only a heap of fine dust. A metal bracelet clattered to the floor and rolled away into the darkness, and a sudden gust of air, that set the torches fluttering, ran along the walls, shaking the sheep-skin hangings and striking every man with a strange chill. And when they looked again, even the heap of dust had gone, nor was Roddhu anywhere to be seen.

Outside a wolf howled, and the men in the hall heard the black cattle crying out in fear. Then the voice of Arminius sounded, hysterical and afraid, "By God, you've slain him! You've slain him! The Senate shall hear of this, I tell you! Rome shall hear of this!"

Part One
CHAPTER ONE
A.D. 33

AS THE SUN rose slowly through the mists, a black cloud in the eastern sky suddenly flamed into gold, and a flock of birds, startled by this angry splendour, took wing and flew, twittering with fear, away to the west.

And from the waiting people massed over the broad plains came a subdued cry of wonder before they turned their eyes again to the great stone circle that stood, gaunt and black, against the reds, yellows and faint blues of the dawn.

Most of the watchers had been waiting in the heather, lashed by sudden squalls of rain and beaten breathless by the wind, since the evening before; and now, almost without warning, was happening that strange thing they had wandered a hundred miles to see. The sun was rising, and soon its first ray would strike inevitably down the eastern avenue of the temple, between the great trilithons, and rest upon the ancient sacrifice-stone.

Standing round the outer circle were the over-lords and the chieftains with their households. Some lived on the plain itself, coming from Sorbiodun; others had ridden along the upland roads for a week, from the most northern limits of Brigantia, to be there. Amongst them and nearest the sun-stone waited Cunobelin's own family; the descendants of the great Cassivelaun and the royal house of the Belgae: his mother, wife and sisters, then their husbands and the boy princes, Reged and Caradoc, Morag and Beddyr, and young Gwyndoc, son of the Chieftain of Cantii, who would be chieftain himself one day, when he came of age, but who was as yet, like his royal friends, only twelve, and so ruled with his aunt as regent.

For the boys it had been a long, dull wait. The cloaked grown-ups stood before them, hiding the blood stone from their eyes, and behind them the royal guard stood in close formation, preventing them from seeing what the massed tribesfolk were doing. Earlier on, an Italian seaman had let loose his pet monkey among the soldiers, and it had hopped about cheekily on their horned helmets, causing the crowd great amusement and sending the lads into fits of laughter. But the monkey had gone. A zealous captain had broken its back with his spear-shaft, and there was nothing at all to see now, only the slow glow in the east.

Suddenly an old woman began to call out and whine. "O King, it is my son upon the stone before you. He did no evil. He loved the gods. Why must you take him, lord?" The boys heard her start to cry and then scream; then she was silent and Beddyr looked with his wide black eyes at a gaunt soldier he knew and said, "What has happened, Pedair? Why is the old woman crying, then?" And the soldier, his eyes still fixed on the blood-stone, said, "It is nothing, Prince. Only an old cockle-woman selling her wares." And before the boy could ask again, a group of black-haired Picts began the long low rhythmic moaning that is the prelude to their death-dances; and a party of soldiers had to break ranks to quieten them down.

So the boys got onto their knees and tried to look between the legs of the chiefs, but they could see little. "He's got red hair," whispered Morag, excitedly. "They always have," said his brother. Then they shrank back, blinded for a moment by the sun's first long ray, that struck inch by inch along the eastern avenue. And when they could see again, Caradoc said to his friend Gwyndoc, "I can see Father's feet. He's dressed like a druid." "What is he doing?" Gwyndoc asked. "He's pushing a stick into the red-haired one! No, it isn't a stick, it's a mistletoe stake! He's having to push very hard, the red one is wriggling so much!" Then they became aware that they were enveloped by a great silence, that no one, the length or breadth of the plain, was speaking or moving, and they fell silent too. And a strange sound came to their ears; it was like a hare when you tried to wring its neck and couldn't quite. Then there was sobbing and gurgling, and all over the plain people were gasping and moving and talking again. The boys turned round and jumped up and down in front of the soldiers, trying to look over their shoulders, but they couldn't see much. Beddyr said to his soldier-friend, "Pick me up, Pedair, then I can see what the people are doing." But he had to ask twice before the soldier shook him away, rather roughly. Then he saw that the man's eyes were filled with tears, and he wondered why.

Then a noise broke out behind the soldiers. It was a party of Brigantes who had got themselves drunk with exhaustion and the local mead, and they were dancing and singing and throwing offerings into the stone circle—belts and bracelets, and even swords. "What's wrong with the Roman?" Caradoc asked his friend, pointing to the new ambassador. He was bent double over the grass, his head almost between his knees. The chiefs were standing away from him, some of them smiling in a crafty, grown-up way. "Why, he's being sick," answered Gwyndoc. "I wonder whatever for?"

"It was something he ate," said a dry-voiced soldier behind them.

"Well, he shouldn't eat it," said Caradoc wisely. "He knows that our cooking is different from theirs in Rome."

And the boys laughed many times to each other about the Roman as they were shepherded to the litter to start the long journey back by stages to Camulodun, where their father had his palace.

As they waited in the semi-darkness of the skin-hung box for the family to assemble they watched the vast crowds slowly breaking up and filing off in various directions across the plain. A bright midsummer sun was shining now, and it was easy to see for miles. It seemed to the lads that everybody in Britain must be there that morning. Then Morag came to the litter, late as usual, but looking strangely worried. "Where have you been?" asked his cousin sharply. "You should have been here, waiting with us."

"I am sorry, lord," answered the boy, "but I was watching Uncle."

Caradoc looked at Morag as fiercely as he could. "Watching my father?" he said. "What was wrong with him, then, that you should take it on yourself to watch him?"

Morag looked abashed as he crept into the litter. When he answered, it seemed that his mind was not on what he was saying. "Nothing, Caradoc," he said. "He was all right, but his hands were red. Right up his arms to the shoulder. Oh, I'm very sorry I saw it, Caradoc." And the lad put his head down and sobbed as though his heart was too full to hold his tears.

Caradoc made Gwyndoc vow not to speak to him for twenty minutes, but both boys were strangely troubled, nevertheless.

After a time the King, Cunobelin, came to his litter, walking slowly and looking thoughtful. At his side the archdruid strode, his hands clasped behind him. They were followed at a distance by the blue-robed Ovates, and then the more privileged subsidiary chieftains. The boys watched the King and the druid get into the litter before them, and at a signal the party started on its way to Sorbiodun, where they were to spend some hours before setting off again northwards for Camulodun.

As they jolted along the road across the downs the boys gradually became more and more sleepy, and soon they were nodding off. From the litters in front, the men's deep voices were going on and on, in a steady monotone. Then suddenly Caradoc came back to awareness at a change in his father's tone. The King's voice had become sharp and, it seemed, almost angry, and the archdruid was very quiet. At last the boy heard his own name mentioned, and then his father's words seemed to come clearer and clearer, till Caradoc thought that everyone in the procession must hear what he was saying.

"It is no good, Bydd, something is bound to happen to us before long, the way things are going. I've done my best to give the south unity; and if they were left alone, the tribes would stick together without quarrelling. They've learned their lesson since the Caesar came: they know that the Roman eagle pecks out the eyes of the stray sheep. We've got good markets in Gaul and half-way along the Mediterranean; we can sell our corn, our cattle, our minerals and our slaves anywhere where there's the Roman Peace, and in many places where there isn't!"

The druid's voice replied patiently but a little wearily, as though he had listened to the King saying the same things many times before. "Yes, brother, I know all that. No one can say that you have not done wonderful things with the clans, and even if you've always avoided a full Roman alliance, such as the Gauls have got, you've helped more than anyone else ever did to spread Roman standards of living in the south-east. And no one could grumble at the money you have brought into the country. That last trade-pact has attracted more Roman capital to Britain than I ever thought existed! You've built a royal city and you've struck a coinage that Rome itself cannot scoff at. The Belgic territory is stable as far as I, or any man, can see. So what are you worrying about?"

The King's voice was almost harsh. "I'm not worrying, Bydd," he said. "I have gone beyond that stage. I am not worrying because I have found an answer to my problem. And the problem is this: I shall die before long—no, don't look so surprised, you've been expecting it almost as long as I have. I'm nearer seventy than sixty, and that cut I got under the breast-bone against the Germans last year hasn't helped me much. I could hardly get the stake in this morning, he writhed so much. It was harder than it has ever been this morning. I couldn't see what I was doing most of the time. As soon as the sun struck along the avenue, my head began to swim and my eyes clouded over. No, there's not much doubt about it: I shan't be officiating at the stones very much longer. And, this is the point, what will happen then? I'll tell you, because I don't suppose your book-learning and mistletoe-grafting have given you much of an insight into politics. This is what will happen: the kingdom will naturally be divided between my sons, Caradoc and Reged. And that sounds all right—but it isn't. The lads will be too young to look after their own affairs and they'll have to have a regent. Now there's only one regent that I can name with justice, and that's Banhir. He belongs to the family of Cassivelaun, just as we do. He has as much right almost to the crown as I have—and he hates Rome as a dog hates a wolf! To make my sons joint kings under him is to declare war on Rome."

Bydd broke in, speaking slowly, "But, brother, you have only got half the story there. Banhir can do nothing against Rome without money. The merchants have the money, the commercial interests in Camulodun and Londinium, and they will never allow Banhir to lose their markets for them!"

The King's voice was almost angry when he replied, "There you go again, jumping to conclusions! Thank the gods that it was I and not you that was elected to rule the Belgae! You see no further than your nose. Yes, of course it's the merchants who have the money, and of course they don't want to lose their markets. Nor would they! They would invite the Romans here before I was cold in my bed, I can assure you. Now do you see what I mean?"

There was silence for a time, then Bydd spoke again, but uncertainly this time. "Then, what can be done? There seems no way out of the difficulty." And Caradoc was surprised and a little shocked to hear his father's great gusts of laughter coming once again. "Why, Bydd, that's where brains come in! The kingdom will not go to Caradoc, or Reged!" The druid's voice sounded horrified: "What, you intend to disinherit your own blood, your true sons? What are you thinking of, Cunobelin?"

And the King said, "I'm thinking of Britain and trade and prosperity first. My sons come next. It's no good handing over to them a land that will crumble before their eyes and leave them paupers or corpses. No, Bydd, I have an eye to the future. When they take their kingdoms, I want them to be secure."

"What is in your mind, then?" asked the druid.

"It is in my mind to nominate young Adminius as my successor. He is my sister's son; his father is a Roman, a citizen of the Empire; and the boy is almost of age to ascend the throne. I shall nominate him king for ten years—and no one will dare touch him, neither Banhir nor the Empire. And he will have all the support of the merchants, what is more! After those ten years are up, Caradoc and Reged will succeed, and Adminius will take a territory in Belgium. He will leave the kingdom stable, and then he'll be out of the way probably sharing a kingdom with Catuval, who'll keep him in order!—and the lads can then carry on as they have seen me rule."

Caradoc heard the druid chuckling. He could not see that there was anything to chuckle at: he felt angry to think that he must wait another ten years before he could become a king. And he hated Adminius for being a coward and a sneak.

His father spoke again. "Ten years. Just a nice time. The boys will have learned a bit of sense then, and Adminius is bound to build up the Roman trade. Best of all, it will get old Banhir out of the way. He's nearly as old as I am. No, he shouldn't be much trouble in ten years' time!"

Caradoc was suddenly so angry that he kicked Morag sharply on the shins. The lad woke up with a start and stared at the prince. "Keep your eyes open," his cousin said. "What's the good of bringing you out if you don't see where you are going?"

Before the litter reached Sorbiodun, Caradoc was fast asleep himself.

CHAPTER TWO

A.D. 34 — A.D. 38

THEN THE YEAR wore on, through harvest-time and fruit-gathering to winter, and on again to the next midsummer day under the great stones, and another, and another, as it had always been, and as, the rapidly growing boys felt, it always must be. The years began with the budding of the oak, and ended with the falling of its leaves. The leaves always came and always went, and the great stones on the plains were always there, timeless and unfathomable, enclosing the holy ground on which none but priests might tread. Each year the druids chose a red-haired youth from one of the tribes to take the part of the Sun-god, and, when he had assumed the shining one's character and attributes, allowed him complete freedom to do anything he chose—to take women, weapons or horses, as he willed—until midsummer morning, when the spirit he had borrowed must be returned to the sun.

One year the youth chosen for this honour escaped as midsummer day drew near. The tribesmen were deeply shocked, especially the red-haired ones, and organised man-hunts with dogs over the southern territory. Caradoc and Gwyndoc were allowed to join the hunt, and their party had the good fortune to find the errant Sun-god. The tribesmen dragged him out of a dense oak tree one wet morning, and his teeth were chattering with cold and terror. He could hardly eat for an hour, until they warmed him with their cloaks. Even then his stomach would not keep anything down for long. When he could speak, he told them that in the week he had been free he had lived in woods, drinking the dew and eating snails and berries and young hares that could not run very fast. He was afraid to light a fire, he said, and so had eaten the creatures raw. He had broken one of his teeth off trying to crack a nut. It made him look very ugly and had given him a great deal of pain, he told them. Some of them felt he deserved it, but nodded sympathetically. The boys were disgusted to find the Sun-god so weak.

Another year a small party of Saxons came in their long-boats, right up to the city wharf, and walked ashore in broad daylight, with their swords drawn. They were all very tall thin men, with pale hair and stupid faces. They had made themselves so drunk with some Greek wine they had captured from a trading-vessel that they hardly knew what they were doing. Cunobelin laughed when he heard about them and ordered the guard not to molest them. Instead he sent a Saxon slave to conduct them to the palace, where he feasted them and made them still more drunk. Over supper they kept the tables rocking with their antics, although none of the Celts could understand a word of what they said.

Everyone enjoyed that night, expecially Morag, who was beginning to develop a grim sense of fun, rather like that of his uncle the King. The Saxons lay down in the straw like beasts, wrapped in their cloaks, and spent the night round the fire.

In the morning they were all dead from the poisoned wine they had drunk, except their chief, who had been sitting by the King's side and so would have noticed if the serving-girls had slipped anything into his glass too.

This chief was even taller than his men, and wore his hair in two long plaits, one on either side of his head. He complained that he felt very sick when the guards dragged him outside, so the King lengthened his life until the late afternoon, when it might be warmer. Some of the court gossips even declared that a young German girl was sent down to the dungeons to him after the mid-day meal, but no one knew for sure. He was tied to a post at the town gate and shot full of arrows as the sun went down. Then his head was set on a spike, the yellow plaits still dangling foolishly, above the King's palace. The boys were present at the execution and were filled with hatred for the Saxon pirates as they saw the chief's long body slump in his ropes.

The King learned, many months later, that this was not a raiding-party, but a trading-mission bound for north Britain, which had got off its course, drunk too much stolen wine, and had only put in to Camulodun to ask where they were.

Odd mistakes like that often happened among peoples who had no common language, and were subjects for amusement when the winter nights grew long, and the tribesmen huddled round the peat blaze away from the wind, telling their long tales to pass the hours away.

There was that other tale of the four Pictish kings, very important personages in their own country, who came down to form an alliance with the Belgae. They had the misfortune to be set upon in the Iceni territory and were left penniless and naked on the moors. Even that would have been all right, but they took to the woods for shelter and were found there later by a Belgic hunting-party that had got well out of its way chasing a stag and taken for wild men. Cunobelin either thought, or pretended, that they were inarticulate savages and had them put into the royal menagerie with the leopards that Rome had sent him from time to time. Only one king came alive out of the cage at the end of the day. When they sat him on a pony and turned him loose, he began to scream so much that one of the guard had to knock him on the head, out of humanity.

But these incidents were, in the main, uncommon. For the most part there was wheat-sowing along the terraced hillsides, ploughing with the great wheeled plough and four oxen, the annual harvest-feast, fishing with trout spears, and hunting— sometimes even as far afield as Anderida Silva, in the country of the resourceful and artistic Cantii.

The boys gradually grew into young men and became eligible to join the secret societies, according to which of the thirteen lunar months they were born in; Caradoc the Badgers, Reged the Owls, Gwyndoc the Otters, Morag and Beddyr the Wolves.

They didn't see very much of Adminius, since he lived an aloof existence with his mother and her court at Dubra; and, in any case, for nearly three years he had been studying religion and philosophy at Dreux, in Gaul. He had written one letter back to his uncle, saying that the druids there were wonderful people and that before long he was sure that their college would be superior to that on Mona. He was studying law and statecraft as well, he said, and had a Roman tutor named Strabius who was reading the classics with him. He also said that he had been, with other students, to witness a sacrifice at Carnac, in Armorica. He thought the stones there more pleasant to the eye, though smaller, than those at home.

In a postscript he admitted that he was coming to doubt more and more the British systems, religions and politics. He hoped to fit in a trip to Rome with his Latin tutor before his stay in Gaul was ended.

When the court scribe read out this letter to the Council, most of the members became very angry, especially about the postscript. But Cunobelin only laughed louder than ever and said that the young lad knew more about preserving British unity than any of them did, in spite of their grey heads and long beards. Which did nothing to decrease their annoyance. In fact, for three days after that letter was received the Court was, below the surface, a seething mass of anger and unrest. Dead animals and refuse were flung through the windows of the house at Dubra, and the cattle were found dead in their stalls. Then the incident was forgotten. The initiation ceremony for the new druids was performed, a bad crop of grain forced the priests to call for a sacrifice of first-borns, and, what with one thing and another, young Adminius passed out of everyone's minds. He certainly passed out of Caradoc's mind whenever there was hunting or feasting to think about.

In a small hollow at the edge of the wood, where the fern grew thickest and lizards darted like flashes of green lightning, the four boys lay through the heat of the summer afternoon. The tall young princes, Caradoc and his brother Reged, leaned on their elbows chewing grass stalks, while at a short distance away from them their cousins, Morag and Beddyr, sat alert, watching them, and never daring to speak unless they were spoken to first.

The tawny Caradoc and his flaming-haired brother made such a violent contrast to Morag and Beddyr, with their black hair and eyes, and their swarthy flushed complexions, that one might not only have guessed they belonged to different families but that they were not even of the same race. Yet the King Cunobelin was their true uncle, and their blood ran as pure and noble as any in the Belgic kingdom, even though at times it did flare up a trifle more quickly than one could have expected from young men of a royal family. Their Uncle Cunobelin often used to tease them on this score. "Lads," he would say, "it would never do for you to let yourselves be made king. Inside a fortnight you'd have lost your temper fourteen times, and if you used the axe each time, you'd have no subjects left in a month." But this afternoon, sleepy with sun and fresh air, the brothers were mild as lambs, anxious only to please their more exalted relatives, to remember their self-imposed function of bodyguards.

Suddenly Caradoc yawned and flung a turf at Morag. The boy saw it coming but refused to duck. The turf hit him, quite hard, on the side of the head, but Morag only smiled at his cousin and bowed his head, as though asking to be thrown at again. And Caradoc would have thrown at him again, but the nearest turf was out of his reach and he felt too lazy to stretch. He just smiled back at Morag. "Morag," he said, "you should not let Beddyr throw turf at your head. It is undignified. You may strike him for doing so." At first, Morag looked back at the prince with a puzzled expression on his face, then he seemed to understand, and turned sharply and punched his brother on the chest. Beddyr smiled at the blow but did nothing. "Aren't you going to hit him back?" asked Caradoc. Beddyr looked kindly at his brother, then reached out and found a stick. He struck Morag so hard on the shoulders that the stick broke, then felt for his hand and held it, half-ashamed of himself.

Reged spoke almost angrily. "What are you playing at, Caradoc? You are acting like a fool, not like a prince," he said. "You are always teasing these two. I am sick of it. I shall go and look for frogs in the wood." And he got up slowly and walked among the trees. "Wait," shouted his brother. "I am tired of these two heathen. I will come with you." But before he could get up, Reged ran quickly into a dark part of the wood and hid. "I don't want any company," he called. "I want to be by myself."

Caradoc sank back among the fern and yawned again. Then he began to throw small pebbles at a ladybird that was trying to cross a patch of bare earth in front of his feet. Morag raised himself. "Shall I kill the ladybird for you, Caradoc?" he said. The prince glanced at him with contempt before he answered, "No, thank you, Morag. I can do my own killing without your help. You make me sick at the sight of you—always wanting to do something for me. I am able to do everything myself. So be quiet!"

Morag's lip began to tremble, and when Beddyr reached out for his hand, he struck at his brother's arm. Then Caradoc said, "Morag, I have just thought. Kill the ladybird for me. It would please me." The boy's lip stopped quivering and he jumped to his feet and trampled hard on the bare patch of earth.

"Good," said Caradoc. "You are a good slave, aren't you?" And Morag nodded his head and knelt to kiss his cousin's sandal. Then he went back to his place and made Beddyr go to Caradoc and kiss his shoe also. Then they all leaned back into the shadow once more.

At last the prince yawned again. "I am fed up," he said. "Morag, will you wrestle with me? I have not wrestled for days." The black-haired lad grinned and began to take off his tunic. "Look after the prince's clothes," he said to Beddyr; and then, half-naked, he began to tread the grass down in the little hollow so that they should have a level surface to wrestle on. After they had both rubbed their damp brown bodies with dust, they began to wrestle, but it was easy to see that Morag was anxious for Caradoc to win always. He neglected to take advantages of openings which the prince left, and even when he had his opponent in his power he allowed Caradoc to twist round and throw him to the ground.

"Damn you," said the prince, panting, "this is not wrestling. You are not trying. It is no fun for me." But Morag only smiled gently at him, like a simpleton, and did the same as before. "Come on, Beddyr," called Caradoc. "Your brother is no good. He will not give me any fun. It is like wrestling with a dead man to wrestle with him." Then Beddyr took off his tunic, and Morag went to guard the clothes. But it was no good. He was just as anxious as Morag not to throw his cousin, and Caradoc became more and more angry, until at last he shouted out, "What do you think I am made of, wax?" And when they both pretended to laugh at this, as though he were joking, he ran at them and kicked them hard, in all parts of the body, wherever his foot could reach. And as he kicked, they stood still, until his temper had worn itself out.

At last he was tired and ashamed of himself, and sat down

again. He could have wept with vexation, when suddenly they
all heard a new voice from the wood, a lad's voice singing
gaily:

> *"The wood is full of shining eyes,*
> *The wood is full of creeping feet,*
> *The wood is full of tiny cries—*
> *You must not go to the wood at night!*
>
> *I met a man with eyes of glass*
> *And a finger that curled like a wriggling worm,*
> *And hair as red as rotting leaves,*
> *And a stick that hissed like a summer snake . . ."*

The prince listened to the impromptu song for a moment, then
he called into the wood, "Gwyndoc, Gwyndoc, we are all here.
Come and cheer us up!" And as he spoke his cousins looked at
each other, and then back at the prince, and their faces were
dark and unhappy again.

There was a rustling of brushwood and dry fern, and then
Gwyndoc appeared, a tall, fair-haired lad, so like Caradoc that
he might almost have been his brother. He was dressed in a
thick sheepskin jacket over his tartan breeches and carried a
stick over his shoulder, on which swung a brace of pheasants. He
came forward to Caradoc and clapped him on the shoulder.
"Hallo, young lord," he said, almost teasingly. "Is this where
you hold your court?" Caradoc pulled him down beside him in
the fern, and Morag looked blackly at his brother and turned
his back on the two friends.

After a while Caradoc said, "Gwyndoc, I am bored with the
sun and these fools. Will you wrestle with me? I cannot get
Morag and Beddyr to give me any satisfaction." Gwyndoc
grinned. "I am rather tired, little badger," he said, "but I will
try, if you wish it." And he slipped off his sheepskin coat and
began to flex the muscles of his arms. Caradoc walked over to
the centre of the wrestling ring and stood waiting, laughing
back at his friend. As Gwyndoc passed Morag, the black-haired
youth spoke, quite loudly but as though he were addressing his
brother. "Gwyndoc will lose," he said. "He knows that he will
lose." Beddyr did not seem to hear the words, and Gwyndoc
pretended to kick Morag by way of reply, as he went on.

Then the two friends circled each other and at last were
locked together, each straining and tugging until the sweat burst

from their foreheads. And suddenly Gwyndoc twisted, caught the prince by the leg and flung him backwards into the grass. Before Caradoc could rise again, his young friend was upon him, pinning him down firmly. Caradoc looked up and grinned. "Your throw that time, Gwyndoc," he said. "But next it will be different." Gwyndoc helped the prince to his feet, and once more they locked. This time, as they strained, Gwyndoc whispered, "I will show you a hold that my father's Greek doctor taught me." Caradoc nodded. "You won't get a chance," he taunted, laughing. But before the smile had left his lips, Gwyndoc had him down again, his face in a clump of fern, his arm twisted high behind his back.

Yet as Gwyndoc began to rise, so that he could assist the prince to regain his feet, Morag and Beddyr were on him, punching and kicking in a frenzy. Taken off his balance, Gwyndox fell sideways and rolled over, as the brothers leapt at him again. "Stop it, you fools!" shouted Caradoc, but they did not seem to hear him. Then the prince shouted again. "Look after yourself," he said, "Beddyr has a knife." Then Gwyndoc was on his feet again, twisting and turning like a ferret. Catching Morag off his guard, he kicked him hard under the heart, and as the lad fell forward groaning, he turned to Beddyr and caught his upraised arm. "Drop your knife, Beddyr," he gasped. "This has gone beyond a joke." But Beddyr's eyes were vacant and his breath came sharp and viciously as he tried to bite at his opponent's hand. Gwyndoc held on to him tightly and looked at Caradoc, asking for guidance. The young prince stared back, his face hard. "Kill him, Gwyndoc, he deserves it." This time Beddyr heard the prince's words. He stopped struggling instantly, all the fight gone out of him, and his eyes lost their vacantness and suddenly came back to earth, full of tears. Caradoc had told Gwyndoc to kill him. The prince had no more use for him then, no more faith in his loyalty, but only wanted to be rid of him, as one would be rid of a hawk that could not be managed or a dog that worried the flocks. Beddyr's head dropped forward as he tried to hide his misery. Gwyndoc felt his taut wrist go limp. As a precaution he gently took the hunting-knife from the lad's hand. "Let me keep this for a time, Beddyr," he said softly. "I like the carving on the haft. It is German, isn't it?"

Beddyr looked up at him, half in shame, half in hate, and nodded. Then he turned without speaking and ran towards Morag, who was now sitting among the tall grasses and scowling as he rubbed his stomach. But as he fell on his knees beside his brother, Morag whispered fiercely, "Why did you not kill him, you fool! He threw Caradoc to the ground." Then he shambled to his feet and walked contemptuously away from Beddyr. After a moment Beddyr ran after him, trying to explain and waving his hands about. Morag pushed him away a time or two, trying to ignore him, but Beddyr followed after him at a distance, like a dog that has been beaten and wants to make friends again.

Caradoc turned to his friend, grimly. "They are my cousins," he said, "but I could wish them both on the great stone at times, with myself officiating at the sacrifice!" Then he smiled at Gwyndoc's look of horror. "Yes," he said, "I know I am too quick-tempered, but they are fools; the sort of fools that will bring trouble to us all, one of these days." Caradoc put his arm round Gwyndoc's shoulders. "And where would you have been if I had not been here to stop them? Eh, my friend?" For a moment Gwyndoc was nettled. "I may have been scratched with this girl's toy," he said, throwing the knife up and catching it by the handle, "but I should soon have sent Beddyr to join his brother."

The prince laughed ironically. "That's what you think," he said. "But if I had not been here they would have attacked more suddenly. I could make them kill you whenever I liked. What do you think of that, Sir Cleverness?" Gwyndoc pulled away from him angrily. "Why, I will fight them together, whenever you wish. I could have hurt them both just now, but for your presence and the fact that they love you! Call them back and let us fight to prove who loves you more. Call them!"

As Gwyndoc spoke, Caradoc's face became serious. He seemed on the point of taking Gwyndoc at his word. Then his frown became a smile, and he slapped his friend hard on the back. "Gwyndoc," he said, "you are my dearest friend. Do not let us quarrel, then." But Gwyndoc began to pull away, the knife still in his hand, when there was a crackling among the dry brushwood, and Reged appeared, his hands cupped over something. "Children," he called importantly, "stop this brawling and look what I have found." The two friends turned towards him. "Be careful, Reged," laughed Caradoc, "or we two will hang you up in the trees by your heels, won't we Gwyndoc?" Gwyndoc smiled, embarrassed, then the two young men bent over Reged's hands to see what he had found. It was a mole, very young and half-dead with fright and suffocation in Reged's hot hands. "A familiar spirit, my friends," said Reged. "You could train a beast like this to obey commands. He would burrow under the floors of your enemies' huts and bring back messages of their intentions. Such an animal is the friend of kings and princes. This one is a specially good creature, for see, on his back there is the sun sign, in white."

The two friends looked carefully at the struggling mole. Gwyndoc whistled. "By Cassivelaun, but you are right, Reged. The mark is plain for all to see." Reged smiled condescendingly. "Yes, I am usually right," he said, "especially about omens and such things. I am more than half a druid already, you see," he said. "Caradoc hasn't the inner eye that I have. That is why he did so badly when father sent him to Mona to take his first degree!" And he turned teasingly towards his brother. But as he did so Caradoc knocked his hands up and the little mole fell into the ferns and thick mosses and was away out of sight with a rapidity that surprised the three boys. For an instant Reged's face clouded, and it seemed that he would forget his even temper and strike his laughing brother. But instead he suddenly recollected his dignity and turned towards the path that led back to the city. "Let us go home," he said, "or we shall be in danger of forgetting who we are."

He began to walk away with a great show of nonchalance. The two boys followed him slowly, giggling at each other, ashamed of themselves. Then Gwyndoc came alongside him and pushed the brace of pheasants into his hands. "An offering, Reged," he said. "Two birds for your mole." Reged looked down haughtily at the crumpled feathers. "Thank you, Gwyndoc," he said, "but I cannot accept your fowl. They are yours, just as the mole was mine." And he looked hard at his brother, who turned his head away, confused by Reged's stare, muttering self-consciously.

But Gwyndoc would not be refused. He stood away from Reged so that the other could not put the birds back in his hands. "They are an offering," he repeated. "You can call them a sacrifice, if you wish." Reged's mood softened. "That is different," he said, pompously for a lad of his age. "As a prince I cannot refuse a sacrifice. Thank you, my friend." And he did not mention the birds again, but held them negligently swinging against his leg as he walked.

As the three came out of the wooded valley into the open they passed Beddyr, sitting alone by the side of the path. His hard young face was streaked with tears. No one spoke to him, and he fell in behind the friends and followed them at a distance. Gwyndoc chose an opportunity to turn and hand back the hunting-knife to him, but as soon as possible, Beddyr flung the knife as far as he could into the bushes and wiped his hand hard on his tunic.

And after a time the sun sank and they came into view of the huts. But they did not see Morag on the path ahead, nor at any other time that day.

CHAPTER THREE

A.D. 38–A.D. 40

T HAT WINTER TURNED out to be the hardest the Catuvellauni had known since they came to Britain. Some new arrivals, seeing the misery brought by the snow and incessant winds, assumed that the island must always be like that and so took sail with the Veneti trading fleet back to Gaul, glad to be in a country where there were stone houses and fuel for all. It was so cold, even in the south, that shepherds were found dead in their huts, while their sheep, buried in drifts, died standing three deep on each other's red backs, fighting for air.

The iron-workers of the south-east, mainly independent Cantii, refused to burn their fuel in the furnaces, hoping to keep it to warm themselves and their families, and in the end the King was forced to send guards who would make them start up the fires again, since there was a constant need for iron wheel-hoops and sledge-runners, without which transport was impossible. As the winter dragged on, village after village evacuated, leaving the cold wattle-huts and moving into the stone-built city with all their belongings. Some of them were fortunate enough to find homes with relatives or brothers of the same society. Others lay down and starved in the streets of Camulodun and Verulum. The citizens of Londinium at last closed their gates against all strangers.

Then the tribesmen manning Mai Dun revolted from lack of warmth and food and sacked the villages near at hand, and this hysteria spread from hill fort to hill fort, right through the south. Cunobelin, this time, was powerless to act, since he could not rely on the support of the various chiefs over whose territories he would be compelled to lead a punitive force. He did not dare to conduct a starving army to the west.

When things looked at their blackest in the south, the Brigantes, who had lost most of their flocks and had gathered only a meagre grain-harvest in the previous year, sacked Eburac and then attacked the riverside Parisii. Not to be outdone, the Parisii came across the frozen estuary of the Abus and foraged left and right among the Coritani, whose chief, Cerdic, a distant relative of Cunobelin, immediately appealed to the Catuvellauni for aid. But Cunobelin had his hands full in his own kingdom, and, apart from offering Cerdic sanctuary in Camulodun, he was able to do nothing more.

Before the spring came, the Saxon pirates had seized another opportunity to raid and had burnt and pillaged five miles inland along the coast from the Abus to Segedun. Then the wolves, made bold by famine, came down from the inland forests by night, and what frost and pirates had not finished they completed. Tribesmen moving into the cities told of whole villages slaughtered by one and the other, and now only inhabited by howling forest creatures.

For the chiefs and nobles the winter was just bearable, for the slaves and common-men it was the last punishment of the gods, and many, half-mad with hunger, prayed that the Romans would come and relieve their misery. Open rebellion was spoken in the streets of the capital, and in the end the King even ceased to have the offending tongues torn out. As he said one night to his closest friends, "If I punished thus every man who had spoken treason, I would be ruler over a dumb kingdom"; and half the tongues in the King's chamber that night seemed to feel the searing iron!

Yet for the nobles the hardships were not too great. Wrapped in their furs, they still sought out the otter, the badger and the wolf. Caradoc and Gwyndoc, being forbidden by their societies to kill the animal whose month they were born in, could not hunt the otter and badger, but they made up for it in the wolf-hunts, much to Morag's disgust.

It was on such an expedition that Gwyndoc was knocked from his horse by an overhanging bough and his ankle broken by the reckless horseman behind him. But for Caradoc's quick action in dragging him clear of the path, other horses would have trampled him in their excitement, for they had just scented wolf and were terrified.

They got the young man back somehow to the King's house, where an inexperienced doctor bound his leg and foot so badly that he stood in danger of being permanently crippled. Even Morag, who had shown an undisguised pleasure when Gwyndoc was first carried in, became sympathetic, and persuaded his brother, who was strangely skilled in medicine and water-divining, to attend to Gwyndoc's leg after the doctor had gone. Even so, it was many weeks before the young chief dared bear his weight on the foot; and before he was out again the winter had gone, like a deathly white dream, and the sky was blue and the buds were beginning to grow along the black boughs.

No more was dissatisfaction heard in the taverns and lanes. Those villagers who had survived returned to their ruined houses in the spring and began to rebuild, clearing away once more the encroaching forest, and borrowing from any neighbour more fortunate than themselves to set up in grain and stock once more.

But the effects of that winter were lasting for many. Quite a number of the nobles saw for the first time that peasants could not all be relied on should invaders come once more to the coast; and some of the less stout-hearted of the minor chieftains began to send gifts and messages into Gaul, destined for Roman officials and soldiers whom they had forgotten for years.

The winter had told on Cunobelin, too. He seldom left his room now, but sat in his high, carved chair before the great fire, wrapped in woollen shawls and furs, giving audience only to those friends he had known the longest, and often talking to himself and his dogs for hours at a stretch.

Gwyndoc, lying convalescent on his couch in the next room, was often disturbed in the night by the King's half-mad voice, sometimes ordering his soldiers to advance, sometimes repeating over and over again the midsummer incantation which he had to speak before the sun-stone, and sometimes begging for mercy, crying and almost whining, in a heart-rending manner.

For a time this worried Gwyndoc, though he hesitated to tell Caradoc of his father's condition. He felt that it would be almost blasphemy, to hint that the King was not himself; for Cunobelin had always been the King, immense, stronger than other men. But two things served to put all dismay from his mind: first, there was Bydd, the priest of the oak, who came to him in a dream and questioned him about all he had heard the King say. And Gwyndoc told Bydd all he had heard, and Bydd made a wry face in his dream and touched Gwyndoc's head with a sacred hare's paw; and when he awoke, he had forgotten all he had heard. But he knew in his heart that the King was ill and that Bydd was already looking for another king to take his place.

The other thing that helped him to forget Cunobelin, even to forget his lame foot, was the girl Gwynedd—or, at least, not Gwynedd herself but another girl whom she brought to Gwyndoc. Gwynedd, the dark-haired, despite her name, was Caradoc's cousin, daughter of a chief of the Parisii, and maiden-in-waiting to the Queen. She was a serious, brown-eyed girl, a year or two older than the boys, and very attached to Caradoc, although he pretended not to notice her. She would often visit Gwyndoc when he lay on his couch of sheepskins in the dark stone hall, and when he was in a fever would damp his brow or change his thick woollen shirt for a fine linen one and sponge him down. He came to regard Gwynedd as a sort of sister, and, like most Celtic noblemen, had no shame of his body and was not embarrassed by her kindnesses. But one day she came with another girl, a tall, golden-haired girl whose name was Ygerne and who, being a noblewoman whose parents had been killed by wanderers in the hard winter, was now under the King's protection and a member of his household. This Ygerne, with her wide, blue, searching eyes was a different person from Gwynedd. She was quick and merry and teasing, and made Gwyndoc go red about the ears when she looked at him.

"I am handing you over to Ygerne now," said Gwynedd, when she had told Gwyndoc about her. "She will look after you as I have done." Then she smiled and patted the young man on the head, as though he had been a child, and left the two together.

At first Gwyndoc was so shy that he half-wished Gwynedd had not brought this stranger to him; then he thought again, and he knew that he was lying to himself and that he wanted Ygerne very badly—so badly that he decided his foot must get better very soon, so that he could show her what a fine horseman and wrestler he was. And he looked up and saw that Ygerne was looking at him and smiling in a strange way. So he looked down again and tried to whistle, but his lips were so dry that he gave that up and said, "All right, girl, don't sit there doing nothing, like a lazy Greek slave. Tell me a story, or something, to pass the time away. A warrior soon tires of lying like a cow under a roof."

And when she didn't speak for a moment, he looked up at her fiercely to hide his shyness, and her smile of understanding made him worse than ever. And when she had teased him enough, Ygerne began to tell him the story of Branwen, daughter of Llyr, who married Matholwch, the King of Ireland, but whose evil brother threw her little son Gwern into the fire. And Gwyndoc became so interested that he tore his bed-coverings and swore that he would have carved the brother into pieces if he had been there. And when Ygerne came to the end of the story and told how the brother took an army into Ireland, slew the Irish king and brought back the suffering Branwen to die in her own country, Gwyndoc's eyes streamed with tears, and Ygerne stroked his head and called him a silly boy and said she would not tell him any more stories if that was how he carried on. But when he looked up at her face he saw that she was crying, too, and he knew for sure then that he loved her above all others, even, perhaps, Caradoc—though he quickly put this thought from his mind. And that night, after Ygerne had gone, and the torches flickered round the dark walls, Gwyndoc became a poet for the first time in his life, and he sang to himself these lines:

> *"Yellower was her head than the flower of the broom,*
> *Fairer was her flesh than the foam of the wave;*
> *Whiter were her breasts than the breast of the white swan,*
> *Redder were her cheeks than the reddest foxgloves;*
> *Whoso beheld her was filled with love for her.*
> *Four white trefoils sprang up behind her, wherever she trod."*

But when he had created the poem, he knew that he was singing of Ygerne and not of Branwen, daughter of Llyr, and all that night he turned from side to side in his bed, almost dying with love for her, he thought, almost mad with anxiety that tomorrow she might not come to see him.

But she did come, to tell him that she must go to visit her relatives in the north, and that she would not be back until later in the year. And as she left him she smiled so gaily that Gwyndoc flung himself onto his face and tore at his pillow covering with his teeth, like a dog.

But Gwynedd came back again and looked after him as before and put up with his sneers and spitefulness, and he gradually got well. When he could ride once more, there was always hunting with Caradoc or fishing alone. And sometimes he would ride out to the uplands where the charcoal-burners lived and help blow the forges for the smiths, while they hammered sword-blades or chariot-scythes or even tried their hands at making gold torques and lunulae, after the manner of the Irish craftsmen whom they envied.

After a while the first ache of his separation from Ygerne died down, and he almost called himself a fool for falling in love with her. And when he got a scribe to write down his poem for him, he tried to alter the words so that it meant a dark-haired girl after all. Then things happened that put the girl still further from his mind. The King, seated at his table one night with his family and dependants, had suddenly been struck down, speechless and gibbering, and had been carried to his bed, no longer capable of movement. Caradoc and Reged had quarrelled over the succession, each backed by strong supporters; and Reged, who had half-playfully drawn his sword against his brother in the presence of the archdruid, had been debarred from the court indefinitely to teach him his manners.

Then in the middle of the ensuing uproar, made more confusing by the common knowledge that the two brothers were devoted to each other, Adminius suddenly appeared in Camulodun, having travelled post haste from Gaul. According to his enemies, he had heard of the old king's illness and had come like a carrion crow for his pickings. But according to himself, he had come as a patriotic messenger to warn the King that the Emperor Caligula was about to attack Britain with a monstrous army; that the assembled troops, with balistae and other military engines, were waiting at Gesoriacum for a favourable wind to carry them across, and that the seriousness of their purpose could be deduced from their great preparations. According to Adminius, Caligula had mobilised all northern Gaul for thirty miles inland, had commandeered all shipping except that of the trading Veneti, and had erected a chain of lighthouses along the Armorican coast.

That night the news leaked out and Camulodun went mad with excitement. Half the population found swords and paraded through the streets with torches, howling for Cunobelin to call the Romans over so that they could get a bit of exercise, the other half packed up their wagons with everything they could put aboard and got out the horses from the stables, ready to make a rapid evacuation.

Caradoc got drunk with Gwyndoc late that night, and the two tipped Adminius out of his bed into a tub of water.

But the Romans did not come then, or the next day, or the next month, and the Veneti, bringing pottery and wine amphorae to the quayside, told them that the Romans had in fact assembled, as Adminius had said, but had then changed their minds and marched south again. They said that when the

invading army was about to embark, Caligula had ridden up on
a white horse and had ordered all his soldiers to fill their helmets
with shells, saying, "These are the spoils of the ocean, due to
the Capitol and the Palatine."

No one understood this, but everyone laughed about it, and
one of the wine-casks was broached on the dockside and all who
cared were free to drink. News came to the people later that the
King was a little better and was resting peacefully in his house.
Then Caradoc and Reged were seen walking in the fields with
their arms round each other's shoulders. And the city settled
down to its every day quiet again.

Adminius went away to the country, with a dead cat tied to
his saddle. He did not discover it until he had ridden through
the town gates.

But for Gwyndoc was the biggest upheaval of all. He returned
one afternoon from hunting to find a slave-girl waiting for him
with a message which said that Ygerne had returned and was
anxious to see him. She had often thought about him and his
wounded leg while she had been away. So that they could talk
in peace, she suggested that they might meet again outside the
city the following morning, if the sun shone. Gwyndoc was so
befuddled by the sudden return of his love for the girl that he
tore off his bracelets and gave them to the slave. It was only
after she had gone, speechless at his generosity, that he remembered one of them was his luck bracelet, without which he would
never be fortunate in love—or at least so an old beggar-woman
had told him!

CHAPTER FOUR

SO GWYNDOC SAT waiting by the side of the old druid
stone. And a lark rose from the heather, almost at his feet,
and soared up and up until his keen eyes lost it in the blue
morning sky. And as he stared after it the bird's mellow song
cascaded down around his ears, like a stream of jewels that had
suddenly been let flow from an upturned treasure-bag. The
young Celt's blood raced in him and he whistled back in
happiness, as loud and as high as he could, trying to answer the
lark.

A sudden wayward breeze started up from beyond the wood
at his back and caught his long flaxen hair, whipping it about
his face and bringing the red blood to his upturned cheeks. And

he felt that he wanted to dance and sing and perhaps swing his
new sword round his head, so that all the tribesmen could see
what a joyous, reckless young chief they had!

Then, as his mood mounted, another bird rose out of the gorse
bushes. It was a windhover, a gallant bird of prey, a warrior of
a bird if ever there was one! Gwyndoc wished that he could
speak its language, as the druids could, so that he might call out
to it and tell it in which direction the pigeon lay or where the
geese nested. But it was useless to try and talk to such a magnificent creature, such a prince among the birds.

So Gwyndoc lay on his back in the heather and watched the
windhover. He studied it against the blue background of sky
until even his sharp eyes ached; watched it rising, poising,
fluttering—an impersonal destiny—death without malice in its
strong eye, its curled claw and its silver beak.

The bird soared, catching a rising current, perfect in its
mastery, and swung round then above the summer fields to settle
for a kill. The broad pinions flickered, and the hawk stood
almost still in the moving air. The young man lay tense as he
watched, both hands shielding his eyes from the rising morning
sun, his long legs stretched out across the turf of the downland.
As the bird soared, his heart moved too; as it poised, his heart
stayed in its galloping. He would have shouted or chanted a
poem if he could have put sound or words to his joy at seeing
the mastery of this hawk, its freedom and skill, its movement
without let or hindrance through the upper air. All that had
ever been chained or confined in his spirit leapt with the bird;
he saw it as a perfect creature at liberty to go as it wished, un-
moved by feeling and unhampered by defeat.

And, as he watched, a missel-thrush rose from his side and
mounted through the clear air until it swung out above the
hovering kestrel. Then it came in to the attack, harassing the
bigger bird. The windhover changed its position, but once again
the missel-thrush darted forward.

Suddenly the magnificent bird of prey wheeled, as though it
did not desire to bicker with such an unworthy opponent, and
fell away down from the hill, into the broad valley and over the
fields of red corn, poising once more, at a lower level, above a
dark spinney. It was hard now for Gwyndoc to follow the
hawk. He held his hand low over his eyes and squinted hard, but
as he found it again he saw a herdsman come out stealthily from
among the trees with a sling in his hand. He watched the man
stoop and select a pebble and fit it into the little leather bag at

the end of the thongs. Gwyndoc would have shouted a warning
to the bird had he been close enough for his voice to be heard.
But it was hopeless. He saw the man bend back and swing his
arm over.

"O lord of the two lights, the greater and the lesser, let the
slave miss! Let him miss, master, and I swear I will sacrifice
three black cocks to you this very night!" Gwyndoc's hands
tore at his cloak fringe in anxiety as he waited. Then he saw the
windhover fall, a tattered rag of bloody feathers, vertically to
the hard ground. He watched the excited herdsman rush out
from the cover of the little wood, waving his arms and shouting
to his fellows. And the young chief rolled over and thrust his
face among the coarse grass. With his hands he tore at the clover
and thrust his nails into the chalky soil. He could have wept or
screamed out. His sandal-toes dug holes in the springy turf.

"My hawk, my friend, I will find the dog," he sobbed. "I
will find him before the sun goes down and have his sling-hand
taken from him. The filthy dung-eater, the scab, the mud-viper!
I will have him for you, I swear, hawk!"

His fingers found a stone, and he rolled over to fling it like a
curse at the innocent herdsman and found Ygerne standing over
him, her golden hair streaming out behind her and a plaid of her
father's clan wrapped close round her tall lithe body. She was
smiling down at him, her big blue eyes half-closed in amusement.
Gwyndoc stared at her, caught half-way between anger at the
bird's needless death and embarrassment at being seen acting
like a headstrong child. As the girl smiled at him, his eyes fell
away from hers and he tossed the stone a little way into the
gorse, as though he had forgotten why he had ever picked it up.

The girl spoke first, teasing and still smiling. "So the great
warrior chief is going to torture a poor ragged cow-watcher for
doing something he has done himself many times in sport!"

Gwyndoc's anger flared up again. "He is a slave," he said.
"He is born to filth and pain. He is not a gentleman, to kill
when he pleases, as we are. Such cattle are born only to be
killed. Who is he to slay a bird like the windhover? He cannot
fight; he is not handsome; he cannot fly!"

The girl kneeled down in the heather beside the young man.
"And can you fly, then, Gwyndoc?" she said.

The young chief went sullen. "That man is a barbarian. He
has no right to act like a lord and kill as the mood takes him."

Ygerne laughed out loud and pointed her finger at the boy.
"Oh, hark at you," she said. "Barbarian, indeed! And I suppose

you think you are not a barbarian!"

This was too much for Gwyndoc. He jumped to his feet and began to wave his arms about, as he always did when he got excited. "I am not a barbarian," he said. "Do I not wear fine clothes? Look at this tunic — it is fine linen. Look at my gorget — it is fine gold. Look at my sandals — they are Spanish leather. Look at my sword, and my belt, and my cloak." And as he spoke he held out his cloak and his sword for the girl to examine. But she still laughed. "That only means that your father bought those things for you. A black African could buy those things if he had enough sheep, or tin, or corn. So you see, it is only the sheep that have bought you your sword and your cloak and your gold necklace. The sheep cannot teach you not to be a barbarian!"

The young man was now almost beside himself with her teasing. "I speak Latin," he shouted. "I know my Grecian history! I have been to Sicily."

But Ygerne was going to plague him to the last. "Yes," she went on, "but you don't speak very good Latin, even I know that. I have heard little Gallic boys speaking it better than you do. And I don't suppose you know your Greek history as well as you know your tribal history! And although you have spent a short trading holiday in Sicily, you have spent longer at your uncle's school for druids on Mona! You are no more a Roman than I am. Not so much, if it comes to that, because I did have a Roman grandmother, although the clan never recognised her."

Gwyndoc hopped about in rage. "You are a woman," he said, "and you cannot be expected to know the meaning of things. You are only fit to have babies and feed the doves! You cannot wield a sword, or wrestle, or swim over the broad rivers! You cannot even —" But before he could finish his last insult the girl took the edge of his long cloak and, catching him off his balance, pulled him over suddenly onto his back. Then, before he could resist, she dragged his cloak over his head and, as he began to shout, stuffed the end of it into his mouth. Then she ran as fast as she could down the hillside towards the stream, laughing.

She did not get very far before Gwyndoc came bounding after her, his hair and great cloak streaming out behind him as he ran. As Ygerne looked quickly over her shoulder she saw that his face was not so serious or angry as it had been. In fact, she thought that he looked really rather handsome, and she liked the way he leapt over any rocks that stood in the way. Although she was just a little frightened that he might hurt her, she began to slow down so that he would not be too long before he caught her.

She heard his feet come thudding up behind her and braced herself in case he swept her off her feet as he passed. But Gwyndoc disappointed her. For a moment or two he ran alongside her, his face set, almost without looking at her, then he pulled away in front of her, racing at top speed down the slope. The girl pulled up, breathless and wanting to cry out to the young man to stop and come back to her, but by the time she felt able to call his name he had gone too far down the hill.

Ygerne sat down on a stone and almost wept that she should have spoiled this first love-meeting. She could have cried with rage, when suddenly she saw Gwyndoc's purpose: he was trying to impress her with his speed and skill. Before him, a flock of sheep were cropping the short grass, a shaggy sheepdog following them up slowly, his tongue lolling from his open jaws. Gwyndoc leapt on, in a frenzy of energy, over the dog's back and right into the midst of the flock! The startled sheep scattered in all directions, and the young man, now laughing like a drunken madman, ran on to the head of the flock, outstripping the frightened animals and sweeping up the flock-leader in his arms with a single movement.

For a few moments the chief continued in his headlong course, until his momentum was spent. Then, with the sheep struggling frantically in his cloak and the dog barking angrily at his heels, he turned and began to run up the hill again towards Ygerne, still laughing.

As he approached, Ygerne called out to him, relieved that he was coming back to her and that she had not spoiled the meeting after all. "Gwyndoc, you fool! What do you think you are doing!" "Bringing a present to a sharp-tongued young woman who had a Roman grandmother," he said, panting hard now.

"Put the creature down, this minute," called the girl. "You will hurt it, and then what will the gods say?" But before the boy could answer, a ragged figure, swathed in sheepskin and wearing a dirty sun-hat of straw, appeared from behind a gorse clump, lower down the slope. For a second or two this apparition watched Gwyndoc's efforts to drag the sheep up towards Ygerne, then, waving a stout crook in the air to emphasise his words, he shouted, "Young Lord Gwyndoc, put that animal down this minute! Do you hear? You'll ruin it! What do you think I spend my time doing, if you please? Tending sheep so that you can throw them about the place like bags of hay?"

Gwyndoc turned in surprise and embarrassment. "Why, it's Dwyggon, my father's old shepherd! I did not know it was his flock!" Then he shouted down to the old herdsman, "Quiet, slave. I'll have your hide taken from you if you dare to address me like that!"

As Gwyndoc spoke these words the old man jumped in the air and began to shamble up the slope, waving his crook menacingly, his face red with anger and exertion. "What?" he roared. "What? Why, I'll turn your breeches down and beat some sense into you with my stick. I've done it before, in your good father's time, and I'll do it again."

The young warrior looked half-ashamed towards Ygerne and grinned. Then he dropped the kicking animal to the ground, wiping his forehead with his sleeve. "By Belcader, and he has done, too," he said, "many a time! I bear the marks yet!" He turned round to face the old man. "Go home, you old dotard," he shouted, "or I'll have the hairs of your beard plucked out one by one!" He made a derisive noise and laughed to see the shepherd's angry expression as he increased his panting efforts to come up the steep slope.

Then Gwyndoc turned to the girl. "Come on," he said, "or the old' fool will try to thrash me! He's soft in the head and forgets that times change! I would not like to have the alternative of bending down while he beat me or of cutting his head from his shoulders!"

Ygerne smiled at his words, for she sensed the young man's natural kindness and softness of heart, and wondered at the effort it must cost him to appear hard and callous, aggressive and imperious, when he was with the other young tribesmen. Like other pastoral peoples, Gwyndoc was by nature a lover of all animals and of the folk who tended them. It was only that tragic Celtic tradition that made him play the warrior's part, that inordinate love of coloured finery and beautiful weapons, an almost feminine delight in textures and decorations, of warsongs and death dances. We are simple folk, the girl thought; we fight only to keep the land and to give ourselves an excuse for feasting and tales. If the Romans were to come and rule us, we should be quite happy after we had got used to the idea. In fifty years' time we should be content to let them do our fighting for us, while we lived like lazy children in the country. She might even have spoken these words to Gwyndoc, but he interrupted her with more violence than she had looked for; and when she realised what was happening, she was over his shoulder and he

was clambering as fast as he could back to the flat summit of the hill. At first she struggled a little, then she lay as still as she could, listening to his feet thudding on the turf and his breath coming fast.

In a little while the old shepherd was out of sight. "You can put me down now," she said. "He cannot catch us now." But Gwyndoc kept on, across the flat stretch of heather, then down the slope to where the river started, on the other side of the hill. "Put me down, Gwyndoc," she said again. "I am quite able to walk."

At first the young man ignored her. Then he spoke. "On one condition, lady," he said. "Either apologise for laughing at me or say a prayer to the ghost of Caesar in Latin!" And he chuckled at his joke. The girl's answer was to kick at his chest as hard as she could. "Apologise to a boy!" she said. "A boy who runs away from an old shepherd because he is afraid of having his behind smacked? Never! We Romans are made of harder stuff than that!" And she kicked again.

Gwyndoc didn't answer. Instead he took a firmer hold on her and scrambled on even faster towards the stream. His strong hands were hurting now, and Ygerne was beginning to feel rather sick as she dangled over his broad back, her head above his heels.

The sound of the stream was quite loud now. "Please put me down, Gwyndoc," wailed the girl. But he did not reply. "I will apologise," she said. Gwyndoc only chuckled. "I will say a prayer in Latin for you," she went on. "But please put me down. I am going to be sick." The young man laughed aloud. "What, in Latin?" he said. "Don't worry, cold water is a sovereign remedy for sickness," he said laconically.

Ygerne pretended to cry. "Oh, do put me down, I feel so ill—and the water will spoil my new dress. I put it on specially for you." Gwyndoc jolted her on his shoulder even harder. "Have no fear, lady, you shall have another dress twice as beautiful as this one, I promise it."

Ygerne began to punch and kick again, and was about to scream in annoyance when she felt Gwyndoc's feet totter and slip, and then they were both rolling in the cold water. Ygerne scrambled to her feet, gasping and groping for some bush or weed to hold on to. When she opened her eyes, she saw that Gwyndoc was standing up in the water, the ripples up to his chest. She held out her hands, and he laughed again and pushed her over, into a shallow part of the stream. By now she was

weeping with vexation and fear. As her hand touched the bed of
the stream her fingers closed on a sharp pebble, and when
Gwyndoc bent over her to raise her to her feet she struck
upwards at his face. Then she shrank back as he still came
towards her, blood trickling from his cheek.

For a moment his face was dark with a surprised anger. Then
he laughed and whisked the girl up in his arms and carried her
up the bank towards the shelter of the gorse bushes. She put up
a hand and wiped the blood away with her fingers, and then
Gwyndoc kissed her, very hard. The blood ran from his cheek
on to her own, and she put both her arms round his neck and
hung on to him.

As they lay down in the heather the sun came out stronger
than before, and steam began to rise from their wet clothes.
"Your teeth are chattering, Gwyndoc," said the girl at last,
"and I feel that I am going to sneeze at any minute. We must
take off our things and let them dry in the sun. We must not go
back to the town with a cold. That would spoil everything."
She smiled at him, showing her even white teeth, and he grinned
back and nodded. Then he crawled round to the other side of
the bush and dragged off his tunic and breeches. When he saw
the girl's long shift spread out on the heather, he called, "Ygerne,
let me know when your things are dry. I'll wait here till you
call." And to pass the time away he began to practise bird-calls
and wolf-cries.

The sun was sinking when they left their little sheltered
valley and made their way towards the edge of the hill. And as
they walked together, hand in hand, Ygerne whispered, "Oh, if
life could always be like this — the sun, the sound of the stream,
the blue sky, the heather, the bees, and the first flowers." She
looked up at Gwyndoc's face and saw the cut that stretched
across his cheek. I have put my mark on him, she thought. He is
my man now by the magic of a wound. Wherever he went that
scar would bring me back to his mind, and he would remember
this day. Now I have marked his face, he is always mine!

Gwyndoc looked down at her. "What are you smiling to yourself about, you sorceress?" Ygerne smirked and said, "I am
thinking what a fierce lover you are, making me love you against
my will, as you have done." Then she looked away, her eyes
cast to the ground in modesty. Gwyndoc felt his heart beat
frantically again, and he wanted to shout and run down the
steepest slope of the hill holding tight to the girl, but she seemed
to divine his reckless intentions and said, "Look below. Isn't it

a splendid view from here? And all ours to enjoy together."

At the hill's foot the broad cornlands stretched almost to the limits of the city, the full ears tossing in the late afternoon breezes, making the plain like a rolling red sea, touched to fire here and there by the last rays of the sun. Little green spinneys, left when the forests were cleared away, for shelter or to house the charcoal-burners, broke the monotony of the landscapes, and far away, almost on the skyline, was the sea itself. The sea from which they had all come in their movement westwards, the sea that separated them from their relatives and blood-brothers in Belgium. As they stared away into the distance, they could even imagine that they saw tall ships putting into port — ships with red hide sails, ships from Gaul, coming for grain or hunting dogs, and bringing gold mirrors, or gorgets, or finely-woven clothes. They even thought they could pick out the breakers lashing whitely against the sides of these ships and the small coracles going out to take off the visitors.

Then they looked again, and all they saw was an evening mist rising after the hot day, and they knew that they could not see the sea, or the ships, or the tiny waves lapping on the wooden planks. They turned their eyes to the city, Cunobelin's capital, where it lay, stretching over the gently undulating countryside, surrounded by crops and herds. Camulodun, straggling without pattern within its broad low walls; the blue wood-smoke rising alike from beehive hut and Roman villa; a shambling, unformed, pioneer city, with its dark alleyways and midden-heaps set cheek by jowl with its pillared baths. A city in process of developing a spirit, where the Royal Mint and the adder-pit were institutions of an equal eminence, a city that housed a proud people, a new people, full of the energies and ambitions that must prompt any pioneer. A city that was being built by a people without fear of any man of the outside world. A city on whom the gods smiled.

Gwyndoc looked thoughtful for a moment. "By all the gods, but if the Romans tried to take this from us we would cut their hearts out and eat them before their eyes!"

Ygerne looked at him archly. "Don't forget my Roman grand-mother," she said, and Gwyndoc took her roughly by the shoulders and kissed her so fiercely that his cheek began to bleed again.

And as they clung together, their cloaks wrapped about them now against the evening winds, a low, mournful sound of horns came up from the houses. At first they could not be sure what

the sound was, for the breeze took it and whipped it away from
their ears before its message could be interpreted. But at last
they understood, as the long blasts echoed and re-echoed about
them, and for an instant they shrank back from each other and
looked almost with horror towards the city.

"The King," they both said together. "Yes," said Gwyndoc,
"we are listening to the horns of death. His spirit is rising from
the city now."

"What will happen now, Gwyndoc," whispered the girl. "Will
Caradoc . . .?" But the young man interrupted her. "Get down,"
he said, "on your face, girl. The King's spirit is passing." And he
almost pulled her to the ground with him.

The melancholy horns still sounded as they crouched, and
suddenly a light rain came in from the sea and passed over the
city. The two lovers heard its swishing sound and looked up to
see it approaching them across the fields of rich corn, bowing
down the laden ears as it came. Then it moved up the hill and
passed over them, leaving their cloaks wet and their faces
glistening. Their eyes followed it over the brow of the hill, and
as they watched a little rainbow showed briefly for a second
above them, and then disappeared as the sun went down.

"He is gone now," said the young man. "We can rise again."
And they made their way to the foot of the slope without
speaking a word to each other. But as they approached the walls
Gwyndoc turned to the girl. "Why is your face so grave?" he
said. "We have each other, even though the Father is gone. We
are betrothed now, so why do you frown?" For a moment
Ygerne did not answer, and when she did her voice was almost
inaudible with foreboding. "Caradoc may be king," she said.
Gwyndoc laughed at her, perhaps a little consciously. "But
Caradoc is our friend, is he not?" he said. The girl shuddered.
"He was," she answered, "but yesterday he offered me marriage
—and I refused him. Now, if he is the Father, he may repeat his
offer, with the fire or the adder-pit as the alternative." She
shuddered again as she spoke. "It is his right," she said.

Gwyndoc laughed again, but the gaiety had gone from his
voice. "Adder-pit, nonsense! Caradoc will give his consent without any barbaric foolery like that! He is my friend, you must
not forget. We belong to a new generation. We are enlightened
people, the Catuvellauni, these days. We do not sacrifice human
life like that now, remember."

They passed within the walls. "Enlightened people," repeated
the girl. "Then what is happening to these wretches now?" and

she pointed to a line of stakes set along the roadside, on the common land where no houses had been built. Tied fast to each oaken post, a man hung head downwards, his breast bared for the knife. Gwyndoc put his arm round the girl's shoulders and turned her face towards him. "Do not look at them," he whispered. "That always happens when a King dies. That is not our doing, it is the druids who order it. And, besides, they are not of us. They are of other tribes — political prisoners, hostages from the Iceni and Brigantes. You must not think of them. They are less than men."

Ygerne began to tremble violently. "They are men, like you and Caradoc. And what if they do not belong to the Catuvellauni —neither do I, do not forget that."

As they passed, one of the wretches heard her voice and called out, thickly and piteously, his words only half-recognisable because of his suffering and different dialect. "Lady, Oh lady, save me! Save me, lady! I have a wife and three small children, lady! Let me go back to them, I have been here so long!"

Ygerne turned towards the creature, but Gwyndoc pulled her back to him. He shouted at the writhing figure, "Silence, you pig! It is a noblewoman you speak to. But for the law I would end your life now, you dog."

The girl tried to pull away from Gwyndoc, almost horrified. "You brute," she sobbed, "you are like the others." But Gwyndoc hustled her quickly away from the stakes, and as they went the condemned man cried out again, "Yes, lord! Kill me! Kill me now if you will not release me! I cannot suffer any longer." And then they were among the houses, and out of earshot.

When Ygerne looked at the young chief again she saw that his face too was wet with tears. His voice shook as he spoke. "Oh, Ygerne, I know it is terrible. It is dark and full of horror for us all. But what can a man do? It is the law, and the druids have eyes everywhere."

Ygerne's loathing twisted to compassion as she looked at his tortured face. "But, Gwyndoc," she said, "we could have loosed his ropes and left him to make his way out of the town. That would have been easy. We could not have been seen."

The young man turned her round for a moment and pointed back towards the stakes. "Look there," he said. And as she followed his pointing finger she saw that a white-clad priest stood beside each prisoner, and that each priest held a flaming

torch in his hand. She looked back quickly. "But they were not
there when we passed," she said incredulously. Gwyndoc patted
her arm. "Yes, they were," he said slowly. "I saw them a long
way off. And they saw us. They were hiding in the long grass,
watching everything we did. If I had loosed your friend, how
long do you think that I should have lived to enjoy your
gratitude?"

They walked further into the town, among the haphazard
huts and rude stone buildings, and everything was silent. The
hand of gloom seemed to have closed over the settlement. No
children rolled in the streets; no beggars stretched out shrunken
hands from the doors of the sheds. Even the dogs had forsaken
the middens and crouched in the darkness, wondering at the
strange stillness that had overtaken men.

From the far end of the town, cattled lowed from some
distant byre, but their mournful cries only seemed to emphasise
the hanging quietude. As the lovers hurried now between the
clustering houses they heard frightened whispers from the half-
open rooms and saw eyes staring out from the darkness at them,
afraid of any footsteps.

At the end of the alley-way that opened on to the newer part
of the city an old cripple woman leaned against her broken
door, too weak to move inside as the other tribesmen had done.
She was wailing to herself, "The Father is gone now. Cunobelin
is gone to the darkness and left us. Oh, the bright blood must
flow in rivers for his spirit's release! Only blood can make his
passage easy, for the gods are greedy! Oh, Master, Cunobelin,
why did you go and leave us now! What have we done to be
punished, Father?" As she wailed, her twisted body rocked to
and fro among the refuse at her door and her frail hands pulled
at her hair in misery.

"I did not think that a man's death could cause such fear,"
said Gwyndoc. "In battle they die and are soon forgotten; but
when they die in their beds all the world must know and suffer."

"We have not seen a king die before," answered the girl.
"And they must go to their graves with many followers to keep
them company."

Gwyndoc looked grimly at the girl. "You speak truth," he
said. "By tomorrow at sundown there will not be a prisoner
or a sick slave left alive in Camulodun. There will be sacrifices
wherever the Catuvellauni live, both in this land and in the
King's lands over the sea."

Ygerne shivered. "But surely it is wrong that one man's death should bring such pain and suffering on the innocent ones," she said. Gwyndoc nodded and shrugged his shoulders. "It is the law," he answered, "and those who disobey it die themselves. I dream of a kingdom where the old ways are forgotten and men live in sunshine, without fear, to hunt and sing as they wish."

"The Romans would give us that kingdom," said the girl, and then fell silent at what she had dared to put words to. At first Gwyndoc's face showed a momentary glimpse of hope, then his jaw set again, and he looked serious, even angry. "I am not a Gaul," he said. "But we are young, Gwyndoc, and we love each other," Ygerne whispered. The young chieftain placed his hand across her lips, so that she should say no more.

For a few moments they stood, half-afraid, before the doors of the great Council House, looking up at the long-dry heads that nodded on spikes above the roof. "They have been there since Cunobelin's father died," said Gwyndoc. "They were Pictish kings who were conducting a peace conference when he died. They waited too long." As they looked up at the roof they saw carrion crows gathering over the city in a dark army. "They always know," went on the young man. "They wait at the edge of battlefields and make their nests in burial grounds."

The girl shuddered, and they went through the great wooden gates into the Council House. Inside, all was chill and dark. Only one torch glimmered in the long room, set in a bronze socket near the entrance to the King's chamber. This door was closed, shutting the lovers away from all sound. But as they waited for a moment in the hall, it opened a little way and angry voices sounded. Many men were arguing, shouting each other down, and Caradoc's voice seemed to be giving orders. It appeared that he was in charge of the meeting.

"He is King," whispered Gwyndoc, "by the sound of his voice. They have elected him and not Reged, his brother. Now the Romans must look to themselves if they dare to meddle with the Belgae! What can have happened to Adminius, then? He stood strong in the King's favour, and older men liked him because he kept peace with Rome."

As he spoke these words the door swung open violently and a short black-haired young man strode out of the chamber, waving his hands about and shouting. Laughter followed him from the lighted room, and he paused for an instant before he went out into the street, turning and shaking his fist towards the maddening voices. "You shall soon know the answer, Belgic fools! You shall know that you have chosen wrong when the galleys come and your miserable hovels are burnt above your heads!" His outburst was followed by another roar of laughter, and he almost ran out into the courtyard.

"That was Adminius," said Ygerne. "He is very angry. I have never seen him like that before. He means evil." Gwyndoc smiled grimly. "Yes," he said quietly, "he has always shown his smooth side while the King lived, but now he is disappointed. But we had better not laugh at his misfortunes; we may have something to curse about ourselves in a moment." "Oh, Gwyndoc," said the girl, "I am afraid of Caradoc, now that he is King. He is sure to refuse his consent to our marriage. He will remember that I slighted him, and he is not the man to forgive an injury."

She looked at Gwyndoc and saw a face that she had not known before. His mouth worked, and his brown hand had crept to his throat-ring and was pulling at the shining metal. "I am a noble," he said hoarsely, as though to himself. "My blood is as good as Caradoc's. My sword-arm is as strong as his. You are my woman, should the Sun himself deny it." She was half-horrified at his blasphemy, but proud of her power over him. He pushed a small knife into her hand. "Hide this in your gown," he said. "I have its fellow. Should he deny me, not one of us three must leave this room again alive. Wait for his answer and see that you strike yourself surely if he refuses. I shall see that he follows quickly after his father; I know his weak spots. Then I shall come with you."

He bent and picked her up with a sudden violent movement. She began to struggle at first with sheer surprise, but when Gwyndoc strode forward and kicked open the door of the King's room she lay still with fright against her lover's heaving chest.

First she heard Gwyndoc's deep voice, respectful yet almost challenging. "Welcome and long life, my King," he said. "Two of your most loving people come to greet you, and to ask you, as their first request, that they may marry and so come to bring you other subjects as loyal as themselves!"

There was silence in the room after these words, and then a great roar of good-humoured laughter. Then, before Ygerne fainted away from fear and excitement she heard the King say, "Blessings on you both, my dearest friends, and may you never love one another less than you do at this moment!"

And Ygerne heard that Caradoc's voice was as gentle and as courteous as it had ever been. She began to cry softly, half from relief and half from disappointment that the King should so soon have forgotten that he had loved her himself.

CHAPTER FIVE
A.D. 41 – A.D. 43

THE BODY OF the dead King lay in his chamber for three days and after that period, despite the embalmer's art learned from Persia, had to be buried because of the heat. Three days gave enough time for most of his relatives to travel to the city for their last glimpse of the paramount chief of the Belgic peoples. They came from Gaul, secretly, to avoid Roman suspicion, and even from Ireland — the tall, fair aristocracy of the western world. Only Catuval, the King's favourite young nephew, did not come. He lay in a stinking Belgian village, on a hide-thong bed from which he was too weak to move, tortured by a fever he had picked up while marauding in Germany. He sent his favourite sword and two deerhounds as a burial offering, and swore by the great stones that he would not disobey the next call from Britain, even though his legs were broken and his heart had ceased to beat.

And Cunobelin was buried at last in a round barrow on the hills above the city. They dressed him in his finest armour and clothing, and sat him in his bronze-plated chariot. Under each wheel they placed a slaughtered foal; inside the chariot, at the King's feet, they laid Catuval's deerhounds and two pigs from the royal farm; and before the chariot they put the King's black stallion, dressed in his silver harness studded with garnets.

Caradoc and his brother wept bitterly to see the tired old animal sink back before the pole-axe. Caradoc held his brother's arm. "Reged," he said, "I have vowed that should I ever lose a battle, I would kill Gallyn under the great stones; but I made that vow in hot blood. After today I know that, should I ever have to keep my promise, you would have to remind me of it and compel me to keep it. I could not do it alone."

When the slaves had shovelled a high mound of earth over the King, the royal family returned to the city, walking barefoot over the harsh gravel and among the cruel brambles. No one ate or drank in the King's house that day or the next, and the names of a dozen slaves no longer appeared on the roll.

Then, after a suitable period of mourning for the dead king, there was a double-wedding. Caradoc married Gwynedd, and Gwyndoc, Ygerne. It was a sunny day and the streets of the city were gay with coloured flags; at every street corner leading to the market-square, servants of the royal house dispensed Gallic wine from great skins for all who wished to drink the King's health. Bonfires were lighted and the celebrations went on late into the evening, and when dusk fell there were still many who could not remember their way home. In the King's kitchens a whole ox was roasted for the servants and slaves, and that day all but a handful of dangerous hostages and other prisoners were granted their freedom.

At the great hall feasting was continuous after the druidic binding-ceremony, and the two couples, seated by the heads of their tables, were as madly intoxicated as any of their wild guests. Only once did even the gentle Gwynedd allow herself to look thoughtful, and then her friend Ygerne pounced on her right away. "What is it, dear?" she said, teasing. "Are you finding a queen's life wearing already? Are you afraid that the crow's feet are coming and your hair is turning white?" But Gwynedd did not answer, she smiled back quietly and with resignation, and Ygerne, following her eyes, saw that they rested on Gwyndoc, and she understood, for the young lord looked more magnificent than anyone who was not a king had a right to do. He stood, with one foot on a bench, glittering with gold rings and bracelets, and his silken-fringed tartan flung back and showing its scarlet lining, his long yellow hair plaited with silver ribbons, drinking toast after toast from a great ivory horn, calling on all his friends by name, the long length of the hall.

And Ygerne felt proud to belong to this man, and yet sorry because of her friend's envy. She leaned over and patted Gwynedd's arm, and a tear stood still in the dark girl's eyes. Then the tear fell, and once more everyone was gay and shouting, and Ygerne remembered the wonderful presents that her godmother, the old Brigantian Queen Cartismandua had brought her: golden mirrors, with enamelled arabesques twisting and coiling round their frames; a silver lunula to wear round the neck at sacrifice-times, set with pearls and emeralds, so that the precious stones formed a spray of mistletoe and its berries; combs of jet, garnished with opals; a little poniard, its coral handle carved like a slim fir-cone and its narrow blade engraved with her name in Greek characters—and so many more lovely things to wear and to use . . . . And Ygerne remembered how she and her party had ridden out one blustering day to greet this queen, to meet her after her long wedding-journey from the north. They had expected her to come with her retinue of warriors and servants, in her famous black litter; but instead they had met a solitary rider, on a squally night, huddled in furs on the back of a shaggy native pony, followed only by a ragged old man who led an ox-wagon laden with bales and caskets. "My dear," said Ygerne, later, telling the story to Gwynedd, "it was fantastic! She had come all that way as I have described! And the old man couldn't even speak! He was an idiot who looked after her garden, not a soldier at all! I tell you, you could still see the straws in his hair! It was ridiculous!"

But the old queen herself, sitting at Ygerne's left hand, was not ridiculous, nor would the girl have dared to make such fun of her in her hearing. She sat, a dwarfish figure, her scanty white hair covered by a tartan shawl, huddled over her plate, hardly eating a thing. But her bright bird-like eyes flickered perpetually on the assembled company. There was not a face she forgot, not a word that did not reach her ears. And she drank cup for cup with the warriors at her table, tipping back wine or mead as the hours passed, the golden bracelets at her thin wrists jangling almost continuously as she raised her arm.

Caradoc's wedding-speech was short. He got to his feet, swaying, and pointed his long finger towards his laughing friends. "My lords," he said, "we thank you for your presence. This occasion will only draw us together once in our lifetime, but this is not the only time we shall drink. Oh no! Give us always your swords, and we will give you occasions to celebrate! We will give you sons, and victories, and deaths — but not of our folk, we hope!"

He sat down then while the horns were knocking on the tables, but half-missed his chair and would have tumbled into the straw had not Gwynedd steadied him. He looked towards her, embarrassed for a moment by her forlorn expression, but Cartismandua relieved him. He suddenly became conscious of her, peering at him with bright eyes through the smoke and the shouting in the hall. She was speaking to him. She had to say her words a number of times before he got them.

"Well spoken, young man," she was saying. "May you always be as brave. But come to me, come to Cartismandua, if your courage ever fails you."

And Caradoc nodded wildly to her, forgetting even to be angry that she should think his courage could fail, laughing all over his face and slopping the mead out of his cup over his wife, his friends and himself with grinning abandon. "Yes, thank you, Mother," he was saying. "I'll come, if I ever need you!"

Then he nudged Gwynedd hard, and she did not catch the spirit of the thing and frowned and rubbed her arm; and Caradoc remembered that she was his wife and he her chosen lord, and he was desperately silent until he caught a flash of Cartismandua's smiling face again.

Then he filled his cup and drank, and loved his friends: all of them who breathed the air; all who walked on two or four legs; all who had eyes to see and ears to hear, and damned to eternal torment any who were not with him in that moment.

And very much later Gwyndoc took his wife to bed, and as they were undressing Ygerne said, "Caradoc was very drunk tonight, wasn't he?"

But her husband was impatiently struggling with the hide wrappings that held his breeches close to the calf. He could not answer for a moment, then he looked up at his new wife as she stood by his bed, only the long, golden hair of her head clothing the beautiful lithe body. He broke the bindings joyfully and stretched out his free hands to hold her.

"Kings! Kings!" he said. "They're born drunk! Oh, Ygerne, thank God we're not kings!" And he stumbled to her side, laughing.

The following morning, even while the many wedding guests were groaning in the straw or holding their heads miserably in the sleeping-chambers, a man galloped his shaggy horse, spattered with mud and froth, through the town gates, and almost fell at the feet of the King's guard as they ran out to meet him. When they could get any sense at all out of him, they learned that he had ridden at top speed from farther down the coast and insisted on seeing Caradoc.

At first the soldiers argued with him, even threatened him mildly, not being at all certain that the young King would feel like seeing this messenger at such a time. But the staring-eyed horseman would not be put off: he flung down the wine they offered him and pushed the soldiers about with such a determined violence that in the end the captain conducted him reluctantly into the audience-chamber and got one of the more coherent noblemen to awaken the King.

Caradoc came almost immediately, his hair tousled, and his eyes full of sleep. He had had time only to fling a shawl about his body, and he was yawning, until the messenger, kneeling before him, gabbled out his story.

And when Caradoc fully understood his words the yawning stopped and the sleep left his eyes. Even the shawl slipped from his body to the floor. He did not speak to the messenger but turned abruptly towards his chamber; then he halted and turned back to the captain of the guard, who had remained present during the interview, waiting with his sword drawn. "Feed this man," he said sharply, "and lock him up safely. His story may be false. Send five couriers to me within half an hour!"

Then the King's door had shut again and Caradoc was already groping among the tumbled linen for his tunic and breeches, knocking over stools, and bumping against the bed in his haste, not worrying now whether or not he woke his wife. He did not even notice that Gwynedd was wide-awake, watching him through the darkened room, her eyes big and questioning.

The captain of the guard assembled his men as soon as he had sent for the five horsemen. "Here's a piece of news for you, lads," he said. "But God help any one of you that lets it pass further than these walls. The Romans are coming!" He looked round at the open mouths and the restless hands. "Yes, they're coming at last. Now there'll be fun for one or the other, and no feast, I'm thinking, for those who can't use a sword!"

"Was that all the messenger said, Captain?" asked one of the soldiers.

"No, but it's all that concerns you," answered the captain shortly. "He'd just got word from a hide-merchant who came over from Gaul in a fast boat. He came over so fast, he didn't bother with a cargo. He says the news has run through Gaul like a forest-fire. Aulus Plautius has assembled the biggest land and sea force Rome has seen for many years. He reckons there are close on sixty thousand legionaries and auxiliaries, as well as fighting galleys and supply barges. What's more, they've started out!"

One of the guard turned round and stretched by the open door. "I'll believe it when I see it. You know what these Gauls are for exaggerating! Hey, where are those couriers off to in such a hurry?"

The captain turned on him, "Get to your post, dog! It's Caradoc's business, not yours, to summon the Belgic Council!"

Gwyndoc and Ygerne, who rose much later, rested and happy, broke their fast in their own room. There was a strange tenseness about the serving-girl who brought them their food, but they paid little attention to her, being still full of love for each other.

And when they had eaten, they noticed that the sun had risen in the sky and that everything outside was fresh, and still green and inviting. Gwyndoc flexed his muscles and breathed the clean air deeply, feeling more powerful, more godlike than he had ever felt before.

"Let us have done with kings and courts for today," he said, "and walk out under the sky, away from fools and walls!" Ygerne laughed and clapped her hands excitedly, like a child; and when they had dressed they made their way out into the courtyard.

As they passed through the gates Gwyndoc noticed that the captain of the guard was watching him, with interest, it seemed. He called the man over: "I shall be away from the King's house today, walking on the hill with my wife. Let the King know that, if he should ask." The soldier stared at him. "But will not the King want you by his side, lord?" he said.

Gwyndoc laughed. "King Caradoc has a wife now—and so have I! Tell him that, if he asks what message I left for him!"

And the two strode out towards the field, leaving the soldier shaking his head in puzzlement.

The morning passed all too quickly by the side of streams, or knee-deep in rushes, or eating oaten bread and drinking the sweet mead in some friendly farmhouse. But at last, well after midday, the lovers turned their steps once more in the direction of the city and so passed again through the tiny straggling hamlet they had seen earlier that day, soon after they had started out.

As they approached the village, hand in hand, the children tumbling in the road ran indoors and the old men who sat talking by the well bowed their heads in silence. Gwyndoc walked on, looking straight in front of him, but Ygerne's face was sad and thoughtful. "What a pity it is, husband," she said, "that the poor ones are afraid of us and will not make friends with us easily. I want all the world to be my friend today and always, now." Gwyndoc smiled, a little grimly. "It is true, Ygerne," he said. "They are afraid of us; and it is good for us that they are, for it makes our rule much easier. I too love them, especially those in my household and my father's old household, but I know that if I could not use a sword I should get short shrift from some of them, especially the older ones who remember other times."

"Oh, why can't all men be brothers, like . . ." began the girl.

Gwyndoc looked at her a trifle harshly. ". . . like the Romans, you were going to say, weren't you?" he asked.

Ygerne did not speak, but hung her head for a moment. Then, ahead of them, they saw an old woman seated by the roadside crooning. "Let's make her talk to us," said Ygerne. Gwyndoc shrugged his shoulders. "Very well, if you wish," he said, 'but I do not think we shall have much luck." As the two came near to her, the old woman pulled her shawl over her face and half-turned away from them, her voice now still.

"She is afraid, Gwyndoc," said Ygerne, loosing her husband's arm. "Let me talk to her. She will be less fearful of me." And Gwyndoc laughed. "You women!" he said. "You pretend to be afraid of men and go to each other for support. Then you spend the rest of the evening tearing each other to pieces! I'd just as soon trust a forest cat as a woman!"

Ygerne pretended to give him a severe look, but in her heart she was glad that he had said those words, for she knew that he loved her, and that he thought she was different from other women. Then she left the man and went along the path to the old crone, and after a moment sat down beside her on a stone and spoke to her in a low soothing voice.

At first the woman did not move. Then she slowly uncovered her face and looked round, and at last she began to talk to the handsome girl who had sat beside her. And after a few moments Ygerne looked back at her husband and nodded to him, to tell him that he could come now and join them.

As he sat down at their feet, the old woman looked at him closely, ready it seemed to cover her face and resign herself again to death. But his smiling face reassured her and she went on speaking, slowly and pausing often, her eyes on the ground as they must be when addressing gentlefolk. She told them that she was very old, that she could remember when the great Caesar came. At first they teased her gently, and said that it was too long ago for anyone, even the druids, to remember. But when they mentioned the druids she caught her breath and began to rock backwards and forwards again and would not speak any more.

Gwyndoc became impatient and wanted to leave her, but the girl unpinned one of her brooches and put it into the old woman's hand. When she saw what it was the old woman shook her head, afraid, and tried to push the brooch back into Ygerne's hand. But the girl smiled at her and closed the wrinkled fingers over the strip of twisted gold. "Do not be afraid, old mother," she said. "We are your friends. We are not from the druids. We are man and wife and are young. We want to hear tales of the old years, nothing more. We wish to harm no one, nor to be harmed. So tell us, mother, about the times of the great Caesar."

The woman looked down at the brooch and sighed. Then she made a slight bow towards the girl and began to talk again, and now she looked over their heads towards the battlemented white clouds that were building up in the blue sky. "It was when I was a girl," she said. "They brought me from Ireland across the western sea because I knew how to spin the flax. My father brought me. A gold worker he was and made the breast-plates for a British king. Cassivelaun it was who ordered the plate to be made. He was a great man and came often to our house. I spun the flax for his wife and taught her ladies the tricks of the spindle. It was hard to teach the ladies for they did not speak Irish. I could not give them all the secrets for I was only a little girl then, and they were very stupid. We lived in a little house outside the King's wall, and in the winter-time the King's forester brought us venison and the King's granaryman brought us grain, and I took wood and peat from the King's yard to make our fire. We were very happy, I think. I was very happy when my father got wounded fighting, or fell down when he was drunk after a mead-meeting. Then I was mistress of the house and looked after him until he was well again."

Ygerne smiled and patted the old woman gently on the arm. "Yes, mother," she said. "But tell us about the Caesar. Tell us what you remember of him."

The old creature rocked again for a time. "We were in the village when he came," she said. "The horns were blowing and we all went down to the shore to see what was happening. He came in big barges with only a few soldiers. They were brave men and were singing when they jumped into the shallows and came up on to the beach. They were fine big men with swords, and they were all laughing at us. We did not know what to do because they were laughing. But we left the dogs to decide."

"The dogs?" said Gwyndoc, showing an interest for the first time. "What were these dogs?"

The old woman passed her tired hand across her brow again, trying to remember. "Dogs," she said, "the great Hounds of the King. They were many and their eyes were red. Round their necks they wore bronze collars and they could kill as they chose.

When there was no flax, I would watch the geese for the village. And sometimes the hounds would come and kill here and there, as they willed; and no man might drive them away, even though the geese were sacred. Once they drove me into a tree and kept me there until moon came and made them afraid. They were giant dogs. Only the forester could call them. But each year, at the time of the burning of animals, one of them was put into a cage with the others and sent into the flames for the gods."

"Yes, yes," said the young chief, almost impatiently, "but what did they do when Caesar came? Tell me that, old mother."

The old woman thought for a moment. "When Caesar came, the dogs broke their bonds and ran into the sea," she said. "They bit the throats of the soldiers as they swam to the beach. And some of them got into the boats. And the king of the dogs was Bran, from Ireland, and he took the great Caesar into his jaws and broke him into many pieces."

As she spoke the old woman closed her eyes and began to sway from side to side, her words rising and falling like the gentle waves at the side of a lake. Gwyndoc winked at his wife and touched the old woman on the knee. "Go on, mother," he said, "your children listen to your words."

"Then Bran called all the other dogs and they came to him in the boats, and he was their king. Then the boats sailed away to the West and Cassivelaun never saw his hounds again. He wept all that night. But I wept for many nights because my father was slain when the first swordsman came onto the beach."

"But that wasn't the end of the great Caesar, surely?" asked Ygerne soothingly. "You remember more, do you not?"

The old woman began to weep. "Yes," she said. "They married me then to an iron-maker, for they said I was too young to be left alone in a house. I was still sad for my father, but the husband they found for me was kind and was like my father in the house. When he was wounded or drunk I looked after him as I had looked after my father. Then my life was happy again. And I had a son one day. But another year my life was sad again, for the great Caesar came again with many men and all the barges that were on the sea!"

Gwyndoc was teasing now. "But, granny, you said the dogs tore Caesar to little pieces. How then could he come again?" And the old woman's voice was timeless and patient as she spoke to him, like a mother speaking to a wilful child. "The great Caesar was a god," she said simply. "When his nine wives saw the little pieces, they wrapped them up in fine linen and

mulberry leaves and took them home to Italy, and all the long
winter nights they sat and stitched the little pieces together
with gold and silver threads. And when spring came again the
great Caesar was a man once more. And he stood on the
pyramids of Egypt and called his armies and they came back to
our shores."

Gwyndoc nodded understandingly, and then absentmindedly
began to flick pebbles with finger and thumb at a grasshopper
that seemed to stare at them from the path.

"Were you happy or unhappy then?" asked Ygerne.

"I was unhappy then," answered the old woman. "For the
druids took my son to the woods so that the gods would defeat
the great Caesar. But they didn't. The gods deserted us and
Caesar stayed on our shores. At first he killed, then he was
merciful and ceased to kill. Then he gave presents and many
wished him to stay for ever as our god. But *he* did not give me
back my little son. Then at last he sailed away again and took
my husband because he was a good smith and loved the horses."

The story was less remote now, and tears stood in the old
woman's eyes. "I cried for many nights by the sea's side," she
said, "and at last the people ceased to be afraid of me and came
and covered me with straw and skins. Then I went to the woods
and lived with the gods. They found me skins to wear and frogs
to eat, and I stayed with them for many years, tending their
geese. Many conquerors came and passed on to the west, but
none of them hurt me. They knew that I was the handmaiden
of the shining ones and they made obeisance as they passed me
in the woods, especially when I came out to meet them at night."

Just then Gwyndoc was lucky enough to strike the grasshopper with a small pebble. He laughed as he watched the
creature struggling back onto its long legs. Then it gave a great
leap and was lost among the grasses.

"Let us go," he said. "We have heard your story, mother, and
now we must go." He made a sign to Ygerne and the two rose,
hand in hand. The old woman bowed her head. When they had
walked a step or two she got up and shambled after them,
holding out her hand to Ygerne.

"Take back your gift, lady," she said, pushing the brooch
into the girl's hand. "I have known enough suffering. I cannot
keep this, for one day it is to know such pain and tears that
would break a heart as old as mine."

Ygerne clutched the brooch, her eyes staring after the strange
creature. She turned at last to Gwyndoc, and his face was

clouded. Together they watched the flapping figure as it moved from side to side back along the path. They saw the old woman's hands stretched out and waving and they heard the sounds she made.

"What is she doing?" asked Ygerne at last.

"She is driving geese for the gods," said her husband wryly.

As they brushed through the tall grasses, the willowherb and cow-parsley that bordered the winding path, gloom hung over them so heavily that they did not even try to shake it off. "It is terrible to be old and afraid," said Gwyndoc. "Not to be able to laugh and leap and fight." Ygerne was still pondering on the old woman's last words. "Yes," she said, "to be full of foreboding and waiting for unhappiness and death. The old live in the shadow of pain. Oh, Gwyndoc, I wish we never had to grow old!"

Her husband pinched his arm muscles, as though to prove to himself that he was still young and strong. Then he put his arm round the girl and held her close to him. "Have no fear," he said. "We shall never be like that old woman. She is alone, but we shall always be together, brave enough to meet anything the gods send." And Ygerne laughed, showing her white, even teeth perhaps a little longer than she needed. They they began to climb the hill that lay between them and the city, and soon they came to the shade of a little spinney, where they lay together for a while. Gwyndoc made a daisychain, pretending to be angry when Ygerne laughed at his clumsy fingers that broke the delicate stems as he twisted and split them; then, while he wove the chain in and out of the girl's long hair, she thrust her hand inside Gwyndoc's blouse and stroked his hard body. Then they sank back into the moss and shielded their eyes as the sun struck through the leaves above them; and at last Ygerne said, "Gwyndoc, tell me again, what is it that you believe in? Now we are married, I too must believe in your gods. Tell me what to believe in, love."

The young man's words were halting and unsure. He put his hands behind his head and stared up through the boughs. "It's hard to say what I believe in, Ygerne," he said. "I believe in the gods — the good ones — and Caradoc; and my own strength. And now I believe in you. I believe in the power we have and in the kingdoms we can build. There is land here for hunting and raising cattle and growing corn. Good land to ride over and rivers to fish in. There are woods to rest and to worship in. There are mountains where the red gold can be dug. And one

day it will be ours, all of it. Already the Belgae have moved as
far as sea and mountains will let them, and everywhere they are
victorious. Everywhere they push the others before them or
slay them or enslave them. And one day they will build a great
kingdom that will stretch from shore to shore of this island.
And Caradoc shall rule that kingdom, and, if the gods are still
with us, you and I will sit at his right hand to make that kingdom
greater still. That is what I believe in, Ygerne. Do you like it?"

The girl moved closer to him. "Do not be angry, love," she
said, "but I do not like it. There is too much of the sword in it;
too much blood and too many tears. I do not want to spend
my life seeing blood, listening to tales of sorrow, knowing pain.
There are other things in life — poetry, and fine weaving, stock-
breeding and embroidery. And, above all, the art of living
together, all of us — the red, the black and the gold — as one
people."

Gwyndoc pursed his lips. "How can that be?" he said. "The
Belgae are my people, not the Scots or the Silures. The corn we
grow is ours, the cloth our women weave is ours, the land our
sword takes is ours. Our fathers did not come here to till the
land for Silurians or beat gold rings for Picts. They came because
they were strong and could take what they needed. To be weak
is to suffer; to be strong is to accept the gifts of the gods and
offer thanks each year under the stones. Surely you can see
that, Ygerne."

The girl smiled a little sadly. "Things will be different now
that the old King has gone. He was a man of sense now. He
knew that Britain would suffer if her people were not bound
together. Now, now that young men like you and Caradoc are
masters, all the good will be undone. You will squabble and
boast and kill each other until the land is tired of you and
surrenders to the next invader."

Gwyndoc pulled her towards him and rubbed his rough face
against her soft cheek. She wriggled and tried to break away
from him, but he held her firmly. At last she was able to turn
her head round far enough to take his ear in her teeth. She
gripped it just hard enough to hurt a little, and held on. At last
Gwyndoc saw that he could not tease her further without being
punished, so he slackened his grip on her body. Then, when she
had loosed him too, he moved his head away and suddenly
caught her again, laughing. "You see, we Belgae are too clever
for you Romans," he said. "You may think you have your teeth
in our ear — but we'll trick you in the end!"

And Ygerne pretended to be very angry, although she did not struggle so hard that he would have to let her go. "Yes, you are like all the Celts," she stormed. "You live and you die by trickery!"

But her husband laughed on, for he knew she was teasing him. Then he moved his body onto hers, pressing her down, holding her hands widespread on the soft grass. He put his lips close to hers. "Say you are a Celt," he said. "Go on, say it, or I will crush you!"

And for a moment Ygerne tried to keep up her pretence; and then she put her lips to his face and said softly, "Yes, my love, I am a Celt, and I am proud of being such. I am as proud of my blood as I am proud of yours, my husband. We are a great people and no one shall put us down." Then suddenly she burst out laughing and pushed Gwyndoc from her. "Oh, oh!" she said. "We must behave ourselves; there's a squirrel with the funniest expression on his face watching us from that tree over there! He looks just like a druid in disguise!" Then they both laughed and sat up.

After a while they left the wood and made their way over the hill, and as they walked, hand in hand above the city, amongst cowslips and bird's-eye trefoil, with a clear blue sky over their heads and the fresh salt breeze tossing back their long hair, they forgot the dark background of their times, the brutish black backcloth against which all moved, in alternating arrogance, terror, whimpering misery and exalted poetry. They forgot the threshing limbs under the great stones, the antlered men whose ghastly faces twitched among the dark forests, the white-robed wolves who annually carried away the first-born or mutilated the cattle with golden knives to bring rain. They forgot the storms and the famines, the black cock's entrails steaming omens before the chief's high table, the fresh blood hardening on some young widow's lintel, and the ruined and ravaged faces that peered out from the beehive slums as magnificent young lords cantered by with cloak floating and bright boar-spears flashing in their jewelled hands.

But at last they were forced to come down to earth again, and the last dreams faded when a company of horsemen swept past them, shouting and waving swords, as they entered the city gates. Gwyndoc pulled his wife to him and pressed hard against the stone pillars to avoid the flying hooves. "They must be mad or drunk," said the girl, trembling. But Gwyndoc did not answer. He dragged her by the hand, after him, towards the King's house, as though she were a calf or a pony going to market. The unglazed windows of the Council Chamber blazed red with torchlight, and even from the courtyard the sound of many excited voices could be heard. Gwyndoc's steps quickened, and in the anteroom he loosed Ygerne's hand almost as though he had forgotten that she existed.

Seated on a bench beside the door were Morag and his brother, the one breathing hard on a helmet and rubbing it with his sleeve, the other lazily kicking his heavy leather scabbard from foot to foot.

As Gwyndoc reached the door he spoke to them. "Hail, cousins," he said. "This is a surprise! Why is the Council in session?" But the brothers looked up at him with a blank stare of enmity, and neither spoke. Gwyndoc paused for a moment, a quick anger driving the blood into his ears. Then Morag slowly bent his head and spat on the floor, and Beddyr stopped kicking his sword and held it in his left hand. Gwyndoc's lips began to twitch and he could scarcely keep his voice down to a whisper. "Cousins," he said, "one day your insolence will find me when I am not in a hurry. Then watch which side of your faces you smile on."

He turned away from them, as they bowed their heads ironically, and passed through the open door. Ygerne waited for him at the entrance to the antechamber, but as the twilight turned to dark he did not come. Morag and Beddyr stared at her from time to time, smiling cruelly but never speaking, until she could stand it no longer. Then she went to find Gwynedd, for she could not bear these barbarians to see her tears and her fear of them.

Caradoc was at first a little angry by his friend's absence that day, but that annoyance was soon forgotten in the general argument and hubbub of the meeting. Before the Belgic Council retired that night they had condemned Adminius to death, in his absence, as a traitor; had sent the fiery crosses out along all the upland roads from Lindum to Mai Dun; had organised an immediate tribal levy throughout the south, and had sent off couriers to Catuval, in Belgium, reminding him of blood-ties and asking for his armies.

As for the Romans let them come if they were so minded. A clash must take place again sooner or later — it was inevitable. They would be allowed to land wherever they chose — though preferably in the southerly marsh country, south of Tamesa —

and then Reged, with the subchieftains and their bog-trotting tribesmen would harry the wits out of them day and night, worrying them to death and preventing them from forming properly. Then, when their determination was shaken, they would be allowed to make their way to the former hinterland, where Caradoc could bring the full weight of his chariots to bear on them and so smash them before they could get their second wind.

The meeting ended at an almost hysterical pitch of enthusiasm. Reged, who was riding off straightway to take over his command, ordered a stirrup-cup to be brought, and the farewell toast immediately turned into an orgy of berserk drunkenness. Only Caradoc and Gwyndoc remained sober enough to strap Reged into his saddle and to pack him off southwards with a guard on each side of him to keep him from falling to the ground.

Then they wandered out together into the streets, arm in arm, laughing with a fierce excitement at the fires that burned brightly throughout the city, calling to the shouting tribesmen and laying their hands on the shoulders of the warriors who ran towards them from the shadows and knelt before them, vowing eternal homage.

By the middens a crowd of youths stood laughing round an old man. As the friends drew near they saw that it was Bobyn, the idiot. He danced in the firelight, uncouth as a great bear in his stinking sheepskins and otter-skin cap. He was singing drunkenly and waving above his head a long sword of painted wood.

Caradoc tapped a young lad on the shoulder. "Hey, boy," he said, "what's happening here?" The lad did not bother to turn round, nor did he recognise the King's voice. "Oh, it's a bit of fun," he said. "It's Bobyn! We've made him a sword and told him the King wants him to lead the army against the Romans!" And the lad nudged Caradoc and went on laughing.

For a moment the King's face was grim, then he smiled at Gwyndoc and gave the lad a cuff over the head that was meant to be playful but which laid him on his face.

When Gwyndoc returned to his room he found Ygerne's bed still empty. She was with Gwynedd, no longer weeping, but cursing the day she had stooped to marry a tribesman, while the dark-eyed girl stroked her arm and nodded patiently, knowing that the fit would pass before morning.

CHAPTER SIX

A S THE FIRST galleys left the open sea and pulled in towards the river mouth the threatened storm broke. Looking back into the Channel, the vanguard saw the following barges swing away from them, like a rope cut in the middle.

Here and there right out into the broad sea of the channel, flaming pitch-balls were shot into the dusk as an indication of position. But the wind had now risen to such a point of violence that it seemed impossible, short of the miracle that happens only too infrequently during surprise attacks, for the full force to proceed as planned.

After a hasty consultation with his ship's captain, Aulus Plautius, in the leading barge, gave the signal for his vessel and the six others that had followed him inshore to lie off the river mouth until dawn. By that time he hoped that the main company would have re-formed and have crossed to join him.

All through the night, blazing pitch signals shot up here and there out at sea, but the attacking barges had their own work cut out to hold their positions inshore against a freshening wind from the land. No fires had been sighted inland; in fact, for all the Romans had seen, this part of Britain might well have been uninhabited. Nevertheless precautions were taken on board and all braziers were doused before the full darkness came. No singing or even talking above a whisper was allowed, and the soldiers, grumbling and bored, at last wrapped themselves in their campaign cloaks and huddled as close as they could to try and get in some sleep before dawn.

But for most of them the light came only too soon. On each barge at first light, non-commissioned officers moved quickly among the ranks, thumping and pushing and swearing when a legionary began to shout. Before the sun had properly risen the invaders were all awake, stretching and yawning and trying to rub the aches of the hard planks from their bruised bodies. Some of them were already complaining of pains in their joints. They looked ashore at the morning mist and cursed the British climate.

For an hour or perhaps more they waited, looking anxiously back the way they had come, hoping to see the galleys coming in towards them with their oars beating up the blue sea and their pennants streaming out behind, or the squat, flat-bottomed barges that carried the tall siege-engines and the horses of the auxiliary cavalry.

But they saw nothing, and as the sun's warmth grew Aulus
Plautius called to his leading galley two tribunes and a few
selected staff-officers and, under the striped awnings of his
cabin, they discussed their immediate plan of action.

The legionaries were ordered to pull sacking tunics over their
breastplates and to carry their helmets under their arms until
ordered to put them on. In the bright sunlight the shining steel
would make their approach too obvious and, if possible, it was
desired to create as much consternation as could be by surprise.
While the legionaries did as they were ordered, grumbling and
shrugging their stiff shoulders, the auxiliaries laughed and lolled
about the decks — narrow-eyed Mongols, brown Arabs, even
black-skinned Africans. These were for the most part archers or
cavalrymen, and wore thick tunics and caps of hardened leather.
They did not need to take precautions like the others.

At last the word came that they would proceed up-river
without the main body, leaving one galley off-shore to hurry
the others up when they did arrive. To wait any longer would
be to invite discovery and counter-attack. One galley, especially
if it carried but a few soldiers, would excite only curiosity if
observed. It was not likely that the land-loving Belgae would
put out to sea in attack, and should they do so in any force the
galley had sails and oars and would carry only a minimum load.

Down below, in the general's barge, the oarsmen got their
orders, and heard the muffled horns sounding the signal to
begin the trip upriver. "What's it like here?" asked a sleek-
haired Sicilian, as he spat on his hands.

The oarsman who answered still bore the remains of blue
caste-marks across his forehead. "Not so good," he said briefly,
and looked through his oar-hole into the water.

"What's wrong with it?" asked the other. "I didn't know
you'd ever been here before."

His companion looked back at him with scorn. "Man, I was
born on this river," he said. "I was born of the Cantii, but they
wanted to put me to the iron and I wouldn't have it. Never
could stand the heat. My father was furious. He threatened to
send me down the mines — so I made my getaway in a trading-
boat to Armorica. I'd built up quite a connection in the hide
business before Claudius ordered that last northern call-up. Now
God knows when I'll get out of this mob. They think this war's
going to be over before the winter, but I know these people.
They've got no idea of fighting as part of a machine, but they

just won't give in when they're beaten. They'll just retreat and then come back when they're ready, time and time again. It must be sickening to real soldiers like our friends up on deck here."

The Sicilian eyed him curiously. "You're a Roman, too, aren't you?" he said.

The other grinned and rolled his blue eyes upwards. "Maybe I am; maybe I'm not. They say I am — but they can't stop me from thinking."

And as the overseer came below and beat out the oar-strokes with his mallet, what the Briton was thinking was that it would be pleasant when the fighting started to leave his oar and jump into the shallows, and make his way back to the downs to see if his old father still wanted him to go into the foundries.

When the sun stood high the barges were still nosing up-stream, and nowhere did they see any sign of resistance. Once, as the heavily wooded river-banks crowded in close on either side of them, they saw a skin-clad herdsman watering his cattle. He stared at them, open-mouthed, and then waved to them. The legionaries could not help disobeying orders: they just roared with laughter and waved back, and one of them shouted out in Belgic, "A fine day it's going to be!" And the old herds-man replied, shaking his head dubiously, "Yes, but it might rain before nightfall, I shouldn't wonder."

After that the soldiers were in fine spirits. Nor would they lie down under the bulwarks as the boats rounded each bend of the river, according to orders. Even the heartless centurions relaxed a little and allowed the men to break into their iron-rations and pass the wine-skins round.

So, as they sprawled about, eating and joking, relaxed and merry, the first flights of arrows caught them quite unprepared. Men fell transfixed in all positions, kneeling to tie up a shoe-string, sharpening a knife to cut another slice of bread, stretching, or yawning. One grizzled old soldier was passing the wine-skin to his comrades when an arrow suddenly pierced it from side to side. The next arrow passed through his breast, and as he died the expression on his face was still one of disgust at seeing the lovely red wine cascading in two streams, to waste on the deck.

Then, as the legionaries took cover where they might, the air became thick with arrows coming from the dense brushwood and reeds which bordered the quickly narrowing river. One shaft passed by chance through an oar-hole and stuck quivering into the oaken seat beside the young Sicilian. He wiped his

brow. "Phew!" he said. "That was too close for my liking." The
British oarsman replied, "It's only a joke. You see, I'll call out
to them. These are my own tribesmen, I can tell from the way
that arrow head is cast. It's a diamond-shape, not pronged like
ours — the Roman's I mean." He put his head to the hole and
called out, bantering. Then he drew back sharply, and swore.
An arrow was sticking in the planks an inch from where his
head had been. He started to push his fist through the hole with
the intention of shaking it towards the wooded bank, then he
changed his mind and swore again instead. "Damn them," he said.
"Nothing but savages, that's all they are! What they want is a
damn good hiding, and with luck we'll give it to them." The
Sicilian smiled ironically. "I thought they were your people."
he said. The Briton spat and took hold of his oar again, but the
time-keeper spoke sharply to him. "Keep your mind on your
job, number four! I've already ordered 'halt'. If you think you
can do this job better than me, you can come and sit up here
and thump this bloody hammer, and welcome!" He had to duck
then for another flight of arrows came over, humming like the
wings of a giant bird.

"Do you think you know better than I do?" he yelled at the
Briton, embarrassed.

"No, Corporal. I was only anxious to get on."

"Do you think you know where we're going then?"

"No, Corporal, I was only —"

"Then shut up and keep still. You blasted cattle!" The time-
keeper glared at the oarsmen and they dropped their eyes —
all except the Sicilian, who nodded at the Briton and grinned,
then winked at the time-keeper and began to whistle quietly.
It was a quaint, jaunty little tune, a song of Mithras that was
sweeping through the legions just lately. The time-keeper found
himself starting to whistle too, then, remembering his position,
roared out, "Who's whistling? Is it you, number six?"

The Sicilian looked at him innocently. "Me, Corporal? '
he said. "Why no. It sounded to come from over there." And he
nodded towards the still-angry Celt.

The time-keeper stared at the Briton. "Well, shut up, whoever
it was, or I'll have you rowing double-time for the next hour."

The Briton suddenly felt a foreigner in a hostile country, but
even he knew that the corporal's threat was an empty one.
The boats stopped: there was to be no double-time, or even
single-time for long enough that day, for the trumpets sounded
and anchors were lowered. Then the auxiliary archers, hawk-

faced men from the Caucasus, took cover and replied into the rushes with volley after volley of arrows. Here and there a man screamed or became visible as he leapt into the air wounded, and after a time there were no more arrows shot from the shore.

The second barge in the line pulled up to the leader and a tribune came aboard for orders. Then he returned to his ship and, under cover from the others, pulled into the river bank with the trumpets screaming again.

But no living enemy was in sight. Here and there among the thick rushes lay tartan-clad tribesmen, their bows or javelins still in their hands, pierced by the Roman arrows, but the others had vanished into the nodding reeds and surrounding woods, and only the low sighing of water and rushes could be heard.

The legionaries stared about them, then back at their captains, in bewildered surprise, and eventually they got back into their barge and proceeded again upstream.

And this happened again and again before nightfall; but always, however swift the landing was, the enemy had withdrawn, leaving the Romans shivering in the evening mists, mocked by the sucking rustles of the marshland and the bitterns' mournful crying.

That night, to give a good impression as well as warmth, fires were lit for half a mile along the river bank and guards were stationed as far inland as there seemed any solid ground. The general held a meeting of staff officers on his barge to decide how the next day's attack should begin in view of their depleted numbers. At the most crucial point of the discussion a light racing boat pulled up to the barges carrying a courier. His message was that the other barges, including horses and engines, were only two hours behind and would join with the general before midnight.

For a time after this news had been passed along the lines there was a revival of high spirits among the soldiers who were not on guard. The bonfires were heaped up and an extra issue of wine and meat was made. The rumour went round later that the paymaster had started his arrangements for paying out in the morning a bonus to all legionaries with over five years' service with the eagles. The veterans helped themselves to another cup of wine and slapped each other's backs. The new recruits shambled round grumbling, and here and there private quarrels began. Then a small group of Parthian bowmen, auxiliaries, still wearing their sheepskin cloaks and fur caps decorated with fox-tails, drank too much of the warm spiced wine and began one

of their fire-dances, shouting and kicking their legs high into the
air. This would have passed off well, but an arrogant young
German laughed a little too loudly, a little too soon, and in the
firelight the dance turned into something else before the
officers could stop it. The young German was flung into one of
the roaring fires, and his friends retaliated immediately by
splitting any head that wore a cur cap. For a time there was a
drunken uproar; then the grey-haired legionaries cordoned off
the area with their long spearshafts, while the non-commissioned
officers went round taking names and awarding punishments.

And as the encampment settled down again to wait for the
arrival of the main force the sentries staring round them into
the darkness saw many small fires start up away inland. They
watched them flickering on hilltop after hilltop, spreading like
hysterical laughter, and they wondered what this meant. And in
the blackness before them they heard the bogs shifting and
settling, and felt the suck and the pull of the wet ground beneath
their feet. Sometimes a zig-zagging bat would come crazily out
from the bushes and beat against their faces, or helmets or
breastplates. Sometimes they would stop breathing to listen to
a rat dragging its belly through the creaking reeds. And sometimes they would stand frozen in alarm, sword-arm quivering
and head shaking, as an owl, or a cuckoo, or a lark began to call,
in the depth of the night, only a few feet from them.

When the relief-guard stumbled away from the bright fires to
take over, half of them, getting no reply to their whispered pass-
words, found the men they had come to relieve lying or kneeling
in the slime, strangled or stabbed or shot with arrows, and the
owls still hooting.

CHAPTER SEVEN

T WO DAYS AFTER the Council had met so merrily, Reged's
horse-messenger brought word to Caradoc that the campaign would be an easy one for the tribesmen. The enemy had
landed the previous night from only six galleys and had been
unable to do more than find themselves fairly dry patches of
ground to pitch their tents on. They had sent out half a dozen
tentative scouting parties but, Reged reported, these had not
returned! So far, he estimated, the Romans had lost over a
hundred legionaries in the marshes, by reason of their ignorance
of firm paths and also because, once they were bogged, the

weight of their armour prevented an easy withdrawal. Those
who did not get themselves drowned in the mud were easy game
for the tribesmen's arrows. By using "ducks' feet" — broad
boards strapped to their shoes — the Belgae were able to move
about as they wished with little danger, using the scanty cover
available to its best advantage. They must have accounted for a
hundred of the enemy, not reckoning the guards who had been
picked off on the first night. Reged speculated that within a
short time the Romans would either withdraw, in which case
they must be met at the river mouth and be wiped out, or they
would abandon their position on the river-bank and try to move
swiftly towards the firmer ground of the hinterland. In this case
they would be forced to abandon much of their stores and
probably their armour. Reged hoped that they would take the
second alternative, for he felt the clans would gain useful
experience from it. He ended his message laconically by telling
his brother not to bother about sharpening the chariot-knives.

The Belgic leaders at Camulodun were beside themselves at
this news, and treated the courier like a prince. Then, when the
first elation had worn thin, it turned to a feeling of disappointment among certain of the chieftains. They felt that Reged was
cheating them of a battle, and some were for leaving immediately
to share the fun that Reged's men seemed to be having. Caradoc,
more cautious, over-ruled this demand, but even so was unable
to prevent certain young adventurers from setting-off secretly
to join the glorious southern tribes.

It was ironical that, even while Reged's messenger was being
made drunk and loaded with gifts, the main body of the Roman
army, delayed by shoals at the river-mouth, had now dropped
anchor under the direction of Aulus Plautius and by superior
weight and numbers was already establishing for itself an
effective, though temporary, bridgehead — the Parthian archers
now sufficiently numerous to hold back the tribesmen in a
broad semi-circle from the waterside while the jack-of-all-trade
legionaries hammered stakes into the slime as a basis for a
protective stockade. Many would die, they knew now, before
they were able to march north to the capital, but there was
sound sense in snatching even a momentary security while the
troops recovered from a rough Channel-crossing and became at
least superficially inured to the island climate. Not that this
mattered much to the north-coast Gauls, who were used to fogs
and sea-mists and slush up to the ankles in the rainy season; but
it was already upsetting the Spaniards and some of the Levantine

cohorts.

When celebrations of Reged's despatch were at their height another courier arrived, this time on foot, for he had come from no further than the dockside. The words he gabbled carried enough force and surprise to put an immediate, shocked end to any drinking and song and to send the befuddled soldiers back to their posts, already fumbling with lance and sword.

A fishing coracle, two or three miles off-shore, had just come in, he said, with the news that a biggish fleet of sailing vessels was standing out to sea, waiting for a wind, it seemed, to head for the port. The fishermen had been too frightened to note any more details — the number of ships, their types, the cut of the sails, and so on. So the immediate conclusion drawn by the Council was the obvious one — that Rome was attacking again, this time with full strength. Now Caradoc thought he saw the significance of the six galleys that Reged had reported. They were nothing but a decoy to draw the main Belgic forces southwards, while a strong and direct attack was made on the relatively undefended capital.

The lords cursed the Romans for crafty foxes, horns blew from every direction, tribesmen were gathered into the city area from the outlying districts and house-to-house fighting was prepared for. The chariots were assembled outside the gates and fire-boats were made ready in the harbour. The royal family and its dependents were then sent some miles out of Camulodun, under a strong cavalry escort, to their hunting lodge at the edge of the upland woods; and they left Gwynedd and Ygerne sullen and tight-lipped, followed by a straggling train of the poorer citizens — puzzled, grumbling cattle, who wanted to share the royal protection but who would have cut the young Queen's throat without remorse for the price of a ram or a new pair of shoes.

Coracle scouts were sent out after dusk, and the tension was relieved when one of them returned with a laughing passenger, armed only with a knife and long Gallic lance, a tall, brown-haired young man whose moustaches hung almost on to his chest and who wore a breastplate of gold-inlaid ebony. As he strode through the torchlit streets to the King's house, snarls turned to cheers as the townsfolk recognised the same tartan as that Cunobelin had worn in the older days: it was the almost legendary Catuval himself, who had left his fleet so that he might come on in advance to offer himself to the King. The

boatman who had brought him wallowed in the admiration of
his fellows, tossing a bag of coins into the air and catching it
again. "He's a real man!" he said. "He nearly knocked the bottom
out of my boat with his spear when he jumped in!" No one
challenged him at any point. He walked from street to courtyard
and into the Council Chamber, where the war-lords were drawing
up final plans for defence. Caradoc turned in his chair as the
heavy door burst open; then, as he saw who had come, he rose
to greet his cousin, both hands outstretched.

But Catuval did not allow himself the familiarity of such a
greeting. He fell to one knee before the King. "Badger," he
said humbly, "your people from over the water pay homage
and offer you their swords. Hail, Caradoc! Hail Belgium!"

The Council took up the hail. Then the King raised Catuval
to his feet and seated him at his left hand, for Gwyndoc was at
his right. And Gwyndoc saw that there were tears in the eyes of
the King and of Catuval: in a moment he felt that they were in
his own, too.

That night even the sulking girls, Gwynedd and Ygerne, so
far forgot their loneliness as to return to be present at the feast
given to Catuval, although they did not disguise their annoyance
when the young chief excused himself half-way through to go
down to the quayside and supervise the landing and billeting
of his infantry. They had found him most attractive and had
hoped, in some way or other, to play him off against their
husbands — just to teach them a lesson!

But there were harder and bloodier lessons to be taught and
learned. By the following day the Belgic Council, reassembled
for an emergency meeting, had voted for a change of tactics,
heartened by Catuval's sudden arrival and by the strength of the
support he was placing at their disposal. So it was agreed that
Reged should be withdrawn from his southern command and
his lieutenant, a skilled old Breton, be asked to take over from
him. The Romans were to be allowed a relatively unhampered
passage through the marshlands and then to be harried, but not
too fiercely, until they were forced to fight a pitched battle
north of Tamesa. There the full chariot weight could be brought
to bear on them in a pincers-movement, Caradoc making a frontal
attack, after the Roman front had been softened by spearmen
from the tribes, and Reged and Catuval attacking the Roman
flanks with chariots supported by Belgian infantry.

Reged, himself depressed by the damp and the poor food

supplies, was only too anxious to hand over his command when the messenger had given his news. Nor did he make any attempt to keep the change of plans secret. Thr result was that many of the young leaders who had followed him south changed their minds now and decided, whether he gave them permission or not, to go back with him to the north, where a pitched battle with chariots and cavalry would provide a better chance of glory and loot. Consequently, when Reged rode off towards Camulodun later in the day, many of the tribesmen were drained from their position around the bridgehead. A long trail of laughing horsemen followed the prince just out of sight, like roguish dogs that do behind their master's back what they would be beaten for could he see them.

This circumstance, together with another on the Roman side, came near to undoing the plans of the Belgic Council even before the first steps could be made to put them into action. Just before Reged was relieved of his command in the marsh area, an envoy came to Aulus Plautius, a little more arrogantly than his subordinate rank warranted, with a pronouncement from the Emperor Claudius, in which the god complimented the soldier on his arrival at the river-bank, but expressed only a thinly-veiled surprise that in so many days more ground had not been covered. The Emperor asked jocularly whether the general felt he had quite enough troops to undertake the campaign success-fully, or whether he would prefer to have another general officer at his side to assist him in making his decisions. Claudius ended by stating his intention of coming to Britain at an early date, bringing with him a special troop of cavalry, which he thought might be useful should the barbarians require a little extra handling.

When Aulus Plautius had heard the message his first impulse was to strike the smiling envoy across the face. But he recollected his position and considered the bad impression such an action would make among the soldiers, especially the half-savage Parthians. So he had the man fed and packed off back to the coast with a bagful of trophies — rings, swords and gorgets — that he had collected during the skirmishing among the reeds. He felt almost inclined to send Claudius a severed blond head, just to show him that this affair was a serious one. Calling to mind the Emperor's terrified expression when a rat once ran across the floor of his tent, he laughed aloud at the prospect and had almost sent off a soldier to bring back a yellow-haired captive. Then he sobered up again and instead went into his pavilion and hacked away at the tent-pole until his rage had passed.

Within an hour the Romans had orders to prepare for an advance, come what may, infantry and cavalry. They made ready almost immediately, and by the time Reged's departure had thrown the defending positions into disorder, the first cohort had pushed its way onto hard fighting ground with scarcely any losses.

During the days that followed, the invading army often called to mind that floating, dreamlike break-through. As they lay flat in the hills covering their bodies with the long shields while arrows flew thick as hail from the dusk about them, or as they pressed hard against each other, helmet to helmet, in the plains while the screaming charioteers swept down on them from all sides and then vanished like howling demons in their own swirling dust, they remembered the fatal ease with which they had marched, victory already between their teeth, along the wooden causeway they had made, out of the marshes. And as their supply-lines lengthened matters became no easier. Food-wagons were bogged or rifled on their way from the riverside, and there were no villages round about worth sacking. Those they came upon were either burnt to ashes or peopled by starving cripples, for everyone capable of holding lance or bow had evacuated the southern area, taking with them the cattle and the season's grain. At night-time, resting round their fires after the long day's march, the legionaries would grumble. "They told me I'd only got to serve with the colours for twenty years and they'd give me a bounty and land to live on when they discharged me," growled an old pikeman who had watched the vultures settle from Egypt to Germany. "Now, when I've only got six months to do, they send me out to rot in this festering island! It's just like them, the long-haired bastards!"

A grinning Arab unslung his sheaf of arrows and slapped the veteran on the head, knocking his helmet to one side, "What are you yelping about, Grandad?" he teased. "I've got to serve twenty-five years — and what do I get when I'm gone in the teeth? Why, Roman citizenship, thank you very much! No five acres and a cow for me, my boy! Why, I only get half the pay you foot-sloggers get and I do all the fighting — me and this!" He slapped the thick horn bow that hung at his side. The legionary looked up, screwing his eyes. "Why, you black monkey," he retorted, "the likes of you don't need pay! All you need is straw to lie in and a bone to chew!"

And then the pair of them began to push each other about, with a heartiness that would inevitably become malicious before long. "Pay!" chipped in a long-legged Greek. "The legions have seen no pay for three months, nor are like to do, from what I can gather! Rome! I'd rather work for a cat's-meat man — I should at least know where my next meal was coming from!"

The veteran turned to him now, "Yes, you'd look well behind a barrow, I must admit! Better than in that armour!"

And so the men joked to kill their boredom and their anxiety. The Greek was wrong about the pay, however, for next morning the paymaster went round from company to company feeling under jawbones for helmet-callouses and paying out accordingly. That day the legions grumbled more than ever because now they had pay and nowhere to spend it! "Wait till we get to Camulodun," called out a standard-bearer, sweating under his leopard-skin. "We shan't need money there — they'll give us anything! And the girls! You've never seen anything like them: they look as cold as ice, but when you get them alone, man, phew! they're hotter than two leopard-skins and an African sun rolled into one!"

And all the time they marched, and laughed, and starved and were killed — ambushed on hillsides, at the edge of gloomy forests, crossing streams, in gullies. The way from the bridge-head to Londinium could be followed by the flapping of crows; and then northwards, towards Camulodun, driven by duty and pride, by the desire for war, by the promise of release or bounty or loot, the vengeful beckoning ghost of Caesar striding at their head, the tottering shadow of Claudius cackling at their heels, nagging like a schoolmaster.

In the royal house, Caradoc and his generals ate and drank and laughed, reviewed the cavalry or the chariots, hunted a little, galloped about a great deal and attended to their last-minute private affairs. Scouts were coming in almost hour by hour, bringing news of the enemy advance. The Council decided that the legions should be halted some ten miles south-west of the capital and there annihilated. Such was the confidence among the tribesmen that Caradoc could not for shame send Gwynedd away to safety this time. She and her ladies must stay in the royal house to keep up the uncertain heart of the citizens if nothing else. But secretly the King took his leave of her, and in their bedchamber he told her that he believed the gods were watching over him, and that before many hours he would be

back again with her. But should the Roman gods prove stronger
— and here his eyes fell, since he did not care openly to slight
the tribal gods — and should he be prevented from returning,
then he had arranged for swift wagons and a big escort of picked
warriors to escort her and her retinue to the west. She must go
as far away from the Romans as possible; he had already sent
an envoy to Caerwent to prepare the Silurian king for this
eventuality.

He kissed her bowed forehead and went from her, and
Gwynedd did not raise her head until the King's steps had faded
from the house.

Gwyndoc, who told his wife almost exactly the same, made a
different exit. Ygerne laughed and wept by turns. At one time
she begged to be allowed to put on man's clothing and cut her
hair and sit alongside him in the chariot; then, when he refused,
her mood changed and she flung herself onto her couch and
kicked and said she was glad the Romans *had* come at last ·
now there would be some real men to rule the country instead
of long-haired boys, and real sense would be talked instead of
mystic savagery. But when she saw that she had hurt Gwyndoc,
who stood silently in the middle of the room, she repented
again and wished him victory and in the same breath asked him
to escape with her to the Brigantes, where her aunt would look
after them. This shocked Gwyndoc more than anything, but she
cut his words short, pushed him through the door and shouted
after him, "I shall be ashamed to tell the child that is in me that
Gwyndoc is its father!"

The young lord whirled round and tried to push open the
door, his face white with surprise, but Ygerne had bolted it from
the inside. He could hear her crying in the room and he called
to her to forgive him, to open the door and let him explain.
But outside the horns sounded and he had to hurry to the
chariots. Before he went he tore off the gold lunula from his
chest and left it by the door as an offering. As he climbed into
the chariot, alongside the King, his face was hard and anxious,
and for the first time he wondered how it felt to be killed in
battle.

Aulus Plautius, however, had no time for emotional specula-
tions of that nature. Claudius' advance guard had landed at
Tamesa with little opposition and were following close behind.
He resented this, for it looked as though the Emperor was spying

on him. But he didn't resent the Emperor's offer of "a new sort
of cavalry" — this amused him, though as a serious professional
soldier he did not allow his mind to run too much on it or on
the Emperor's orders concerning its employment. It went all
against the text-books — but it was fun! If nothing else, it
would teach these barbarians the contempt with which Rome
regarded them.

And, protected from view by tall screens, this new sort of
cavalry followed in his wake towards the battlefield, trumpeting
and snorting and causing the Parthian horses to rear and stamp.

CHAPTER EIGHT

JUST AS THE Council had planned, the chariots swung into
line, four deep, and cantered up the rise to the brow of the
slope. Each chariot, drawn by two chargers, carried its leader,
his companions, a spearman tied to the central shaft, and footmen
hanging onto the tailboard, ready to leap off into the press and
use their axes when the chariot struck.

Not a word was spoken or a banner raised as the slow movement was made, but all looked towards the royal chariot, which
was leading, ahead of the front rank by twenty paces, its red
dragon standard trailing behind it, not to be raised until the
charge was begun. And the following tribesmen saw the King,
dressed now in his scarlet cloak over his gold breastplate, lean to
his nearest companion and embrace him. From the silver bull's
horns that stood high from the warrior's helmet they knew that
this was Gwyndoc, and all the young chief's clansmen felt proud
that their leader should be so favoured by Caradoc.

Soon the chariot mass had gained the head of the hill, and at
a sign from the King halted. The rear ranks, still below the rise,
were unable to see what was going on in the plain, but the
King's chariot, positioned above the battlefield, commanded a
perfect view of the action. The sun stood high in the sky now,
and wherever the eye looked it saw only confusion and a tangling
mass of bodies as the tribesmen harried the attackers. The ear
heard only shouts, warcries, screams of men and horses, and the
savage, rhythmic hiss that swordsmen make as they slash again
and again. Already the crows were hovering over the swaying
chaos, and at the farthest edges of the field outcast dogs snapped
avidly at each other's mangy ribs as they moved impatiently up
and down, waiting.

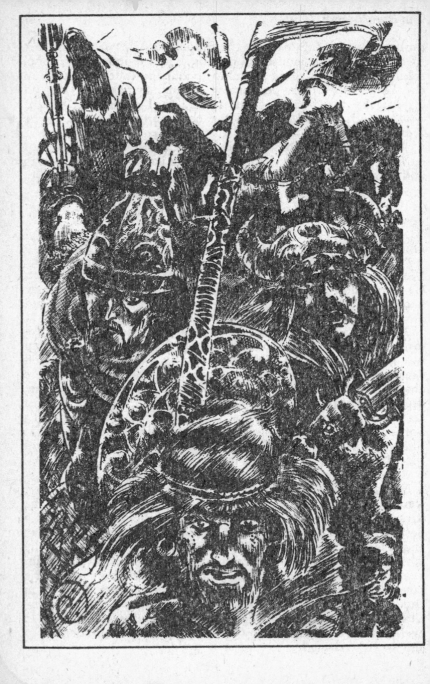

Gwyndoc, at his lord's side in the great gilded chariot, looked about him as they drew up to the brow of the hill. A company of long-haired Cantii were in the thick of the fighting, right under the feet of the cohort that protected the Roman general, Aulus Plautius. They were hacking and thrusting, all swordsmen, and giving no inch of ground. Gwyndoc recognised their chief by his tartan and tried to shout to him, asking him to go easy on the Roman general as he, Gwyndoc, wanted a bit of fun. But his voice was drowned in the other noises of that day. Caradoc heard him, though, and looked down at him sternly. Then for a time Gwyndoc was silent. He looked away from the King's eye and watched the battle intently. And, as he stared, he saw a strange, unpredictable thing happen that held him fascinated as it took its course, like something in a dream. The Roman shield-wall suddenly unlocked and swung open like a great door of living steel, leaving the ranks behind it uncovered. At first Gwyndoc thought that the legionaries were crumbling, but soon he saw the purpose of the movement: the Roman archers were waiting to go into action. They were arranged, neatly as a boy's toy warriors, in three tiers, the first kneeling, the second crouching above them, and the third standing upright and clear of their comrades. Each archer had his bow held before him at the ready, an arrow already fitted to the string, waiting. They were a magnificent spectacle of military efficiency. Gwyndoc gasped at their precision and coolness, then he heard a brisk command, and each archer drew his red-hackled arrow to his ear and waited again, motionless as a statue. The harrying tribesmen halted for an instant, taken off their guard by this unexpected movement, and, as they stood amazed, there was yet another command, this time more urgent than before, and the bowstrings twanged in a ghastly, vibrant unison. Yet hardly had this sound died on the ear when it was repeated again, and then again. Three flights of arrows had flown into the mass of the oncoming attackers while a man could have counted three. And, as Gwyndoc stared, the Cantii melted and fell into a huddle of writhing forms before his eyes. Then the shield-wall closed again and the terrible bowmen were hidden.

Gwyndoc glanced up at the King's face. It was pale and tense. Caradoc had seen, too, and his long fingers twisted and untwisted the gold bracelet on his left arm. He spoke, or rather whispered, so softly that his friend could not be quite sure that he had heard correctly. "We must attack soon or the footmen will lose heart, and then our cause is lost," he thought the King said.

To the left the Trinobantes were working hard with their knives and long lances. Again and again they broke upon their section of the shield-wall like the savage breakers of a ravenous sea. Singing their own war-song, a desperate and melancholy dirge, the tall spearmen prized open the long Roman shields while the shorter, more agile knifemen ran in quickly and stabbed right and left at throat and arms. As Gwyndoc watched, they surged once more against the motionless wall, and suddenly their song grew louder and louder, becoming derisively victorious, rising to a shriek as the shieldmen crumbled and retreated before them. The Romans were breaking formation! They were falling before the knifemen at last!

Then, with a forlorn attempt at the precision they had shown before, the shieldmen tried to swing back like a great gate. They tottered and fell, lying on the ground helpless while the Trinobantes thrust at their faces and their sides, howling now like wolves, and already looting helmets and swords as they passed on. The remnants of the Roman defence stood gallantly, re-forming even as their neighbours died, and then pulled to one side to show the archers once more, as magnificently ordered as before. But even as they drew their long arrows the spearmen were upon them, thrusting and yelling. That volley of arrows was never fired, and Gwyndoc bobbed up and down on the chariot floor like a man possessed as he watched the green tartans rolling in, and on and on, almost too tired with slaughter now to howl their song, keeping their strength only for maiming and mutilating, drunk with glory, right in amongst the enemy. Three hundred men at least went through that shrieking gap, with victory already in their wild hearts. Then the shield-wall closed again, almost as solid and impassive as ever. For a few seconds Gwyndoc still heard the spearmen's chant, and here and there the shield-wall quivered and shook, as though it were being attacked from behind. A few shields fell from their places. Then there was no movement at all, and nothing more was seen of the Trinobantes. It was as though they had never been.

Gwyndoc plucked excitedly at the King's kilt. "Let us attack now, lord," he said. "To the left, where the spears went in. It must be weaker there." But Caradoc's blue eyes were sweeping far to left and right, away from the battlefield, towards the distant hill and the woods. He made no sign that he was even conscious of his friend's presence.

Then Morag began to swear, as he stood on the central shaft of the war-chariot, turning his dark face up at the sun and chattering, imploring, the muscles of his tense throat moving up and down within his gold gorget. "Let us go now, lord of the greater light! Let us attack them now! I do not ask for victory, lord, only for sword-meat and the mist of blood in my eyes! I do not ask—" Caradoc suddenly stiffened and struck Morag full across the mouth with the flat of his sword-scabbard. The King's cousin gabbled on, insensitive to the sharp blow, still staring up and mumbling towards the sun. Blood trickled from the corners of his mouth into his black beard. Then the King struck him again, this time on the neck, and a low hiss of awe rose from the assembled charioteers behind who had seen the blow.

Morag turned this time, spitting out blood from his wounded mouth. He shouted, almost in the King's face, "Attack! Attack! Bite with your sharp teeth, Little Badger, for the Sun-god gives you his leave." His hands fumbled at the broad strap that bound him by the waist to the chariot shaft. He intended to leap from his post and run among the enemy. He was battle-mad, and Gwyndoc, infected by Morag's hysteria, half rose and had his sword almost out of the scabbard to join him when Caradoc spoke. His voice was cold and hard as he half-turned to the axe-men. "Tie him up! He's useless! The Roman magic has curdled his brains." But before the axemen could drag Morag down from the shaft he had cut one of them deeply in the shoulder and had almost severed another's wrist. Then they tied his arms and ankles with belts and flung him, still snarling and yapping like a dog, on the floor of the chariot, at the King's feet. But Caradoc did not look down at him once. Only Beddyr seemed to show any concern. He flung a cloak over his brother's face to keep the sun from his head and then turned again, apparently unconcerned, to watch the battle.

Then came the signal they had been waiting for; two long blasts on the horn, one from the left, beyond the sheltering wood, the other from the right, over the crest of the far hill. The claws were about to close! And even as the sad misty sounds hung on the wind, a light shower passed over the field, and then a great rainbow shone out, brilliant and prophetic.

Caradoc raised his voice and laughed for the first time. "An omen!" he shouted to all near him. "At one end of the bow, Reged; at the other, Catuval! We must be victorious this day!"

And as he spoke he touched Gwyndoc on the shoulder, and the red dragon banner was raised and stood fluttering magnificently in the sunlight. As Gwyndoc, the standard-bearer, thrust the thick shaft into its socket in the chariot floor, he was conscious of the Catuvelauni all around them, their faces turned towards the royal chariot, like dogs waiting in silence for the order to attack. They all seemed so confident, so proud, that Gwyndoc wanted to weep with happiness. His stomach suddenly seemed light, and he wanted to dance. For the first time that day his mind was completely free of Ygerne, free of his possessions every one — his lands and his houses, his clothes, and his weapons. He stood, in the King's chariot, almost a disembodied spirit, his whole identity concentrated in the length of his sword. Rhashidd, with no thought any more for safety or comfort, food or warmth, no regrets for the past or hopes for the future. Light-headed with slaughter, the young man was gloriously dead and alive at the same instant, a throbbing cipher in isolation from all emotions but the desire to kill.

Suddenly out of the corner of his eye he saw one of the men in his company break ranks and run forward, laughing and shrieking. It was Bobyn, the idiot, still swinging his long wooden sword! The excitement had turned his head completely, and he ran across the broad expanse of heavily-trodden ground that separated the chariots from the Roman formations.

As he gradually approached the shield-wall the tribesmen could hear the Romans beginning to laugh. Even the shield-bearers had lowered their wall so that all could see this strange mad Briton who could not wait to strike his blow at them. Gwyndoc could see their white teeth glistening in the sunlight as they laughed aloud. He would have shouted to Bobyn, threatening him with death, but he turned and saw that Caradoc himself was smiling. Gwyndoc gnawed at his knuckles and fumed. Still Bobyn raced on, no longer the shambling, whining imbecile of the midden-heaps, but a bright warrior, racing towards death and victory!

Still the Romans laughed at him, their shield-wall wide open; and as the screaming man came nearer, they leaned forward as he attempted to poke at them, thrusting and slashing with the wooden sword that the village-boys had given him, being pushed and buffeted jocularly among the roaring legionaries. . . .

Gwyndoc groaned, and tears of shame stood out in his eyes. "Look!" said Caradoc, placing his hand on his friend's shoulder to comfort him. A man of the Bibroci had stripped himself naked of his tunic and breast armour and was leaping, his short sword held firmly in his teeth, towards the cluster of men round

Bobyn. "That must be one of his lodge brothers," said the King, "for he bears the same blue mark between his shoulder-blades."

As he spoke the Roman humour changed suddenly. It was one thing to humour an idiot, another to let the enemy send dangerous fighting-men one by one into the lines. An archer stepped forward and took careful aim, and his arrow picked off the berserk clansman when he was less than six yards from Bobyn. The man ran on for a few paces with the arrow sticking from his neck, tearing at his throat, and then dropped and lay still. How confident these legionaries were! As Gwyndoc looked, the Roman standard-bearer came down from the dais, where he had been standing with Aulus Plautius, bowed ironically to Bobyn and offered him the golden eagle. The madman stretched out his hands to accept the trophy, and then the horns sounded again, louder and clearer, in a final signal, and the King raised his hand in the order to advance. The long lines of chariots began to move, slowly at first, each one decorated with bright paints, some with heads hanging by the hair from the shafts, some even decorated with flowers, and each one carrying its own coloured pennant. The shield-wall closed as if controlled by pulleys, and Bobyn's end was never known. Then the chariots began to canter, then to trot, and at last to gallop in an immense and magnificent wave down the long slope that kept them from the waiting army.

And Gwyndoc, his cloak flung back to free his sword-arm, and his great helmet with its silver horns fastened securely over his flaxen head, noticed as they charged that the rainbow which had promised victory had now disappeared.

In the rear of the cohorts, but strongly protected by infantry and cavalry, stood the great screens. The Numidian slaves who had carried them for some days now squatted on their haunches, showing their big white teeth as they yelled to each other above the noises of the battle, their high-pitched African voices making a strange contrast to the babble of Latin, or German, or Gallic, that sounded everywhere. To each side the black carriers saw only the legs of men and the feet of horses, and before them the legs of more men and still more men, and then the great dais on which the general stood.

They did not mention the general's name: he was a god. They hardly dared to think of him, and when they did they bowed their heads, automatically, woodenly, like puppets. It was possible to know of whom they were thinking even though their eyes were shut and they spoke not a word.

From time to time they laughed and pointed in amusement when the men before them surged. Sometimes stray arrows fell amongst them, piercing the screens or vibrating in the hard ground. But only once did an arrow strike one of their company. It struck in his backside as he turned to make a joke to the next man down the line. He howled till a legionary kicked him in the ribs and then removed it. Then he just rubbed the place and sat on the other cheek. But he did not joke any more that day.

They were children in their hearts and minds. They hated no one, they loved no one — at least, not in this damp land, where the sun hadn't enough strength to strike through their dark skins. But they had been put in ships and taken across the seas and so they were in Britain. All they had to do was to lift the screens and march forward when bidden by their Arab slave-master. He was almost as much a god as the general. His visitations were certainly more frequent. He had told them, "When I say 'Move', get up and carry your screens forward in time to the drum. I shall quarter with meat-hooks all slaves who do not march in step. But, in your anxiety to please, do not run into the general's dais." The slaves noted that he did not bow his head when he said "general". "You must move to the side of that. If any slave approaches within five paces of the general's dais I shall have his teeth knocked out, his ears torn off, his eyes burnt with needles, and his arms and legs broken in three places — immediately!"

When they heard these words the slaves grinned amiably and nodded their heads in understanding. They made up their minds not to knock against the general's dais, whatever might happen. Most of them had known Abu Yussef long enough to listen to what he said. And they laughed again in the cold British sunshine.

They were still laughing when men began to tumble over them, with red all over their heads or their arms flapping in the air like a scarecrow's sleeves. They were laughing as the javelins split their skulls or broke their ribs, when horses and wheels and knives suddenly broke into their pallid sunshine; dust in the nostrils and the smell of dung, the thick cloying blood splashing the face and mouth, and the yellow-haired men coming in from every side, laughing till the blood spurted from their mouths, hacking with long swords till their hands fell to the ground, thrusting with their crimson spears till their legs broke under them and let them tumble beneath the grinding, screaming wheels. . . . Then Abu Yussef stood up and patted his burnous straight. "Move!" he said.

Caradoc saw the shield-wall growing bigger and bigger. He stood upright only with difficulty, for by now the chariot was racing over the bodies of men. For a moment he put his arms round Gwyndoc and kissed him on both cheeks. Then he gave Beddyr the order to untie his brother, who was now quiet again, and Caradoc turned as the chariot swayed and bumped, and smiled to his cousins. He had only just time then to prepare himself for the clash. Setting his feet in the two niches, he tensed himself and shouted loud. Not words, but just sounds to convince himself that he was brave and alive. Then his chariot, the first of them all, struck the shield-wall. As in a remarkably clear dream, he saw to the left of him Catuval's chariot, its lord driving like a handsome demon in ecstasy straight for the Roman flank; to the right Reged's chariots bearing down in an orderly fashion, his brother standing bareheaded and smiling with the reins round his body and his arms held up to the sky. . . .

Then it was shock after shock, and mist before the eyes and gratings in the skull like teeth being drawn, and Caradoc hacked with his sword and saw blood on it and his chest, then he turned and went back, but only with difficulty, and made another charge, and it was the same again only not so violent. Then the mist cleared and he said, "Where are the Belgians?" And as he spoke he saw Catuval's chariot, his black and gold chariot, blazing on the ground, and his chargers lying on their sides, full of spears. Then he turned and shouted, "Reged! Reged! Where are you now?" And it seemed to him that a croaking raven swooped down from the blue sky and screamed in his ear, "Look, King! Look! Reged is only a few yards from you, still standing in his chariot! But he won't stand for long! He can't! There's an arrow sticking through his throat! Look, Caradoc, he is calling for you! The blood is coming out of his mouth!" Then, weeping in his nightmare, the King heard a strange thin voice, not a Roman voice, yell "Move!" Then the tall screens moved and fell away and an obscene scent came into his nose and his mouth. Then his horses snorted and screamed and pawed the air and became unmanageable. They turned against the rein and swung away from the fighting; but as they turned, Caradoc saw what they were fleeing from, and what he had smelled — the elephant and camel "cavalry" of Claudius, moving relentlessly forward, their heads swaying heavily, like the heads of idiots, stepping mincingly, their lips thrust out arrogantly, like flea-bitten whores! Claudius the Emperor had attacked with his cavalry and Caradoc, looking back on the chaotic mass of men and horses, sobbed and fell to his knees in his chariot, broken and ashamed.

At last he felt a hand holding his and he dared to look round at Gwyndoc, who lay by his side. Then they both got to their feet and saw that they were racing in the middle of a broad stream of chariots, away from the field. But no chariot was being driven.

Then they were on the road leading to the capital, a road littered with dying men and horses and broken chariots. They wept no longer, but whipped on the terrified horses. What had happened? Was Reged dead? Dead, with a mole in his hand, talking about philosophy and barbarians? Caradoc began to laugh brokenly. And Catuval — he in his ebony breastplate, wearing Cunobelin's tartan — was he dead too? And all the others? All dead? Just because of the Romans and their half-witted Emperor with his elephants and his camels? It could not be: fighting was not thus. Fighting was gay and spirited, and one always returned home in glory with one's brothers and uncles, to feast and sing and boast, battered and sometimes a little hurt — but always gay and victorious. . . .

And at last they clattered into the courtyard they had left so recently. Gwynedd and Ygerne were at the door, both pale and weeping. The King almost fell from his chariot and laid his head on his wife's breast. "The battle is lost," said Gwynedd quickly. "They are both dead, Reged and Catuval. We must do as you say and go to Caerwent."

And Ygerne ran to the chariot and took Gwyndoc's trembling hand. "Husband," she said, "thank God they have not hurt you! Oh, my love, look up! We shall fight them yet and conquer them!"

CHAPTER NINE

IT WAS AN hour or more before Caradoc could think plainly of what had just happened. Gwynedd sat patiently by his side as he told again and again of the battle, of the rainbow and the charge, of Bobyn, of Catuval's horses tangled in their own entrails, the Belgians lying dead or being hunted as far as the eye could see by yelling horsemen. But now he could not bring his tongue to speak Reged's name. Always, as he came near the end of his story, his voice broke and he stopped, the sound of the ghastly raven in his ears again. Then Gwynedd held his hands and nodded, as though she understood what it was like to see a brother with the arrow's feathers sticking out from under his chin and his hands still raised towards the gods.

Gwyndoc sat dumb by his king, his head hanging in shame and shock. He hardly heard Ygerne as she told him excitedly again and again that they were young, that what was lost could be regained — that life was not ended by one defeat.

At length the two men looked at each other again and clasped each other's hands, trying to smile. And after they had drunk a glass of wine and forced themselves to eat a little, Caradoc said, "Ygerne is right. We shall come at them again. We shall win back what we have lost. And may the gods destroy me and mine if I do not one day go as far as Rome to meet this Claudius!"

Outside in the courtyard, Caradoc called together all the lords who were still loyal to him and ordered that they must forget their defeat. "It can only remain a defeat if we accept it so! It is my wish that we do not accept it. From this moment until we gain our revenge, let this day be forgotten by you all."

As he spoke the words, Reged's face grew big before his eyes, and he turned away from his followers to busy himself with preparations for the next move.

When they had arranged for the safe conduct of their families and kinsfolk, leaving behind a body of picked warriors to protect them on their journey to Caerwent, the royal party began their long flight to the west.

Caradoc rode the black stallion Gallyn, a splendid creature in red harness set with great coral stones. Behind him he led the white horse Mapi. Gwyndoc, at his right hand, mused sadly on Ygerne and the child she was carrying for him. He did not feel right at leaving her, but he knew that his only allegiance at this time lay with his master, and secretly he felt proud that she should be in the Queen's party, following them. Morag and Beddyr rode grimly some paces behind with the other lords, leading the armed men.

As the party clattered through the open gates of the city the feeling of depression and despair still hung over them and no one spoke. The place was deserted, since all who wished to leave had already gone on hearing the news of the defeat. The others, who were unafraid of, or even friendly towards the Romans, and there were many such, mainly traders in hides and cattle, were quiet behind bolted doors, waiting for their moment.

Above the gates a white figure waited. It was Bydd, the druid. He had not left with the others for the island Mona. Caradoc reined in his horse and called to the old man, "Come with us, Uncle, we will take you to the west with us. The enemy vanguard will be here before the sun sets." But the old man shook his grey head and smiled down. "No, King," he said. "Here in this city is my shrine; and I must stay by it to prevent its desecration. But have no fear for me, I have that power in me which will turn a few Roman eyes to stone before I am done. Farewell, and the gods ride with you!" The druid waved, and the royal party cantered on again.

Outside the city, where the road became narrow and wound uphill, a beggar, perhaps an ex-soldier by his mutilated arm, spat as they approached and then turned his back on them. Morag raised his eyebrows, swung round in the saddle, and, waiting until the range was suitable to his aim, shot him cleanly between the shoulder-blades. The armed men riding behind nodded approval at this bowmanship but no one spoke, and as the horses mounted the rise and approached the open rolling country-side the spirits of the party rose and there seemed to be hope in the future. Beddyr began to sing softly a Mess song about two fleas who retired and invested in a dog, and soon everyone had joined in and was singing or roaring with laughter. When it came his turn, even Caradoc, the King, entered into the spirit of the thing and sang a verse that no one had heard before.

But this mood was fleeting. As they topped the rise they saw, perhaps a quarter of a mile below, a man riding madly on a white horse, his hair and cloak streaming in the wind. The sun glinted on his horned helmet and body armour and he waved a sword about him, but in a half-hearted manner it seemed from the distance. Well behind him, and breaking in a disordered rabble through the bushes, came running half a dozen footmen shaking lances and swords. One even stopped in the chase to draw a bow at the fugitive, but this arrow went wide of its mark.

"What do you make of that?" asked Caradoc, pulling his horse up. From the skyline the Catuvellauni looked down on the horseman and his pursuers. "That man seems to be a chief-tain by his dress," said Gwyndoc. "It is impossible at such a range to see his tartan, but I would say that he is retreating like us from the battle and has been waylaid by these carrion. They are the men who snatch prizes from those who die honourably in battle — Picts and sometimes Saxon bands that work their way inland."

As they watched, the horseman drew away from his enemies and, turning in the saddle, waved to them ironically. Even as he did so, another band of men, more numerous than before, burst from the cover of a spinney ahead and surrounded him. The watchers saw him strike about him with his sword, but the attackers closed in on him. One clubbed at the white horse's head, and another, taking the lord by a leg, dragged him from the saddle. Then the two bands closed in like terriers worrying a rat.

"Lord, let us ride down and save the horse," urged Morag, pushing forward to the King.

Caradoc smiled wryly and shrugged his shoulders. "It is too late now, the beast is dead. But you might save the rider if you are quick."

They looked and saw that the lord had somehow regained his feet and was thrusting and slashing savagely at the mob about him. Then the bowman, taking the risk of hitting one of his companions, took close aim and released his arrow. The knight fell, writhing, and the squabble for his arms and clothing began

Morag turned and rode back to his position. "He deserved no better death," he said. "He was not a real warrior. I would not risk myself for such. But he rode a good horse."

Then the royal party put their horses to the downward slope and rode into the valley, their lances at the ready. The robbers must have caught sight of them as they stood on the skyline, for when the horsemen reached the plain they had disappeared. Both horse and rider were stripped of everything that might be valuable. But as they passed the tumbled corpse Gwyndoc gasped and tugged at Caradoc's arm. "Do you see who it was?"

"Yes, it is Adminius. The Romans have not kept their dog long, then! He must have been running from them, just as we are doing now." The leaders bowed their heads for a moment over the broken body; Morag and his brother caused some amusement in the rear by wiping mock tears away from their eyes with their sleeves.

At last the party moved off again heading westwards away from the open country towards the wooded hinterland. Sometimes, in the distance, they saw clouds of dust raised by great trekking-wagons and their attendant horsemen; and sometimes solitary riders would appear from nowhere, galloping like the wind, but always skirting the armed party cautiously as they

rode on again towards the west. Once they overtook a group of
soldiers who stumbled along the flint road on dragging feet,
many of them carrying Roman shields or wearing broken
Roman helmets. These drew to the side of the path as the
mounted party came on, and stared sullenly before them as the
King passed, no one speaking a word of greeting but all tottering
like men in the middle of a cruel dream, fearful and hopeless.

Before nightfall the horsemen reached the uplands. By now
every man lolled in the saddle, weary and anxious to rest, and
the horses became slow and disinterested, moving faster neither
for whip nor spur. The King turned to Gwyndoc and said, "This
used to be your father's country, the place of the Trinobantes.
Can you remember any villages here?" But Gwyndoc could not
recall this countryside, however hard he thought. He had hunted
on its outskirts as a lad, but for the most part had spent his time
south of the great river, among the rich farms of the Cantii. So
Caradoc turned in his saddle and shouted back to his followers,
"Does any lord remember a village in these parts?" And one
youth, whose head was bound with a bloody cloth but whose
voice was still gay, called back banteringly, "Yes, lord. There is
a village beyond this hill. The food is fit only for crows, but the
girls, oh, the girls!" And he blew a kiss from the tips of his
gashed fingers. Even Caradoc laughed back at him, and they
rode on.

But when they reached the hilltop there was no village. Only
desolate heaps of smouldering ashes lay in the little valley.
There was no sound of cattle or sheep. The villagers had taken
everything they could with them in their flight for safety from
the invaders.

At first it looked as though the smoking ruin was deserted,
but as the cavalcade made its way through the settlement an old
man rose from among a pile of tumbled masonry and came
towards them, wearing the cloak of a chieftain and holding his
right hand upwards in greeting.

"We cannot offer you hospitality, gentlemen," he said. "You
have come too late. My people are all visiting their relatives
somewhere in Hibernia, I think! They went so fast I made sure
they must be going so far, and must get there before nightfall."
He made a wry grimace at his own joke and smiled up at Caradoc.
Gwyndoc spoke to him sternly, "Do you know to whom you
speak, old man? And do you know who we are who come to
your village?"

The old man shrugged his shoulders and smiled again. "Young

lord," he said, "I should indeed be a dull old fool if I didn't recognise young Caradoc. He's been a nephew of mine for twenty-four years now! And as for who you are, I assume you are Cimbri from Germany by your tartan! Who else could you be?" Gwyndoc looked so discomfited that Caradoc gave him a dig in the ribs, and Beddyr rocked in his saddle to see the chieftain so teased.

"Yes, Uncle," said Caradoc, "that's what we are now, Germans, or Scythians, or anything except Belgae — and Romans! But if there is nothing for us here, let us travel on. Come with us. One of the men can let you have his horse. We are going westwards to raise the tribes again. Come with us to help put a new heart into the clans."

But the old man shook his head. "No, Caradoc," he said. "I don't fancy the west. It rains too much there and they tell me the Silures eat only frogs and have shocking habits! No, I'll build myself a comfortable little pigsty here from among the ruins, and I'll get the village ready for you when you come this way again."

Caradoc argued with his uncle, telling him that food would not easily be come by and that the invaders would surely find him and make him a slave in time. But the old man would not be dissuaded, and in the end they had to leave him.

As the moon rose they reached the heavily wooded hill-country and, exhausted by their long ride, made an encampment in a glade, building shelters from the night winds from fallen boughs and bracken. It was long before Gwyndoc could sleep. The hard earth and the rising mist troubled him, and thoughts of Ygerne kept coming to him. He wondered whether she would be safe after all, and whether he had done right in leaving her side to follow the King. He heard the bracken creak from time to time and knew that some of the others were awake too. They would be troubled, like him, about their own lives — their people and their possessions. Remembering at night their wounded or killed and the mad retreat from the field, they would be wondering perhaps whether this was the end of all things in spite of the singing and the enthusiasm with which they had set off.

Away in the depths of the wood, branches crackled. Gwyndoc heard a vixen crying, and once an owl hooted from above his head in the blackness of the thick foliage. And later, when the moon shone out full along the avenue in which they lay, he saw Morag leaning on his elbow and looking at him with wide staring eyes, like a wolf too tired to take his prey.

Gwyndoc shut his own eyes then and tried to forget the battle and the heaped bodies and the long sad ride that stretched ahead of them towards nowhere and nothing, and he tried to believe that he was just sleeping out in the wood for fun and that a few miles away, in the valley, everything was as it had always been — sunshine and mead, hunting and the strong kingdom of Cunobelin, and, above all, Ygerne. Ygerne, the tall girl with the blue eyes and the quick laugh who washed him down with warm water when he came in drenched after chasing the stag with Caradoc, who insisted that he wore his thick sheepskin jacket when he had to ride out to Council meetings in winter-time. . . .

But it was no good. That world was ended really. The Romans had put a stop to that life of fields and woods, or careless hunting and drinking and making love. They were stronger than anyone else in the world; stronger even than the druids, Gwyndoc thought. Then he said a hurried, frenzied prayer to absolve himself from blasphemy, for he thought he had heard someone breathing up in the oak tree above him.

He looked at Caradoc, lying stretched out beside him, all but his head covered by the broad green riding cloak. "King," he whispered at last, not hoping to be heard, "I am a traitor to my heart to be with you now. I wish I were a hundred miles from this spot."

And to his surprise Caradoc's eyes opened and looked at him long and understandingly. "Why do you say that, Gwyndoc?" his king whispered. And Gwyndoc forced himself to speak. "Because my wife Ygerne is with child and perhaps needs me," he said.

For a moment Caradoc smiled. Then he whispered back, "I understand what you must be feeling now, friend. That same thought keeps sleep away from me, for my own wife Gwynedd bears the same burden." Then Gwyndoc felt Caradoc's hand gripping him hard about the wrist, saying more than any words could of the bonds that held them together. Gwyndoc felt too full to speak: he wanted to make a death dance then, swinging his sword in the moonlit avenue against demons as massive as the rocks. He wanted to sing a song that no one had heard since the world began its journey through space. He was suddenly a Celt and a poet again, knowing death as but another stage in life, seeing the coloured flowers as but another step towards ashes and decay, and all beautiful and rare. But his king still held his wrist, and the tears trickled down Gwyndoc's face because he could say nothing, could do nothing. And at last he heard Caradoc whispering again in the moonlight, hoarse and urgent. "No barrier divides us, Gwyndoc, we are of one mind and spirit, closer to each other than blood-brothers. Closer even than dear Reged and the gallant Catuval had ever been to me. You know, then, as well as I, that this world's glory is a thing of worthlessness. We are here now, confiding in each other, because yesterday the Roman brought his African creatures to frighten our folk with smells. They ran like children to safety away from the noise and the strange sights. And because we are lords, grown men and the conquerors of the gods, their rulers, we must go after them and force them to turn again and destroy these Italian mountebanks." And as the King spoke Gwyndoc forgot that the Romans were the strongest people in the world, he forgot the grim charging phalanxes and Reged calling out in his agony, and he whispered back, "Yes, lord, yes. We are rulers! We shall destroy them!"

Then Caradoc's voice softened. "Friend," he said, "I know your sufferings. We both await our first-born, who shall have hair like corn and eyes like the sky, and shall hunt with us and fight with us, and live to get other sons like themselves when we are gone! I know your pain at leaving Ygerne, for Gwynedd is comely and loving also. But we must do these things — fight and ride, starve and suffer — for their sakes. It is not that I wish for my crown above all things, or you your lands. They are only trumpery toys. But we wish for another day of pride and peace, when we can ride out in safety with our sons and rule the dark people like gods." Then he was silent and Gwyndoc could only nod. At last they were both asleep, the King still holding his friend's hand.

And Morag, who watched this like a whipped dog and who had no son to follow him, wept until the first long light shone between the trees, and pulled at his hair till it came out in his hands.

That morning the grooms were up as the birds began to sing, scouring and polishing breastplates, cleaning harness and watering horses. One of these men, searching for brush-wood to light a fire, plunged his hands by accident into a nest of adders and died soon after, writhing on the grass, surrounded by his fellows. This they considered to be a warning from the wood-gods that their presence was un-welcome, and when they began to shout that the lords were leading them into danger instead of saving them, Beddyr, who had not slept very well because of his brother, took his sword scabbard and beat them. Their cries wakened the rest of the party, and Beddyr spent the rest of the morning sulking because of the things Caradoc had said to him about camp discipline and the need for efficiency in all things. But at last all preparations had been made, a roe deer was shot in the wood and roasted over a great fire, and then later the horsemen mounted and struck off again, this time with the sun at their left hand, keeping as far as possible within the heavily wooded area for the sake of cover.

After they had been riding for an hour the King's horse trampled by chance upon a hare sitting quietly in her form, and the men-at-arms were at first worried that this might be another omen, since their gods forbade them to kill this creature. But Caradoc tore off one of his bracelets and wound it round the dead animal's neck as an offering. So they felt that everything might turn out all right after all. Then they struck the Icenian upland road and headed to the south-west. Towards sundown they made a wide detour to be sure of skirting Verulum, which would be full of Roman troops by now. It was lucky they did so, for soon they came upon a group of refugees from that city hiding in the woods, whose spokesman told the King that Aulus Plautius himself was there with the pick of his cavalrymen and that a house-to-house search had been going on all day for anyone who had been in the big battle. About a dozen young men of noble blood had been found hiding in taverns or grain-sheds, and they had been whipped to death in the market-square. Some of the refugees who had horses and looked hard were allowed to join the royal party, after they had sworn over a sacrifice that they would serve Caradoc with their last drop of blood.

Then later in the day the party ran into a wagon-train heading west from Londinium who told the same story: although the city had surrendered without much trouble, on the whole, there were some elements faithful to the Belgic king, and they were either being executed or being sent to Gaul as slaves. It seemed that after two ineffectual attempts to occupy Britain the Romans were determined now not to allow anything to ruin their chances of a complete conquest.

One wrinkled old warrior almost wept as he spoke to the King. "Their Caesar says he will forbid us, on pain of slow crucifixion, to wear tartan or warpaint," he said. "But he must

create sheep that grow no wool and plants that carry no woad
before he can stop us. We are not Gauls!" The King put his
hands on the old man's shoulders and kissed him and asked him
if he would ride with them. And the old man fell to his knees
on the marshy ground and wept, and swore that he would never
wash his face again where his King's lips had touched. All the
party, except Caradoc and Morag, laughed at this. But for the
King it was a symbol of hope in the resurgent spirit of his
tribesmen and in the new kingdom that he would one day
create.

At nightfall the gradually increasing band came out of the
woods and struck a sheep-track that led them down to the River
Tamesa. The ferrymen had fled, but there was no difficulty in
persuading the hardy fighting ponies to take to the water. On
the south side of the river they met a troop of Belgae who had
come from the far west to fight but had arrived too late. They
were overjoyed at being still of some service to their new para-
mount-chief and led the horsemen to a hidden valley they knew
where the villagers made them welcome, offering them girls and
wine and even cattle to drive along with them when they left.
And during supper in the thatched hall the village headman,
more than a little overcome by the situation and the thick
honey-mead, called for volunteers to travel with Caradoc.

The following morning, on counting up, it was found that
every man in the village had volunteered, but as this was practi-
cally foolish the King agreed to take with him only those
between the ages of twenty and thirty who had already fought
in three battles and were unmarried. Even so, when the party
was well on its way into the land of the Bibroci it was found
that one volunteer who had persisted in wearing his tartan over
his head was no less than sixty years of age and, on his own
laughing confession, had at least three wives in various parts of
the country. Caradoc, who happened to be in a cross mood just
then, threatened to have his teeth drawn for deceit, but in the
end was so overcome by the rogue's good humour that he let
him ride with the grooms on condition that he mended his ways
and took no other girl to his bed. They were not troubled with
the old ruffian long, however, for later in the day he complained
that one of the servants had tried to poison him by putting fox-
gloves into his broth, and at the first opportunity he straggled
behind the party and was lost among the trees. No one turned
back to look for him, and in an hour he was forgotten.

After that, for two days there was only riding, eating fresh flesh cooked over open fires and drinking stream-water, and sleeping wrapped in riding-cloaks under some boulder, or in the bracken, or in a hollow away from the wind, and rising to the song of birds, or the bright sun, or, more frequently, to the driving rain of morning.

And at last, when even Morag longed for a soft bed to sleep in, they came in sight of the great stone temple, the one solid and unchangeable symbol in their lives, and they halted while Caradoc went on alone to make the sacrifice he had promised long ago to Reged. No one watched the King at his devotions, but all rested in a hollow in the rolling plain. The skins were cut and Gwyndoc superintended the distribution of the rich Gallic wine. Each man was allowed half a helmetful, and all who had big heads had to put up with much teasing that day.

At length the King returned, and his friends saw that he had been weeping. He came on foot, carrying Gallyn's magnificent red harness over his shoulder and the stallion's bright blood staining his hands and arms.

The grooms saddled the white horse for him then, and the party rode on towards their first resting-place, Sorbiodun. As they passed through its stone gates the great bronze gongs were roaring, and from every house came the sound of women wailing.

CHAPTER TEN

JUST WHEN CARADOC'S horsemen moved into the mourning city of Sorbiodun, the first Roman cavalrymen heading the triumphal procession into Camulodun, their cloaks pulled up against the driving rain, clattered through the high gateway, scattering the scavenging dogs and chickens before them.

The preparations for the entry had started the day before, when a red-crested herald, escorted by a squad of German auxiliaries, had stalked through the main streets during the morning to announce, in four Celtic dialects besides Latin, from a dais in the market-place, that the Emperor himself, Claudius the God, would soon be visiting them; that all arms, including butcher's knives and trout spears, were to be piled in the public square; and that no man of military age was to occupy a place in the front line of spectators.

When the herald and his bodyguard had marched off out of the gates again, the city went into a paroxysm of unrest. News of the Caesar's arrival spread from house to house like fire, from the wattle farmsteads outside the walls right down to the white stone houses by the wharfside, where sky-blue trading-vessels, with their gilded vine-carved prows, still unloaded their cargoes of wine and pottery and bronzes into the bobbing coracles.

At first there was uncertainty and fear among the population; women wept, and men buried their swords and arrows. The richer farmers, unwilling to leave their granaries and cattle until the last minute, now became panic-stricken and, loading their wagons with everything they could carry, began to leave the city. Most of them did not get far: foraging squads of Romans or lurking bands of outcast marauders — escaped slaves and camp-followers — saw to that.

But, as the day wore on, the city settled down again. The population was a mixed one: Belgae, Iberians, Germans, Italians and even Greeks, and few of the city-dwellers felt that burning loyalty to the chieftain which the inland tribes did. Many of them were too close to Rome, in blood or custom, to fear Claudius as much as they hated the druids. If the city was to change its master, well, better to change to Roman government than to Silurian or Saxon. Where the Romans went, their trade followed them! Down at the docks the Latin-speaking Levantine community locked their money chests and put up their shutters until such time as the invaders needed their services.

In the great houses of the merchants the cooks were hastily lectured in the preparation of Roman dishes, the best Italian wine and Gaulish pottery were brought out, and the heads of households practised wearing their cloaks like togas, while the children went busily to their revision of the Latin tongue.

The ordinary folk shrugged their shoulders and clustered in the taverns. There was no point in working until one knew exactly who was to pay for the work. In one cabin, where the vine leaves hung before the door, the farm-labourers, dressed in their poor best, some of them Gaulish deserters from the legions years before, sang songs as they drank rough wine and fermented apple-juice from terracotta cups:

> *"Caesar came to Britain*
> *With soldiers in his galleys;*
> *Let him come and live here*
> *If he'll fill our bellies!*

> *Claudius brought his camel*
> *To mount Caradoc's cow;*
> *The fun begins tomorrow —*
> *But where's Caradoc now?"*

By late afternoon they had drunk and sung themselves stupid, and lay in tumbled groups over benches and tables, and even snoring in the gutter, where they were walked over by cattle, daubed with mud by young boys, and defiled by roaming dogs. The tavern-keeper finally rolled the last one out into the street and shut his door. He was an old campaigner who had lived long among the rough coast-wise Armoricans. "Briton or Roman," he said, "it's all one. Give them drink and they forget themselves." He turned to his son-in-law, the herdsman Barwch, who sat in the corner carving a staff. "What say you, son?" And Barwch laughed, showing the gaps in his mouth, for he was an incorrigible fighter. "Give dogs a bone and give men mead: then you can skin the one and rob the other with safety," he said. He laughed and spat in the straw and tried to carve a stag's head on his stick; but the knife slipped and spoiled his design. He swore and flung the stick onto the fire and got up to punch his father-in-law playfully in the ribs. The two wrestled and rolled each other about until they woke the baby. Then they went out guiltily by the back door and lay down in the grass until a meal was ready.

And in the pillared brothel by the waterside the girls got out their coloured finery of silk and coral, brushed and dyed their hair with henna, and painted their faces before long metal mirrors. A tall German girl plucked the eyebrows of a dark Scythian. "Now we shall have fun, Sasha," she said. "Real soldiers to visit us and give us presents from half over the world. Precious stones from Africa and bracelets from India, not like these blue-faced monkeys! Why only yesterday I had a drover from the hills to see me. He said he had no money, but could I do with a couple of sheep instead! I soon sent him packing — the hairy barbarian!" And the Scythian laughed to cover her tears as she remembered her father's herds and the tented village where she had once been happy. Of them all, only little Bronwen, daughter of a hostage from the Ordovices, refused to make herself ready for the Roman arrival. She lay on a couch and wept, from time to time thrusting a thin dagger into the cushions. "You bitches," she sobbed at her companions. "You have no loyalty. You think only of money and your own miserable bodies." The German tried to soothe her. "But, Bronwen, we must. We are outcasts, after all. Our country is the world, and our loyalty is to ourselves. You must remember that, dear." But Bronwen kicked and stabbed more fiercely than ever. "I won't remember it," she wailed. "I am a Brython. If my countrymen come here, they can take me for nothing, all of them — all the tribes! But if the Caesar himself came, offering me the wealth of his Empire and a seat on his throne, I would spit in his eyes!" The other girls could do nothing with her, and in the end had to send for the old Greek lady who managed the establishment.

And so the day passed, and the following morning the city woke to find that the rains had set in. The skies were grey and the smoke blew back down the chimneys, filling the rooms with soot. But although the streets were at first deserted, as the morning drew on, crowds gathered shielding their heads with cow-hides and sheepskins, and lined the street from one end to the other, jostling and elbowing and sometimes singing. Once or twice there were false alarms. "Here they come!" someone would shout. Then the street would be hushed and necks would crane, and those who stood on flat rooftops would begin to wave their coloured flags. Then, when the expectancy was at its highest, a tinker would clatter through the gates on a donkey, his pots and pans jangling behind him, and the crowds would rock with laughter and forget for a moment that they were a defeated people.

But at last the Romans came. First, in the distance, there was a thin scream of trumpets, then a long pause. Then a body of mounted swordsmen raced like the wind through the tall gates, slashing left and right, sending the yelling crowds back to the shelter of the buildings. And before the horsemen had disappeared in swirls of dust and mud the legionaries came marching in, each man walking head erect, like a machine, his long shield held in position on his left arm. With the infantry came spearmen, who broke ranks on passing through the gates and stationed themselves before the crowds, along the street, holding their javelins horizontally to push back the swaying spectators.

Then, between lines of legionaries, came the officers, mounted on black horses, whose manes were trimmed short, like hogs bristles; first Aulus Plautius in his scarlet cloak, and then his staff officers, and finally his infantry commanders. All of them looked straight in front of them, as though they were moving in a deep dream of military ascendency. Some of the young officers wore bandages, and one who had been wounded in the back by a spear thrust had to be supported in his saddle. He was very young, but his white face was proud and noble looking. When the crowds saw him they forgot themselves and cheered loudly. Some of them, the older folk, even wept. The Roman spearmen guarding the route saw this and were puzzled. They joked with each other about it and said the Britons were women, but in their minds they were troubled, for they could not understand how these islanders could fight so terribly and savagely one day and weep so easily the next. Weren't they savages, and didn't they burn their hostages in wicker cages? No, the Britons lacked all sense of proportion. Perhaps Claudius could understand them — but his soldiers couldn't!

Then there was a great hush as the Emperor's archers appeared, first the Roman contingent, tall, smiling men, followed by his eastern bowmen, grim-faced little Parthians, riding shaggy ponies and wearing high sheepskin hats. When the camels appeared, swinging awkwardly between the ponies, the street-watchers whistled through their teeth, but when the first elephant came through the gates, his black mahout almost on a level with the top of the city wall, gasps of wonder broke out the length of the main street, some of the more timid breaking from the crowd and rushing away behind the buildings, and the religiously inclined ones falling to their knees and saying that indeed the gods had arrived in Camulodun.

After the first impact of the elephants, the Emperor himself caused comparatively little stir. Was this small, huddled figure with the clown's face and the hunched back really the ruler of the world? Carried on a great purple palanquin by four tall Nubians, he looked smaller than ever, an ineffectual puppet, a mere mouthpiece. And some in the crowds suddenly remembered Cunobelin, and how he had once stunned a horse with a blow of his fist.

Then followed a vast rabble of prisoners — Britons, Gauls even Persians, gathered together from many campaigns for this moment. They looked tired and disspirited in the rain. A few of them, however, those leading the lions and leopards, mainly negroes, were healthy and vigorous — for they were professional slaves, men whose livelihood it was to walk in such processions, decked with trophies.

By this time the leading infantrymen had reached the end of the long street and had halted, in close order, so that the

Emperor's palanquin should now be positioned in the public square. The trumpets screamed again and the procession shuffled to a standstill. Claudius coughed and fidgeted in his robes, and finally called out in a thin, stuttering voice for his secretary. The crowds tittered that so great a man should sound such a fool. The secretary ran along the line and pushed a roll of skin into the Emperor's hand and then began to assist him to the ground.

The Britons jostled and pushed to see what was going to happen. "He's going to sing a song," chuckled one fat tribesman, and all round him the watchers laughed. But the spearman keeping order in that quarter turned swiftly and smashed his lance butt into the tribesman's face and he fell to the pavement, spitting out teeth. After that there was silence as the Emperor's high voice began.

But at this moment Barwch, who was watching the proceedings from the tavern roof, thrust his fingers into his mouth and went spluttering down the stairs. His father-in-law, anxious not to offend his new masters, bobbed down out of sight and then followed his son-in-law. But when he got down below, Barwch was nowhere to be seen. He had run out at the back of the tavern, chuckling, and was lost among the outbuildings.

Under the city walls, well away from the main street, he halted, breathing hard and still laughing. "Romans!" he said. "Camels! I'll show them!" Then, half-drunk, he ran on to the great circular enclosure where the King's bulls were kept. As royal herdsman, he knew every nook and cranny of the place, and, choosing a long fork from a barn as he passed, he leapt onto the stone wall of the corral and looked down on the animals below him. They were all shaggy long-horns, a breed left by earlier inhabitants, and they were wild. In the turmoil of the last few days no one had thought to feed them, and they pushed and gored each other, almost mad with hunger, rolling their red eyes up at him as he watched them, slavering and trying to get their horns down to wound each other.

Barwch, safe on the wall, began to talk to them, quietly at first, and then louder until his thick voice rose almost to a frenzy. "Little bulls! Little brothers! Look who's come to see you! It's Barwch! Yes, Barwch! You remember me, don't you? I used to feed you in the King's time, little bulls. But he's gone now. Didn't they tell you? He's gone to seek his fortune among the rocks. He's gone to make friends with the badgers and the eagles! He's gone and left you. Yes, and Claudius has come to take his place! But you won't get far with Claudius, little red brothers! No, he's brought his own bulls — bull-elephants! They wear their horns lower down, not like you, little barbarians! They carry no ugly hair like you, little beggars! Oh no, he won't like you, anybody can see that! You've lost your master now; no one wants you! No one wants you!" Barwch began to leap about on the wall, smacking his pole down heavily on haunch, and horn, beating time to his words and sending the cattle almost crazy. Then, when they had begun to rear up and bellow, half-mad with hunger and fear, he stopped beating them. "I'm going to open the door and let you out!" he shouted. "Then you can go and see for yourselves what sort of man this Claudius is! Go and tell him what you think of him and his camels! Go now, go swiftly, little beasts, and tell him I sent you!"

Then he leaned down and quickly pulled away the long wooden bar that kept the bull-pen closed. The gates swung open and the terrified animals pushed through it, crushing each other against the posts in their frantic haste to be free. They swung into the lane behind their leader, and then galloped madly between the houses, coming to the main street just as Claudius was ending his peroration. The crowds, hearing hooves thundering behind them, turned in fear to see a tight-packed mass of bulls, their horns tossing madly, and scattered to left and right, some even breaking past the astonished spearmen and into the road. An adjutant, annoyed at this sudden turmoil, spurred up to give the soldiers a piece of his mind. He intended to have a dozen of them thrashed for not keeping better order when the Emperor spoke. But even as he opened his mouth to restore peace the first bull was upon him like a whirlwind. Man and pony were sent crashing down, to be trampled on by the following beasts.

Foot-soldiers, who had raised their shields against more deadly opponents in all parts of the world, ran in all directions, dropping swords and shields as they went. Cavalry horses reared and screamed, breaking through the infantry ranks and trampling the guard. . . . Then the bulls were amongst the elephants and camels, and the crowds now clustering on roofs and walls saw the bloody thrust of horn and tusk, heard trumpeting and the camel's terrified scream. The last they saw of the Emperor was his heels as he tumbled into the palanquin, too hastily raised by the frightened negroes. Then the Imperial Guard had formed round Claudius, shields close-locked and swords out.

Somewhere a whistle sounded, and the javelin men were seen marching in a single broad line, their lances out, relentlessly stabbing at the now exhausted cattle. In half an hour the last bull had been encircled and hacked to death. But the Emperor's entry was ruined. In the square, wherever one looked, lay bulls and horses, some of them still twitching. Five of the camels had been killed outright and three of the elephants so badly injured that the archers had to destroy them. Only one man, the unfortunate adjutant, had been gored to death, but many were quite seriously wounded.

As for Claudius, his nerves were in such a state that the Syrian physician had to administer a sedative before he could be carried back by his grinning black men to the royal pavilion.

Barwch, on the other hand, had never felt better. During the first tumult he had slipped into the crowd and had been fortunate enough to save a Roman officer from being gored to death. The grateful soldier had put his name on record as one of the Emperor's friends and had promised him a position in the royal stables.

And so the Romans took Camulodun. A public holiday lasting for three days was later announced by the herald, and before the sun had properly set over the western uplands the whole city was drunk either with elation or with the free issue of Roman wine dispensed from huge skins at every street corner in the centre of the city.

CHAPTER ELEVEN

CARADOC'S BUSINESS DID not keep him long in Sorbiodun. In the rambling thatched house of the local chieftain, Gwyddion, the horsemen refreshed themselves before the King went out to speak to the people in the open market-place. Here, for the first time since he had begun his journey to the west, he was among his own folk — true Belgians, part-Celt, part-German, the tall, fair people of Europe. There was not a black or a red head to be seen in the market-place as he spoke. And as his voice gained in strength and passion, these yellow heads nodded in approval of his words and the woad-streaked hands hammered on their bronze shields in applause.

Caradoc told his story simply: the Belgae were great, he said, their future was a noble one. That the mongrels of Rome had torn their hides once was no reason for despair. That Camulodun had fallen was no matter for desperation. To build a new city, a new capital, was easy work for willing hands. A city was a thing of stone and timber, a thing which might be destroyed by a tempest or any chance fire. But the courage of the Belgae was another thing. No storm or fire could break that down. No power in the western world could vanquish that, not even Rome. Caradoc ended by telling the tribesmen to make ready without delay, to unite without friction and bickering, to be prepared to maul the Roman busybodies as they came westward, which they were bound to do within a short space. He told them that he was riding on to visit his other people in the south-west and to give them the same message, and finally that he was leaving the majority of his cavalry party in Sorbiodun to form the nucleus of a Royal corps, named after himself, over which Gwyddion would assume complete command.

When he rode out of the city gates on the following morning, many of the tribesmen who had followed him from Camulodun tried to take their places again in the company, but Caradoc shook his head and thanked them and asked them to serve him by giving strength to his loyal subjects in Sorbiodun. Then he rode on with fewer than twenty horsemen in his train.

So, heading always towards the sea, to the country of the Durotrices, the King stopped here and there at the small hilltop forts, carrying the same message and always finding the same unhesitating loyalty, until, when they could imagine that the sound of the sea was almost in their ears, a strange thing happened which was to have results that no one thought of at the time.

The royal party, travelling in single file because of the narrowness of the way, found themselves in a sunken road leading to the fortified hill of Mai Dun. The foremost rider, topping the hill, could already see the great ramparts rising before him when Gwyndoc's horse suddenly cast a shoe. He called out to the King that he was dropping behind so as not to spoil his stallion's feet on the sharp gravel, and that all would be well with him when he reached Mai Dun, where, he knew, there were expert blacksmiths who would be able to match the other shoes without any difficulty.

So when the first hail of arrows and javelins fell upon Caradoc's party from the thick woods that hung above the road, Gwyndoc was not there. Four men tumbled dead from their horses, and the King's thigh was pierced deeply by an arrow before the standard-bearer could hoist the red dragon to establish the identity of the royal party.

And so the King was carried bleeding and half-conscious through the massive eastern gate of the fortress, past rampart after rampart, until the upper levels of habitation were reached and he was lodged in the wattle-hut used by the keeper of the fort.

This officer wept as he knelt and told his story to the sneering and impassive Morag: the royal party had appeared without previous warning, he said. The over-anxious outposts had thought they were Romans and had attacked straightway. He would do anything, he said, to atone for his mistake and he assured Morag that Caradoc ruled no more loyal subjects in the whole of southern Britain than the great garrison at Mai Dun.

When the soldier had worn himself out in hysterical protestations, the King's cousin signalled the others from the room and was left alone with the garrison commander. The King had fainted now from loss of blood and was being attended by a doctor from the fortress. They could do nothing but obey Morag's orders until Caradoc had recovered. And so they left him alone as he commanded.

A short time later he summoned them back to hear, he told them, a confession from the lips of the treacherous keeper. They noticed that those same lips were now broken and bleeding as the soldier told how Gwyndoc had forced him to arrange this ambush so as to destroy the King and, indeed, the whole of the party, and they lowered their heads in sympathy as they recognised the terror that suddenly sprang into the commander's eyes as he told his broken story.

Before the King gained consciousness, and before the puzzled Gwyndoc made his way up between the ramparts to the wattle-huts, the headless body of this unfortunate commander was flung, by two of his own brothers, over the high walls into the ditch at the foot of the hill.

Two days later, when Caradoc had sufficiently regained his strength to sit in a saddle again, the depleted and wondering party began its ride northwards towards the wide estuary that separated them from Caerwent; and although none of the lords who had been present when the dead man's strange confession had been made fully believed the words they had heard, something kept them from speaking to Gwyndoc as they had done before. They rode in silence when he was with them, or looked down at the ground when he spoke to them. Only the King still treated him with friendliness; but even he seemed troubled by some change that had come over the party.

As they rode on through downland and marsh and over lonely heathland, the temper of the weather seemed to change.

It was as though winter had decided to strike in the middle of autumn, and the russet fullness of the countryside around them disappeared, giving place to dying colours under grey skies. Again and again they were overtaken by sudden squalls of rain, far from any shelter, and rode hunched in their saddles like brooding dwarfs.

Once, as they passed through a marshland village, set high on piles away from the ooze, an emaciated old woman looked down on them and screamed some words they did not understand; then she made the Pictish finger sign against evil and pulled her black shawl over her head so that she should not see them any more. This troubled Caradoc, who was still weak from his wound, and Beddyr, the slow, morose watchdog, would have set fire to the whole village had not his brother, sober and thoughtful for once, restrained him. As it was, Beddyr contented himself by shooting arrows into every beast he found grazing a little further along the road on the common-ground. He did this openly and the King made no effort to restrain him, but looked away, tired and discouraged, until the bowstring had ceased to twang.

And once, as the little party made its slow way over the moors in a beating rain, soaked and half-blinded, a flurry of gaunt shaggy ponies swept down on them out of the mist, almost brushing them from the saddle and spattering them with mud. Their own mounts snorted with fear and reared madly. Morag's stallion flung himself back so violently that his rider was pitched into the sodden heather and escaped being trampled only by a miracle, while Caradoc, unable to grip his charger, groaned with pain as he was thrown to and fro. And as the wild squadron swept past them and on into the mist again, one of the soldiers, staring after them, cried out, "Look, they carry men!" And all saw that each pony had a rider, dressed in skins and looking as wild as the beast he rode, either clinging to the side of his mount or hanging almost underneath its belly.

"They are the wild ones," said Gwyndoc. "The first men whom our fathers met many lifetimes ago when they came to the island." The King nodded to him, but no one else seemed interested in his words. That day they rode on long after darkness, until they were well away from this spot, and finally made their camp on the slope of a hill that ran gently down to a rushing stream. Few of the party slept, for the air was thick with sounds they did not know, and all were hungry, since that day they had seen no creature, not even a wolf, that they could have killed for flesh.

Gwyndoc, wide awake, lay close to the King, with his arms about him, for the night was damp and a thin rain still fell. Until the first streak of grey dawn, Caradoc's teeth chattered yet his face ran with perspiration as fever gripped him. Then quite suddenly, when Gwyndoc could have howled with the pain in his stiffened arms, the King shook his head like one who wakes from a dream and sat up, stretching his arms and rubbing his legs. "Friend," he said, "I am well again. The fever has passed." He smiled at Gwyndoc for the first time for days, and then they both rolled over onto their sides again, to sleep until the men-at-arms had saddled the horses and prepared oatcakes.

That morning was no brighter than the rest. The sky was over-cast and heavy with rain, though a wind had sprung up just before dawn and had given a short respite to the drenched horsemen. Nor did they find hospitality at any of the miserable hovels they passed as they headed northwards. Here and there they saw smoke blowing gustily from a chimney-hole, or at the mouth of a cave, but when the riders galloped up to ask for food they found only an empty shed and sodden ashes, nor, though they searched round about in anger like wild beasts after an elusive prey, did they set eyes on any human creature. In the late afternoon, however, Morag made a wide detour when smoke was seen rising from a little storm-swept copse. He came back later leading a young black calf, which the soldiers slaughtered and roasted before they went on. And as Morag tore at the fresh meat, Caradoc noticed that he was wearing a necklace of bear's claws: "Where did you get your necklace, Cousin?" he asked. "You had not got it when we set out this morning." Morag grinned and flung a bone at his brother. "I got it from the lord who presented us with this calf, King," he said. "He wished his loyalty to be known to you. He also sent you this." And Morag tossed a little bundle over to Caradoc, who caught it and unwrapped it and then flung it away from him in disgust. Morag scrambled after it and, wrapping it up in a fold of cloth, carefully tucked it into his belt. "Such a charm against the evil eye of this country is not easily come by, King," he said. "Nor should it be treated lightly. It is not like a blue eye, you know! Dark ones are scarce, and hard to come by!" Caradoc looked sternly at him but did not speak; and for once Morag did not seem overawed by the King's gaze. He slapped his brother on the back just as he was swallowing a piece of bread and made him choke. Then the two began to wrestle and the incident was forgotten.

Gwyndoc, watching them, was again aware of the new feeling in the party. These two, Morag and Beddyr, seemed to be daring more, as though they were conscious for the first time of their own power. Often when a remark was addressed to the King, Morag would be the first to answer it; and frequently Beddyr would take it into his head to curse the riders for being too slow, or too fast, as the mood found him. And Caradoc, especially since the wound in his thigh, would sit huddled in his saddle, ignoring them and speaking to no one, as though he had lost all his powers of command. As for Gwyndoc, although the others sometimes smiled at him furtively, for the most part he was left alone, as though he were outcast, almost, or at least as though the mark of death was on his forehead.

After they had eaten, the rain quickened, and shortly the storm was upon them again. They mounted their dripping horses and rode on into a blustering rain-belt, with the black clouds almost on their heads. When darkness fell they came to the edge of the desolate, hawthorn-choked heath they had crossed for the greater part of the day. Their track rose to the top of a moorland stretch, up which the tired horses stumbled miserably. At the crown of the rise they halted in a small body and looked down before them. There stretched the river that they must cross, misty and leaden-coloured in the dim light. From where they stood it was impossible to see to the far bank, it was so broad. But all the air was filled with its rushing, gurgling voice as it ran, swollen by the rains, to the nearby sea, over the drowned kingdom of Lyonesse.

Morag rose in his stirrups and, shaking his sodden cloak from his arm, pointed into the dusk across the estuary. "There lies Caerwent," he said. "There lies the King's new home till such time as we people of the sun shall rise again."

As he spoke a flash of sheet lightning struck through the clouds and lit up the rushing water, and all around them the thunder rolled. The riders wrapped their cloaks about their heads, and some of them mumbled prayers to the thunder god, as they set their horses to the slope and clattered round over the slimy pebbles to the water's edge.

Here they halted again, the stream up to their horses' fetlocks, arguing with each other. Some were for making a camp there on the shore until the sun came again and let them see how broad the river was. Others were in favour of riding along the river bank as far as they could, while any light lasted, in the hopes of coming across a boat. Morag and Beddyr did their best to persuade the riders to put their horses to the water and swim them over, but by now there was not a man in the party who did not sway in the saddle from sheer weariness, and no one was willing to take such a risk in the darkness while the storm wraiths were whispering about them.

So, after some half-hearted discussion, the tribesmen began to ride along the stony riverside, their eyes down-cast and their legs hanging limply from their stirrups. Most of them were inland Belgae, with little love of the sea. Now, in a strange land, away from the comrades they knew and the families they loved, they were saddened and depressed. The sight of this great river that lay before them and which they must cross came suddenly like a symbol of their defeat. They were fatigued and hungry; most of them had eaten little for days and their stomachs had revolted against the half-raw flesh Morag had found for them earlier that day. They were all soaking wet and covered with the filth of travel. Some of them had wounds gained in the battle for Camulodun which they had not admitted to and which were festering for want of proper care, and all were saddle-galled. But, worst of all, in many minds was now growing a nagging doubt; were the Belgae invincible, after all? Had Caradoc's power failed him? Would they ever see their wives and lovers again? Were they not merely defeated cowards who were riding away to forgetfulness and death?

Gwyndoc rode beside the King, silent and unhappy. Morag and his brother, as sensitive to atmospheres as all savages, spurred their tired horses back and forth along the file, patting men on the shoulders or slapping their horses' rumps, shouting and singing all the time that this river was no bigger than a baby could make, and that by and by they'd drag Claudius there by his ears and make him drink the whole damned lot of it at one gulp!

But this time their high-spirits only aggravated the exhaustion of the party. Tempers grew hot, and one lord who had fought side by side with Gwyndoc's father in Germany turned in his saddle and almost kicked Beddyr's teeth out with a sudden back-hander. Swords were flashing all along the line, and it is likely that the Belgic party would have slain each other that night but for a strange act of providence, for, even as the horsemen closed, the dark shape of a long flat barge swung round a bend in the river and came towards them, its bottom scraping on the sharp flints of the shallows. It beached and waited for a moment as all eyes turned towards it. Then a short, black-cloaked figure rose in the prow and called towards them in a high voice, "Hail, Caradoc! Hail Belgae! Your servants welcome you and wait to carry you to the other side of this river."

For a moment the riders hung back, amazed and a little afraid that their identity and purpose should be known by the old ferryman; then the King rode forward and spoke to the little black figure. "Greetings to you also, little wise one; but tell me, how do you know our names and our destination?"

The old man in the boat bobbed up and down in amusement; then the watchers saw his white face turned up to the King's. "My ravens brought word from a certain battlefield that you would soon be coming," he said. "I have waited for you these three days and nights."

"Who are you?" asked the King, almost angrily, as his followers drew close to him on the shore.

The old man pulled his cloak over his head and made ready to push the barge out into the stream again. "I am known by many names, King," he said. "Some call me The Rain-maker, others The Black Ferryman; and in your father's time at Camulodun, men simply called me Roddhu! But it is no matter, I am the same, whatever I am called!"

He laughed when he had spoken, and the tribesmen drew back. But Caradoc turned to them sharply and bade them dismount and get into the barge. Half of them crowded into the narrow seats, keeping as far away from Roddhu as they might, holding their horses by long head-halters. The King and his immediate friends watched the boat push off and then sat down on the stones to wait for the ferryman's return. They watched until the low dark shape of the boat and the horses' bobbing heads merged into the mist, and then began to sing to pass the time more easily. Morag tried to start them off with a loud war-song, but Caradoc was in no mood for heroics and stopped him after a few bars. Instead they sang a low lilting melody, against which the higher voices set another tune that moved away from the air and poised like a sea-bird before it settled again with the other voices in the closing phrase. The refrain they all sang in unison, softly and with feeling, repeating the sad words again and again, against the background of the restless river and the lowering mist:

> *"Two lovers sat beneath the moon*
> *All night in their cockle-boat;*

> *They heard the lonely grey seal croon*
> *And watched the green weed float.*
>
> *Their tears streamed down as warm as blood,*
> *Their kiss was cold as ice;*
> *But they dreamed the dream of the broken word*
> *And shrank from each other's eyes."*

As they sang Gwyndoc felt the tears coming to his own eyes as he thought of Ygerne. He would never break his word to her, he thought. Nor did he fear that Ygerne would break her word to him. She was to bear his child and that, above all things, bound them together. The child, the glorious blue-eyed son-to-be, was the word they would not break — the word made flesh. And before the song sank back to silence Gwyndoc was wondering where the great wagons were now; how far they had got, travelling straight, on their journey to the west. Had they met trouble from ambushes or broken wheels or poisoned horses? Perhaps he would know when they reached Caerwent, just across the river. Perhaps Ygerne might even be there, waiting to greet him, with the golden bracelets shining on her slim brown arms and the sharp points of her breasts thrusting at the coloured stuff of her dress.

Gwyndoc looked at Caradoc by his side and saw that the King was thinking too, his tangled head turned away from the grey water. Then they both heard the suck and slap of the oars as the barge pulled in to take them across the river, and the King rose and sat in the stern, with his long cloak wrapped tightly round his body, silent and gazing towards the far shore.

First of all the boat pulled up-stream against the current, until they were half-way across the broad river; then Roddhu rested a little on the oars and let the water carry them down towards the other horsemen who were waiting. The horses scrambled to the bank, whinnying with relief, and the King's friends followed them. Caradoc stood now in the stern of the boat and all heard his words: "Thank you, Roddhu. What gift can I make you for your loyalty?" They saw the King put his hand into his pouch to take out gold for the ferryman, and they saw Roddhu shake his head in refusal and turn as though to push out the boat again. And once more the King asked, "What gift can I make, Roddhu? Tell me and you shall have it." Then Roddhu turned his head again towards Caradoc, and said in his sneering, sing-song voice, "I am not a ferryman such as you have

known before, Badger. I am no slave of any but the gods. What I do I do for them and for myself — but not for you." On the river-bank Morag and Beddyr began to mutter and to loosen the swords in their sheaths, but Roddhu went on, "Since you insist on paying me, Badger, I will say this to you: I want no land, other than that which my feet cover in walking; I want no wife, other than the mandrake root; and I want no gold, other than a lock of your own gold hair!" And he held out a thin hand towards the King's head.

The brothers were thigh deep in the water. "He shall not touch the King," they shouted. "It is an omen. He means evil. Bend, Little Badger, and we will take the head from his shoulders!"

Caradoc shrank back from the curling fingers and the laughing mouth, and as he did so Morag tried to clamber into the boat. It rocked suddenly and violently and Morag fell back into the water with the King almost on top of him. Then the boat was off-shore and well out of striking range, and as the two men waded onto the beach the ferryman laughed back at them and called: "Very well, Caradoc. It shall be known wherever men talk that the King of the Belgae does not pay his debts!"

Beddyr cursed him in a howling voice and flung stone after stone at the little dark figure. Gwyndoc, in a sudden rage, unslung his bow and sent arrows whistling after the barge, but the light was now too bad for him to sight his mark with any certainty.

Once more they heard the old man's mocking laugh come floating to them across the water, and Caradoc, trembling now with passion, called out, "Laugh your fill, Roddhu of the red hands! Yes, laugh, for tomorrow the dogs of Caerwent will be fighting over your entrails!"

Then out of the mist they heard Roddhu's voice again, but strangely clear and piercing, for all the distance that lay between them: "First find Caerwent, broken King, before you talk of the dogs! And when you do find it, see that you do not enter it like dogs yourselves — on the end of a rope!" And the long, high, cackling laugh seemed to sweep round the horsemen like a tormenting bird as they stood on the desolate rain-swept shore; then it left them and followed the dim shape of the boat over the river and into the grey sea-mists.

In the shadow of a rock they built a fire from what drift-wood they could find and tried to dry their sodden clothing before they went on. Beddyr lay on his face among the weed and pebbles, almost insane with rage, while his brother stormed and cursed at everyone within reach, men and horses alike. Gwyndoc gnawed his knuckles and could not speak as he watched the King hunched up before the weak fire, brooding.

At last Caradoc spoke, to no one in particular, but low so that only Gwyndoc heard him. "Broken King, he called me. And that was Roddhu, who has always been here, even before the first folk came. He speaks with the authority of the gods themselves. Broken King. And what if he is right, after all? What if our power did come to an end on the field before Camulodun?"

Gwyndoc moved towards the King and put his arm round Caradoc's shoulders to comfort him, but the King shook his head and looked away, and the other had not the courage to leave his arm there.

At length the King looked round at the others squatting behind him and chose a young lord, a boy famous for his ability as a path-finder. "Go inland," he said, "and find Caerwent. Find the city we have come to rest in and bring us to it." The young man saluted and set off along the bank, leading his horse.

When he returned, breathless and exhausted, long afterwards, the wind had risen again and the lightning played about the sky until the men were blinded by its flashes. "There is no city, lord," he said. "There is no habitation that a man might live in for many miles, not even a shepherd's hovel."

The King's head sank on his breast. "Roddhu has cursed us," he said. "We are a ruined people, and I am its broken king. We have outlived our time! Oh, Reged, oh, Catuval, my brothers! I would be with you now, for yours was the glory of a warrior's death!"

Gwyndoc could not stand the sight of the King's despair. He pulled his cloak about him and tightened his belt. Then he bowed his head before Caradoc and said: "Badger, I will go now and find Caerwent. Or, if the gods keep me from doing that, I will at least find some place away from this cursed river where we may come again to remember that we are men of a great people. I go now, Caradoc, but when I come back it will be by the black-bird's call that you shall know I have succeeded." And he almost ran from the spot where the warriors sprawled or squatted and where the tiny flame flickered among the damp ashes. No one wished him luck, or showed any love for him when he went; but after he had gone, men began to talk to each other once more, as though they had found hope. Morag and his brother lay together and seemed to sleep. Even the King looked up and watched the lightning as it pierced into the blackness over the wide estuary. And all waited and listened for a bird's crying, for in their hearts they had faith in Gwyndoc.

Then, after this first hope, the rain came down as heavily as ever and the river began to rise, creeping slowly up the pebbled beach towards them; and once more the men lost heart, being unable to see that any human creature could battle with the gods on a night like this; and the King sat down again, his head in his hands, shuddering and talking to himself as he had done before. A great fear settled on every man; they saw with their own eyes that they were a defeated race. It did not matter whether they lived or died. Their King had lost his power and the gods were no longer with him. Nor were their other leaders likely to bring them better luck. The King's cousins were bloody-minded men, happy only in killing, whoever it might be. And the King's friend was a scheming traitor who, even now, was probably planning to bring down some other wild ambush upon them.

CHAPTER TWELVE

THEN, WHEN THEY all knew that warmth and comfort would never be theirs again, that they must go to their deaths with the intolerable scream of wind in their ears and the cold hands of rain searching every inch of their exhausted bodies, a dark shape detached itself from the surrounding blackness and came slowly, stumbling and groping, in their direction. For a time they looked at each other, and Morag's hand sought his brother's. And no one spoke. Then Caradoc whispered, "It might be Gwyndoc. Whistle like a blackbird, Morag. It is his call." Morag put both his hands about his lips and whistled, at first softly, and then more boldly as his courage returned. They saw the figure stop, cautiously, and listen; then, to their relief, between gusts of wind, they heard the answer come back, the cry of the blackbird, and they saw the dark figure move again and come as quickly towards them as his fatigue would allow. "It is Gwyndoc," said the King. Beddyr grunted and turned his back on the panting chief. "He has been long enough, too," said Morag, "leaving us here to wait for him." The King turned and looked at the grumbling tribesman, and Morag, who could see his master's eyes in the dark, was quiet again.

Then Gwyndoc staggered among the men and squatted down

in the lee of the great rock, away from the piercing gusts. "It is
well, Caradoc," he said, breathing hard. "I have found a place,
a great cave, big enough to shelter an army, and not more than
a mile from this spot. There we might lie hidden for as long as
we wish."

"Rest awhile," answered Caradoc, "until you feel strong
enough to lead us to this cavern. You seem to have done well."

And Morag punched his brother savagely in the chest and
then began to whistle the blackbird's call with all the strength
of his lungs, a distorted and grotesque version of Gwyndoc's
signal, while Beddyr rubbed his chest and rolled his bloodshot
eyes round like an imbecile.

The way to the cave was difficult, even dangerous. Once one
of the men-at-arms stepped off the narrow mountain way and
fell into an unsuspected ravine. Hearing a sheep bleating far
below him in the mist, he found strength enough to hold onto a
tree root while Beddyr and his brother knotted their cloaks
together and made a rope to drag him back to safety. After
which the party went on in single file, each holding the hand of
the one in front like blind men. When they were almost unable
to move any further from cold and hunger, Gwyndoc halted
and whispered back along the file, "Listen, friends, and you will
hear the wind howling at the mouth of the cave." The tired
clansmen waited, and at length, as Gwyndoc had said, a long
low howl came to their ears from the darkness ahead. "Let us
go forward without delay," said Caradoc. "The cavern cannot
be far away now." And he began to stumble on, but Morag's
hoarse voice called out from the end of the column, "No,
cousin, we will not go on. That sound is the voice of death. We
are walking into a trap with our eyes open. Gwyndoc has
betrayed us all." Beddyr took up the call, like a crazed beast,
half-laughing, half-sobbing, "Yes, Caradoc, he is a liar and a
murderer. He would kill his king and take his kingdom. The
cave he speaks of is the home of devils. We will not go."

Caradoc, even more tired than his followers, stood like a
statue for a while. Then he spoke, quietly and evenly. "I shall
not order you to follow me. You are my people and should
know your duty. I have no time for soldiers who know not their
duty. As my close kinsmen I wish you farewell and an easy
journey. As my officers, under oath to obey, I wish you nothing
but death. I shall speak no more." Then, in a harsh voice he
shouted to the bodyguard, "Run them through now and throw
their bodies into the chasm." There was some scuffling in the

dark, and the King moved on towards the cave. But after some minutes, Morag and Beddyr were at the tail of the column again, carrying between them the guard who had tried to carry out the King's command. The man was but slightly wounded from a blow of Morag's axe handle and felt quite grateful to the brothers for carrying him. Caradoc never referred to the incident again, but as the party halted before the great entrance of the cavern both Morag and Beddyr came to him and, bending into the sodden grass and heather, touched his shoes with their foreheads.

The cave was an immense one. Passing through the high, arched entrance, the wanderers took flints and tinder from their pouches and lit a fire of dry bracken which they pulled into a heap on the floor. They saw that they were in a sort of ante-chamber, circular in shape and as tall as ten men standing on each other's shoulders. The roof of the cavern was quite smooth, as was the floor, and, as they looked, Gwyndoc turned to the King and said, "This is the work of men, Lord. No wind or weather ever carved out a place like this." Morag, standing close behind the two, heard these words and looked over his shoulder at the awestruck men. "Did we not tell you that it was a place of demons?" he whispered. Caradoc turned on him and pointed to the opening of the cave, like a man sending away his dog. Morag bowed his head and went to the cave's entrance. Beddyr joined him, unbidden, and together the two stared out into the black night.

The King's action brought calm once more upon the party, and soon a big fire was crackling in the centre of the cave and the clansmen had pulled together enough fern and dry leaves from the corners of the great cave to make beds for themselves. Three of the soldiers unpacked the provision bags and set about making bread. The lords took off their outer clothing and held their tunics and cloaks before the great blaze, trying to get the rain out of them before retiring. Only the brothers stood away from the fire, wrapped in their wet clothes still and saying no word. From time to time they glowered at Gwyndoc, but the chief pretended to disregard them and went about his business of making a couch for the King.

Then, when all in the cavern felt at the least temporarily relieved by this warmth and shelter, this promise of a safe home, a wolf-like howl from the darkness at the end of the cavern hall brought every man to his feet. It started low and gradually rose till it sounded like the exultant cry of a devil. Then, before it ended, other voices took up the howl, until the sounds of the ghastly crying echoed and re-echoed about the high cave, filling every man's ears. Morag leapt back into the open, his sword out. "Come back, all of you," he shouted. "It is as we said. We are betrayed! Little Badger, here is my sword out to defend you." Caradoc looked for a moment at his cousin, then at Gwyndoc, half-doubting him. Then he dragged a flaming branch from the fire and flung it, crackling, towards the end of the cave, into the darkness. The tribesmen followed the blazing arc, and as the bough fell to the ground, still burning fiercely, they saw that the cavern floor sloped upwards towards another, low opening in the far wall.

"That door must lead to another cave," called Gwyndoc. "Yes," said the King. "Who will come with me to find out what lies on the other side? Who will dare the howling of the wind?" For a moment Morag and Beddyr looked at each other, then they stepped forward with the others to Caradoc's side. The King and Gwyndoc took torches from the fire and, sword in hand, led the way up the sloping floor. One by one the men passed through the opening, the taller of them having to bow their heads as they went, and found themselves in a low tunnel, hardly high enough for a man to stand upright. As the party moved cautiously forward the howling died away to a low moaning. Then that fell away to nothing, and the only sound to be heard was that of the clansmen's breathing and the shuffle of their sandals along the stone floor.

The tunnel was a short one, hardly more than ten yards long, and Gwyndoc, ahead of the rest, was the first to come out of it. He suddenly waved his torch above his head and then fell back with a gasp of horror. "By the gods," they heard him say, "a cave of death!" In an instant the other men had pushed forward, their swords and axes ready. Then they too saw what the chief had seen and fell back aghast.

The room they had come into was many times larger than the great entrance hall of the cave, and so high that its roof could not be reached by the flickering rays from the torches. It was in the form of a vast, roughly circular bowl, round the walls of which ran galleries as high as any eye could see, and round all the walls and along all the galleries sprawled human creatures, some dead or dying and some still alive. Each one was secured by a neck-ring to iron sockets in the rock walls, and near to each one was a rough clay or wooden bowl. Only the bowls of the dead contained any food, and that food a scrap of rotting meat or a dry bone.

The Belgae stared in horror at this gallery of death, their swords now pointed at the ground and their limbs shaking. Before them men and women, old and young, lay contorted into every ghastly shape and posture possible to a madman's nightmare. A blind old woman lay moaning, twisted across a creature whose sockets held no eyes and whose skin had the hard gloss of an ancient parchment. A young man, whose filthy rags showed a body covered with sores, was gnawing in a frenzy at his wrists. The tribesmen, sickened to the heart, watched him for a moment before they turned away in disgust; but all had seen that his arms ended in ragged, bloodless stumps, from which the hands had gone.

Only Caradoc kept the power to speak. He turned to Beddyr. "Go back and bring more torches," he said. "There is work for us to do here that needs a good light." The tribesman went, and as he moved it seemed that every head still capable of motion turned towards the visitors. Only the wretches who lay slowly falling to dust made no movement. But no sound came from any mouth; even the dying ceased in their groaning, silenced by the sudden terror of lights and men who walked upright and free.

Then Beddyr came back with fire-brands, and, as the great charnel-house was flooded with light, a rustle started among the bodies, increasing in volume until it sounded as loud as a summer breeze in a field of barley, and as the tribesmen followed the sound they saw a wave of grey and black sweep over the floor and on into the darkness at the furthermost end of the cavern. "Great God!" almost screamed Gwyndoc. "Rats! We are in the feeding house of the rats!" Beddyr stumbled forward to his cousin, his throat working violently. "Caradoc," he groaned, "kill me now, but do not order me to go on in this place. I have a stomach for most things, but I cannot bear to look on this." The King stretched out his hand to comfort the man, and Beddyr fell on to his knees and retched. The other men turned away, some of them covering their eyes and ears with their hands.

Then the King spoke again. "My friends," he said, his voice shaking now, "we are in no house of spirits. This is a prison-house, where hostages and war-captives are kept. There is nothing but pity to be felt for these creatures. They are put to death by darkness and starvation — and rats. Some of them, you see, are cripples. Here, in the country of the Silures, such unfortunates are doomed to death, since there is not enough food in this stony land to support both the sick and the healthy."

Gwyndoc pushed to the King's side. "What are we to do, master?" he said. "We cannot leave these things here with the rats, now we have seen them." The King looked at him gravely. "Yes, you are right," he said. "We have a task to perform, though some of you may have no stomach for it, and I shall not blame those of you who have not. We must take our weapons and fight a battle against suffering. This is a battle we know we can win. These poor devils are not Romans." He smiled grimly as he spoke. Then he stepped forward and with one sweep struck off the head of the blind woman. Behind him his soldiers gasped in horror, and he turned, angry as a wolf. "What, you craven women," he hissed, "will you deny these suffering things a quiet sleep? Then may you rot too, for I have no more use for you." And he went on along the gallery, striking left and right, swiftly and accurately. Then the tribesmen followed, their eyes averted from the eyes that waited for them and the hands that reached out towards them. And for a time nothing could be heard in the cavern but hard breathing and dull blows. Not one of the wretches groaned as the sharp steel struck. And at last the clansmen were together again on the floor of the great cavern. They did not speak as the King made an obeisance to the still figures. Then they all turned and filed out again into the tunnel, towards their blazing fire. And as the last man left the vast shambles the rustling of rats' dry feet sounded again in the darkness, now louder and more urgent than before, and before the last flicker or torchlight had left the tunnel the air was full of a thin squealing and the crunching of small teeth.

For a long time Gwyndoc lay amongst the rough bracken, the light of the great fire shining full in his face, its warmth striking hard through his clothes and seeming almost to scorch his body. At first sleep seemed impossible to him with the heat on his face, the charnel-house smell still in his nostrils and the tearing of dry flesh still in his ears. And always the great river lapped and gurgled about him and the little black figure snarled and gibbered from a barge that drew rapidly from his eyes into the swirling mist and then, as he breathed again in relief, came forward towards him, faster and faster, until the dark prow seemed about to cleave its way into his breast.

Around him lay the huddled figures of the other riders, some of them still and silent, others snoring and beating the air with their hands, as though to ward away some oppressive evil that threatened to choke them.

Gwyndoc's bones and muscles ached to the point of pain with the day's riding and the damp. His hips could find no comfort in the cavern floor, in spite of the thick layer of ferns on which he rested. He turned onto his back and for a time gazed above him at the shadows that jigged about the high roof like the sword-play of ghosts and at the long stone icicle that hung down above him like the finger of a threatening god.

With his hands pillowing his head, Gwyndoc sank slowly into a troubled sleep, like a man caught in a salt-marsh, conscious until that last inch before his eyes are covered by the inevitable, callous slime. As he sank, Roddhu was waiting for him again, crouching like a cat to spring at him from a dark corner, his pointed teeth showing in a white smile. And as the old man sprang, Gwyndoc woke with a ghastly start, the sweat beating out of his forehead, his mouth wide open but only painful air coming from it. His wild eyes told him that the cave was almost dark now, that the bracken fire had burned down to ashes, that he had slept for longer than he had thought; and, as he fought for his breath, he knew that a man's strong hands were locked hard about his throat. Morag was looking down at him, so close that his long black hair fell into Gwyndoc's eyes, and whispering to him as he strained. "Good night, Gwyndoc, the Otter! Go quietly on your journey and do not disturb the King with your cow's bellowing! I have waited a long while to let your spirit from your body. Now I am doing it! Good night, Otter, and pass quickly!"

Gwyndoc's eyes turned in agony, and to the side of him he saw Beddyr, standing with folded arms, looking down on him and smiling gently, as though he were watching a child's first laboured attempts to walk.

Gwyndoc tried to move his arms, but Morag's knees were on them, painful and heavy. He tried to twist his body, but the other was firmly seated on his stomach. He tried to shout, but the long fingers only dug deeper into his throat.

The cave began to swing round, and the gaunt stone icicle waved above him like a sapling in the wind. The fire began to crackle again, flinging off many-coloured sparks. And far away Gwyndoc heard the King singing softly to the harp, but the words were strange ones, like those a crow speaks, and the harp was the sound of many bows twanging in chorus. Then there were trumpets and the swinging of elepants' trunks, and the obscene smell of camels. But, above all, the white pain of imprisoned blood howling to be set free through ears, or nose, or eyeballs. . . .

Then, all at once, the sun was shining again and the mountain wind blowing into his face, and he rose, up and up, until he swung out like an eagle above the dark forests and the blue lakes. . . . And the new air swept back into his lungs, full and clean, and he tried to swallow it down as a subterranean tunnel swallows a river. . . . Then his eyes cleared and he was standing, gasping, in the cave again. Two dark, painted men clothed in dangling skins were holding his arms down to his side and grinning in his face, showing their broad broken teeth. Sprawling among the bracken, pinned down by others, Morag was struggling and cursing. Gwyndoc cast his eyes quickly round the great cavern: it seemed to be swarming with these skin-clad savages, and not one of the Belgae but was either held down or tied with leather thongs, even the King.

Suddenly Gwyndoc turned and the pain of Morag's murdering fingers rushed back into his head, and with a great heave he flung off the two Silures who held him, and was stamping with the heel of his riding-boot into Morag's mouth, crushing and hacking with all his force. The shouting in the cave stopped as all turned to watch the tall madman. Then Gwyndoc's guards had him again as he paused for breath; but once more he broke away and was upon the screaming Morag, his thumbs feeling for the wide dark eyes, tearing and gouging in the bloody mist of frenzy. But Morag twisted in terror and suddenly struck up with his knee at Gwyndoc's groin, and the madness passed and he fell back breathless, with his captors upon him again.

For a moment there was only Morag's groaning to be heard; and then one of the dark men, decorated with bears' claws and wearing the antlers of a deer, leapt into the middle of the floor and gave his orders: his harsh, crackling words sounded foreign to the Belgic ears, but with just enough likeness to their own language to be recognisable. "To Arrad-Bwlch with these foreign cattle!" he said, and pointed to the cave entrance. The Belgae were dragged to their feet and pulled or pushed out into the open again. By now the first signs of daybreak were showing over the eastern hills.

Herded like sheep, the captives were driven along the hillside for a time, and then were turned through a narrow cleft in the rocks, just wide enough for a man's body to pass through, into a narrow, steep-sided gulley. The Belgae looked back, wondering what would happen to the horses, then they saw that the Silures in the rear of the file were carrying the harness, some of it broken now, and a few of the lords began to shout out in anger, asking by what right their horses had been taken from them. But the little black-haired warriors grinned and stuck their spear-points into the legs of those who shouted, so the outcry died down.

Gwyndoc walked like a man in a dream for a time, but at last the cold morning air revived him. It had stopped raining now, and a fresh mountain wind was stirring. He looked up and saw Caradoc striding at the head of the file, his arm round Morag, who stumbled along with his chin on his chest. Suddenly Gwyndoc wanted to run to them, to tell them that they were all walking through a ghastly dream and that tomorrow they would wake up and find that nothing of it was real. But the two tribesmen who walked at his side clutched him roughly by the shoulders, and one of them struck him at the back of the knees with a bronze axe, not too hard, but hard enough to show him what his punishment would be should he try to break away. Then his throat began to hurt him again, and he knew that this was no dream.

At last the gully became shallow, and then they came to its mouth. Before them lay a great natural bowl, bounded on every side by rising treeless land. Everywhere was grey stone and sheep-dung. They made their way in the faint light to the farthest side of the hollow, passing crude shelters of slate or stone from time to time — moss-grown and insecure, the slabs resting against each other without joints or mortar, rather like the trilithons the Belgae had seen among the more northerly Celts. Here and there smoke rose from chimney-holes, but no one came out as they passed. Beside a few of the buildings goats or cattle were tethered, but they were mostly dwarfed and emaciated creatures, useful, it seemed, neither for milk nor meat.

When at last the party reached the tall cliff-face at the farther side of the valley, the captives saw that the rock was pocked with a number of regularly placed holes at ground-level, just big enough for a man to enter them if he stooped. They appeared to be cave entrances. The Belgae were roughly pushed into these, in twos and threes, and boulders then rolled against the openings. Gwyndoc pulled at his bonds and tried to get into the one Caradoc was being dragged towards, but he was struck in the neck and thrown savagely into another prison-cave, and after him were flung two others, both ordinary men-at-arms. Then the light was blocked out by the boulder and the prisoners were left.

For a time Gwyndoc had no desire to speak, but at last he was forced to ask his companions to try and move, so that he could shift his weight onto the other side of his body. They attempted to turn, but found that any movement was impossible. The cave was only big enough for two men, nor was it high enough to allow a man to stand. After a while the darkness became oppressive and the air thick and stifling. Gwyndoc did not complain, because he was a chief, but at last he fainted off. When he became conscious again he heard the others talking painfully, grumbling that they were free-men and not slaves; that Caradoc had no right to expect them to suffer like this for him; that they had wives and children who were worth more to them than a king. Gwyndoc tried to order them to be silent, but he found that he was too weak to raise his voice, and he lay back against the cold stone, the breath whistling in his wounded throat.

At length his mind left him again, but before he fainted this time his ears, made keen by light-headedness and the darkness, caught the sound of a repeated low moaning. He listened as hard as he could, trying to fasten his shifting mind to this one reality. It was coming from the next cave, he was sure, and it was Morag's voice.

Gwyndoc bit his lip with misery until the salt came into his mouth. Then he moved his hand and touched the tribesman nearest to him. His body was limp and heavy.

As time wore on, Gwyndoc fainted and revived many times. He could not bring his mind to say how many. Now the only thing he feared was having to become conscious again. Once, when his head cleared for a short time, he heard someone screaming out thickly in the hole beside him. He knew only that there was a sound, but he was not sorry or afraid any longer.

When the stone was rolled away, darkness had come again. At first Gwyndoc could not believe that he was breathing fresh air once more. He lay back and gulped, his eyes gradually seeing that great fires had been lit somewhere outside. His limbs were cramped and ice-cold and did not belong to him any more. No one moved in the cave. Then one of the soldiers was dragged out, feet foremost. As the body was moved, it slumped across Gwyndoc's chest, and he felt a faintly warm mess across his face. He knew without seeing that the tribesman had cut his throat with a hidden weapon or a flint. The other warrior revived and crept out of the narrow hole. Gwyndoc saw him fall a number of times and then disappear behind the boulder.

When his captors eventually pulled him out, his wandering eyes saw the Belgae, kneeling or lying in every posture of despair, about a big fire that threw its crazy shadows half-way across the broad valley.

So they stayed for a while, until the little men were on them again, prodding and kicking them to their feet. They were shouting excitedly, "Arrad-Bwlch comes! Arrad-Bwlch comes! Stand, you cattle, so that he may see what his children bring for his fires!"

There was a flourish of bulls' horns beyond the firelight, and suddenly Gwyndoc remembered the early days on his uncle's farm near the narrow sea. There would be such orders from the overseers to the stockmen: "Stand up there, man. Let the lord see you're fit to work among his cattle!" Or, "If you don't hold your head up I'll take the skin off your back. The chief'll cut my wages for underfeeding you!" Then his uncle would walk through the stockyard, tall and aloof, in his bright tartan, asking the bailiff questions about this and that, prodding a cow, glancing inside the granary, pausing to ask one of the slaves if he liked working for a Belgian, and so making his way back to the home farm to taste a new brew of mead or to watch the cream being taken from the milk and sample honey from one of the new stocks. . . . These things passed through Gwyndoc's mind, almost bringing the tears to his eyes, as he stood by the blazing bonfire, staring into the dusk.

But when Arrad-Bwlch, King of the Silures, came in sight, those friendly pictures faded and Gwyndoc was back among savages, in a dark country of careless agony. The Silurian hobbled towards a great wooden chair set at the edge of the biggest fire — a small, wrinkled figure hung about with greasy sheepskins. From the stretched lobes of his ears hung massive bronze rings, and his black hair, held in place by long pins of bone, was knotted in rolls above his head. In his right hand he carried a long wand of white wood; his left arm, made useless by an old wound, hung shrivelled and dangling at his side. Partially supporting him was a tall brown-haired young man, dressed in what might once have been a tartan tunic but which was now faded and threadbare from long use. From time to time as they moved towards the chair, the King half-turned his head to speak to his attendant, who seemed anxious to please and who nodded back and laughed at the slightest word.

The Celts looked at each other when they saw this and wondered who the King's friend could be. Then Arrad-Bwlch eased himself into the tall chair and the dark-skinned tribesmen flung themselves on their faces, calling out his name again and again. At first the Belgae, taking their lead from Caradoc, stood still, looking straight before them and over the Silurian's head; but soon they were beaten and kicked and forced down to their knees, while the shouting went on.

Then at last there was silence, and Gwyndoc saw that the King was holding up his wand. He heard Arrad-Bwlch call out in a harsh, cracked voice, and then Caradoc was being dragged forward, his arm still about Morag. At first the Silurian seemed to ignore the Belgic king, but fingered the cloth of his cloak and his kilt, almost in wonder it seemed, leaning back occasionally to comment on it to his tall smiling attendant. When he had tired of examining the woollen cloth, his eyes rose to the ornaments on Caradoc's arms and at his throat. He spoke sharply, and before Caradoc could move, his guards had torn bracelets, gorget and brooches from him to lay them at the Silurian's feet.

At last, with an infinitely offensive slowness, Arrad-Bwlch looked up into Caradoc's twitching face. He stared at the Celt for a while, and then his broad lips moved in a twisted smile. He turned to his companion and spoke. "Whose dog art thou?" asked the tall young man, interpreting for the King, and glaring at Caradoc as he spoke.

For a while not a man moved or whispered as Caradoc flung back his head and stared back at his questioner. Then at length he spoke. "What carrion crow lifts his voice to the Badger?" For an instant the young man's face grew wild, then he controlled his voice and said, "I am Commius, the friend of the war-eagle, great-grandson of Commius of the Atrebates, brother-in-arms of Gaius Julius Caesar, Lord of the Western World and Conqueror of Britain."

The Belgic king smiled grimly and then with a studied insolence spat at the feet of Commius. "Midden-dog," he said, smiling into the other's face, "I am Caradoc, son of Cunobelin, son of Tasciovanus, son of Andoco, son of Cassivelaun, King of all the Belgae wherever they be. My father pulled the Caesar's nose and threw his jackal Commius where he belonged, onto the dunghill. What say you now?"

There was a stir of laughter among the Belgae, and wonder in the faces of their swarthy captors, who only half-understood the words that had been spoken. Arrad-Bwlch looked up at Commius, cynically smiling, and then addressed Caradoc, haltingly but with interest. "You who call yourself Badger," he said, "listen to me. I speak your language with pain, but you will understand me. I had reserved your body and those of your friends for my fires, and the wicker-cages are even now ready. But I am a merciful man, as you shall learn, and I like the sound of your words. Show me that you are indeed a better man than my adopted son, Commius, and I shall let you and all your party go free from the flames."

Commius nodded excitedly, and Caradoc bowed his head in assent. "It is not my fashion to use a sword on sucking-pigs," he said. "Give me a knife that cuts meat and I will be satisfied." Commius started at the insult, but the Silurian patted his arm. "Give him your hunting-knife, Commius, my son," he said. "We shall shortly see which of the two is a sucking-pig!" Then Commius flung his long bronze knife down at Caradoc's feet, but before the Celt could bend to pick it up, Beddyr had called out, "Badger, take care, you should not fight when we are here to defend you. Let Morag or me take up the knife. We are your wolves!"

And Caradoc half-turned towards the fire and said, "Thank you, Beddyr, but I shall need you in the days to come. You will be king when I am gone, and Morag is blind."

Gwyndoc heard his friend's words and lowered his head in shame. He had gone from Caradoc's mind. He was no longer the King's brother, but an outcast whose very existence was ignored. He wanted to break away from the sharp clutching fingers of his guards and fling himself before Caradoc, asking his pardon for not being wounded before Mai Dun, begging his king to blind him for having blinded the Prince Morag; but his heart failed him, and he looked on apathetically as Caradoc flung off his heavy cloak, tried the point of the hunting-knife on his thumb, and stepped into the circle that had been cleared at the edge of the fire.

And as Caradoc waited, the glow of the flames turning his golden hair to crimson, Commius snatched a long-handled axe from one of the guards and, swinging it round his head, ran into the ring, laughing madly and calling on Arrad-Bwlch to have faith in his son. Once more Caradoc smiled, and said so that all should hear, "Yes, we flung him back onto the dunghill where he belonged!" The Belgae laughed again, and this time even their captors joined in, hardly knowing what they laughed at but sensing that this Caradoc was a man to fear.

Then the fight began, slowly at first, as the two circled each other in the leaping firelight, then faster and faster as each man feinted and rushed and dodged. Commius had the advantage, by the length of his axe, but Caradoc, holding his knife short and close to the body, drew first blood. His opponent had moved swiftly towards him, swinging the axe from side to side, but Caradoc, stepping under the whirling blade, put out his foot and sent the taller man almost sprawling into the fire. Then before he was back on his feet, the long hunting-knife had sliced through the guide of his right arm, rendering it useless. As the blade bit, Commius howled and staggered back onto his feet, clutching the axe in his left hand, his face twisted now and sweating. "The advantage is with you now, Belgian," he said. "But before I have done the starlings shall make their nests in your skull-bone!"

As he spoke the dark tribesmen hissed with admiration. Then he ran forward again. This time Caradoc did not try to meet him but backed away from every stroke he made, attempting to tire him now that he could only use one hand. And, after the men had circled each other for a while, it seemed that Caradoc's plan had succeeded, for Commius, breathing loudly and painfully now, let his axe rest on the ground for a moment so that he could lean on it. Even as he did so, Caradoc was on him; but this time Commius was ready. With a quickness that no one expected from him, he drove the haft of the axe upwards into Caradoc's body. The knife went spinning from the Celt's hand, among the ashes of the fire, and as Caradoc doubled with pain his opponent swung the axe viciously against his legs. As bone snapped, the Silures yelled and the dark king beat against the side of his chair with the white wand. "A leg for an arm! Bravely done, my son! We shall hear what songs the Belgae can sing to the fire-god, after all!"

Commius smiled as best he could towards the voice, but the pain from his arm was almost more than he could bear now. The fire was swimming in his eyes, and it was becoming more and more difficult to focus his writhing opponent. But at last he stepped forward and raised the axe over his shoulder, bending to watch where it should strike. As he bent, Caradoc rolled painfully to one side and, clutching his opponent's dangling hair, dragged him to the ground with his last rush of strength. The axe fell out of reach, and for a moment the two enemies lay side by side in the hissing circle, too spent from loss of blood to move. They breathed in a harsh agony, in unison, almost like brothers. No one spoke, but all leaned forward into the fire-

glow to see what would happen next. They saw Caradoc's hand
clutch again, deep into their champion's long hair. Then they
saw the King's other hand take him by the breast of his tunic.
Slowly Caradoc dragged his bleeding body on top of Commius,
pinning him down with the dead weight. Then again the two
were still, and somewhere in the direction of the hills a horn
blew sadly and a wandering dog began to howl. Slowly Caradoc's
head fell until he seemed to weep on his enemy's breast, and the
assembled tribesmen, Belgae and Silures, bent forward to watch
the end of this strange battle; and in the silence the dog howled
again. Then Commius's legs began to twitch, at first slowly and
then in a convulsive frenzy, and at last they lay still and contorted.

And as the watchers gasped, they saw Caradoc raise his head
painfully and look towards the fire, and his mouth and beard
were red with the blood of his enemy.

For a long time then there was a quietness broken only by
the Celt's deep sobbing breath. Then the voice of Arrad-Bwlch
called, cold and cruel, from the big chair. "So the Badger has
made good his words upon my only son and has left him fit
only for the dunghill. No one shall say that Arrad-Bwlch does
not keep his word, therefore. I said that I would free you from
the flames, and I shall keep my promise. You shall not burn,
not one of you. Instead, you shall each die as my son here has
died. May your journey be short and your path strewn with
flowers!" Then he turned and called to his bodyguard, "Bring
the dogs, slave! One dog for every prisoner here, and see that
they come on the strongest leashes, for tonight they will dine as
they seldom have before."

As he spoke, Caradoc raised himself again, and began to crawl
back towards his clansmen. Morag began to cry out for him in a
high, childlike voice, "Badger, Badger, I smell blood. Say it is
not yours, Badger! Say, Badger!"

And Caradoc stopped for a moment, seeming to hear his
cousin's voice only faintly. At last his lips moved and he said,
"No, Morag, it is not my blood you smell. Have courage, little
wolf!"

Then he fell senseless on his face among the dead ashes of the
fire. And as his body rolled over stiffly, the hounds began to
bay excitedly from the distant stone houses, and, even as they
did so, the full blare of horns was heard again, now right on the
edge of the great crowd of tribesmen. And the Belgae looked up
from their King's still body to see the Silures fall back to left
and right as they let someone pass. In the firelight Gwyndoc

saw that it was Gwynedd, with Ygerne by her side, and after
them rank after rank of the picked warriors they had left
behind in their doomed city, their lances at the ready, their
body armour glinting magnificently in the flames.

Before the humped figure in the chair the women halted, surrounded by their warriors, and no one spoke, until at last Arrad-
Bwlch smiled up at them and said, "Welcome!" Then Gwyndoc,
his heart beginning to leap again, saw Gwynedd, the gentle
Gwynedd, lean forward and take the dark king by his beard and
spit in his face; and, as she did this, two golden Celts belonging
to the royal household took the old man by the shoulders and
forced him to his knees before the Queen of the Belgae.

And Gwyndoc began to cheer and sing and weep, all in one
breath, and when he became conscious of his fellows again he
heard that they were doing the same. At either side of him his
guards were on their knees, and his hands were free once more.
And everywhere he looked the Silures were prostrate, silent
only because they did not know by which name to hail this
strange strong woman who had tumbled their god from his
wooden throne.

Then Ygerne turned and, searching among the crowd for
Gwyndoc, ran towards him with her arms outstretched. And for
long enough they held each other close, laughing and weeping.
Then Gwyndoc fell down by the side of Caradoc and called his
name and stroked his tangled, bloody head with tender hands.

Part Two
CHAPTER THIRTEEN
A.D. 44

THAT YEAR THE Celts suffered many unaccustomed hardships, living now as the Silures did. But when spring came
again and they had had time to find themselves dark-skinned
wives and to plant their cornseed, they began to feel more
settled. Besides, as Caradoc had told them, hobbling round from
farm to farm, this was only a temporary measure. One day,
perhaps very soon, he would collect all the tribes and ride back
to the lost kingdom. Then the Romans would be thrown out
and there would be rejoicing in Camulodunum once more. At
least that was what Caradoc had said; and though some of the
more cynical had seen a look of doubt in his eyes as he spoke,
they had all nodded and slapped him on the back, Gallic fashion,
and called him "Good old Badger" affectionately.

In most ways they were not unhappy. The Silures bowed
down to them, especially as more and more Belgic refugees
came in, red-faced and touchy, to offer their swords to Caradoc.
Besides, their old king, Arrad-Bwlch, was virtually a prisoner
and could no longer perform for them their power rites or make
their wives bear men-children. He stayed most of the time
crouched over the fire in his smoky stone hut, mumbling to
himself that he was the god-king who had been called on to die
for his people. But the Belgae would not yet allow him the
privilege of martyrdom. His food was always served by a Celt,
so that he might not take the easy way of poisoning himself
with foxglove sauce; and whenever he chose to walk abroad, a
group of tall golden-haired guards walked with him — at a
respectful distance of course — their swords slung to the front
and ready, partly because they rather hoped Arrad-Bwlch would
try to escape and partly to impress any stray Silurian rebels who
might consider an attempt to recapture their king.

These precautions were, in the main, unneccessary, since the
old man, a chronic asthmatic, barely survived the hard winter.
He died in the night, humped in the darkest corner of his
suffocating hut, on the eve of the spring-sowing festival, when
the rest of the village was dancing, tipsy with mead, about the
fires, and the dark girls were choosing their spring mates among

the thatched hovels.

After a perfunctory ceremony, performed mainly by his own followers, Caradoc was made King of the Silures, and given all the magic of Arrad-Bwlch, together with his six wives. He accepted the first, as it was no liability, being so infrequently practised; but the wives were rather old and their swarthy charms unattractive to one whose standards had been cultured among a corn-haired race. Those older Celts who needed a woman about the house were given the pick of Arrad's faded treasures. The two wives who were not claimed were pensioned-off by the Badger and allowed to live out their days untroubled by domestic cares.

Caradoc was perhaps the least happy of the Belgae. Every week new messengers came in, some riding on stolen horses, some limping painfully, wounded by wandering lawless men in the great forests that lay between Camulodunum and Siluria, and each told the same tale: that the Roman disease was spreading like wildfire through the land; that the Romans were daily bringing in fresh soldiers, building forts, making roads for the rapid movement of troops, and all the time fanning out westwards, almost to within two days' ride of Siluria. And perhaps the worst news of all was that the tribes in general had gradually come to welcome these invaders. Chieftains whom Caradoc had known from boyhood were now bowing the knee to Claudius or to his general. Just as though they had never been taught about Vercingetorix or old Cassivelaunus! It was sickening. And just so that they could go on sitting in the same chair, eating as before — but no, not even that! Only last week a freckle-faced runner had brought in the news that Roman fashions were becoming all the rage in London, and even in Camulodunum, which the Romans had given a new name and were in process of rebuilding, Roman-fashion, with public baths, temples and a square market-place! There were times when Caradoc wondered whether he himself had done well in standing out against the new order of things. But he confessed these doubts to two men only — Morag and Beddyr. Not to Gwyndoc.

Sometimes his chieftain's new coldness towards him hurt Gwyndoc; but often, as he watched Morag groping his twilit way between the overhanging thatch of the huts or fumbling for his drinking-horn at the feast-table, he felt that Caradoc's silent hostility was the justice he must expect for ever raising his hand against the royal blood, even to defend himself. But then, Gwyndoc had other things to think about. At night, sprawling on the skins beside his own fire, he would watch Ygerne as her fingers embroidered the soft woollen clothes that their child should wear, then they would look at each other, the grey eyes meeting across the leaping flames, as though after long rehearsal, and often they would both begin: "I think we might call him [always "him"] . . ." and then the names would cross in the air — Bran, Gwyddion, Llew, even Catuval — but never a Roman name, never Julius, or Brutus, or Balbus, or Adminius . . .

But sometimes, especially if he was walking alone on the hills or fishing in the broad river, Gwyndoc would be overcome with doubts. What if the child were born dead, or blind, or deformed? What if he could never have the warrior son he yearned for? Or, worst of all, what if Ygerne did not survive the birth?

When such thoughts came over him, Gwyndoc would drop his lines, or slip his bow back into the case, and run or gallop back to the village without delay — one never knew when the gods were sending their warnings — just to reassure himself that Ygerne was still alive, still healthy and even happy, still almost bitterly in love with him. Then, at these times, Caradoc's lack of faith in him shrank back to nothing, and he did not mind if Morag and Beddyr were the favourites now. All he wanted was to be left alone with Ygerne, to wait for this miraculous birth.

Gwynedd was not so happy or so well. Something had happened to her husband's feelings towards her since the flight into Siluria. It was almost as though Caradoc had become another man. She began to realise how much he had depended on his position as Belgic chieftain to give him stability, even identity. He was a man in love with a kingdom, it seemed, for whom his fellow creatures were not so much sensitive men and women as pawns and counters, useful or useless, and treated as such, without overmuch feeling or insight. Gwynedd now saw that she mattered to him only because she would bear the son who would succeed him one day in the Belgic territories. And that didn't please her at all; she had learned now the power she had in her, the royalty and command. At times she remembered that night by the great fire, when she cowed Arrad-Bwlch and forced his warriors to their knees by the dominance of her spirit. And when she was specially angry with Caradoc she sometimes felt she would like to tell him that but for her he might not now be sitting in his halls, the ruler of the Silures. Indeed, he might not be anywhere, unless he was fortunate enough to be reborn into some casual mistletoe berry and cut by a druid at full-moon or, more likely nipped off by some stray starling as he perched in the oak tree. . . .

But Gwynedd never mentioned Caradoc's debt to her. It was merely something she thought about in the long lonely hours while she waited for her child to come.

She was brought to bed one morning in early summer, and her child, a girl, lived only until the afternoon. When her women dared tell her the evil news she turned her face to the cold wall and sobbed almost unceasingly, without relief or even full understanding, for hour after hour.

Caradoc was away hunting when word was brought to him. At first he stared at the frightened messenger as though he would run his knife into him, but he never spoke or moved for a time, and the man crept away into the thicket, vowing silently not to return to the village again. Then Caradoc's fury overbore him and he lashed his horse cruelly about the head, then galloped away, laughing hysterically, his horse rearing and caracolling madly among the overhanging boughs.

He did not return that night. Nor dared any of his henchmen follow his tracks through the forest. At dawn a herdsman saw him standing up to the waist in the cold river, calling on the water-god to drown the world and to swallow up his pain.

He came back to the village late in the evening of the second day, his hair tangled and torn out at the scalp, his clothing ragged, and without his arm-rings, weapons or horse. No one dared ask him where he had been or even dared to tend his wounds, for his arms and hands were covered with deep cuts, as though he had slashed himself with his hunting-knife.

Ygerne, her own time near, did her best to comfort Gwynedd, sitting with her for hours at a time, singing by her bedside or saying hope charms. But it was difficult, for Ygerne had not enough strength for both of them now, and Gwynedd's eyes always looked beyond her, as though she no longer belonged to this world or was interested in its workings.

Then on the evening of that second day Ygerne, half-dozing by the bedside, was suddenly conscious that a new shadow was dancing on the wall-hangings. She looked up and saw Caradoc standing near the low doorway. His face was that of a dead man, but cruel like the gods. He waved his hand, and the slaves crept away, afraid. For a moment Ygerne stared back at him, until even she could not stand his eyes any longer.

At the doorway she looked up to plead for Gwynedd, but

the King turned his eyes on her in such a way that she knew then that the spirit of the shining one had entered into him, and, weeping, she made her obeisance and hobbled painfully back to her hut to tell Gwyndoc what she had seen.

The next day they learned that Caradoc had put his wife away into a druid-house until such time as she might be clean again. And at a specially called council meeting Beddyr announced that Gwynedd had been the victim of a curse, either put on her by the foreign gods for the way in which she had treated Arrad-Bwlch that night by the fire or by their own gods because she had associated too freely with one who had lifted his hand against the blood royal. In the firelight Caradoc looked towards the seat where Gwyndoc sat, and all men's eyes were turned on him for a while. No one spoke a word of accusation, but from that day the warriors turned away whenever Gwyndoc or Ygerne came towards them, and only slave-women could be persuaded to pass through Gwyndoc's door to help Ygerne in her labour.

Three weeks after Caradoc's daughter had died, Ygerne brought a fine boy-child into the world, safely and without too much pain. And Gwyndoc, whose life had been heavy upon him since that mute accusation, suddenly felt the weight of guilt fall from his mind as he swept the howling baby up in his arms! Now here was a new warrior! One who should live through the bad times and, if needs be, make the king see reason one day!

Only Ygerne seemed doubtful. "We may have to go away," she said suddenly one night, the child at her breast. "If the two should persuade the Badger that a sacrifice of first-borns was necessary to make Gwynedd clean again . . ." And that night neither of them slept. Ygerne lay staring into the dying fire from her sheepskin couch, while Gwyndoc prowled about, gathering together their few valuables — pieces of cloth, drinking-vessels and ornaments — and wrapping them into a bundle in case they should need to leave suddenly, without further preparation.

But in the morning, when the new amber light fell in a broad shaft across the floor of the hut, and the boy Bryn lay crowing in his mother's arms, Gwyndoc lost much of his fear, and even sang again as he put a new edge on his war-axe. "I know I have a son," he thought, "and now fear has left me, for I know the gods are on my side. I feel their strength in all my blood and bones! And I know that if all the Badger's spearmen came for me the gods would give me the power to meet them — aye, even

Badger himself — and to strike them down."

Ygerne heard his song and read his thoughts in the axe as he threw it into the air and caught it easily again. And she smiled back at him, for she felt something of the same power — although with her the joy was mixed with pity and love for Gwynedd, and perhaps with a new sort of hatred for Caradoc.

Then, as though to prove to himself that he was right and that the gods really were with him, Gwyndoc strode out of the hut, swinging the axe and singing, looking for a cow that should give them milk to break their fast. Looking also for any man who would so much as turn his head or seem to sneer, or spit in the dust as he passed.

But he met no one. And when he came back to Ygerne with the pitcher full, she told him that the King's messenger had already been to the hut with greetings from the King and a little gold gorget for Bryn, which could only mean that Caradoc had accepted responsibility for the boy's upbringing and would stand as his father-next-to-Gwyndoc.

When he heard this, Gwyndoc clutched the baby to his chest and called him "King's son" and "my lord" and pretended to do him obeisance, until Ygerne called her husband a silly old fool, and told him he'd make the boy as stupid as he was if he didn't stop it all immediately. Then Gwyndoc fitted the gold trinket round Bryn's neck and laughed like a madman, while the child bawled at the touch of the cold metal, and started with fear each time his father roared out. But Ygerne, really impatient now, snatched Bryn back and boxed Gwyndoc's ears really hard. So hard that for a moment he too was cross. Then he stooped and picked them both up and ran round the hut with them till they were all dizzy. After which Gwyndoc placed his wife and the child gently on the bed and almost ran out towards Caradoc's hall.

Inside the stockade, Beddyr met him, his eyes two dark stones in his head, his jutting lip forbidding, his hand on his dagger. Gwyndoc greeted him freely now, and would have passed into the hall, but the King's cousin drew his short knife and stood in the way. He stared above Gwyndoc's head as he spoke, and his voice was as cold and impersonal as his eyes. "Caradoc is sleeping," he said. "No one shall disturb him." But even as Beddyr spoke, Gwyndoc saw the King pass through the hall, buckling on his riding-cloak as he went. "No," he said, smiling. "The Badger is well awake. I saw him walk even as you spoke just now. He is wearing his red tunic and the silver sword-belt."

Beddyr's face was as harsh as a thorn-bush. "The Badger is sleeping, Gwyndoc," he said. "He tells me to say that to you he will always be sleeping now."

Gwyndoc suddenly felt a pulse beating madly in his forehead, but he tried hard to keep calm. "How can that be," he said, "when the Badger has only this morning sent my new son a neck-ring? How can the Badger be sleeping towards me, Beddyr?"

The man's face was smiling now, a strange smile, like a small fissure coming without warning on a dangerous chalk-slope. "The Badger sends to your son Bryn; not to his father, Gwyndoc! And the father, Gwyndoc, would do well to go back home now and make his obeisance to his son, who is the King's son, whenever the Badger shall care to claim him."

For a moment Gwyndoc's fingers moved to clench themselves round the tormentor's throat and to squeeze and squeeze until that vicious tongue burst out. But then he saw Caradoc, in the high doorway, staring at him, his face as cold and hostile as Beddyr's. Then Gwyndoc knew that the other's words were true.

Smiling bitterly, he looked past Beddyr and gave the royal salute to Caradoc, who made not the slightest movement of recognition. Then Gwyndoc turned and strode out through the stockade and back to his hut, his head high. In the doorway he stopped. Ygerne was rocking backwards and forwards, singing softly. Bryn was sound asleep, still clutching her white breast. "Gracious one," said Gwyndoc, "we must go tonight. It might be too late tomorrow."

Ygerne nodded. "We shall not travel alone," she said. "After you had gone, Mathwlch of the Trinobantes came here openly. He did not look to right or to left but entered this house directly. He for one is not afraid."

Her husband looked at her, amazed. "But Mathwlch, of all the warriors, has sneered the most. It seemed to be Mathwlch who led the others in turning from me."

Ygerne shrugged. "Even Mathwlch can be wrong," she said. "Gwynedd is dead. Mathwlch was there — at least, he accompanied Morag to her house at the Badger's orders. Morag was to take her a message, he said. Mathwlch was to take him to the door and then to wait outside. He swears he heard Gwynedd's voice as Morag entered. Then she was suddenly quiet, and when Morag came out he was trembling. Mathwlch led him back and noticed that there was — something on his sleeves. But he did not dare ask. Now the councillors are told that she died last night in her sleep, unforgiven by the gods . . ."

Gwyndoc put his arm round her shoulder as she began to weep. "And so Mathwlch of the Trinobantes dares to accuse Caradoc, the Badger of the Belgae, and would be rid of him?"

At first Ygerne did not know how to answer her husband. She could sense below his words that loyalty to a chief, against all reason, which so often had destroyed the Celts even in their moment of victory, no less than of defeat. She said, "Mathwlch's people say that you were ill-accused and that neither Caradoc nor his kin should rule us any longer. He swears that they would follow you if you asked them . . ."

For a long while Gwyndoc was silent. "They are not Belgae," he said. "They do not know what true allegiance is. They have not taken the blood-oath to the Badger as I have done."

Ygerne looked through the doorway into the sunlight. "They know enough," she said. "They know that the Badger is a sick man now, and has been so since the battle. They know that this releases every true man from the oath. They know that with those two royal imbeciles, Morag and Beddyr, beside him, no man's life or property are safe. They know that if Rome is ever to be turned back, they had better find one stronger than the Badger now . . ."

Suddenly Gwyndoc raised his hand as though to strike her. She did not flinch, but looked back at him, the child in her arms. Then, remembering himself, Gwyndoc put his hands over his ears so that he should not hear what she was saying.

Then Bryn woke and began to whimper, pawing like a blind puppy at his mother's breast. Ygerne bent her head and rubbed her cheek against the child's warm head, and her eyes looked over him, grey and fearless, at her husband. For a moment there was no sound in the hut but the baby's cries. Then Gwyndoc straightened his shoulders and held up his head. He pointed towards Bryn.

"That is my first allegiance now," he said, and looked away from Ygerne. "We will go tonight, and should Mathwlch offer us his sword, so much the better."

And Ygerne nodded and smiled gently, as though she had known he would say this all along.

CHAPTER FOURTEEN

WHEN THE MOON had fully risen, Gwyndoc banked up the fire in their hut, so that the glow should shine out through the window-hole, and, keeping in the shadow of the house walls, he led Ygerne through the village towards the place where Mathwlch was to wait for them. Bryn they wrapped closely in a hide, so that his cries should attract no attention, and Gwyndoc carried him close to his chest, ready to put himself in the way of any assailant who might spring out on them.

But they saw no one, except a tipsy Silurian, who staggered out of a turf hut, gave Gwyndoc the royal salute, and then fell to his knees by the roadside. They passed by without answering him, afraid that their voices might be known to him and that he would later give the alarm. But as they went Gwyndoc wondered about that royal salute. Did the man imagine he had just met Caradoc, or was it an omen?

Outside the straggling cluster of huts, they cut across the pasture fields and down the slope that led to the river, towards the wood's side where Mathwlch and his tribesmen were to wait for them. Once Gwyndoc stopped and half-turned back. "Is this the right way?" he said, almost to himself. But Ygerne pulled at his cloak, urgently. "Remember whom it is you carry, Gwyndoc," she said. And her husband turned again and went on towards the trees.

At first they thought that Mathwlch had betrayed them, for they saw no one. Then from under the overhanging spruce boughs, two men suddenly stepped, heavily cloaked and carrying swords. They stepped forward swiftly towards Gwyndoc in the dusk, peering at him, the moon holding the edges of their uplifted weapons Mathwlch, the tall grey-haired warrior, wearing the bull's horns on his bronze helmet, looked at Gwyndoc for a second, then, raising his sword, said, "Well met, King that shall be!" His companion raised his sword at the words, and Gwyndoc shrank back, half in shock, half in embarrassment. Just then, Bryn cried out in his wrappings, and Mathwlch's face lost its gravity. "Welcome, too, you king's son, who cannot yet give back the greeting!" And as he spoke Ygerne heard the rustling of many swords behind the speakers, inside the wood, and saw here and there the glitter of metal.

"Your people are waiting?" she said. Mathwlch nodded, proud, it seemed, that his promise should have been so promptly kept. "The cattle are waiting for us five miles along the river, in a spinney, with men to guard them. Gwyndoc, I give you king-hail — and a warrior-band to take you to what safety you wish, you and yours."

Gwyndoc slowly handed the child to his wife, thinking, his mind swinging this way and that. At last he spoke, quietly and almost with reverence. "This thing we do, Mathwlch — is it the right thing? Do we not tempt the gods in breaking with the Badger? I would like time to think it over. I am not satisfied yet."

Ygerne made an impatient movement, but Mathwlch held up his hand. "Gwyndoc," he said, "you must make the choice for yourself and for your own kin. We are not bound as you are. We shall go, whether you come with us or not. We have decided, and our gods have promised their help. But you must choose your own death — and the deaths of your lady and her child. It is not our place to advise you."

In the wood, feet rustled and twigs fell with the sound of a light breeze. There was a tension in all the moonlit air. And every man could hear his fellow breathing.

Then Gwyndoc spoke again, into the heavy silence. "Mathwlch, I give you thanks for your friendship; it is more than I expected. More even than I want, in all loyalty to the Badger. Your way and my way may be different, or it may be the same way. I do not know, nor shall I know yet awhile. But I must know before I can come with you."

Ygerne came forward and held out the sleeping child. "This is all the reason you need," she said. "This, and the memory of Gwynedd. Now will you come?"

Suddenly Gwyndoc swung his heavy cloak about him and turned to them, his hand on his sword-hilt. "Mathwlch," he said, "wait for me but a little while. If I can, I shall return and come with you. If I do not come before the cocks crow again, leave this place and take my wife and her child with you. Treat them well, and forget that Gwyndoc was ever one of your company."

He stepped back and turned from them and began to walk quickly up the slope into the clear moonlight. "Wait for me, I must come with you!" called Ygerne. But he did not wait, and only shouted out over his shoulder, "Look to the child. I go where he is envied." And then he was too far away to follow. Ygerne felt Mathwlch's strong hand on her arm, and she followed him into the wood where his tribesmen were waiting, already thinking that she had now only the child, that she might never again see her husband.

And Gwyndoc, as he strode away, topping the hill and coming upon the lights of the village at the other side of the pasture-fields, also felt that he might never see his wife or his son again. "Oh, Light One, guide me," he said. "I am a man outside the Badger's law now, a traitor to my oath of fealty. What shall I do? Go back to Mathwlch, or make my peace again with the Badger?"

He stopped and looked up into the moon, and it seemed that a mocking face appeared inside that silver disc, and a voice seemed to whisper along the night wind, "Go back to Caradoc, Gwyndoc. It is right that you should make your peace with him. Then at least your wife and your son will be guiltless, whatever may become of you."

Gwyndoc dropped to one knee and bowed his head. And when he got up to make his way onward to the village, he seemed to see Roddhu sitting in his path some yards away, casting a long shadow in the moonlight. And Roddhu seemed to grin up at him and whisper something in a hoarse voice. Gwyndoc stood still so as to hear the wise one's words. And at last they seemed to say, "Do not go back with a sword, Gwyndoc. The Badger must not be visited with a sword tonight. Put away your sword."

Then Gwyndoc's sight cleared again, and he only saw a gorse bush where Roddhu had been sitting. He unswung his sword and dropped it into the midst of the gorse, and went on, still wondering.

Reaching the village, he made a wide detour and approached the King's hall from its open side. Everything was strangely still, and there was no guard at the gate. Gwyndoc hurriedly wrapped his cloak tightly about his left arm, so that it might serve as a shield should it be needed, and walked into the hall. The fire had sunk down and the torches had guttered into their sconces. But screwing up his eyes he could see that the room was empty.

At the end of the hall, under the thick hangings, a thin strip of light showed that the King's private room was lit. Gwyndoc stood outside and called his own name, and after the space in which a man might count twenty he heard the Badger's voice, quiet and gentle, telling him to enter.

Caradoc was sitting in his chair, his head sunk in his hands, his sword far away from him on a table. He looked up as Gwyndoc parted the door-hangings and smiled, and his face was the face Gwyndoc had always known in the good days.

"So you have come back again, Gwyndoc," the Badger said simply. "I thought Mathwlch might have tempted you away, with his talk of a crown." And then he smiled again and was silent, as Gwyndoc stopped in amazement before the royal chair.

Caradoc still smiled, even as he spoke, and Gwyndoc suddenly felt that the King's sickness had passed and that now things would be always as they had been.

"Badger," he said, "you know all?"

Caradoc seemed to hold out a hand towards him. "Yes, Gwyndoc, all," he said softly. "I have been waiting here for you all this night, knowing that your oath was stronger than any promise Mathwlch could make, knowing that your oath was even stronger than your love for Ygerne — or Bryn." And as he spoke this time it seemed that some devil was coming into his narrow eyes. But Gwyndoc only knew that Caradoc was his friend again, and he did not watch the Badger's eyes as he might have done had he been in his right senses.

Then Caradoc was speaking again. "You have come without a sword, my friend," he said. "It is a good thing to leave the sword behind when one comes on a mission of peace."

Gwyndoc bowed his head. "Roddhu counselled it," he said. And as from a great distance he heard the King's voice, "Roddhu is my good friend, Gwyndoc. His oath, at the least, is above suspicion."

And Gwyndoc remembered the broad river and the barge, and Roddhu pulling out into the stream and threatening the Badger. "How have you made your peace with him, Badger?" he said. "What sacrifice did you make?"

"Have my sacrifices not been great enough," he heard Caradoc say. "Were not my daughter and my wife enough, think you, Gwyndoc?"

Then Gwyndoc saw that the King was holding out both hands towards him, his face friendly, his eyes full with tears. "Come, Gwyndoc," he was saying. "Kneel before me and place your hands in mine and take the oath again, as you did before. Let us make all new, and this time remember our promises to one another."

And Gwyndoc went forward, like a man in a trance, and placed his hands in the Badger's. But just before his head dropped in obeisance, he saw the devils come again into the King's eyes, and this time they were the devils of the knife. And he felt the

King's hands close over his own like a blacksmith's pincers. Then he heard the hangings behind him rustle and knew that Beddyr was there to strike as he knelt.

And Gwyndoc roared like a bull and shouted, "Ygerne and Bryn!" as though he was in battle, and the King fell back from him, his chair overturned by Gwyndoc's sudden violence. He saw Caradoc's feet go upwards and backwards, and then flung himself flat as a great weight came at his back. Then Beddyr sprawled on top of him, casting round for the chance to strike with the long axe he carried. But Gwyndoc knew what to do now. The Badger had broken his faith, and Gwyndoc was no longer in fear of his gods.

"Die at last, Beddyr," he shouted, and picking up a burning log from the open fire, struck with all his force at the dark head before him. Beddyr put up his axe to parry the blow, but the charring pieces flew down into his face and his hair and his eyes, and he staggered back from Gwyndoc, half-blinded, and cursing with pain. Then Gwyndoc saw that Caradoc had reached his sword on the table, and he turned and ran from the room, unwilling to fight with the King. At the door he stopped for a moment. "The oath is broken on both sides now, Badger," he said. "Let who will, prosper in peace." And as he spoke the last word he tossed the flaring log over their heads into the thatch and ran through the hall and across the yard.

Past the grazing-fields, he stopped for an instant to get breath and to drag his sword again from the gorse-bush. As he did so, the moon went behind a cloud, as though hampering him; but he thrust the blade into his belt and ran on.

At the wood's edge he halted and called Mathwlch softly by name, but there was no answer. At last Gwyndoc pushed his way through the overhanging branches and came into the small clearing where the tribesmen had been waiting for him. They were gone, but here and there among the tussocky grass and short bushes lay men, hacked about the head or shot through with arrows. Perhaps a dozen men, all of them dead. In what light there was, Gwyndoc recognised their tartan for Mathwlch's, and then it came to his mind why the Badger's hall had been empty of warriors. They had cut off Mathwlch, even while Gwyndoc had been talking with Roddhu, or the gorse-bush.

For long enough, Gwyndoc stood in the clearing, shaking with terror for his wife and Bryn, and anger at the Badger's treachery. But at last he began to make his lost way towards the heath again, and as he reached the edge of the clearing, one of the warriors raised himself on his elbow. Gwyndoc saw that two arrows had passed deep into his chest, leaving only the feathered flights sticking out from his leather tunic. Gwyndoc went towards him in compassion, but the man waved him away. "You have no power to help me, lord," the man whispered. "I travel beyond love or treachery. I only wait to tell you that she is safe. Ygerne and the little king-child." The man stopped and fought for breath, but the blood flowed up into his throat again and he gasped. "Where are they, comrade?" said Gwyndoc tenderly. "Are they still with Mathwlch?" The man found strength to nod, and even to smile.

Then as Gwyndoc bent to touch his face, the warrior looked with yearning towards the lord's sword, sticking in his belt. He made a cut across his own throat with his finger; then the strength had gone from him and he could only lie back again among the gorse-thorns.

Gwyndoc smiled down at him again tenderly, and, standing so that he kept the moon's light from the warrior, he quickly slipped the sharp blade under the man's breast-bone and waited until his writhings had ceased. Then he straightened the warrior's legs and walked away from him along the wood-side, taking the route he knew they were to take, Mathwlch and the Trinobantes.

CHAPTER FIFTEEN

BY DAWN GWYNDOC reached the limits of the wooded country, and, coming over a hill-top, looked down across a broad rocky valley. High up the slope, on the further side of the dried river-bed, he saw a long column of men and cattle slowly winding their way between the great boulders towards the hill's crest. Even from that distance his eyes, made keen by anxiety, picked out the shape of the totem-pole that the leader carried — a bear hugging a warrior — and he knew that this was Mathwlch. He strained to see whether Ygerne and Bryn were in the column, but though he could distinguish a number of figures, heavily wrapped and riding ponies, he could not be sure that his wife and son were there.

No longer looking in fear behind him, he ran forward down the scree slope, sometimes staggering among the loose stones, sometimes falling, but never noticing his hurts, and always running on, his heart beating wildly in his breast, his hair, unplaited now, blowing into his eyes.

Half-way down he almost fell across the body of a tribesman, one of Mathwlch's oldest followers, a cadaverous man with a withered left arm. Gwyndoc knew him well as a good board-man and a great mead-bibber, a man who would challenge any-one in his cups, although he could hold no shield and must both attack and defend with his one sword-arm. Gwyndoc halted for a moment, and then saw that he had received heavy wounds the night before and had carried them to this spot. He had been left for the wolf or the eagle, as befitted a warrior slain in battle, and not burned on the pyre, as he would have been had he died in his bed.

Gwyndoc stayed to thank him, and then ran on again. And almost an hour from first sighting them he stood among Math-wlch's men again, hugging his sleeping son and praising the gods for protecting Ygerne, whose relief at seeing him was no less than his own.

Only Mathwlch seemed a little less than joyful. At first he did not dismount, but sat on his half-wild pony and glared down at Gwyndoc. "We have paid a heavy price for you, Otter," he said. "That boy of yours had better make a good king or else we shall feel that we have perhaps paid too much."

Gwyndoc looked at the grave faces about him and knew that they all felt as Mathwlch did. At first his pride stood in the way, and then he looked at Ygerne and the child again and knew that Mathwlch was speaking fairly, as he saw it. And Gwyndoc knelt down before the wild pony and, drawing his sword, went through the ritual motion of suicide. Then he looked up at Mathwlch and said, "May this, and more, come to me, if the Otter does not repay his friends a hundredfold!"

For a time the travel-stained faces about him made no sign of friendship. Then Gwyndoc rose and offered his sword to their leader, saying, "If I have not pleased you, strike now, Mathwlch, and go your ways happy again."

Then Mathwlch swung himself from his pony and knelt before Gwyndoc and put his hands in his, and all the tribesmen shouted and beat their swords upon their ox-hide shields. And Ygerne came forward, the fear gone from her face, and knelt to Gwyndoc too, the child still in her arms. Then the warriors shouted Gwyndoc's name and that of Bryn, louder than ever, and the wild creatures of the rocks shrank even further into their hiding-places, wondering at men who could sound so powerful and yet so happy.

Then one of the lead-ponies was brought for Gwyndoc, and

he and Mathwlch rode at the head of the column, with Ygerne close behind them in a litter. And as they went, Mathwlch told Gwyndoc that until such time as they might come back again to the country of the Silures, it would be best for them to find Madoc of the Ordovices and put themselves in his hands. For Madoc was a great chieftain and had married one of Mathwlch's distant cousins, and so would feel the bond of blood, even against Caradoc of the Belgae.

"But don't trust my cousin," he said. "She is beautiful — if you like women with red hair — but she is ambitious. Madoc means nothing to her as a man, but his kingdom does! And if you, Otter, stood in the way of making yourself a greater shadow on the earth, she might well forget Madoc!" Then he laughed as he saw Gwyndoc's scared backward glance. "It would take more even than Ygerne to put her off," he said. "Or the boy. She knows how to produce boy-children too. Her age can be counted on four hands, with a year or two to spare, yet she has given Madoc three sons already! And she will want a picking for each of them, too!"

Gwyndoc said, "You did not tell me this earlier."

And Mathwlch replied, "I did not think it necessary, then. Now I am feeling I would like a woman myself, and so it comes into my mind."

After that the two men did not speak for a while, and when the column halted to break fast, Mathwlch chose one of the younger Silures and took her with him farther along the slope, where there were bigger rocks and even small caves in the hillside.

Later in the afternoon, riding beside Gwyndoc, he said, "My young bitch-cousin isn't so bad, perhaps; but she once crippled a hawk of mine with a bodkin, and I've never properly forgiven her."

He did not say any more, but Gwyndoc thought about her often, until at last she went out of his mind, under the stress of tent-pitching, hunting for small game, and occasional fishing.

On the evening of the third day, still striking northwards, one of the forward scouts came back, red with excitement, holding his finger to his lips, and told them that beyond the next ridge there were men camped about a great fire. Gwyndoc and Mathwlch, taking their bows, crept forward to see what these men might be, and from the ridge-top found that the fire was what had once been a farmstead. Black smoke still rose from the cow-byre, and wafted in the night-breeze towards them was the heavy scent of burnt flesh. Down below, lit up by the flames that still danced, they saw men, twenty or thirty of them, sitting about carelessly, eating and drinking, their weapons stacked, Roman-fashion, in pyramids.

At first Gwyndoc began to fit an arrow to his bowstring, but Mathwlch held back his arm. "We need all the horses," he said. "These would make an easy picking."

But he had been over-enthusiastic. An hour later he found that the sudden swoop from the ridge-top had cost him five horsemen and three horses, transfixed on long Roman spears that had not been as far away from their wielders as it had seemed from above. And in return they had twelve prisoners — the rest had fled or lay among the still-smouldering beams of the farmstead.

These twelve were a curious assortment. Germans, Scythians, Italians, even Africans. And all dressed in the leather jerkins and marching-boots of the auxiliary footmen of the legions. It was hard to make any sense of them, and for a while Mathwlch almost gave in to his tribesmen's requests to shoot them full of arrows out of hand. Then, of all things, the dark African began to speak to them in Gallic. He had been stationed, he said, on the southern shores by the middle sea for fifteen years, but had forgotten his tongue in the excitement. That is, until he saw Gryf, Mathwlch's best and bloodiest archer, fitting a fire-arrow to his bowstring.

Then they got the story. These men were deserters from the legions; not because they were afraid, they stressed, but because there was not enough looting allowed now that the invasion looked like establishing itself. Why, they said in disgust, Aulus Plautius had even issued a high command decree that they were to respect the Celtic gods and leave the temples alone — such as were left. And as for touching a married woman — well, look what happened to old Gennius! And they called to mind, half-laughing about it, one of their Scythian comrades, a big strapping fellow with all the instincts of the bull, who had taken a young girl from her school — and only found out when it was too late that she was the youngest daughter of a councillor in Dubra. They shook their heads as they remembered him hanging, three javelins in his belly, outside the town-gate. "Aye," they said, "for three days. And he didn't stop groaning till the evening of the second. A constitution like an ox he had. Oh, what a man!"

The Trinobantes were not shocked. Indeed, there was something in the story that appealed to them. They offered the

Romans the mead cup, and later Mathwlch took them into the
band, for he acted now as Gwyndoc's lieutenant and made all
military decisions for him.

Ygerne was not quite sure that this had been a wise move,
especially when she looked up from her bowl to see two of the
Germans eyeing her and nudging each other. Later she told
this to Gwyndoc, and he sought out the two and knocked the
taller of them to the ground. Then he stamped the shaft of his
throwing-spear into the man's mouth as he lay and broke out
many of his teeth. After that the newcomers did not look up
when Ygerne passed by; and the following morning Mathwlch
made them all take the blood-oath and swear eternal fealty to
Gwyndoc, his wife, and his son.

On the sixth day the party came again into well-wooded
territory, and Mathwlch warned the scouts to keep a strict
watch, for now they were in Madoc's kingdom; and Madoc
was a touchy man who seemed to be in the habit of killing his
unannounced visitors and asking about their business later.

But late on the sixth day, as they sat in a wide circle about a
cooking-fire, their bowls in their hands, a horn sounded without
warning behind them, and a tall man, dressed in Madoc's tartan
and half-covered in a herald's wolf-skins, strode into the firelight and walked right to the fire.

He stood silent for a while, as they all gazed at him, then he
turned and swept his gaze round the full circle. All remarked
his great boldness, his arrogance and the nobility of his face,
and there was silence, even from the Romans.

Then the herald spoke, quietly and with a confidence that
almost sounded like contempt. "I come from Madoc," he said,
"whose dog I am. I speak for the ears of one Mathwlch, whoever
he may be among you." He paused and turned his eyes upon
the smaller Roman, a Scythian of disgusting food-habits, who
was at that moment gnawing at a bone and spitting the sinews
before him into the circle.

Mathwlch's face worked. He whispered to Gwyndoc, "I will
have one of his ears for that." But Gwyndoc quietened him, and
the herald went on, still addressing the Scythian, who could not
understand and continued to pick his bone happily.

"Madoc bids you welcome, if you come in peace. He offers
you a quick passing if you come in war. Do not hope to get
your weapons, for the hills around you are full of Madoc's kept-
men, and they are anxious for practice, not yet having had the
pleasure which I think most of you have lately enjoyed — that

of meeting Rome in the field."

At this a murmur ran round the circle from the Trinobantes. But Mathwlch held up his hand and stood in the firelight, his face working, but his voice under control.

"Comrades," he said, "you must not let these words anger you. This is the customary address sent out by Madoc, my cousin. He is a warrior of a strong humour, and his jests are intended for laughter, not dismay."

The herald turned slowly towards him as he spoke and stared above his head, proudly. But Mathwlch bowed slightly towards him, and as though addressing a child said, "Speak on, master herald, and tell us more of your master's humours."

Then the herald smiled and bent his knee to Mathwlch, and said for all to hear, "My lord, and cousin of my greater lord, I come in peace. Bid your people follow me and I will lead them safely to the king."

Mathwlch flung his poorest arm-ring at the herald's feet and waited until the man had wrily put it on. Then he said, "Gwyndoc, my liege-lord, is it your wish that we should accept my cousin's shelter?"

And Gwyndoc smiled and nodded and threw down an old ring made of copper that he had never really liked.

CHAPTER SIXTEEN

IN THE HIGH mead-hall the great fires burned brightly, and the thick spruce-boughs that lined the walls, amber in the light of flames, flung down their heavy scent across the two long tables. At the smaller high table, set above the other two, Gwyndoc sat at Madoc's left hand, and the cousin Mathwlch at his right. The air was full of song and story and reeked with spilled drink and the smells of roast meats. Along one side of the hall the harpers lounged, stringing their instruments, humming over new airs that had suddenly come to them as the mead-bowl passed, stroking the strings in febrile sweeps, secretly, lest the next man should hear the fresh-minted flourishes.

And Gwyndoc, already in his cups, stole another glance at his new friend, Madoc, over the top of his drinking-horn. There was something about him that reminded Gwyndoc of his uncle, old Cunobelin — except that Madoc wasn't old, of course! Hardly more than in his early middle-age, as yet. But there was the same set of the long, proud head, the same forked red beard,

though the red was perhaps a sort of delicate auburn rather than
the old king's blood-red! But what struck Gwyndoc most of all
was Madoc's sudden way of shaking the two red plaits from his
shoulders onto his back when he became heated in argument.
That was the old king to the life! Gwyndoc decided that he liked
this side of the King of the Ordovices. But there were other
things he was not sure about yet; that sudden sly sidelong glance
and the smile behind the hand; the rather effeminate interest in
clothes and perfumes . . . Gwyndoc was not sure about these
things in a warrior — or a comrade. But he let that pass for the
moment and drank deep again, finding the spiced heather-honey
rich and powerful, too rich and powerful, holding him down in
his chair, fettering his tongue, causing the smoke-whirls in the
roof to take on strange shapes of bulls and bears and wolves . . .

Far down at the end of the hall, Ygerne sat with Gylfa, the
wife of Madoc, a pale-faced girl of eighteen or so, with two
thick strands of red-corn hair that reached, even braided, below
her slim waist. Her green eyes and wide wound of a mouth had
interested Gwyndoc from the moment he met her. Now he
could understand how she had come to kill Mathwlch's hawk
with a bodkin — and even, perhaps, why he hated her. There
was something so beautiful and yet so cruel in her — a streak of
waywardness, of thoughtlessness, that not even her three children had drilled out of her, either in their coming or their nursing.
Gwyndoc looked across the hall at her, but caught his wife's eye
and smiled shamefully and raised his drinking-horn to toast
Ygerne. Even from that distance, and through the smoke, he
could discern that she was not deceived; and it was almost a
relief for Gwyndoc to see the two ladies rise and leave the hall
shortly afterwards to go to their own bower. Already he noticed
the fixed cat's smile that Gylfa gave his wife as she stood aside
to let the Queen of the Ordovices pass.

And then his attention was taken up once more by Madoc
and the mead. And Madoc said, "My two cousins, Mathwlch
and Gwyndoc, you are much more than welcome. The time has
hung heavy here for a year or two, and we have been kept much
at home with the three sons coming so soon, one after another.
I have often wished we might have had such visitors as yourselves. These Ordovices are a stupid lot — not like us, who have
a more northerly strain in our veins! We know what it is to live
and to fight. But their thoughts seldom soar higher than pasture-
land or the raising of the corn . . . "

Gwyndoc let the reference to the corn pass, though he

thought at the time that Madoc might have chosen his words more carefully. There were those along the tables to whom the corn-god was perhaps more powerful than Mapon, even, and in any case it was not wise to speak so carelessly where the gods might hear. But he held his peace and said, "Yes, Madoc, no one loves the sword-whistle more than you, every man knows — and that is partly why I am here — I make no excuses for Mathwlch, he would have come without me, as he nearly did."

Madoc looked at him, smiling, courteous, questioning, his red eyebrows raised.

"I serve Caradoc," Gwyndoc began. Madoc's eyes widened. "But surely this is old history," he said. "Mathwlch has told me all. He has told me that you are here only to wait your time, before returning to the Belgae as their full king. The Badger can't live for ever, friend! And he has no son. Have courage. I could send a man this night who would bring you back his head and want never a deal more than your kingly thanks at the end of his journey."

He smiled at Mathwlch, who nodded back with enthusiasm.

"I had hoped," said Gwyndoc, biting back his first words, "that together the Ordovices and the Belgae might have flung back Rome."

Now Madoc's smile was less than ever bearable. "And so they shall, Gwyndoc," he said. "But with the Otter, not the Badger, to lead them! The old hairy grey one is too gone in the jaws to make the clean kill — the lither water-beast will bite with sharper fangs, surely, Gwyndoc?"

"There is still my oath . . . " Gwyndoc began. But Mathwlch cut his short. "Caradoc has broken his to you. You are absolved of fealty."

Gwyndoc, heavy with drink, wanted to say so much, but his tongue was now a useless instrument. "I have dreams," he said. "The Badger still stands in them as the king of beasts. . . . "

The two began to laugh at him, and he felt his hand closing about the haft of his knife and knew then that he must control himself. He knew also that for the moment he could not look to Madoc for support on behalf of Caradoc. He remembered the sunlit days under old Cunobelin's apple trees, when he and the young Badger, yes, and even Morag and Beddyr, used to play together, and wrestle and sing — aye, and even put their arms round each other in the thoughtless friendship of youth. With the hot fire on his face, and the warm wine in his body, he was overcome by his emotions and could have wept. To save his face, he rose from the board and went back into the stables, pretending that he wished to relieve himself.

Entering the thick air of the hall again, he was conscious that something had changed. The gaily drunken atmosphere had given place to one of tenseness, and the hall was alert with anger. He sat at the board again, when the herald in his wolf-skins rose suddenly and jumped onto the table at the left side of the room, his face red, and turned towards the high board, towards Madoc, almost appealingly.

"Madoc, liege-lord," he shouted, his voice clear, so that all could hear his words, "am I to tolerate this Scythian bone-chewer any longer? Am I to sit and smile at him while he spits his offal into my face?"

Madoc turned to Gwyndoc. "The Scythian is one of your men?" he said.

But Mathwlch answered. "No, a Roman," he said, and smiled behind Madoc's back. Gwyndoc felt the blood rising again in his forehead, and began to speak. "He has taken my oath, Madoc. He is no longer a Roman." But somehow the words would not come out — or if they did, they could not rise above the herald's clamour.

"This is a good chance for us to see what manner of men these Romans are," said Madoc. "Besides, the feast has been a little dull up to now! Usually we have three fights before the day is out and at the least one corpse to burn on the morrow!" Then he raised his voice. "What is your wish, friend?" he called to the herald.

"Let him defend his manners with his sword," replied the herald, flinging off his wolf-skins and standing for all to see, dressed only in a short kilt and light deer-skin shoes.

Then all at the tables shouted and cheered and called to the Scythian to stand up and show himself. At last, grinning foolishly, and hardly understanding what the noise was about, the short, thick-set legionary stood. His hair hung thick and black down the sides of his face, greasy and unkempt; his heavy arms were tattooed in blues and reds and were naked of any ornaments. His rough linen tunic was now much soiled with mead and meat-fat. And he was so befuddled that he could hardly keep on his feet without the support of his few friends.

As he stood, the hall rocked with laughter. Madoc turned to his cousin. "This will be a poor fight," he said. "The Roman is badly outclassed. The herald is one of my ablest swordsmen — and that is saying a great deal in a country whose men take more easily to the sword than to any other weapon."

Then he began to laugh again, for the Scythian, understanding now what was required of him, had reached under the table and dragged out his short ash javelin.

"It looks as though your swordsman may not have the advantage after all," said Gwyndoc, with spite. But Madoc looked at him smiling. "The herald is a swordsman, and a swordsman is the equal of any man, and assuredly the better of a Roman!" He looked hard at Gwyndoc, as though waiting for him to bridle at the retort, but Gwyndoc had learned now to smile back at Madoc, whatever he felt in his heart.

Then the tables began to shout, "Let them fight, Madoc! Let us see the Roman fight!" And Madoc, smiling like a father at his children, nodded his head and waved the two towards the open space between the tables.

The herald came forward in the silence and saluted the King with his sword, and Madoc bent over his table and kissed him on the cheeks. The Scythian watched this, and grinned, and then stuck the point of his javelin into the earth and danced round it, heavily, like a bear, enjoying the drunken applause of the tribesmen. But all the time Gwyndoc noticed that the man's eyes were sharp and missed nothing in the room.

Then the two went into the centre of the room, near the great fire, and began their opening passes, trying each other out, watching for weak spots, testing for strong thrusts. And the herald's long iron sword snaked nearer and nearer the Scythian's face time after time, as he judged the distance between them, and each time the rough ash spear flicked up, deflected the bright blade by a mere inch at a time — but always deflecting it, never letting it approach nearer than it need for safety. And so the two circled about the fire, and the hall was still. And Madoc turned to Mathwlch and said, "The Roman is not the fool he seemed." And his cousin answered, "Wait, King. The Roman is drunk, and the herald is sober. We shall see soon who is the fool." But Gwyndoc said nothing aloud. He was praying silently to the Otter Father on behalf of the Roman, though he did not know whether the Roman's gods would let his prayers pass unhindered.

Then suddenly there was a low whistle from the tables, and he saw the Scythian stumble on a drinking-cup that lay in the straw. In an instant the Celt was on him, thrusting as viciously as a snake, but the Scythian righted himself and pushed upwards with his javelin, knocking the sword aside. And when he had

driven the herald back again, all men saw the damage that the
sword had done in that brief interlude. The Scythian's breast
was slashed across, so that his linen tunic parted to show the
long shallow wound, and his left arm hung almost useless by his
side. But the man was still grinning, in his drunken way, as
though he had scarcely felt the thrusts.

Madoc stood up then and shouted out, "Which of you will
call this enough?" The herald looked back over his shoulder and
shook his head, and as he did so the Scythian stepped a pace
forward and thrust out, under the blind sword. The tribesmen
groaned and shouted their anger at this act of treachery, and
Madoc's face clouded. "He does not understand your words,"
said Gwyndoc hoarsely. "He is a Scythian, he forgets his Gallic
when there is fighting to do."

But Madoc was still staring at the herald, who had tottered
back, his left hand clutching his side. And he saw that the Celt
was bleeding from the mouth and nose now. "By all the gods,"
he muttered, "that was a deathly blow." Then he raised his
voice again, "That is enough, I say. Some of you see to the
herald!" But, even as he spoke, the herald regained himself and
went forward at the Scythian, who was gasping for breath now
from exertion and loss of blood. Then suddenly the Scythian
dropped his javelin.

"The herald has him! Down with the Roman!" shouted the
tribesmen. And then they saw the Scythian half stoop, so that
the sword passed over his head, and with the same movement
scoop up a handful of burning wood-embers. And even as the
herald poised for the kill, they saw the fiery particles fly into
the swordsman's face and watched him stagger back, blinded.

"A foul trick! A Roman trick!" the tables screamed, and
some men even got to their feet to put an end to the Roman.
But before they could have reached him the grim entertainment
was over. For the Scythian was still groping, weakly to pick up
his spear from the floor when the herald shook his head and
cleared his sight for the necessary instant. The long sword swept
round, and the Scythian's head bobbed up from his shoulder
and bounced down the table where the two had first sat. Then
someone took it by the long greasy hair and pitched it across
the hall towards the harpers. An old man caught it and pretended to kiss the still smiling lips.

For a moment the Scythian's headless body stood, and then
sagged limply into the ashes of the fire. The herald watched it
fall, turned towards the high table, his face still arrogant, and

fell foward into the straw.

Men rushed to raise him, and Madoc stood, his knuckles white on the board, gasping like a man who has fallen into icy water.

When they rolled the man over, his face was set in that last smile, and they saw that the Scythian's thrust had cut through all his ribs on the left side.

Gwyndoc, watching the King, was torn between contempt and pity as he watched the wild mouthings. The Madoc's repeated words became clear to him suddenly, and he only knew pity, a strange tearful pity that almost drove Gwyndoc to run out and kiss the dead man's face himself. For Gwyndoc knew now what the King must be suffering. "He was the first son of my youth," Madoc said. "The very spring-time of my blood, to be killed by a blow from a midden-churl!"

When they had moved both of the bodies, and the mead was passing once more along the tables, Madoc turned again to Gwyndoc, his face still white, but his mouth now attempting a smile. "That is your answer," he said. "I will lose every man of the Ordovices to drag down Rome! Whether you or the Badger lead the Belgae. Tonight it has become my quarrel, too!"

And much later both the King and Mathwlch were carried, sick with mead, from the hall. And Gwyndoc at last levered himself up from the table and staggered to the hide-partitioned bower that had been set aside for him and his wife.

There he found Ygerne still awake, sitting up in the straw bed and waiting for him. And he knew that she was going to ask him about his feelings towards Gylfa. And he knew that he would just laugh and then make love to her, and that in the morning they would both be too sleepy to remember what their quarrel had been about.

CHAPTER SEVENTEEN
A.D. 45 – A.D. 50

FIVE YEARS IN a life can be eternity; can be the length of a
summer's afternoon. In Madoc's tree-hung Hall i' the Forest,
time flowed away almost before Gwyndoc had noticed it, for
there was so much to do, and, at times, it seemed, so little time
to do it in. Once Madoc's fury against Rome had died down —
which it did within a few weeks, when he realised fully the
practical implications of declaring a war on such a powerful
neighbour — and once Gwyndoc had inured himself to waiting
for Caradoc to make a move, the problem was fairly simple. It
was now only a matter of accepting life as it came, of putting
oneself in the hands of the gods and waiting. Gwyndoc had his
new friend's assurance that when the time came his Ordovices
would march with him or with the Badger — but march they
would; and that, for the moment, was enough for Gwyndoc.
The years of anxiety, the months of defeat, and the treachery
of Caradoc, had exhausted him emotionally. Now he must wait
until something, someone, outside himself made a decisive move.

There was hunting, feasting, the sowing and the harvest rites.
And there was, for a while, Gylfa. At first Gwyndoc had no
eyes for anyone but Ygerne, who was now more beautiful than
he had ever known her, full and ripe and mature since the birth
of the child. And of course there was Bryn; Gwyndoc had never
seen much of babies before, and as he watched Bryn learning
to spoon his porridge into his mouth, or attempting his first
tottering steps across the great mead-hall, or at last pretending
to be a grown warrior and inventing a sword for himself from a
stick, and an enemy from a sack of oats, Gwyndoc felt that life
could hold little more for him, even if Rome were cast down.
And once, on a summer's evening, he looked from the window
to see his small flaxen-haired son standing in the middle of a
field full of daisies, just looking down at them, bewildered by
the magnificence of these treasures; and Gwyndoc began to
weep, not knowing why, but suddenly full of a strange bitter-
sweet emotion that he had never known before. Then, before
the day was out, he rode alone into the woods and killed a wolf
with his short knife, just to prove to himself that he was not
getting too tender.

Yet there were times, a little later, when he could no longer stand out against Gylfa. Not that she had made any outright advances towards him, but she always seemed to be about, in some tempting attitude or situation at the times when Ygerne was not there or not feeling generous. Sometimes Gylfa would merely be combing her long hair under an apple tree at the back of the house, or reaching up to pluck a pear, her skirts tucked up into her girdle for easy movement. And then she would do no more than smile, like an ordinary friend, as Gwyndoc passed by. But one evening, when Madoc was away at the house of a kinsman near the coast, Gwyndoc, riding late, came on her as she bathed in the stream that ran below the orchards. At first he would have passed by, but she called out to him suddenly, in alarm, and said she thought a snake had slithered in among the bushes by the side of the water. She said that she dared not come out until it had gone. He answered that he would pass his spear through the bushes and show her that the snake had gone — if there had been a snake at all. But she covered her eyes and began to cry so loudly that he was afraid someone would come and find them together. And when he dismounted and tried to reason with her, she held out her arms towards him and said that if he was a man, if he was Madoc's friend, he would wade into the stream and help her out. And she stood facing him, the water only to her knees, holding out her arms and smiling at him mockingly, the long red hair thrown back and hanging down out of sight.

And for a time Gwyndoc forgot Ygerne and Bryn and took her at her word and helped her out and in among the tall grasses. And later he dried his wet tunic and breeches before the kitchen fire before going back to the bower he shared with Ygerne.

Yet this didn't happen often, and not at all when Madoc was at the house. And when Ygerne at last told her husband that Gylfa was going to have yet another child, Gwyndoc felt almost a sense of relief. That is, until one night, as he and Ygerne were lying back in each other's arms, when suddenly she said to him, with the cat's spirit shining openly in her eyes, "What if Gylfa's baby should have gold hair, and not Madoc's red, Gwyndoc? What then?" And Gwyndoc was so startled that he was quite unable to achieve what it had been in his mind to do, for a time at least. But later he realised that she was only teasing him and did not really know what had happened.

Hall i' the Forest was a long house of one storey, built with two wings that came forward at each end, so that there was a sheltered space for the children to play in. It stood at the crest of a hill, but was surrounded on all sides by trees — oak, and ash and pine. Beyond the trees lay orchards and grazing-fields, and behind the house a warren and a heronry. It was the home of such peace as Gwyndoc had never known before. It was the home of such secluded forgetfulness as he would never know again. In it, five years passed like a troubled dream, mostly happy, sometimes a little bitter, but never too sad to be borne. And when little Bryn was three years old, Ygerne brought another boy into the world, and they named him Caradoc — against his mother's will, for she could never forget Gwynedd — because Gwyndoc often had twinges of conscience, during which he accused himself of unfaithfulness to his only lord. Then for a time, until the new baby could get onto his feet too, Gwyndoc was tied down by the helpless attractions of the baby. And though he had grown to love his job as nursemaid, sometimes, when he was drunk at a feast, he thought of his two sons and even of his wife as being the obstacles which the fates had placed between himself and his fidelity to his true master, the Badger.

Then, if there was no one about to stop him, he was liable to tear off his feast-robes and challenge anyone in the room to fight him. But as time went on the tribesmen got to expect this, and to treat it as a pardonable eccentricity in one who was some day to be lord over all the Belgae. At first there had been some takers; and though Gwyndoc had always come off best, being a head taller than any man in the country, he had collected for himself a number of scars and a broken bone or two to show for his still-living allegiance to one who had betrayed him. But latterly, since the clans had come to disregard his outbursts of loyalty for Caradoc, he had taken to cutting himself on the arms with his meat knife or running outside and banging his head against the apple trees. When this happened, all turned away from what would, in another man, have been enjoyed as a spectacle of entertainment; and only Ygerne was allowed to fetch him in and tend to his hurts.

And this was the troubled part of the five years' dream; a dream which, one day, Ygerne knew would have to be broken. And so at last she said to Gwyndoc, as they were riding together at the tail of a hunting-party, "Now no one can hear us talk, my lord, I must tell you what is in my mind."

And he tightened his coral-studded rein and sat looking at her in surprise. At first she could not speak, he looked so fine a sight, his light hair bound back with an Irish gold fillet, his great heavy red woollen cloak swinging down from shoulder-pins of jet, and the light-blue linen tunic she had embroidered herself for him, with the Otter in silver thread, writhing against a flaming sun in gold.

"What is on your mind?" he asked, perhaps a little frightened.

She smiled at him. "The same thing that troubles you, husband," she said. "The Badger."

At first he made a movement of impatience, and was about to whip up his horse. But she held up her hand. "Never fear," she said. "I know the worm that bites daily deeper into your heart. I know that the life you stagger through now is a shallow stream to you, without meaning or any river-mouth to reach. I know that he is still your lord, and that though Mathwlch helped you to a kingdom, you would always feel in your heart that you had stolen it from him — even though he were a dead man."

Gwyndoc's eyes begged her to be silent, but she was determined now to go on. "Gwyndoc," she said, "there is only one way for you to clear your mind of this thing. Go back to the Badger again and see if the gods are still with you."

Then he looked at her with wide eyes and almost gasped, "But what if they should be with — Morag, or Beddyr?"

She smiled resignedly and twitched the edge of her green riding-coat. "Then we shall at least know one way or the other — and no longer shall I have a half-man to live with."

He raised his hand as though he might strike her, but then the movement became a salute and he swung his great horse round, turning from her so abruptly that he did not even have time to notice the tears that had gathered in her eyes.

And when she looked up again, his red cloak was flying behind him in the wind and his long silver spurs were beating hard against the flanks of his black horse. So she turned and followed the hunt, and when they asked her, said that Gwyndoc had suddenly remembered an old oath that he must keep the following day and was forced to ride hard to keep it.

As he rode, Gwyndoc turned over in his mind many things that had happened, to ease the journey and so get Ygerne's last words out of his memory. The present did not look well for the Belgae; each year new and evil tidings had come in of one great people or another that had gone over to Rome — Brigantia, under Cartismandua, that went without saying now; but there were also the fickle Iceni of the eastern seaboard, with their king, Prasatagus, tumbling over himself to enjoy the arid favours of Rome; and even the king at Chichester, Cogidubnus, who

should have known better, but who now had taken the names
Tiberius Claudius, and was styled by Rome herself as "rex et
legatus Augusti in Britannia". What a mouthful — and what did
it all mean? Why, that you became the snuffling lapdog of that
imbecile Claudius, in return for which he, or his man Plautius
(the same thing, only Plautius was stricter), allowed you out of
his sublime grace to keep a third of what was yours by right
anyway.

And they were always pushing on with their roads. That was
the devilish thing. They were relentless, these soft Italians! No
one had suspected they could be as hard as that, as tough as
they were. Now their roads were creeping up through the
country, from Londinium to Lindum, and across from Londinium
to Viroconium — only a stone's throw, as it were, from Madoc's
kingdom itself. And down to Gloucester, and, oh, everywhere
almost! Soon there would be no sanctuary from them. . . .

And Gwyndoc pulled himself up with a jerk that he should
be thinking of sanctuary at all; he, whose dream it had always
been to die in battle, with the arrows sticking proudly from his
chest and the mark of his axe on ten men lying about him!
Then, as he set his horse, hour after hour, at the rough slopes,
or trotted, head low, under the overhanging boughs, he began to
feel very tired, and blown, and chafed. And it suddenly came to
him that he was getting older.

He had never thought of this before; life in Madoc's house
was soft and uninterrupted, it let the years flow by without
trying to hold them back; in it one grew a little older and softer
every day without knowing it.

Gwyndoc looked down at his white and jewelled hands. They
seemed like a girl's, he thought. He turned them over and looked
at his palms. Soft and unmarked. And almost in sorrow he
remembered when his hands were red-raw from the chariot
reins and calloused with the axe's shaft. And he regretted those
days, as a girl must regret her unwrinkled throat in the days
before she was a woman. . . .

As the sun went down, the air became chilly, and he wrapped
the great cloak about him and lay down under a bush at the
edge of the wooded country to sleep, if he could.

By dawn he was up and off again, up the scree slopes, hungry
now, and almost wondering why he should be riding southwards
at all. Shortly after sunrise he half-frightened a shepherd-boy
out of his wits when he hammered on the rough oak door of a
wattle hut and demanded food and drink. And that night he

slept in a flea-ridden bed belonging to an old goldsmith, only an hour's ride from Caradoc's country. That night sleep flowed round the edges of his room, but was a long time in overwhelming him. As he got nearer the end of his journey, the more foolhardy it began to seem, and now he began to blame Ygerne for forcing his pride to undertake this ride. He was not even properly armed. True, he had a short axe and a hunting-knife and a small bow capable of bringing down a fallow-deer, but what was that against the javelins of the King's guards?

He woke unrefreshed, and ate lightly before he mounted his tired horse again. Well away from the hut, he bowed down and said a prayer to all the gods he could call to mind, and flung his bravest ring into a cleft in the rocks as an offering to whichever god might wish to help him now. Then, only slightly reassured, he went on his way.

And towards noon, as he was riding precariously along a narrow pathway, high above the valley, with an almost sheer drop below him, he heard the sudden call of the hunting-horn and saw, with something almost like horror, the Badger's hunting standard towering above the low scrub trees below him. Perhaps a hundred yards down the slope from where he rode was another path, obscured by stunted trees and thick bushes; and now he saw that this foliage half-hid a hunting-party, riding in single file and going in the same direction as he was himself. The sweat stood cold on his brow as he thought how, had he galloped down a little further before finding a path for himself, he might have ridden in on them without warning!

Then the leader came into view. It was not Caradoc! Gwyndoc's heart pounded like a hammer at his breast, until he saw that the first young horseman, a boy he didn't recognise, was leading the second with a long thong. And the second was the Badger — but such a Badger as Gwyndoc would scarcely have recognised had he now worn the tartan. The King had lost much of his hair, and what he had had greyed so that he looked like an old man. His face was heavily lined and his back bowed. He sat, a gaunt, humped figure on his pony, his legs dangling in apathy at the creature's sides, his hands hanging down, almost in hopelessness.

Gwyndoc remembered that last chariot charge again, with the Badger standing up above the fray like the war-god himself, splendid, fearless, immortal. And now this. How long ago was it? Six years only — just a summer's afternoon, but leading now to a long and bitter winter's night it seemed.

The next horsemen to emerge from the trees were no less moving. Beddyr was leading his brother's pony, gently, almost lovingly, and Morag sat still, staring ahead vacantly, silent. Gwyndoc saw now that the brothers were dressed poorly, like wandering singing-men, not princes. Even their horses were thin and ill-kept, like the beasts of men who had lost interest in life and saw no purpose in keeping clean any longer since the worm was waiting for all flesh, be it clean or foul.

Now Gwyndoc knew that he could not go to them as he was. The strange thought came to him that they might even have forgotten how to speak the tongue he knew and had shared with them once.

And as they slowly passed below him, a perverse thought came over his mind that now they were in his power! Even with his little deer bow he could pick off, say, Morag — and Beddyr! A small shaft, well-planted, could leave the way clear to a new friendship with Caradoc. A Caradoc who had lost all his fight — and wanted a friend, perhaps? But was that the sort of friend that Gwyndoc wanted now? The Badger, his youth and god-like perfection gone, his spirit shrunk to the bare essentials of existence among stone-harassed savages? Was that any longer a dream to be followed? To be the friend of such a man? And, in any case, to think of shooting Morag, blind Morag, was somehow almost indecent. . . . Morag and the hot-blooded brother of his who now moved as gently about his charge as a woman with her first baby.

And as Gwyndoc watched the straggling party emerge and wind along the narrow path, the servants and slaves following at a respectful distance, he began to feel bigger than all of them; the pattern of his life suddenly unfolded itself on a grander scale than it had done before; he felt almost mean and small at having even thought of punishing them — and at the same time laughed at himself for feeling so mean and small, when now, he saw, if he chose right, he might well come to be greater than any of them. For an instant he almost stood up in the stirrups and shouted for all to hear, "Behold, Badger, here is Gwyndoc, the lord who dared displease you, the lord you taunted and tormented, the lord who shall be your lord before the tale is told!"

As the drunken blood swept through his head, he might well have done this. But suddenly, from nowhere, a partridge scurried out of the bush and mounted, heavy-winged, up the slope. And Morag, blind Morag, swung round in his saddle, the shaft on the string, and by hearing alone drew his bow and shot.

It happened almost before Gwyndoc had time to take it in. The bird fell, transfixed, near to his feet, still fluttering. He stared at it, aghast. Had Morag wished to pick him off, he could have done so, it seemed.

And then a slave began to scramble up the slope towards the bird. And Beddyr was slapping his brother on the back and calling him the prince of archers, and Morag was smiling his strange, black, blank, hunched smile — deep as a burial-pit, as hard as the rock he rode upon. Gwyndoc knew then that his pity was wasted. But more than that, he sensed that he was in danger now more than ever — for now his new confidence had made him careless. Quietly he backed his horse; then, covering his tartan breeches with his long cloak, so that he might be unrecognised, he turned his horse, as soon as he could, and galloped back up the slope and over the hill, not once looking back to see whether the slave had noticed him.

For a second or two it seemed to him that the voices below him had become loud and menacing. Then, realising that he had the start of them, he slackened down and began the long ride home.

CHAPTER EIGHTEEN

TWO DAYS OF hard going brought Gwyndoc back to Hall i' the Forest, tired and hungry and needing sleep almost more than anything, but now clear in his mind, the old cramping dream and delusion of loyalty mostly gone.

When he had handed over his spent horse to a servant, he strode stiffly into the bower, hoping to find Ygerne alone, so that he could tell her what he had seen and how he felt about Caradoc now. But the bower seemed to be full of folk! Ygerne was sitting by the fire playing with Bryn and suckling little Caradoc, while at her side sat beautiful Gylfa, rocking her latest little red-haired son and smiling through the firelight with her green cat's eyes at Gwyndoc. And by the wall sat Mathwlch, at last back from his long journey to Ireland after gold lunulae, in the middle of some fearfully long story about an Irish witch who had a competition with a druid. And intently listening to him, though more than half-tipsy, Madoc, his best tunic on, and his hair beautifully bound in alternate strands of gold and silver. And, lolling on the long pearwood side-table, a young Roman officer, unhelmeted and wearing his armed tunic wide open at the neck, for all the world as though he had nothing to fear!

As Gwyndoc stalked in, flinging his cloak into a corner, Madoc rose and the Roman bowed stiffly. He turned out to be the second-in-command from Ostorius' garrison at Viroconium. He had looked in early that afternoon and had stayed to eat meat with the Celts and drink some of Gylfa's best elderberry wine. They had nothing like it in Rome, he said, and Ygerne, who seemed to like him, had smiled perhaps a little ironically; but he went on to say that they neglected the good natural things there, and seemed to go for the artificial, the over-cultivated — in vines as in all else. And that bit of humility seemed to put things right again with the Celts.

But as Gaius, the Roman, looked at his host, Madoc, he was less and less sure why these folk were called "barbarians". Why, the man wore enough gold on his arms and about his neck to buy out a couple of averagely wealthy citizens! And who in Rome these days could have afforded to wear that fine silk tunic and those silver-latcheted soft-hide boots? And who would even dare to walk in public in that coral-bossed belt of Spanish leather? A man would need an armed escort to stroll round the Forum with such treasure on his back! And yet these "barbarians" seemed to take it as a matter of course that no one would knock them down and strip them naked on the highway! As Gaius took his leave and rode back towards his camp, he began to revise his own ideas about barbarians and citizens! But, of course, he had only been in the island a few weeks. . . . He thought of the blue woad caste marks on Madoc's forehead — but then, their own African auxiliaries delighted in slashing their chests to form raised scars as tribal decorations — and that was nothing to some of the things the Egyptians did for the same purpose! Surely woad was a more sensible idea, altogether, barbarian or not!

When they had seen him safe through the stockade, the three men walked back to the bower and sat once more near the great fire.

"Why did the Roman come here?" asked Gwyndoc, at last. The other two looked at him carefully, as though wondering whether they might with safety tell him the truth. Then Madoc said, "At first it seemed like a social visit. Then he teased us and said he had come to requisition Hall i' the Forest for the general and his staff."

"Tell him the rest, Madoc," said Mathwlch. "He can bear it

now, I know."

Madoc looked doubtful, then said, "Caradoc has been causing trouble in the south. Night raids, and so on. The legion at Gloucester has given him enough rope, since they know what he suffered in losing his kingdom. It seems they are reasonable down there. But now they are getting tired of it. They say they can't afford to lose good trained soldiers purposelessly, like that. They are going to teach him a lesson." Then he stopped and waited. Gwyndoc looked up from the fire and said, smiling, "Yes, Madoc, go on."

And Madoc said, "That young Roman who was here knows more than we thought. He knows that you are the king-elect of the Belgae — should anything happen to the Badger. He knows that the Badger is aware that he has gone too far at last and intends to come here with his most trusted warriors, Belgae and Silures, to keep out of the way, and later to persuade us to go in with him on a last throw."

Gwyndoc looked keenly into Madoc's eyes. "What is your answer to that?" he said. Madoc fidgeted with his rings and looked into the fire. "These Romans seem a reasonable people," he said, "if a bit simple and crude, perhaps. They do not ask me to join them against the Badger. They say they know that is not right and proper, when one of us has sworn the oath under the oak. But they suggest that we do not join Caradoc actively either; that we merely go about our own business and leave those concerned to settle their own quarrel. They do not ask for our allegiance."

"Do you trust them?" said Gwyndoc, at last.

Madoc smiled cynically. "I do not trust anyone," he said, "not even my own she-cat over there, with her children! But I like her none the less for that!" Gylfa bowed ironically. He went on, "And there is much that I like about Rome, although I don't necessarily trust the Romans. For instance, I would like the boys to be educated there and to have a better chance in the western world than I could give them under the old tribal dispensation. As Romans, the whole world would be theirs for the asking. As Ordovices, they have little chance of seeing anything or having anything."

Mathwlch began to protest that they would always have Ireland to draw on, and there was a lot of gold-stuff there. But Madoc cut him short and said, "Our trouble in the past, Gwyndoc, has been that we have too often sacrificed the broader interests for reasons of tribal or even religious custom. That is a thing of the past. We are living on the doorstep of the new times now. And it is up to us to move with those times."

"It needs much getting used to," said Gwyndoc. "What have the Romans offered you to keep out of this affair?"

"Nothing," said Madoc. "They have merely stated that if I go on without interfering, I shall be allowed to continue in my own way, among my own people, in my own hall."

"And if you join Caradoc?" said Gwyndoc. Madoc shrugged his shoulders. "Then they will treat me as they treat Caradoc," he said. After a pause he said, "You see, they are not offering me anything that isn't mine. They are not bribing me, Gwyndoc. They know my allegiance to the Badger is too great to be bought with a bribe."

In the firelight a smile seemed to flicker over Ygerne's face — and as she looked across the room, she saw that Gylfa was smiling too. For a while there was silence, then Gwyndoc said slowly, and almost hesitatingly. "When they have broken the Badger, what then? Who shall lead the Belgae?"

Mathwlch reached over and patted his arm. "Never fear, Otter," he said, "the Romans know a good man when they see one, even if the Belgae don't. Gaius promised on his solemn oath, before you came, that should Caradoc persist in his stupidity and, as is inevitable, be defeated, they will establish you as chief in his place."

Gwyndoc's smile was a little better. "And you, Mathwlch?" he asked. Mathwlch looked at him steadily. "I am to be your successor," he said. Gwyndoc shrugged towards his children. "What of them?" he said.

Then, for the first time, Ygerne spoke. "They will not be kings. They will not have that hanging over them. Like Madoc's sons, they will be citizens of the world, the new world, and their minds will be free of this treachery and the blood-oath that so nearly destroyed their father."

Gwyndoc turned and looked hard at her, but she returned his stare boldly, and he knew that the others were with her in this. He turned back and said, "Very well. I may not alter it. But, mark me, the full guilt is not my own for what we do. It has come on us from stronger gods than ours."

Then he rose and went into the kitchens for some food, but before he could finish what the kitchen-slave placed before him he heard some commotion in the bower, and, going back, found that a messenger had come in from the outer territory to say that Caradoc was coming, dressed for war, with his warriors and their wives and children.

"It looks as though you made up your mind to become a Roman only just in time, Madoc," said Gwyndoc. And Madoc took him by the shoulders hard, so that even Gwyndoc winced. "My friend," he said, "you too are a Roman now. Do not forget it."

"Will the Badger come here?" said Gwyndoc, after a time. Madoc spoke as one who knew the future. "No," he answered. "His pride is as strong as ever, even though it seems his brain has softened! He has sent by the same messenger the word that he would rather offer his entrails to the ravens than share the same roof as Gwyndoc. He has asked that a sheltered field be given him, where his people may set up their own tents. He does not even ask for food and drink."

"There is something that one can admire in such pride," said Gwyndoc.

"Is there?" said Madoc, smiling. "I think the time for pride went after the defeat at Camulodunum."

Gwyndoc held his peace and soon went to his own room, behind the hide curtains, where Ygerne lay waiting for him, wanting to hear what had happened since he left her in the hunting-field.

Before dawn they were awakened by an unfamiliar sound, as though all the trees were sighing and all the beasts of the byre lowing. They recognised the last as war-horns, carried on the damp wind. Gwyndoc rose in his bed. "Caradoc is come," he said. "Lie still, Roman," said Ygerne. "Caradoc marches to his death. You now have a life to live."

All night long the grim procession passed by Hall i' the Forest: tall, golden Belgae, dressed in whatever finery remained to them, and most of them wearing the skins of animals now, in the place of the great cloaks they had once carried; small, dark Silurians, strangely bitten with the hunger to devour Rome, equipped as well as they were able, some in jerkins of horse-hide, some in the rusting cuirasses that had once shone on the breasts of Roman foot-soldiers. Behind them all straggled the pack-horses and the heavy wooden wagons, laden with food and arms and tents. And last of all came the long drays on which sat the families, the women and children and slaves of the warriors who were marching and riding to bring back the Badger to a throne worth sitting on.

And as Gwyndoc and Ygerne watched them from the roof-tree of Madoc's hall, hidden by the steep slope of the thatch,

they noticed that, almost to a man, the Belgae turned away
their heads as they went past the King's house. There was something about that pride which touched the watchers and made
Ygerne move close to her husband and put her hand in his and
say, "Remember your promise, man. Think of your children
now."

Then, at last, after long waiting, came the royal party, Beddyr
and Morag leading, heavily cloaked and sitting upright on their
shaggy ponies, then a band of young lords, and then, riding
alone and followed at a distance by other young men, the
Badger himself.

And this time Ygerne's hand clenched tighter, for the Badger
sat his great charger like a king. Gone was the slackness, the
tiredness and decay that Gwyndoc had seen among the hills;
now he sat straight, staring ahead, as though he knew he was
being watched, his armour perhaps too big for him, but burnished
and lordly, his sword balanced across his strapped, tartan thighs,
his lance glimmering as it stood in the stirrup-notch, with the
badger pennant fluttering from it in the morning breeze.

"He is a king, after all," Gwyndoc whispered, looking away
from Ygerne. "He is one a man could still follow and find
honour in following."

Ygerne gave a heavy sigh of disgust. "Before you shall follow
him again," she said, "I will open a vein in my arm and take the
children with me, too."

Gwyndoc gave a shocked start and looked at her in terror.
"Have no fear, mouse," he said. "All that is over. You have
heard my promise. Tell me when Gwyndoc broke a solemn oath
before?"

She looked at him, a little tired. "The Belgae has passed,"
she said. "Let us go back to our beds." And she began to
clamber down.

Gwyndoc stayed a while, echoing her words in his head. "The
Belgae have passed — to their death. Let us go back to our beds
— to the slow oblivion of warmth and ease. To the gradual
death of invalids — and women! Oh, God, and I who was once a
warrior!"

CHAPTER NINETEEN

WHEN THE DAY came, it came without warning. A Roman spy had demanded audience with Madoc the day before, to tell him, with a strong threat against his life and the lives of all his household if he divulged the secret, that the garrison at Viroconium was in battle order and would march without delay — in fact, just as soon as The Second, from Gloucester, was within striking distance, should the Belgae prove too obstinate. Some sort of pincers movement was projected, with Caradoc between the jaws. And Madoc was reminded of his promise to abstain from making any move in any direction.

He gravely thanked the spy and repeated his promise to Rome. Then, when the man had gone, he gave the gist of the Roman's message to an old stableman, in passing, as it were, and so went about his business, looking over a few outlying farms that belonged to him and having amusement with the girls who saw to dairy matters.

By chance, almost, it happened that the stableman had once worked for Cunobelin, and as soon as the King had passed through the stackyard he borrowed a pony and rode to the great meadow where the Badger and his warriors were encamped.

So it was that the garrison from Viroconium found their task a little more difficult. Caradoc had moved perhaps a mile away, to a hill that sloped stiffly to a summit perhaps four hundred feet high, rocky, and covered with gorse bushes that would give enough shelter to make an archer's work trying. At the bottom of the hill, a deep stream curled, covering almost two-thirds of the approach. The advance-scouts of the legion observed this, and reported that it was a good spot that the enemy had chosen. They might almost have been warned of the Roman attack! But Gaius, leading the first cohort, knew that this was quite out of the question.

To make matters worse, the Badger had had his slaves working hour after hour building up a circular wall, about twelve feet high, almost at the summit of the hill, enclosing a space big enough to protect the wagons and the noncombatants, and even the warriors, should they retreat. Of course, such a fort was ultimately untenable — food and ammunition were expendable, after all, and women and children were a liability on a job like this — but a wall like that could give a lot of trouble, could cost a number of valuable Roman lives. And the Senate was liable to take too great an interest in that side of the business and to require a commission to inquire into losses. Then it could be awkward for commanding officers. They had a horrid habit of disappearing suddenly after such inquiries — and they didn't all go back to staff headquarters in Rome either.

The battle broke at midday, just three days after Caradoc rode into Madoc's kingdom. Gwyndoc and Madoc sat astride their chargers, with Mathwlch just behind them, a quarter of a mile from the Roman left flank, sheltered by a small hillock, looking down on the stream. With them they had one picked company of Ordovician spearmen, just in case, as Madoc had said. And they were all very impressed by the Roman array, and very quiet in consequence.

At the back, one tribesman said hoarsely, "A horse against a sword that the Badger will stand up to the first charge! Any takers?"

Madoc turned in his saddle. "I'll take you," he said. Then he turned again, and the men were silent, half-afraid since their king had spoken.

Gwyndoc only smiled grimly. "Are you remembering the herald?" he said. "The first-born of your youth?" Then, when he saw the look of pain in Madoc's face, he was sorry he had spoken.

But after that there was little time for jibes or for sorrow. The Roman trumpets sounded, the Celtic horns replied through the warm air. Then the legion rolled forward!

Even from where Madoc's party sat, the Belgic laughter came clear along the wind, as their arrows struck down row after row of legionaries even before they reached the stream. But those who had the misfortune to leap into the thigh-deep torrent were both shot through with poisoned barbs and drowned. The poison was an idea that a Silurian sub-chieftain had passed on to Caradoc, who felt that with an enemy like the Romans, a less-than-human foe, even poison was a good idea. Though secretly the Badger hated the Silurian from that moment and decided that he should be crucified when they had won the battle.

The trumpets snarled again, and the legion drew back. From where he sat, Gwyndoc saw Gaius ride over to the officer commanding the next cohort. And, clear through the summer air, clear as a thing is impossibly clear in dreams, he saw a grizzled old centurion throw his sword on the ground and stamp on it, and watched his lips moving in curses as he did so — even saw

the look of gratification on the faces of the men who stood in
the ranks near him. . . . Mathwlch laughed. "I know just how he
feels," he said. "I remember when I took a company into Gaul
— it would be before your time, Gwyndoc — and exactly the
same thing happened then. The Germans were placed on our
right flank . . . " And the rest of his story was drowned when
the legion split into two groups and began to move again.

This time the shield-hedge went over the stream, and every
man kept his footing against the current, even though the hail
of arrows rattled thick above. The second detachment went
about, to a ford higher up the stream, and approached the hill
from the left flank. Some of the Romans were so close that
Gwyndoc told himself he could see the sweat running down
their faces under the heavy helmets. Then he lost them as they
passed round the hill.

The forward detachment, however, was always in sight. This
time there was to be no mistake. Up, up, up they went, brushing
aside the javelins, catching the arrows in their shields, falling
only when bush or rock betrayed them, or when the long stone
bolasses wrapped round their legs. And few men fell if they
could help it, for once down, the end came swiftly and without
reprieve — with shaft or spear or the quick dagger-thrust.

The Celtic horns wailed, and the Roman trumpets shivered
the air, and Gwyndoc was suddenly conscious that the nails of
his hand were embedded in the palm. More than that, he was
conscious that by no effort of his could he set them free again.

Then, through the blurred picture, there came a scream,
starting first from the women and children on the hilltop and
spreading hoarsely down the bloody slope. The long, low misty
sound of horns tremored on the air for a space, turned into a
high shriek of terror, and then broke in mid-air, and Gwyndoc
saw the Belgae running back up the hill, falling as the Romans
had done, against their own rocks, or transfixed by the arrows
which the cool and laughing archers were sending up from the
far side of the stream.

The whole thing was a shambling nightmare. The whole movement by either side was upwards, towards the summit. As he
watched, Gwyndoc saw one grizzled old Belgian, a warrior he
had known since he was a small boy, stop and turn back again.
He was a man as broad in the shoulder as a barn-door and with
arms like the legs of a bear. He was a man who years before had
taken an old horse shoe in each hand and had bent them into a
narrow hairpin with the pressure of his fingers. Gwyndoc had

watched him do it. And now he watched him turn round, carefully wrap his cloak round his left arm, and charge back down the slope. At first the Romans laughed. Then they heard the old man's death-song, shrieked in a high womanly voice as he ran towards them, and they began to edge to the side to let him pass. Three ranks did this. And then he was in the middle of the enemy, hacking and slashing, screaming and kicking. And at the last, just screaming. Then the legion moved on up the hill.

Madoc moistened his lips and spoke. "I am glad I am not in this today, my friends," he said, with a grin towards Gwyndoc. But he saw that the Belgian's face was grim and white, and that the tears were streaming down his cheeks. He changed his tone. "Brother," he said, "there is nothing we can do now. Let us go back to the hall." But Gwyndoc didn't seem to hear anything now, and when Mathwlch moved forward and took him by the arm, the Otter shook off his friend's hand, angry, almost vicious.

Then the Celts were within their stone wall, and for a moment the fight went slower. But once again the silver trumpets spoke in the valley, and now the shield-wall was formed again, and behind it went row after row of engineers with grappling irons and picks. Right up to the wall, even though the women had prepared hot pitch and red-hot irons in the meantime to throw down on them.

If the legion lost twenty men at the storming of the wall, that was all. And then the grey stone barricade was down, down for ever, and the little soldiers were clambering over the rubble, in among the women and children, thrusting and hacking without discrimination, and all the while the trumpets down below howling and howling, in derision it seemed.

Suddenly Madoc heard a sob and what was almost a scream beside him. He turned, but Gwyndoc had gone. "Come back, come back, you ever damned fool!" he shouted. "You have given your word to Rome. You will be crucified, you bloody idiot! Come back. I am responsible for your life!" Then he stopped, for he knew Gwyndoc could not hear him. He looked at Mathwlch, and was horrified by what he saw in his cousin's eyes. It was something as cold as the northern seas, and as deadly.

Mathwlch spoke first. "I intend to rule what are left of the Belgae well," he said. Then he laughed scornfully and turned back to watch the end of the battle.

CHAPTER TWENTY

THERE WAS NOTHING that could be done now to help Gwyndoc. To expose their position, and that of their armed men, would be to invite an attack from the victory-crazed Romans.

Madoc turned and gave the order to move back down the hill, out of sight. He looked at the tribesman with whom he had the wager. "The Badger outlasted the first charge," he said grimly. "My friend, I owe you a sword. Come for it this evening!"

As he led the troop away, he cursed himself for not watching Gwyndoc more closely. He should have seen that the man was going berserk. It was his duty to notice things like that, after all.

But it was doubtful whether he would have seen the madness coming on; it came so quickly. Gwyndoc didn't even feel it coming himself.

All he knew was that suddenly he had noticed Morag standing above all men, the arrows whistling round him, his arms thrown up, his head back — and screaming. Gwyndoc couldn't hear what he was saying, or singing, but somehow he knew as by instinct that Morag was offering himself as the sacrifice that should turn away the wrath of Rome. And he suddenly felt envious of the blind man.

Then Gwyndoc saw the sun come out from behind a cloud, immediately behind Morag, framing the wild, black figure with its brilliance. And then a lark rose suddenly, almost from under the feet of the legion, and rose, rose, rose, above the little stone fort at the summit of the hill. And its song mingled with Morag's long howling. Then it seemed that the battle stopped for an instant, and everything was still. Even the Romans stood, listening to this strange wild man whose voice shared the summer air with a lark's limpid song. Then the attackers rolled forward again, and, as Gwyndoc watched, the sun behind Morag seemed to grow and grow, and come closer and closer, faster and faster, roaring like a waterfall, until it seemed to enter his own head, to explode with great heat and an intolerable light. . . .

Then at last he was conscious of his horse's galloping movement. He heard someone — was it Madoc? — shouting behind him; but now that was unimportant. He felt the horse's flanks heaving beneath him, and found that he had made the detour round to the other side of the hill. Up and down the rocky slope, he saw the Belgae, in small knots and groups, the battle for the wall forgotten now. Some were kneeling, some setting their swords among the rocks and falling upon them, some grovelling while their comrades performed the last service of hacking their heads from their shoulders. The women and children were sitting or lying about, their hands over their eyes, wailing or imploring the gods to give back the victory.

As Gwyndoc rode, he saw before him, almost half a mile away, Caradoc, followed by two horsemen, galloping eastwards, towards the thick forests. So the Badger was safe at least. Then, as he passed along the base of the hill, Gwyndoc saw the wall on his side break, and the wagons topple over it, rolling down and down as splintered wrecks. And then a great torrent of men surged down, weeping, shrieking, tumbling, striking at each other, mad with fury and despair. And Gwyndoc suddenly found himself in the centre of this torrent, heads swirling round him like angry waves, mouths cursing him for a traitor, hands striking up at him or trying to drag him from his horse. And Gwyndoc drew his sword, and struck about him, at last clearing some sort of path round his horse's head. He began to move away once more, but a great hand reached up and took his bridle-rein firmly, pulling his horse round. And Gwyndoc, terrified, struck with his sword, and heard a man scream. Then he galloped on, and suddenly saw that a red hand was still clutching his rein. He bent and unclenched the stiff fingers and the hand fell, and he rode on.

So he came clear, and the forest lay before him. And, bent low over their horses, he saw Caradoc and the two cousins riding beneath the hanging boughs. Then Gwyndoc rose in his stirrups and shouted and blew his war-horn until his chest almost burst. But they did not look round, and he sank back into his rocking saddle, exhausted and afraid.

After that a heavy cloud descended and filled Gwyndoc's head and he rode through a howling nightmare of darkness for day after day, it seemed; a darkness that made his heart stumble and blinded his eyes, letting him see clearly only in occasional flashes.

And in one of these patches of clarity he thought he saw a fire blazing in a glade and seemed to gallop through it, scattering men to right and left. He saw the terror in the whites of their eyes and lashed at them as he passed. . . . At another time cloaked men seemed to leap out at him from the shadows of

trees, and he heard himself singing and laughing as he thrust
them back with his boarspear. . . . And again, he seemed to be
lying cold and shivering on a narrow rocky edge, high above a
wide plain, watching a broad river marching below through the
misty dawn. . . .

But always through these nightmares echoed the names of
Caradoc, Morag and Beddyr. Always they seemed to be just a
few yards before him. Yet whenever he reached the place where
they were they had gone again. . . .

And so it was that at last he saw before him the walls and
rooftops of Evrauc, Cartismandua's capital; the great town of
Brigantia. His head cleared for a while and he knew that he had
ridden from one side of Britain to the other. He looked down to
pat his horse and to praise him for coming so far, for galloping
so gallantly. But he did not recognise his own charger or the
harness. This was another horse. A roan, and not the black he
had started out on. It was not his own embossed saddle, either.
This was a dirty sheepskin, lashed to the horse's back with a
rough hide thong. And the reins in his hands were rope. . . .

Then he saw his own clothes. They were soiled and torn
almost past recognition. His cloak and helmet were gone. His
hands and arms were scarred and caked with black, dried blood.
The sword, dangling at his side, was hacked and notched and
bent — a useless thing.

And so he passed through the stockade of Cartismandua's
capital. The two guards laughing at the gate stepped back to let
him enter. Then he heard the gates shut behind him and the
laughter rise; and he rode on, only half-aware of the curious,
mocking eyes that stared out at him, from all the doors and
windows, right across the beaten earth parade-ground before the
old queen's hall, and into the royal house itself. . . .

Then he stopped, and someone lifted him from the saddle
and took his wrist and held it. And the hall was full of the
sounds of armour and laughter. He looked round, through a
haze, and saw that rank upon rank of Romans lined the walls,
their dark eyes hostile from under their burnished helmets. He
turned but they were behind him too, close and smiling harshly.
He heard a sharp order, and the javelins came up on guard, all
pointing towards the centre of the long room.

And at the end of the room, on a dais, seeming taller than all
of them, despite her shrunken old body, stood Cartismandua,
the Queen of the Brigantes, her arms above her head as though
she was prophesying, her pale eyes turned up towards the roof.

And at her feet Caradoc, the Badger of the Belgae, was kneeling humbly, supplicating, his eyes turned up to her merciless face.

Gwyndoc remembered the far distant wedding-feast and suddenly heard himself shouting, "Badger! Badger!" But Caradoc did not turn. Then Gwyndoc felt a spear-butt jar against his ribs, and he was silent again.

Then there was an order that Gwyndoc could not understand, and six soldiers detached themselves from the ranks and marched up the hill in perfect step. They stopped at the dais and dragged the Badger to his feet, holding him roughly.

Then Gwyndoc heard Cartismandua begin to laugh, and he tried to shake off the hands that held him, to go to the Badger. But his sword had gone, and when he tried to make the war-shout, hands came over his mouth, hard fists punched into his face and neck. . . . Gwyndoc fell, and saw only trampling feet. Then he was up again. Caradoc had reached the door and was going out, the soldiers hemming him about. He looked fine still, head and shoulders above his captors. Then Gwyndoc shook his head to brush off the hands about his face, and bit into hard fingers and yelled, "Morag! Beddyr! They are taking away the King! Save him, they are taking the Badger away!"

But there was only laughter and cruelty. "Badger! Badger! My Badger!" he screamed, but Caradoc never turned his head.

Then Gwyndoc heard Cartismandua's laugh again, and saw that she was going out with them too. He cried out with all his strength, "You barren bitch! The carrion of the air shall have you, Cartismandua!" But she smiled in his direction, and a Roman kneed him hard in the belly and he fell again.

Then he felt that they were dragging him along passages, through low doors, and could smell that they were approaching the kitchens. "Where are they taking the King?" he gasped. A hard-faced Roman laughed and said, "To Rome, my friend! Where else? But you are going to Jagoth, the slave-master. He will look after you!" Then they flung him through a doorway, and he saw the women among the fires and boiling-pots stop their work to turn and look at him. And he saw a big black-haired man come forward swiftly towards him, his bearded face smiling cruelly. And behind him he heard the Roman say, "Here he is, Jagoth! Treat him well, he looks like one of your kings!"

Then Jagoth punched him hard in the mouth a number of times while some men in horse-hides held him upright. And they stripped him of his clothes and ornaments and struck him on the body with spits until he fell to the filthy floor from pain and exhaustion, bleeding and groaning.

And after that they kicked him, some lightly, some brutally, but some with cunning and skill. Then they left him.

And Gwyndoc lay alone by the dying fire for many hours, half-delirious, bleeding from the mouth and ears. And he thought he was leading the chariots of the Cantii down the slope once more, against the glittering shield-wall. Once when he was half-conscious, he heard himself screaming, "Bobyn will save Britain! Put your money on Bobyn, my friends!"

A long time afterwards a kitchen slave crept in by the grey dawn light to clear the dead ashes from the fireplace. He found the cold shuddering body and shrank back from the blood that choked Gwyndoc's nose and ears and mouth. Then he went away and told some scullions what he had seen, and two of them came and dragged the body into the other kitchen where the fires were burning. There he was left for the rest of the day, naked and shivering, even though they had thrown him so close to the great furnace that one of his legs was burned from hip to ankle.

At eventime one of the slave-women forced a cup of greasy broth into his mouth and covered him with an old hide. He slept deeply that night. And on the following day, when his hearing began to come back to him and he could see a little, they showed him how to cut a hole in the hide and put his head through it, wearing the skin like a tunic, gathered in about the waist with a length of rope.

Part Three
CHAPTER TWENTY-ONE
A.D. 51 – A.D. 56

A S THEIR CORACLE bobbed up and down towards the rocky shore, the two men turned their heads, staring back over the dawn-lit waves, to where the great rollers of the Channel marked the open sea. Beddyr could just make out a faint grey shape, low in the water; he could not distinguish the colour of the hide sail or see the oars beating against the head current. Morag, humped close behind him in the flimsy shell, could see his own hands on the wicker-rail and the water lapping almost up to his fingertips, but little more; the rest was a blurred shadow, through which broke the sudden cold gull-cries and the sound of the sea.

Then they felt the rough sand beneath their craft, and Beddyr jumped out into the white foam and dragged the coracle onto the beach. Putting his arm round his shoulders, he helped his half-blind brother out, and then, bending, pushed the frail coracle out once more among the waves. For a time, as the bitter morning wind tore down the sand and the chill water still broke over his soft-hide shoes, he watched the little boat caught on the ebb, bouncing up and down, until it was far out to sea again. Then the brothers began their climb over the rough boulders and up towards the cliff face that towered above them.

They were lucky to find what had once been a watercourse, and holding on to whatever tuft or stunted branch they could find they made their way up it slowly and without speaking. When they were perhaps half-way up the cliff-side Beddyr stopped and looked back over the leaden waters, shading his eyes, and at last pointing. "I can just see her," he said. "She is heading south with the wind in her red sail now. If you could see, brother, you would weep to watch them go — the pick of the tribe. All that are left now. The Belgae!"

Morag snuffled, pulling his ragged cloak about him in the icy wind. "I would not weep for any but the Badger," he said. "They have their freedom and their eyes. They will sell their swords to Egypt or Greece. They will have gold again to wear on their throats and silks for their backs. They have life before them. We have only a dream of a king who has gone from us.

We have only a long wait in the dark before death comes on us, too."

Beddyr turned back and looked at the tears on his brother's cheeks. The wild gulls wheeled round them as they stood a moment longer in the cleft. "Have courage, Morag," he said. "We are in Gaul now. The gods will take us to Rome one way or another, and then we shall see whether it is their wish that Caradoc should be freed from his enemies. That is our duty now, to Badger and the gods."

Morag did not speak at this, but slowly pulled off his last arm-ring, a pretty piece of chased silver, set with sea-pearls, and twisted into the shape of a water-snake. He held it close to his eyes for an instant, then he whirled it out into the grey air, and Beddyr watched it as it swung for a moment in the strong breeze and then fell, without making a ripple, into the oncoming waves.

And they both remembered their mother fastening the thing on the young boy's arm, once when he had come back successful from a hunting-trip, bringing her the skin of a red deer for a new bed-robe. Beddyr recalled that he had brought her an otter's pelt at the same time, but that had only earned him a smile and a kiss. Now the silver bracelet had gone back into the sea, and it didn't seem to matter any longer whether one had a gift or a smile, whether one brought a red deer's skin or an otter's pelt. Nothing seemed to matter much any more, only finding the King, wherever they had taken him. Just finding him. Beddyr dared not think any further than that.

"I hope the sea-god will like your gift," he said.

Morag smiled girmly. "He has pearls enough," he said. "But it is all I have to give now."

Then Beddyr took him by the hand, and together they struggled on towards the coarse grass that jutted out above them and marked the summit of the cliff.

At the top they stood for a while, getting back their breath and turning their faces towards the sea once more. When they turned again, a man was standing twenty yards from them, half-hidden by a gorse-bush, his arrow drawn to the head and trained on Beddyr's heart.

Beddyr looked at him helplessly, noting the Roman helmet and the heavy iron-plated leather jerkin. He glanced at Morag, who had not seen anything but seemed uneasy, sniffing the air like a dog.

Beddyr held up his hand, showing that he carried no weapon.

"Hold!" he called in as quiet a voice as the wind would let him use. "We come as friends. We are wanderers without a lord. We mean no harm to Gaul."

The man in the Roman helmet smiled, sneering. "My orders are to shoot anyone who lands along this stretch, friend or no!" he said. "Gaul has no friends now. It has only Rome to care for it!"

Something in the man's voice made Beddyr say, "You speak better Gallic that most Romans, friend."

The watcher bridled. "I am no Roman," he said. "I am a professional soldier now."

Beddyr said, "Your voice reminds me of Catuval's. Catuval was my cousin — but he is dead. I am Beddyr, and this is Morag, my brother."

The man in the Roman helmet slowly let fall his bow and slackened the string. "If you are liars," he said, "I will blind you with gorse-spikes."

Morag laughed bitterly. "You will need to blind only one of us," he said. "Gwyndoc has saved you half your trouble."

Then the man came towards them, amazement marking his face. "Now I know you speak the truth," he said. "We know of Morag the blind here, and of the vow he made to revenge himself on Gwyndoc. A wanderer told us of it round the fire one night, a bard."

Beddyr said, "Was it Roddhu?" And the other nodded. Then he said, "I was Catuval's bowman. I rode in his chariot. I was at Camulodunum with the Cantii on the day that Rome broke the Belgae."

Then he smiled. "If you had worn your tartans," he said, "I should not have threatened you."

And Morag said, "We wear the tartans of the birds and beasts now — only hide and feather! The last shred of tartan blows in a thorn-tree on a hill above Viroconium, and soon the crows will carry it away to line their nests."

The watcher said, "Are the Belgae broken at last, then?" And the brothers nodded their heads. "Where is Gwyndoc?" he went on. "Is he dead too?"

Morag said, "He followed us from the battlefield. He was at the bitch's hall when they took Caradoc. Perhaps he is dead now. We do not know."

And the watcher said, "Why are you not dead, then?"

Beddyr bit his lips and then said, "The Badger made us stay outside the stockade when he rode in to meet Cartismandua. He told us to wait for Gwyndoc and stop him. But we did not see him. He entered at the second gate."

The other looked at him steadily. "How did you get here?" he said. Beddyr nodded back towards the sea. "We took a long-boat, with the rest of the Belgae who came across to Evrauc, and sailed down to Gaul. They went on to the middle sea, they said. They set us off in a coracle and we let the tide bring us inshore."

The watcher said, "Where is the coracle?"

Morag answered, "It has gone back to the sea-god. We turned it back into the waves."

The watcher said, "That was a foolish thing to do. A coracle is worth something. Now if it gets washed ashore again someone may be suspicious. They will think someone has landed, you see. And no doubt your coracle was a coastwise one from Brigantia. They make very singular boats. You can tell them a mile away. It is the way the wickerwork is framed before the hide is stretched over it. A Roman would know that without a doubt. They are sharp ones, these Romans. I give them credit for that. They wouldn't have got as far as they have if they hadn't had their heads screwed on the right way!"

Beddyr frowned at him. "It is done now. We cannot undo it. But perhaps by the time the coracle is washed ashore we shall be on our way to Rome."

The man in the Roman helmet said, "That's where they have taken him — Caradoc. He came past here four days ago, heavily guarded, in a wagon."

Morag turned his nose towards him, "Was he chained?" he asked.

"Yes," answered the watcher. "They had chained him heavily, and there were twelve picked soldiers in the wagon with him. He will not escape now. That is the end of him. Claudius will treat him as Julius did that other one."

Then he smiled, and Beddyr seeing that smile shuddered. "What is your name, friend?" he asked.

The soldier shrugged. "It does not matter now," he said. "I have stopped using my Belgic name. I am called Gracchus now on the army lists. But a name is only useful to me on pay-days — and they come seldom enough on this part of the coast. All the best jobs are in the south or in your country now. That's where I would be if I were years younger. But I can't stand the damp now."

Morag had not been listening, and he said, "How did the folk hereabouts treat the Badger when he came through? Were they good to him?"

The soldier laughed. "What have they to be kind about? They owe the Badger nothing. He killed many of their sons and husbands who had been taken over to Britain as auxiliaries. No, they didn't strew flowers before him. Most of them either threw dung at him or spat at him, if they were near enough! That's how it was! That's how it is with every hero once they have been dragged down."

As he spoke the thin note of a trumpet sounded through the morning. He stopped. "You will have to take cover," he said. "There is a detachment of legionaries camped half a mile from here. They do a morning patrol along here. It would be bad for me if they found you here."

Beddyr said, "Can you hide us? We do not know where we are." For a moment the other surveyed him from top to toe, noting his rope belt and his toes showing through the ends of his shoes. "You have nothing to pay, Beddyr," he said. "It would be more profitable for me to hand you over. They would at least give me a copper or two blood-money. You are princes, after all!"

Beddyr did not move to strike him, as the man had expected, but just shook his head from side to side. "You will not get blood-money," he said. "Blood-money is only paid for live prisoners. Morag and I will fling ourselves from this cliff if you make any sound to signal our whereabouts. Either that or you will have to kill us for attacking you!"

Then Gracchus came forward and put his hand on Beddyr's shoulder. "You are a broken man, but still one of the Belgae. I am a Roman kept-man, but I still remember Catuval."

For a moment they smiled into each other's eyes. Then Gracchus said, "Quick! I can hear them forming up. Follow me to the village!" He set off without looking behind him, and the brothers followed. When they had traversed the heath, they looked down on a small cluster of huts built round a central farm. Their guide stopped and indicated a deep bed of bracken. "Lie in there until I return," he said. Then he ran on down towards the farm.

As they lay in the fern Morag whispered, "When he returns I will hold his arms to his side. Then do you take his knife and slit his throat." Beddyr punched him in the side. "Do not be a fool," he said. "He is our only friend."

Morag muttered, "He laughed when he said that they spat on

Caradoc. I do not trust him!"

Beddyr said, "He has an honest face. He was Catuval's bow-man."

But Morag answered, "I cannot see his face. I only know his smell and what his voice says behind the words he uses. Besides, Catuval is dead long since, and with these cattle loyalty dies when the master is not there to enforce it."

Beddyr punched him again, but harder now. "We will not kill him, yet," he said. "We must wait till we have rested and know the way we shall take towards Rome. That is good sense, brother. Yours is madness."

Morag was still grumbling inarticulately when Gracchus returned and told them to follow him again.

"I have arranged for you to lie up in the farm," he said. "I know the old woman who runs it. Her husband fell out of a tree last year and died straightway. I look after her and her young daughter now, when I can; see that soldiers don't get billeted on them, and such like. They repay me as well as they can. They always accept my friends as their own."

In the village the three moved under the walls of the huts, not daring to risk the open spaces. But no one was stirring at that time, except the Roman party, whose feet could be heard now from the road above the village as they marched towards the cliff.

The farm house was solidly built, some rooms of stone, others of wood; very different from the farmhouses in Britain. The windows were shuttered and the doors stout and well-bolted. Beddyr noticed these things as he was led into the low hall. It was a place where a man could feel fairly safe for a time at least.

In the hall, seated by the fire, the old lady was waiting for them; she did not rise when they entered, but touched her fore-head with the back of her hand, in respect, for Gracchus had told her she was to entertain princes of the Belgic blood. Her daughter, a girl of sixteen or so, knelt beside the fire, stirring the broth-pot. Her black hair was heavily braided and her hands were fine, but her face wore the sullen look due to a heaviness of jaw that so often characterised the Parisii. Beddyr had seen it among the Brigantes, and now it looked familiar, as if they were back in Evrauc again. But then the girl looked up and smiled, and Beddyr saw that she was a friendly thing who perhaps needed someone to talk to. It was a lonely spot for a girl of quality, he thought. And the old lady looked the domineering type.

Morag had strayed into the room and was sniffing. "I smell broth," he said. "Bring me a bowl of broth, you lady, whoever you are."

Gracchus turned and went to the door. "You will be safe here," he said, "and when the coast is clear — perhaps tomorrow — I will set you on your way again. Rest here till I come." Then he went out, and Beddyr noticed that the girl followed him with her eyes as though she loved him.

After they had eaten they were taken out into one of the barns, where they lay among the straw through most of the day, on the off-chance that a squad of legionaries might decide to call at the farm. But when darkness came the old lady came into the barn and told them politely that they might come back into the house and rest the night there.

In the flickering light of the fires they lay down on pallets of hay, draped over with old robes and the skins of deer. After a while a woman in a nearby hut began to moan, in sleep or child-birth, they did not know which. A man's rough voice swore at her, telling her to be still, and so she was silent until the pains or the nightmare came back. Morag could not sleep but lay listen-ing to her, his dull eyes wide open in the firelight. Then from the other side came the distant howling of a wolf. Morag saw his brother's dark body rise, and he knew that Beddyr was sitting upon his pallet listening too.

After a while Beddyr became aware that the girl, at the other side of the room, was watching him, her eyes shining brightly as the last flames caught them. In a far corner the old woman lay huddled fast asleep and snoring from time to time. Morag saw his brother dimly stretch out his hand and beckon towards her, and, shading his eyes, he looked through the gloom and saw a quick movement from the other side of the hut. Then he lay back in his bed and pulled the coverings over him, biting his wrists as he lay in the darkness.

Beddyr watched the girl come towards him and saw that she had thrown off her shift. She stood still for a moment by the side of his bed, rising above him, her shadow thrown past him and onto the wall. Then she moved in beside him, gently, almost apologetically, a peasant beside a lord.

For the space that a man would need to count fifty he lay still, his heart racing with the unfamiliarity of a warm body beside him; it seemed that he had been a warrior so long, so long accustomed to the harsh embrace of an iron breast-plate

and the chafing of a shield-strap that his senses had unlearned
their sensitivity to touch. Then her hands moved over his
shoulders and down his arms, across his breast and down his
stomach; stroking, feeling the hard muscles tightening and then
relaxing, knowing the harsh wolfish power that lay in them,
waiting for the last touch to set it free. And when that touch
came, suddenly and almost wickedly, Beddyr swung towards
her and clutched her so fiercely that she would have screamed
but for the old woman snoring in the corner.

Then at last they fell away from each other and for a space
lay still. When they were aware once more of other things outside themselves, they heard the woman moaning and the wolf's
cry coming from the spinney just outside the farm stockade.
The girl shuddered and reached out her arm again towards
Beddyr as though for comfort. And so again his body possessed
her, brutal, as though, warrior-like, he would destroy her.

And at last the girl bit her lips until the blood ran slowly
down her chin, and she wondered that a man could so approach
a god and yet walk on the simple soil of Gaul! And in the end,
when the night began to seem a long tunnel through which a
haycart tried to pass, but so overladen that many men had to
push it from behind and the bales scraped so strongly against
the walls that the stones began to fall and the tunnel to crumble
in, then Beddyr pushed her away roughly and said, "Go to my
brother. He is weeping and needs comfort." And when she
listened she heard Morag's sobs and then knew that Beddyr was
sleeping again, his head flung back, his arms dangling at the
sides of the pallet.

And she lay beside Morag, trying to be still, trying to let the
rest of the night pass quietly by. Then Morag turned to her and
put his arms about her and rubbed his rough face against her
breasts. And she waited; but there was nothing. Only his low
voice seeming to call for a mother and the hairy face nuzzling
her breast. And at last he was still and the crying stopped and
she crept quietly from his bed and went back across the room.

But even while she was putting on her shift again, feet sounded
on the earthen pathway to the house. She sat up in alarm, for
she knew the sound of Roman marching-boots, and she could
hear that these men were armed as javelin clanked against
shield-boss in the dark. So she rose quickly and ran across to
Beddyr, shaking him and whispering that he was to be silent. He
sat up, puzzled, then he heard the feet and shook Morag into
life again. The girl pointed to a wall-hanging and told them to

go through and hide in the straw. Then, as she was shaking the old woman, they heard the spear-butts hammering on the door and they lifted the hangings as she had said.

Behind the rough matting they found a stout door, which opened easily. They shut it quietly behind them and found that they were once more in the barn they now knew so well. Morag went to his old place and covered himself completely. Beddyr saw that his brother was hidden, then he squeezed himself behind a wagon into a heap of sacking and lay still. From the other room they heard the women's voices, as though suddenly wakened from sleep, querulously arguing, demanding to know why good citizens of Rome should be treated in this fashion. And they heard the reply of the centurion in charge, and they knew that this was a man who would not be balked by so much as an inch. For a while the argument went on, and Beddyr remembered enough Roman to know that they were all discussing the two pallets by the fire that they had so recently left. The girl was saying that they had been made up to accommodate a cousin and his wife who were supposed to be visiting them from the Ardennes. The centurion asked where they were, and the girl answered that they had not arrived. Perhaps their horse had gone lame. A soldier answered that it could not be as lame as her story, for the bedding was still warm!

Beddyr felt the hackles rising on his neck as the man said these words. But then he heard the girl laugh and say that she had had the coverings on her own bed, since it was a chilly night, until she had heard their knock, then, thinking it was the cousin and his wife, and not wishing to appear inhospitable, she had flung them back onto the other bed as she went to open the door.

The centurion laughed at this, but Beddyr shivered at the laugh, for it was that of a man who knew the truth in his heart but could not prove it for the moment.

Then he heard the house door bang again and feet marching round the side of the barn to the door that led onto the stack-yard. Then he felt a cold blast of air and could see the light of torches flickering on the beams above his head. For a time no one spoke, then he heard the voice of Gracchus. "They must be here. This is where they hid through the day. I know that. I looked in through the window and saw them before the sun went down, both of them, the blind one and the big one."

From outside the centurion said, "Your story had better be a truthful one, Gracchus, I don't like bringing men out at this time of night on a fool's errand. Prod the straw, my lads, and see if this dog is lying! No, start from one end and work to the other. That's it!"

Beddyr heard the men grunting with effort as they moved slowly down the barn, and he waited trembling for Morag's scream. But nothing seemed to happen. And still the feet moved down the barn. Then the centurion said, "It looks as though you will know the Roman lashes before breakfast, my friend. Three hundred should give you an appetite, eh?" And he heard Gracchus say, "You Roman bastard, do you think I would lie about this? They killed my lord, Catuval. They put him into their battle-line and let him die! But for them he would have been living now. He would be my chief still — not a snivelling Italian like you, who can neither read nor write, nor even hold a sword correctly!"

Beddyr heard the centurion roar, and then the prodding into the straw seemed to stop and there was some scuffling. "Hold him!" cried a sudden voice. "He's armed!" Then there was a scream, and the centurion said, "Cut him down; the man's mad! Here, let me get to him. Stand back, I have my sword! I'll show him whether I can hold it correctly — and we can let the reading and writing wait!" There was nervous laughter, and the voice of Gracchus starting to cry Catuval's battle-charm. Then his voice went very low and he began to gurgle in his throat. For a moment no one spoke in the barn. And at last the centurion said breathlessly, "Roll him over there. Yes, take his helmet and arms; they will come in. We can leave the women to dispose of the body. Less expense for Rome!" There was laughter, and the centurion said in a softer voice, "Well, Gracchus, can I hold a sword, think you?" But this time no one laughed.

And Beddyr sat stark, listening to the silence swirling through the low place, beating in waves on his eardrums till it sounded like the throbbing of his own heart or the sea.

Then he heard the centurion say, "All right, lads. There's nobody here. Gather the others from the house and make your way back to camp. There will be no roll-call for you in the morning."

Beddyr heard the sound of marching footsteps outside, and then there was silence in the room beyond the wooden wall. He sat still, on and on, waiting, for he sensed that there was still someone in the barn. At last he could bear it no longer and slowly moved his head so that he could look below the wagon. The centurion was still standing over the body of Gracchus, muttering now. "You bloody fool! Now I shall have to make out a report — and you were right, I can't read or write! I could have stood the bit about the sword if you had not said that! Oh, you Celts, will you never learn when to keep your stupid mouths shut!"

There was something in the man's tone that appealed to Beddyr. This centurion was a warrior of his own sort, he thought. Then the man seemed to look up suddenly, straight into his eyes, and Beddyr sank back into the shadow again.

Then the centurion said, "That was a rat, if I ever heard one," and the man's feet shuffled through the straw towards him. Beddyr sat, turned to stone, like a rabbit as the stoat closes in on him. He saw a long spear-point stab beneath the wagon, a foot to his right side, and heard the Roman curse.

Then a pink mist seemed to come over his eyes and a strange smell came into his nostrils and ran down the back of his throat. And he felt his teeth meeting through the sacking and his nails breaking against the wooden floor. And the white-hot point slid easily into his groin and through the lower part of his stomach. But he had fainted away before he could scream through the thick fabric that filled his mouth.

Then the soldier went through the door with his torch and the cold air swept through the barn again. And Morag crept slowly from his hiding-place across the floor in the darkness, calling his name again and again, reproaching him for lying still, telling him that the Romans had gone. That they were safe now.

CHAPTER TWENTY-TWO

THROUGH THE AUTUMN and the winter Gwyndoc un- learned the past and became, as well as he was able, a beast of burden, dragging in logs from the fuel-yard, heaping up the great kitchen fires, scooping the mutton grease from the iron pots and emptying the privies with hands that had once worn gold and glistening stones.

Although his hearing returned to some extent, he was no longer sure that he understood what he heard, and held his head to the side if he was spoken to, which at first was seldom; a broken lord has few friends, and Gwyndoc was to find that in Brigantia the Belgae had none. Until the other slaves and serving-women gradually accepted him, he was something of a figure of fun. His dialect was unfamiliar and his speech thick and blurred, to make it worse. Often the same women who crept to his side beside the great fires at night taunted him by daylight that his teeth were broken and his right leg lame. He had the Roman spearbutt to thank for the one; for the other, the witless kindness that had left him lying too long at the edge of the roaring furnace.

As Gwyndoc moved away from the lashes to fill or empty kitchen-bowls, it was his leg that perhaps troubled him most. He remembered the days not so far away when he would have been faster in the field than any of them; when he could have leapt fully armed into the saddle from the ground; when he could have danced the midsummer festival through without feeling the slightest fatigue. Then he would rub his withering limb and weep, and the old hag who supervised the kitchen-women would nudge the one next to her and pointing at him cackle that the chieftain was thinking about Caradoc again! She would tell him not to worry, that Caratacus was probably grinning down from a pike along the Appian Way now, and not thinking about his Belgae at all! Either that or he was dining in some rich Roman hall, taking his pick of the scented women and laughing that he had ever ridden with those woad-painted savages, Gwyndoc and Beddyr! Then, after the women had laughed at him and the men had grinned, Gwyndoc would perhaps spit at her, or name her as a dried-up cow with poisoned teats, and this would be enough for her to call in one of Jagoth's henchmen with a whip.

Later, when he was lying among the kitchen offal, stiff with wounds, he would weep again, and would dream of the things he would do to the old woman when he was free once again.

But at last even this dream left him. As the snow came and the floor was daily thick with slush and the air streaming with drying skins, he began to forget freedom and to believe that this was now his life, that never again would he see the world beyond the tall pine stockade. And soon he began to forget what that world was like altogher.

Only at night, when the pain from his leg kept him awake in spite of his exhaustion, could he picture Ygerne and the children clearly. Then his tears were bitter and sore, for he felt that they had deserted him; and he began to yearn for a sight of Bryn and Caradoc, just a glimpse of them, no more, if the gods would allow it, from a distance, if need be, or through a window — sometimes when they were playing or talking or just sitting still by the fire looking up at their mother. But when he thought these things his tears would come more painfully than before, and he would roll on his wet pallet, cursing and muttering, until the slave-master on duty would kick him in the mouth to quieten him.

At last Gwyndoc began to answer to his new name, The Cripple, and the day that he first did that was the end of his old pride; thereafter he was one with the other lice-ridden, inarticulate creatures who struggled and screamed for the half-eaten garbage that was sent back from the feast-tables of Cartismandua.

Only once while he was a kitchen-slave did he see the queen who had betrayed Caradoc. It was the middle of the long winter, and without warning she decided to inspect the kitchens. Jagoth himself came down among the spits and fires, ordering that this and that should be done before the great one appeared. Gwyndoc shrank from him in fear, as all the others did, and stumbled here and there to carry out his orders. In one dank corner of the place a slave-woman lay groaning in labour, bearing the child of a palace guard who had often visited her through the cold nights. She made the mistake of moaning while Jagoth was making his final rounds, and it was given to Gwyndoc to drag her outside into the knee-deep mud of the stackyard so that Cartismandua might not be disturbed by the noise. But before the queen came the woman took a chill and died, howling, before the day was out.

As the slaves waited, dressed for the occasion in coarse linen tabards, Gwyndoc heard the woman's thin high voice, mingled with the lowing of cattle, and for a moment the mist cleared in his head and he had a sudden blinding picture of Ygerne just before Bryn came, and for the space of five breaths his arms and hands and shoulders ached to slash and crush and crumble all about him, slaves and their masters and even the great one, Cartismandua. When his head was whirling and the red mist was crossing his eyes again, a slave-woman standing by him seemed to sense what was going on in his heart and punched him sharply in the side. "Keep still," she whispered hoarsely. "If you move when she comes they will think you are going to attack her and they will hold you while Jagoth cuts the sinews of your wrists and ankles! Keep still, lover!"

He half-turned to her, curiously, but a guard saw him from the corner of his eye and swung the lash across his face sharply. Gwyndoc took the blow full in the eyes and fell to his knees, groaning. Then there was silence in all the kitchens, for Cartismandua, supported by two of her warriors, had entered.

The slaves gasped as she turned her hawk's eyes towards the kneeling cripple. Then she said in a voice as weak as a child's, "Who prays there, when a Queen of Brigantia enters the room?" And nodding and slavering the old creature hobbled in his direction, the slaves parting before her as she came, and the guards swearing under their breath that she should have noticed that mad fool of the Belgae!

But Gwyndoc was still fighting the pain in his head and did not know who had come to see him. The old queen stood swaying above him, noting the blood that trickled down through his fingers, recalling something familiar in the broad back and the thick neck.

"He does not raise his head to greet me," she said. "Do you help him, my friend, for the man seems sick." The guard who had struck him stepped forward and, taking Gwyndoc's hair, jerked his head upwards so that the red face and torn eyelids were turned to the roof-beams.

The Queen looked down on him for a moment. Then she said, "I remember this one. He was once at a wedding-feast in Camulodunum! An ill-mannered scullion he was then, and it seems that his temper has not improved. Jagoth, I command you to bring order into his heart. We can afford to have no pride among the slaves in my house. Rome will permit no pride but her own, and we are the children of Rome now!"

As she spoke Gwyndoc tore his head away from the hand of his captor, and his mind became crystal-clear and strong again for a spell. His voice came back to him, the voice that he had used in chariot charges or in giving the halloo in the hunt, and he spoke so that all should hear him, even the numb-fingered soldiers outside, keeping guard over the tall stockade.

"Cartismandua," he said, "bitch of the Brigantes, mother of naught but treachery, hear me. . . . " But Jagoth himself struck him in the face and toppled him over into the straw.

Then in the silence the old queen spoke again like a cat, quietly, sure of herself, sure of her cruel power. "Jagoth, the man shall speak. Let no man say that Cartismandua turns away her ears when her people call on her. Raise him up, I command you!"

Two guards dragged Gwyndoc to his feet and turned him towards the queen. "Speak," said one. "The Queen commands you." But the fire had gone out of his heart and his gaunt body began to shiver and shudder until he was a man possessed by a fever. From the corner of his mouth a thin thread of blood trickled down as his teeth closed on his tongue to keep it still.

Then the Queen spoke again. "Gwyndoc," she said, and everyone was horror-stricken that she knew his name, "had I the strength, they should bring you to my hall so that I might educate you. But I am an old woman, pitiful and without power; I must leave your education in more expert hands."

And then she moved on through the kitchens, and all the slaves fell back from Gwyndoc as the guards held him still.

And when the Queen had gone back to her hall Jagoth came and made them form up into three long lines so that they might see the education of Gwyndoc and so become educated themselves.

"This is now the Sun-god of the Belgae," Jagoth told the shuddering wretches. "He must be shackled for his own protection or else he would fling himself into the fire there before we had prayed to him enough!" Then he nodded and two of the blacksmiths ran forward with an anvil and the iron chains. With the lash about their own backs, they wasted no time, but hammered on the bonds while they were still red from the fire. But Gwyndoc only shuddered the more, and made no sound but a long groan, so low that the slaves were not sure if they had heard him or not.

When the anvil had gone, Jagoth said, "You see, fire does not harm him. Such a god eats fire as we ordinary folk bite at a piece of bread." Then turning to a guard he said, "Feed the god! No one shall go hungry here!"

As the white iron seared his mouth, the slave-women who had stood by him when the Queen entered shrieked and fell in a faint. It was then that Gwyndoc stopped shuddering for a space and opened his eyes slowly. He looked straight ahead and seemed to see Jagoth clearly. And all heard him say, "One day I shall crucify you, Jagoth, on a kitchen midden." Then his eyes closed and he fell senseless to the floor. And Jagoth laughed and made the guards burn him across the breast, and deep under the armpits with sharp spits.

And when they had done this they opened his clenched mouth and laid the iron on his tongue until all the heat had gone. Then they dragged him outside and flung him among the cattle in the winter byre, still shackled and unknowing.

In the night one of the women, obsessed by what she had seen, flung herself into the main fire and was hopelessly hurt before her companions could pull her out; and later, while they were still tending her, a kitchen-boy began to shout out some gibberish about a sacrifice to the flaming one and swung a lighted pinebranch into the thatch before the duty guard could stop him. Thereafter, everyone was too occupied to pay much attention to the lad as he ran out through the open door and into the yard. Later, the slaves learned that he had got as far as the heath outside the citadel, but had perished in the night from exposure in the hard frost that came down when the moon had risen.

As cold as a corpse, Gwyndoc began to stir as the fever was quelled by the frost, and from somewhere far back in the caverns of his mind a trancelike memory came to him of a golden-haired girl who stood close to him in a stream and gashed his cheek with a stone as he kissed her. And his burnt lips almost formed the name, "Ygerne", before he sank back again in the mouldering straw, unconscious of the pains that gnawed into his breast.

And just before dawn, two herds, Graig and Arddog, crept out to him with mutton-fat they had stolen from the kitchen and rubbed his flaring wounds and covered him with their own blankets. His eyes flickered for a while as they told him they were slaves captured, as he had been, after the Belgic defeat. They told him they were Mathwlch's men, Trinobantes, and that Mathwlch had been killed by the Romans for stabbing Madoc after the battle because he was a traitor, Mathwlch had said, to the Belgae. Now Madoc and Mathwlch were dead, and the Roman captain had turned Gylfa out of Hall i the Forest and was living there himself. And they told him that they were now his men, Gwyndoc's men, and they took the oath of allegiance there in the straw as the frost bit them to the bone and the wolves howled in the woods outside.

But Gwyndoc did not know what they did. His pulse fluttered weakly, like the heart of a dying bird, and only the slightest particle of consciousness still held him to earth, with his memory of Ygerne's face as she bent over little Caradoc, with Bryn by her side, standing wide-eyed, his yellow hair tousled over his broad forehead, staring at his new brother. . . .

And Graig, a raw-faced pikeman with an axe-slash that split his nose horribly below the bridge, whispered to his friend, "This is our only lord, Ardd. If he goes, we are lordless men, and the carrion of the air will be free to pick out our eyes."

And Arddog, who was a gentle man, a chariot driver unused to sharp weapons, wept and said, "Graig, if the gods will save him I will give a set of leather harness every year till I die, under the great stones near Sorbiodun. I swear it, or may my mother come from the fire and sit with me every night!"

And they began to stroke the tormented head as gently as women might have done; and as the first cocks began to crow from the old queen's yard, Gwyndoc began to breathe softly and regularly and the red fever seemed to drain from his wounds.

And the sun broke out in the east, above a low bank of purple cloud, and shone through the gaps in the cow-byre wall. And Graig, his eyes lit now by the new promise, said, "Arddog, it is Lugh! The shining one has answered the prayer. The harness shall go to him, and I will give a sword of iron each year."

CHAPTER TWENTY-THREE

WHEN THE FIRST signs of spring came to Gaul in the plover's cry and the new sun's kindness on the shoulders, Morag began to stir and to move beyond the stockade of the farm. At first he went only a short way, fingering a path for himself along the close-set stakes. And then at last, when the leaves began to spring and the streams to run warm, he would walk as far as a hundred paces from the house to sit and brood over his slain brother, under a little circle of stones on the slopes that led to the cliff.

The villagers, seeing him there, head bowed, his stick tracing its accustomed patterns in the sandy soil, would pass far off on the other side, murmuring a charm against the dark one, and treating him with respect. But their children, knowing he was a lord from the other Gaul, sometimes brought him gifts — plovers' eggs and sprays of heart's-ease and, less frequently, a stolen hen. They would lay these at his feet and run away laughing, but softly so that they should not disturb one who had known the great.

And the old woman had grown used to him by now and called him son-in-law, for no longer did the girl bother to make up two beds for them. Morag had grown to forget his mother, it seemed, and was no less ardent than the one they had found in the barn with the hole in his belly.

But Morag himself seldom spoke, only to ask for food or for the girl Myfan to come to bed. His sight was better, they could see, and now he could dress himself and even find his way across the room without falling into the fire. So everything was, in its way, stable and almost comfortable. The old woman began to forget the time when Morag was not one of the household; and as for the Romans, they did not know him — they were a dull, uninformed lot in these parts, recently posted from some flea-ridden end of the Middle Sea, and more knowledgeable about the dancing-girls of Syria than the lineage of real folk like Morag and Caradoc and, of course, the old woman, whose grandfather had carried a spear for the only real king, Cassivelaunus. . . .

Gracchus had not lasted long, after the wound he got that night, so he didn't bother them any more. In fact, things couldn't have turned out better, as it happened. . . . Except that sometimes Morag got restless, especially when the wind was in the south; then he began to remember names he had never mentioned before and to mumble that it was time they were getting on, or they would miss the Triumph.

At first the old woman pretended not to understand what he meant; and then even she saw that the thing must have its logical end, so she said one bright morning, "Son-in-law, there is a baggage-train going south tomorrow to the far coast. If I used my influence I might get you a seat in the wagon with the women and children. You are a strong man, and discomforts like that would mean little to you."

And Morag, putting down his knife, and gazing at her with dull grey eyes, said, "Old woman, you catch me at the heart. That is where I want to go. And as for women and children, they are nothing to a man who cannot see them. I only know now what I touch, and if they do not touch me I shall not know them. Can I get to Rome from the far south coast?"

Then the old woman went to her bed and felt under it, and came back with a bag full of coins and pieces of broken gold that had been gorgets and lunulae.

"A ship will take you for these," she said. "But you must promise on your lord's word that you will come back. The girl isn't pregnant yet, the fool, and I have a longing to start a new house of chieftains in this wind-bled part of Gaul!"

And Morag had laughed for the first time, and had pulled the girl onto the bed. "We will start now, grandmother," he said.

But the girl had shoved him back and said, "If he goes to Rome, so do I. It's time I saw a bit more of the real world than this spot forsaken of the gods!"

And the old woman had said, "That's just what I thought you would say! And I shall not be sorry to see the back of both of you for a few months! When you get to my age, it's enough to live your own life without having the stags rutting in your bedroom and groaning their way through what should be a gentle pastime every night. I need sleep, rest, nothing to disturb me. You two are worrying me to death — bringing back to me memories that I thought time had killed. Go, both of you, and be damned! But come back before the year is out. I need company when the snows begin to fall."

And that was all the word they got from the old woman. And that was the word that the young girl wanted. But it was only the look in the warrior's eyes that spoiled things — for now he was beginning to remember what Caradoc looked like again, and already the raw smell of the sea was in his nose, and only a wagon of the gods could have carried him to the coast fast enough.

CHAPTER TWENTY-FOUR

COMING BACK TO life through the chilly winters of despair and agony, warmed only by the patient meat-bearing slaves — two things of nothing who daily risked the lash to come to him secretly — Gwyndoc began to sense hope again as the hairs on his white arms rose in the new glow of the spring sun.

It had been a long winter of nightmare and vomiting, of always-breaking flesh, and then the slow knitting together again; of faces surrounded with knotted hair looking down on him in the half-darkness, pityingly, in secret; of violent nights when Jagoth reeled drunken about the byre trying to find where he was hidden, lashing out left and right with a long bull's-pizzle and swearing he would crucify him by cockcrow. . . .

But now it had passed and he could almost walk again, almost talk again in a language that other men could understand, almost see again. And though they dared not associate with him openly, there were always those two good friends Graig and Arddog behind him, somewhere, in the shadows — perhaps only in his own mind — but there. He was no longer alone.

And now Gwyndoc had forgotten the past, the warrior-past — Caradoc, Madoc, Mathwlch, the tribesmen who had died on the hill that afternoon. He only remembered Ygerne and the two boys now and his two friends, the herdsmen, the slaves of the byre, who treated him like a king.

It was as though he had grown a calloused skin of suffering over all his nerves. Nothing could frighten him any more, not even Jagoth. For Jagoth, he thought, one day it will be the slow death over hot stones; and as for the old sow, Cartismandua, she can wait, and for her it shall be the death of the hooks. . . . How she would scream when she saw the real colour of her own heart as it hung down on her breast. . . . And so Gwyndoc hobbled about, fetching and carrying as he was told, or just standing in the new sun, waiting, feeling the strength coming back to him, slowly, every day, as the summer came nearer. And as the year grew, something new grew inside him too, almost a new hopefulness, a new courage. Hope for the first time in his life, now that disaster had burnt his mind clean of all former allegiances. For the day Jagoth burnt his body was the birth-pain of Gwyndoc's new self; but it had been a pain he had hardly been strong enough to bear.

So one evening when the birds were calling in their clear voices from the trees outside the walls, he lounged beside the kitchen door and watched a squad of Roman soldiers march in through the great gates without curiosity or fear, only noting how confident they looked and what a fine young fellow their decurion looked in his new cuirass and leopard-skin.

And Graig joined him, standing a few feet away from him, and together they nodded, and Graig said, "The tribes have had their day. Look at the discipline of these men! They march like that whether they are going through a farmyard or through a line of tribesmen. They do not know fear. If I could get out of this place I would feel like joining them myself."

Then Gwyndoc turned and said, "Yes, Graig. A young man might do much worse than that."

And a little later a slave-guard came out to the door-way and said, "You, the cripple, I mean! The Romans have come for you. Ten of them. They must think you need guarding carefully! They don't know what Jagoth has done to you, eh?" And he began to laugh, and took Gwyndoc by the hair and dragged him through the kitchens towards the hall. And, as they went, the kitchen-women stared and then whispered together and speculated on the new torments that the cripple would endure. And Graig and Arddog stood in the doorway and watched him go, not daring to shout that whatever happened to him now, they would always remember him.

In the hall the decurion had his men formed up and waiting. There was no one else there but the slave-guards; even Jagoth was absent in his wattle-hut, half-drunk with imported Gallic wine.

And the young decurion stepped forward smartly as he saw Gwyndoc, and said, "They told me to bring irons for you as you had the reputation of being dangerous. But I think they must have meant another man. I shall not bind you. Give me your word that you will make no attempt to break away."

Gwyndoc said, "I promise that I shall go with you. I am not very interested in escaping now. I must go where I am told."

The decurion said, "That is sound sense. I hope you mean it. You see, if you did break away we should have to put a spear through you and then carry your body back — for I am ordered to return with your body — but that would cause us trouble. It would spoil our order of march, too, and you will appreciate we have a certain reputation to keep up in the city."

He smiled as he said this, not unkindly; but the slave-guards slapped their thighs and guffawed. Gwyndoc bowed his head gravely. "I do not need explanations, decurion," he said. "I am accustomed to the rules of war. I myself like to see a smartly-turned-out squad."

The decurion half-bowed to him and led him to his position between the ranks. Then they turned about and marched out of the palace yard. "I am sorry to go so slowly," said Gwyndoc. And the decurion smiled. "Please walk as you wish," he said. "But my men must march properly. I would have ordered them to slow-march for your convenience, but that would look altogether too funereal and might give the wrong impression in the town!"

They marched for a time along the main thoroughfare, where the spectacle of the Celt, so heavily guarded, fetched the folk to their doors and held up what traffic there was in Evrauc. But at last they turned into a side way and so down in the direction of the river. And at last they halted outside a rather fine stone-built house that stood in a small garden away from the other houses. The men stood at ease and the decurion took Gwyndoc by the arm and led him through the door and into the hallway. There he handed him over to a young officer who was sitting on a bench filing his fingernails. Gwyndoc thanked the decurion for his courtesy, and the man gave him a salute.

"I may not see you again, sir," the man said, "but it has been a pleasure to escort one who is so obviously a soldier." Then he went out, and the young officer yawned and stood up and nodded to Gwyndoc to follow him. And when he found that Gwyndoc had to take his time in climbing the flight of stone stairs, he sighed impatiently and said, half-under his breath, "Why the devil they give me jobs like this, I don't know. The man can hardly walk!" Then turning to Gwyndoc, he said, "I am a front-line soldier, not a serving-man."

And Gwyndoc said, "It is strange how appearances cheat the mind." Then the officer blushed and said, "I do not welcome your wit, sir." And Gwyndoc bowed and said, "Forgive me, I have lived too long in the kitchens." And the officer smiled and said, "I am sorry, too, but the new commander is a little trying. He makes hardly any distinction between officers and men. A rough type from the west, I believe."

On the landing, outside a marble-pilastered door, Gwyndoc said, "What is his name?" But the young officer was tired again now, and said, "Oh, I fear you wouldn't know him. It does not matter, does it?" Then he knocked on the door and gently pushed Gwyndoc inside the long high room.

For a moment Gwyndoc hardly knew where to look, his eyes were blinded by the comfort and the brilliance of the place; at least twenty rush-lights were burning in their sconces, and the walls were painted a gay vermilion, striped with gold. But from among the lights at the far end, where he had been sitting at a gilt table, a tall young man rose and came towards him, an officer of high rank by his cloak and the ornaments of his breast-plate. He smiled and held out his hands to Gwyndoc, and said, "Have you forgotten me? I am Gaius, who talked with you many months ago in the house of Madoc."

And Gwyndoc stared at him and said, "I seem to have forgotten so many men I once knew. You must forgive me. What do you want with me here?"

Then Gaius said, "I have come to take you back to your own people, if you choose to go."

And Gwyndoc said, "Am I free, then?"

"Yes, within certain understandable limits," said Gaius. "You are released on parole — my parole. But to all intents and purposes, as long as you do not plot against the Emperor, you are a free man again."

"That does not mean I am to be a Roman?" said Gwyndoc. And the other smiled. "I do not think they would like that," he said. "Your past record is hardly an appropriate one for a citizen! But never mind, you are no longer a slave, and that is all that concerns us now." Then he sat Gwyndoc down and a slave brought him food and wine, and after a decent interval other slaves came and washed his body and dressed him in clean clothes. Then Gaius said, "If you would like some of your own neck-rings or bracelets, I have them here in this chest. It might make you feel more like yourself!" But Gwyndoc waved them aside and said, "How did you get them?"

Gaius smiled and said, "Ygerne sent them. She lives under the protection of the garrison at Viroconium. Yes, and the children are well — I was to tell you that. They are all looking forward to seeing you again."

And Gwyndoc said, "Why are you doing this for me? What payment have you received?"

Gaius smiled and said, "I am not surprised that you ask that! But really there was no need to. I should have told you in the end. You see, Madoc being dead, as you may have heard, I have married his wife, Gylfa. We officers are allowed a little freedom in that direction, you know, and in any case I intend to settle down here when I have served my time. Hall i' the Forest makes a comfortable home for me, and, all told, I don't think I could do much better anywhere in the country. Gylfa is a charming girl — and very attached to you! In fact, I don't think I could have persuaded her to take me on if I hadn't agreed to arrange your release!"

"Then it wasn't Ygerne who persuaded you?" said Gwyndoc.

The Roman grinned. "Both of them! Gylfa wouldn't let me sleep with her until I did. And Ygerne threatened to poison me or have me ambushed if I didn't. Between the two of them, I became so worried I almost lost my command!"

Gwyndoc sat silent for a time. Then he said, "I have two dear friends among the slaves in Cartismandua's hall. Two old warrior friends. They have kept me alive these last months. Can you have them released?"

Gaius said gently, "Officially, no; but they shall come with us if you want them. I have the general's seal-ring here and will write out the order for their parole now. I will do it myself; I do not trust the scribe they have supplied me with here! Forgive me a moment."

And after a while he rose from the desk and came towards Gwyndoc with the paper.

Then Gwyndoc said, "Who will go to fetch them?" And Gaius answered, "The young officer who brought you up. He comes of a noble Roman family, and needs disciplining. He shall take twenty men, and your friends will be safe. Dare you return with him to identify them? It would be annoying if he brought the wrong men — and he's just the sort of person who seems liable to do that if he isn't watched."

And Gwyndoc said, "I should be glad to fetch back my friends. May I wear a sword?"

The Roman looked at Gwyndoc gravely. "That is one thing I may not allow you," he said. "That is the price you must pay for your freedom — never again will Gwyndoc be allowed to carry a sword. Does that distress you, friend?"

But Gwyndoc shrugged his shoulders. "No," he said. "Perhaps you Romans know best, after all. It was little enough good I did to myself or to anyone else when I did carry one. I will go without one, Gaius."

Then Gaius slapped him on the back and called downstairs to the duty-officer to make ready with two horses and twenty soldiers to return to the hall of the Queen.

Gwyndoc heard the young man grumbling below, and in a way began to sympathise with him. Gaius had rather a loud voice and he hadn't spoken to the noble young soldier very kindly!

And so they made their way back through the main thoroughfares, Gwyndoc riding a white horse and sitting beside the officer, who grumbled part of the way and then began to whistle nonchalantly, as though the whole affair was really not worth bothering about.

After they had made their purpose known and the two herdsmen were safe in the midst of the Romans, punching each other and giving praise quite blatantly to the Celtic gods, the party turned round and rode once more towards the outer gates. There Gwyndoc reined in his white horse and turned to the officer. "Sir," he said, "I realise that it is against orders, but as one gentleman to another, might I have your permission to go back into the farmyard again, to say goodbye to a . . . ?"

The young man grinned. "Certainly," he said. "I am not one to stand between a man and his sweetheart!"

Gwyndoc smiled and said, "How well you understand, sir!" And the other bowed in acknowledgement of the compliment. Then Gwyndoc wheeled his horse and rode past the flank of the squad, and as he went he bent swiftly and whipped out the sword of the end soldier almost before the man had noticed it. He saw the surprised look in the man's eyes, but as he galloped on he noted that the man made no outcry.

Hens fluttered under the white horse's hooves as he swung into the stackyard. Ahead of him, in the gathering dust, he could see the slave-master's wattle hut. He reached the shelter of its walls and dismounted, and saw lying in the doorway Jagoth's great mastiff. As Gwyndoc moved towards the hut the dog raised his head suspiciously. But before it could get to its feet the man had stepped forward and struck hard into his neck with the short sword. The creature made no sound, but sank back dead into its sleeping position, and Gwyndoc stepped over the body into the hut.

Jagoth, lolling on a stool before his fire, looked back angrily as he heard the door-skins rustle. He would teach these dogs to enter without announcing themselves, he thought. But he saw Gwyndoc, his cloak flung back, his sword already dark with blood; Gwyndoc who stood still, watching him, half-smiling, slowly pulling open his fine linen tunic to expose the deep scar where once Jagoth's iron had tortured the flesh of his breast.

The slave-master saw not the wound but the death that looked out of his eyes, and he opened his mouth to shout for his dog. But Gwyndoc shook his head and passed his finger across his throat. Then he came forward, still smiling, and the slave-master, no longer frozen with fear, sprang from the stool and backed away. "Lord," he said, in an even voice, "you are a man and a warrior. Allow me to show that I am the same. Give me leave to reach my sword before you strike. I beg you."

The man began to move towards his bed where sword and javelin lay. For a short instant Gwyndoc was impressed by Jagoth's courage. Then he shook his head. "You allowed me no weapon when you burnt me," he said, without malice and almost gently. Then, as he finished speaking, he was upon the slave-master, and gripping him by the throat he stabbed him once, carefully and without haste, with a low upward thrust. Then he stood back and watched the man fall.

Jagoth groaned, his hands to his groin, and his body gave a series of shuddering starts. His face took on an amazed, almost a shocked expression as he lay.

Gwyndoc stared at him without emotion. Then Jagoth began to gasp and to make frightful disjointed movements, trying to get up. "Spare me, lord," he whispered. "Have mercy, my lord! You have hurt me enough!"

But Gwyndoc never spoke. He bent over the wretch, quietly, as though ministering to him, and struck him many times, methodically, about the face and neck like an inexpert craftsman first shaping a piece of wood, crudely and without love.

And the dying creature groaned with each stroke and tried to cover his ruined head with bloody hands. But Gwyndoc struck and struck until he could not see what he was doing. Then he stopped and gave a great groan and passed his hand over his face. Then, spattered with blood to the waist, he went outside and mounted the white horse and galloped back, his eyes staring, to where the impatient company waited for him at the gate.

Gaius was booted and spurred when they arrived, waiting for Gwyndoc in his room with the vermilion and gold walls. The young officer stepped inside and saluted. Then in a shaken voice he said, "The Celt is not himself. I regret it, sir, but I am to blame. I allowed him to visit the huts again, unguarded." Fear stood in the young man's eyes. Gaius would certainly cashier him, perhaps even flog him in public. He watched the colonel's face.

But Gaius wasn't looking at him; he was staring at Gwyndoc's hands and arms and blood-splashed face. And his voice was gentle as he spoke. "Who was it," he said, "Cartismandua or Jagoth?"

And Gwyndoc replied quietly, "Jagoth."

Then Gaius said, "I am sorry it was that one. We could have executed him on a technical charge. The other one is more difficult. I wish . . . " Then he saw the amazed look in the young officer's eyes. "Forget what you have just heard," he said. "And be thankful I haven't court-martialled you." The young man saluted and said, "Very good, sir," and went to the door. Gaius called after him, "And don't forget, you are morally responsible for this affair. The Roman courts would hold you more guilty than this lord, who, after all, according to the Senate, is not entirely answerable for his actions!"

And the young man saw that both Gaius and Gwyndoc were smiling, so he smiled too, and went downstairs whistling — though he knew it was against orders.

And when he had gone, Gaius said, "For God's sake wash that off your hands and change your tunic. We must burn this. When the old queen knows she will suspect us all. This isn't my territory, and I haven't the influence here that we might need. So move quickly and get ready. The sooner we are on the road to Viroconium, the better."

Gwyndoc nodded and tore off his tunic. "When do you wish to start?" he said. Gaius flung him a fresh shirt. "The mounted guard is already waiting with provisions. I have given your friends the herdsmen two of the swiftest ponies in case they need to leave us and make their own escape. But we must be started before the moon gets up. The darkness will give us cover."

Gwyndoc smiled and said, "Permit me to rub a little of this wine over my face, and I am ready."

CHAPTER TWENTY-FIVE

THE HIGH ROMAN moon rode silver among the turreted spring clouds, and by turns flooded the city suburbs with a thin unearthly light or withdrew to throw the villas and their gardens into semi-darkness. The scene resembled a stage-set, in which tall purple-grey hills rose across the backcloth, towering above all else, but distant; in the middle-distance, a row of poplars, regular and disciplined, ranged on either side of a long low villa, porticoed and single-storeyed, its open windows ablaze with the light of many candles. In the foreground, a granite balustrade that cast a strong shadow forward as the moon came out from the scudding cloud-masses.

All was silent, save for the occasional hooting of an owl from somewhere behind the house and the sudden squawking of the hens as they dreamed on their perches of marauding foxes. Occasionally a sleepy young soldier, a junior officer, strolled round the garden balustrade, humming or yawning, or, to break the monotony, foining with his short campaign sword at the undraped statues that stood at intervals along the wall, staring blankly through the moonlight towards the house.

Once as he drew near the darkest of the shadows, close by the low, ornamental gate, he stopped and went on guard with his sword, but seriously, right foot forward and left arm up as though he bore a shield — a routine drill movement that hid his fear. He coughed menacingly and said, "Who goes this night?" But no one answered from the shadow, and after a second or two he laughed at himself for his nervousness, and then, hearing a shout of laughter louder than anything that had come over the night air before that evening, shrugged his broad shoulders, sheathed his sword and vaulted over the gate. He did not once look behind him as he strode up to the swinging curtains of the main door and went inside the house.

And when he had gone, Morag said from the shadow, "Get up, girl, and see if the coast is clear." And out of the deepest point of blackness, at the foot of the balustrade and so near that she could have touched the urn that stood on her side of the gate, Myfan stood, in her boy's clothes, her dark hair cropped short, and stared through the moonlight towards the house. "There is no one about," she said.

Morag rose then, his thick body swathed in a dark-brown cloak and his head half-covered by a hood. "It has been a long wait," he said. "After two months on land and sea to get here, my patience has been shredded a little."

Myfan said, "It is always the last stage that is the hardest to bear in a rescue like this, or in love!"

Morag, who was in a good humour, in spite of his stiffness, pretended to strike at her. "You little strumpet!" he said. "Will you think of nothing but your trade?"

And the girl laughed and said, "Had I not known my trade, my mother's trinkets would have done us little good! She always thinks in terms of last year's prices, before the army of occupation, with all those wealthy foreign legionaries, put things up! You would have got no further than the coast but for my skill, dear husband!" She made as to put her arms about him, but he backed and said, "For God's sake, child, you'll wear me out! Can't you see that there's a right and proper time for your tricks? We must keep our minds on the work in hand now! There'll be time enough for foolery when we have the Badger with us and the straw of some friendly inn to hide ourselves in!"

The girl smiled, looking more like a boy than ever, with her heavy Brigantian jaw and her long thin legs exposed below her tunic.

"What if I take a fancy to the Badger when I see him?" she taunted. But Morag laughed back. "I shall be angry with you if you don't," he said.

"What would you do?" the girl replied, putting her finger into the dark hood and tickling the side of his face.

"I should beat you first," Morag said. "Then I should drag you back to your old mother and tell her, and she would beat you."

The girl laughed softly. "I am not afraid of her now," she said.

Morag said, "Well then, I think I might leave you in a German garrison for a night or two, and that would bring you to your senses!"

The girl slapped him lightly on the face. "But I mean punishment! What punishment would you make for me?"

And Morag suddenly swung round and said seriously, "Down, girl, there is someone coming out into the garden. Get down, you will be seen."

For a while they crouched in the shadow, and then Morag whispered, "Look carefully, and tell me how many men there are and describe the man who seems to be the leader of them all."

Myfan rose gently and peered over the lip of the balustrade for a short time. Then she whispered, "There is only one. He has come out to relieve himself and is alone. He is a tall man, but gaunt. His hair is grey and dressed Celtic style, with two plaits."

She could hear Morag's breathing quicken, and he said, "Quick, fool, tell me more. Where are his ornaments?"

She said, "I cannot see well in the moonlight, but he seems to wear gold on wrist and upper arm and a broad collar of gold at his neck — wait, he limps a little on the left leg as he moves. . . "

Then Morag was standing beside her, his head above the wall. "It is the Badger himself," he said. "Praise to the gods who have let him come out alone and without a guard! Oh, they are careless, these Romans!"

Then Myfan heard Morag make a sound that sent a chill along her spine, a sound that she had never thought a man's mouth might make; it was the low night call of the dog-badger, hunting, low in the throat and weird in a man's mouth, for it was the voice of a four-footed creature. Behind the house a chained dog suddenly whined in terror and the hens in the yard scuttered about the straw in fear. And still Morag made the sound, deep and urgent, his thick voice throbbing back from the white walls of the house.

And the tall chieftain stopped a few yards from the door, still arranging his clothing, and turned towards them, scenting the air, it seemed, like another badger answering the call.

Then he came over the short grass like a man in a trance, his head held back, his arms out; and when he was within five yards of where they stood he stopped and said in a trembling, confused voice, "I am here. I come at your call. What would you have me do, lord?" And they saw that his eyes were wide open but staring past them into the light sky, and the moon rode in his pupils, so that his eyes burned like amethysts.

For a moment Morag could not speak, but Myfan felt him shuddering against her, and she could hear his throat working as he swallowed again and again. At last he whispered hoarsely, "It is Morag, come to fetch you away, King, back to your own folk."

And Caradoc slowly let his head drop until he was looking at them, and his eyes were cold grey now, because the moon no longer swam across them, and he said, "Morag — but you are dead, my friend. Where have you come from?"

And Morag said, "No, lord, I am no corpse. I live still. It is Beddyr who is dead, Badger."

And Caradoc lowered his face. "Poor Beddyr," he said. "I thought that he of the two of you might live to see better times. How did he die, my cousin?"

And Morag said, "A Roman spear ran through his belly as he lay under a wagon in Gaul."

And Caradoc said, "I hoped he had died for me among the Brigantes. That would have been a warrior's death, a death to remember."

And Morag said, "He died for you in the worst way, Badger, waiting like a cow in the slaughterhouse."

Then Caradoc said, "Why did you not die, Morag?"

And Morag said, "I lay in the straw and the spears passed on either side of me, but only tore my shirt. When I knew that Beddyr had died, I cursed the gods that they had taken him and had left me. If they would set him here this night, I would gladly go back with them to the place where they have taken him."

Then Morag began to cry like a woman, not even bothering to wipe the tears from his face. And Caradoc said, "Poor Morag, and it was all for this, for nothing. Truly, the gods are harsh with us."

Then Morag said, "Not for nothing now, lord. We have come for you, and we shall find the Belgae and make them into a great people again and drive the Roman dogs from our cities."

And Caradoc came close until he stood on the other side of the wall, and he looked over at them in the bright moonlight. "Morag," he said, "that is a lost dream now. It is all finished. I cannot come with you. I must stay here now until the end of my life."

And Morag stared at him as though he did not understand the words he heard. "Caradoc, Badger, come now. I have a boat waiting at the coast that will take us back by way of Spain. It is all arranged. Come now, and Beddyr will not have died for nothing."

But Caradoc shook his grey head sadly. "I cannot come with

you," he said. "I have given my word to stay with them. I am the guest of Claudius himself and live under his protection for ever."

But Morag would not listen. He said, "They have broken their word to us, Caradoc. The gods will forgive you when you break your word to them. Your oath is one between you and the Roman gods; our own gods will not hold you to it."

Caradoc smiled patiently. "They made me swear by my own gods. They would never forgive me." Then he held out his arm for them to see. A thin gash half-circled the wrist of his right arm. Morag looked closely at it and said, "You have taken a blood oath. With whom was it, Badger?"

"It was with Claudius himself," he said, "and I cannot break the blood oath."

And Morag shrank a little away from him. "You are a Roman, then," he said slowly. Caradoc smiled again, sadly, but, even through his sadness, defiant.

Then they were silent for a moment, until Morag said, "An oath under duress is valueless. Come now, Badger. I think little less of you for your oath to him. No one need know but us, and the girl is safe."

And Caradoc said, "No, Morag, I do not wish to come back. Now at last, as the summer of my life falls away, I know peace and comfort for the first time since my father cared for me. I have no wish now to go back to the hills, with the cold night winds blowing over me as I try to sleep. Now I lie in a warm bed and know that a guard stands at my door through the night. I have dreamed that dream, and it is over. I am a Roman now."

Then Morag was at him, clawing and spitting, but kept back by the wall. Caradoc stepped back, wiping his face with his silk sleeve. "Go your ways, Morag," he said. "The journey has made you overwrought. Go back to where there will be peace for you too, and forget me. Goodbye. Try to learn tolerance before you come to the funeral pyre."

And the girl, seeing the pain in Morag's face, said, "Are you a lord to follow to the death? They told me you were a man, Caradoc."

But Caradoc only laughed at her. "You are a woman and do not understand the ways of princes," he said. "Take your man away now, lest the guards hear him and come to see what wild beast has broken into the garden."

Then Morag said, "Badger, we have walked many painful miles to fetch you. Through Gaul and across the Middle Sea.

For you, my brother lies a heap of carrion in a land he did not love. On the hill above Viroconium lie all the man I ever loved. And all that was for you! Once more, will you come?"

And Caradoc said, "The Celts will destroy themselves by tribal treacheries. They are already a dead people, if they could only see it, I could not leave this place to go back and rot with them now that I have known the other way of living."

Morag said thickly, "Is that your last word, Badger?"

And the King nodded gravely. Then the moonlight caught the quick flash of Morag's hunting-knife as it flew over the low wall, and Caradoc fell back, the blood spurting from between his fingers.

In a voice that became almost a shriek, Morag shouted, "I deny you before the gods, Badger! You are a traitor to your people. Die now and pay your debt to Beddyr!"

But the King regained his balance and stood swaying on his feet, the red oozing down his face and on to the white silk of his feast-robe. "Go, Morag," he said. "Your blindness has spoiled your aim. Go, before I blow my whistle and call out the guards."

And then he spoke to Myfan, who stood trembling beside the blind man. "See that you take him to his boat," he said. "He is a wild thing, and must not be allowed to trouble peaceful citizens. Lead him away, girl, before he does himself an injury. I shall set my dogs on your track at dawn. You have till then. Go!"

Then Morag began to sob, weakly, all his strength gone with that last throw. And Myfan took him by the shoulders and led him back along the way they had come, down between garden walls, where the cypresses leaned over the lane, giving them cover.

And when she looked back, before they took the turn which would shut out the villa from their eyes, she saw that Caradoc was still there, his hand to his face, staring after them, smiling bitterly it seemed. And she pulled Morag along with all her young force, and now he was too broken to resist her any longer.

CHAPTER TWENTY-SIX

AS THE SUMMER matured, Gwyndoc slowly came back to health in his mind and in his body. Now the dreams from which he had wakened screaming in the night came less and less frequently, and he began to walk quietly, alone, without looking back over his shoulder at every step he took.

At first Ygerne would not let him out of her sight, but gradually she became confident of him once more and would let him go to watch his cattle grazing and turn back into the house where the children would be needing her attention.

The Roman administration at Viroconium had given them permission to live in the small farmhouse that lay beyond the orchards of Hall i' the Forest, on the twin conditions that Gwyndoc renounced all claims to succession as chieftain over any tribe or any body of men, and that he gave his solemn oath always to go unarmed, save during hunting, where he might carry a skinning-knife and a small deer-bow. As the adjutant had put it, when Gwyndoc reported to the garrison to take the oath, "Now you are no longer a tribesman. You are a dependent of a great military power, which reaches over half the world. You do not need weapons, my dear sir; *we* are your weapons!" And Gwyndoc had bowed his head gravely and had knelt to take the oath before the small bronze statuettes of the Roman gods, but translating them, as he spoke after the adjutant, into gods of his own. Then they had drunk a glass or two of a thin tart wine — from grapes grown in the adjutant's own vineyards, he had proudly said. And after that Gwyndoc went back to the farm, pleased that the guards at the garrison gate had given him the royal salute, although they knew they were not supposed to! It was at least some comfort to know that one's story had got round, even among the ordinary soldiers! It gave one a little backgound and helped to make one feel a real person still!

The little farmhouse lay, one-storeyed and thatched, within a circle of trees, almost in a forest glade. One path from the house turned to the left, through the trees, to the long low cattle-byre. And beyond that a little way lay the guest-house, a wooden hut set out with beds and a table and stools where travellers might rest — wanderers who might not appropriately lie in the house itself.

The other path, leading right from the house, descended steeply to the fields and the river, and it was this path which the family took when they went riding. Then Gwyndoc and Ygerne would go first, both riding white horses, followed by the two boys on small shaggy ponies. Bryn was quite a big boy for seven, and could already sit his pony well, his woollen cloak swinging behind him — a little chieftain. But Caradoc was only four and had to be strapped in his saddle with broad deer-hide thongs to keep him from jolting out of it when the ground was rough. Usually the boys rode happily together, but sometimes Bryn could hardly resist pointing out to his brother that when he was a big boy, too, he would be allowed to ride without the straps! And then little Caradoc would fly into a temper and ride at him, trying to get close enough to bite him. And sometimes, in the middle of an exciting run, the party had to halt while such a situation was straightened out. Once Gwyndoc would have flown into a violent rage at such an interruption, but now he would sit back on his horse and just laugh at the children and tease them into forgiving each other again!

And once, when Ygerne commented on this change in him, he said, "Dear one, life has been harsh enough to us all. But at last we have been given the chance of peace and love; and I will not be the first to break down the walls of such a heaven. Let the boys kiss each other again and ride on as friends! The deer can wait. There will be other, fatter deer for us to hunt before the day is out. And if there are not — why, there's always tomorrow!"

He seldom spoke crossly to the children now; in fact, Ygerne became rather concerned by his manner towards them. "Why don't you put your foot down, Gwyndoc?" she often said. "They must grow up to respect their father. You respected yours and I respected mine. We aren't any the worse for it. Besides, it throws all the work onto me! I have to slap them or send them to bed, and they think I am a cruel mother to them. Only yesterday Bryn said that he was sure I was a cruel witch and not his proper mother at all! Then for the rest of the morning he and Caradoc ran round the yard calling 'witch!' after me whenever they saw me!"

And Gwyndoc laughed and said, "Well, you are a witch, aren't you?" And she laughed too in the end, and said that he was as bad as his brats!

Usually when the household went riding, Graig and Arddog left their work as herdsmen and rode too, at the tail of the party. On them fell the work of skinning the deer after Gwyndoc had given the coup and of carrying back the tenderest part of the creature on their saddle-bows. The children spent much of their time with the two herdsmen, and Bryn especially loved Graig and often asked him about his funny broken nose and said he wished he had one like it because it looked so fierce and warlike. But it took little Caradoc some time to get used to Graig's face, and for a while Ygerne thought they would have to send the man away, the baby screamed so much when he came to the house. But Gwyndoc said that Caradoc must learn to love him; there would be harder things for the boy to do in life than that later on. And, anyway, Graig was almost a member of the family now, and it would be very wrong to send him away. Then at last, seeing Bryn so much attached to Graig, Caradoc became more daring, and in the end spent much of his time riding pick-a-back on the man's broad shoulders as he went about his work in the fields.

And sometimes Graig and Arddog would make the children little toys. Graig was a good smith, and while he was beating out a small sword for Bryn, Arddog would be carving a wooden horse and chariot for the younger boy.

Arddog was obsessed by chariots, and when Graig was teaching Bryn to use a bow he would insist on the boy standing on a log which he would sway from side to side. "You cannot call yourself a bowman until you can shoot from a moving chariot," said Arddog.

"Give the lad a chance," said Graig, "you old warhorse! There are foot-soldiers as well as charioteers!"

But Arddog shook his head. "It is only right that a chief's son should think in terms of chariots," he said.

And Graig answered, "But as things are, how do we know he will ever be a chieftain himself?"

And the other said, "We know nothing, Graig. But we have to prepare for the future we desire, nevertheless."

Sometimes the children would get very dirty or would tear their clothes when they were learning to be archers and charioteers, and then when Ygerne called them in to supper she would box their ears, and Graig and Arddog would come up too to have their ears boxed while the children watched. "It's only right," said Graig, when Arddog drew back proudly once. "She is the woman of the house, and we must submit to her. It sets a good example to the lads." So Arddog came forward and Ygerne gave him an extra hard one, but smiling as she did it.

And Bryn jumped for joy to see the leather-faced charioteer wince and clap his hand to his head, as he did.

Only once was there a break in the happiness at the farm, and that was when the children, following a stray cow, had wandered over the old battlefield on the hill. They came back that evening with the hilt of a broken sword; a hilt studded with small bosses of ivory and jet. Bryn took it to Gwyndoc, and then shrank back at the look which came over his father's face, for he thought that Gwyndoc was about to strike him with the thing. But Ygerne went forward and took the hilt and flung it far among the trees outside, so that it was lost in the grass and small bushes.

"That sword belonged to Morag," her husband said.

She took his arm. "It is broken, like Morag, like the Badger, like the past. It is no more. You must forget it now. This is a new world we live in, and the past has gone for ever."

After that the children were forbidden to go to the old battlefield. And even Graig and Arddog got cross when Bryn tried to wheedle round them to take them there.

From time to time Ygerne and Gwyndoc went up to Hall i' the Forest, leaving the men or the serving-woman to look after the children. And sometimes Gaius would call with military news at the farm. The Brigantes, he said, were in a state of unrest. It seemed that they were no longer content to serve two masters — Cartismandua and Rome. Two lots of taxes a year were too much, they argued; and besides, Rome did more for them than the old queen, who only took and took without giving back in return, as a good chief should do. It looked as though there might be trouble later in the year, as the Brigantian harvests had been none too good and supplies in Gaul had been pretty well absorbed by the Roman army there. "We're lucky to be living quietly over on this side of the country, Gwyndoc," he concluded as he rode away. And Gwyndoc smiled and said that he agreed with all his heart.

But that day he found Graig and Arddog and spent much time talking to them, urgently and almost fiercely. Ygerne came upon them, sitting on an upturned wagon in the barn, and she saw Gwyndoc's hands raised again and again as he presented his argument, and she noted the intensity of their faces as they nodded at each point he made. But when they saw her they stopped talking, abruptly, and began to look round and say that the roof needed mending before the winter rains came on. And Gwyndoc's hands stopped waving, and he called her over to them and asked her opinion about keeping goats next year.

That night she said, "What are you up to, husband?" But he only smiled at her and said, "What mischief could I be concerned in? You know I have given my word never to carry a sword again."

She was not satisfied with his answer, but she knew that it would be all she would get until he chose to tell her himself.

For a few days Ygerne's peace of mind was clouded by the secret that was being kept from her. Then she laughed at herself, thinking that she was making mountains out of molehills and that the men were probably just reliving some story again, a story in which they had perhaps been actors, a story of their dark months of slavery in the old queen's house. . . . Then other things came to take her mind from the incident. Bryn would fall and cut his knees, climbing among the boughs of the pear trees; or Arddog would run a splinter into his hand and need her attention; or Gylfa would come to the farm, with all the news from the garrison. . . .

One bright morning, they were all in the kitchen drinking the fresh milk from Gwyndoc's dairy-herd when Gylfa rode up and came indoors, her deep yellow cloak flung back from her tight-fitting long green dress. Gwyndoc noticed the gold braid in her hair and gay flush of her cheeks. But Ygerne noticed something else.

"I have brought you a basket of apples," Gylfa said. "We picked them only this morning. The children will like them." And Bryn and Caradoc whooped out of the kitchen to the door, where the great basket stood. Bryn looked at the green and the red and the gold of the fruit and said to his brother, "Apples always remind me of Aunt Gylfa. They are her colours." Then the boys sat down to eat what they could before their mother came and took away the basket.

In the kitchen Ygerne said, "We are so glad, my dear. Do you hope it's a girl, this time?"

And Gylfa said, "Yes, but I expect it will be another little boy-brat — with black hair this time, though! A little Roman! Gaius wants a lad of his own — though he's completely in love with Madoc's children. I'm quite fond of the man, you know, Ygerne. I didn't think I would be when he first took me. He was so different."

She smiled pleasantly at Arddog and Graig, who were standing with their milk-beakers in their hands, sheepishly trying not to look as though they were listening.

Then, as though to shock them still further, she said, "Of course, we Celts are a little old-fashioned in these matters! The Romans have so many curiously interesting ideas on the subject! Really, Ygerne, you should get Gwyndoc to let you come up to the hall and learn about it when Gaius has his next leave! Then perhaps you would produce a little black-haired boy to grow up with Bryn and Caradoc!"

Then Ygerne pretended to be very angry, although they could see she was laughing all the time; and she took up a small chicken that was being dressed for the table and chased Gylfa out through the door, calling her "slut!" and "Roman strumpet!" and other things that amused the herdsmen.

The children, their mouths full of apple, joined in the chase, but Gylfa was too agile for them all and reined in her horse by the wood's edge to call back, "All right, Ygerne, if that doesn't suit you, what about sending Gwyndoc up some time, and I will teach him the game!"

Then Gwyndoc, smiling, flung a Roman penny after her and she galloped away laughing; and they went back into the kitchen to think of names for the child when it should come in the new year. . . .

But towards autumn the shadow came back to Ygerne's mind, for the men began to leave the children behind and to go out together each day, riding side by side and talking in whispers. And then, at last, when Gwyndoc came to her as she was making bread one afternoon and told her that they were going to ride on a hunting trip for a few days, the men alone, she was not surprised, but more anxious than ever. She stood, with the cornflour up her arms, wiping her hands on her smock.

"When you went before," she said, "the ride came near to killing you. Have you forgotten Jagoth's irons so soon?"

But Gwyndoc smiled and said, "This is another thing, a different thing; and Jagoth is dead. I killed him."

And Ygerne said, "You are a madman. They broke your body before, and the gods have seen fit to mend it again. Next time the gods will neglect the fool who tries to destroy their handiwork. I know you are going where men will destroy you. I can read it in your face. It has been in your face since the day you were talking to the men in the barn and I came on you unawares."

Then Gwyndoc put his arm round her waist. "Ygerne," he said. "I have waited for this day since Gaius brought me from the kitchens of the old queen. I swore an oath then which I must carry out now, or I shall never be my own man again. Try to understand that this time it is different; that unless I go this time the dark places of my heart will never know light again. Try to believe that this time I leave you for a few days at the most, and that when I return I shall kneel before you and swear another oath which I shall keep as surely as I intend to keep this one — never again to leave you and the children, never again to go against whatever you wish for me, never again to call my body or my soul my own — but only Ygerne's. Will you give me your permission to go now?"

Ygerne put her hand on his head and looked at his face. She saw the long scar her stone had made when they were very young together and struggling in the stream.

"My mark is on you, Gwyndoc, isn't it?" she said. "I suppose that it might act as a charm if I prayed to the gods; charm to keep you safe from all other wounds. Yes, I will ask the gods to do that."

Gwyndoc took her floury hand and held it to his cheek. "I would rather go with your permission and laughter than without it and you in tears. For this is a joyful errand I go on, that shall make us all the happier in the years to come."

And Ygerne said nothing, but only wiped the flour from his cheek with the edge of her tunic. He rose and said, "I shall be away so short a time, I shall not wish the children goodbye, for that would trouble them. We shall rise tomorrow, early, before you are up. We have far to ride."

Then Ygerne said, "Is there a message for — anyone?"

And Gwyndoc said, "Tell Gaius that I pursue the other quarry this time, but that now only I am responsible."

The following morning she did not rise when he left the house but lay in her bed pretending to be still asleep. She heard the men outside making ready, as quietly as they could, and looked through the window as they rode away. It was a bright sunny morning, and she saw that Gwyndoc rode with his cloak open so that all men should see he did not carry a sword. But both Arddog and Graig rode with their cloaks wrapped round them as they descended the steep slope that led away to the old battle-ground and the rising sun.

CHAPTER TWENTY-SEVEN

BY EARLY EVENING on the third day Gwyndoc and his henchmen reached the neighbourhood of Evrauc. They had eaten little since they started out on their last quest, and the rough country and thick forests had tired them. So when they came within sight of the beehive huts clustering round the looming grey structure of Cartismandua's house, they halted and lay at the edge of a wood, having tethered their horses in a clearing, and watched. For they were close enough to the settlement for them to see the smoke rising from the chimney-holes in the wattle roofs and even to see the Brigantes moving about in some of their more open streets.

At the wood-side they made a meal of oat-cakes and the hard dry meat-strips which they had carried with them, for they did not dare light a fire. Arddog, looking round for nests of stray hens that might have provided eggs for them to suck, found a little stream, and they went back to it in turn, always leaving one man on watch. And since they had no cups with them they knelt down at the water's edge and lapped like dogs.

Only once did anyone from the town approach their hiding-place. Just as the first cool evening winds began to blow, two children, a boy and a girl, ran through the gates and came zig-zagging towards them, playing some chasing-game. From the colour of their hair and the similarity of the tartan tunics they wore they must have been brother and sister. As the children, laughing and shouting, headed in the direction of the wood the three men were forced to creep back under cover of the trees and to crouch in the bracken. "Little fools!" muttered Gwyndoc. "They do not know the danger they run."

"Danger for all of us," said the broken-nosed Graig, his hard face belying his anxiety, for he once had had children of his own, yellow-haired and noisy like that. He reached for his strong bow and fitted an arrow to the string. The others looked at him silently, their eyes full of fear.

Then Gwyndoc smiled again and put his hand to the arrow-head, as though holding it back. "They are going away," he said. "They have not seen us."

And Graig wiped the sweat from his forehead and said, "I owe the gods a sheaf of arrows for that!" and he gave Arddog a punch of relief that bowled him over into the fern.

When dusk fell, and few folk seemed to be stirring in the township, the three men left their spinney and made their way over the fields, slowly and cautiously, stopping at each sound of bird or beast that might be a signal from one watcher to another. As the night came down, black and moonless, they lay underneath the high wooden stockade at its nearest point to the Queen's house.

At the far corner of the settlement there were lights from fires and torches, and many voices were now singing to the accompaniment of flutes and drums. It seemed as though a tribal dance might be in progress, a celebration of one thing or another — a boy-child or a litter of black pigs. The waiting three grinned at each other. "They will soon be drunk," whispered Arddog. "Then it will be easier for us!"

Graig's broken face wrinkled. "I'd rather be getting drunk with them there than lying here shivering," he said humorously.

Arddog said, "Be quiet, you ox! You will not wish you were there when we start! Remember what you are about!" and half-seriously he took Graig by the throat and shook him, repaying him for the punch in the wood. So for a while Graig did not speak a word, but rubbed his throat carefully, where Arddog's hard fingers had pressed the gorget into his neck. He vowed he would get his own back, all the same, when they had finished the work of the night. That Arddog ought to keep his horseman's hands to himself!

Soon afterwards a villager passed within three yards of their hiding-place in the ditch. He was a tall lithe man, and from his round hide shield and long javelin he seemed to be on patrol duty round the stockade. But this night he did not seem to be very watchful. He stumbled and swayed from side to side, and once dropped his heavy shield with a clatter and had to make many attempts before he could pick it up again. As he passed the tribesmen he was laughing quietly and talking to himself in the flat nasal tone of his people. Then he stopped, slapped his thigh, shook his long spear at the sky and shambled off again.

"He has been too often to the mead-jar to be very dangerous," whispered Gwyndoc grimly. "It will be long enough before he passes us again." But as he spoke the guard whistled, a high piercing sound, and as they faced each other in alarm they heard an excited snuffling and the padding of a dog's feet. Gwyndoc looked up and saw that a hound, a great wolf-hound, had been following the patrol round the stockade.

The dog came close to them and stopped, looking in their direction and sniffing. They could see it clearly now, not many yards away, a big grey creature whose eyes shone even in the darkness.

The guard whistled again, more distant now, and as the hound began to howl Graig took careful aim and shot it through the head. Then Arddog reached out and dragged the writhing body into the ditch beside them. After a while the whistling stopped and the hound's legs ceased to thresh. The three men waited a moment longer, then they scaled the wooden wall, mounting Graig's shoulders and dragging him up after them.

Below them all was still and deserted. They dropped down into the thick grass and lay still for a moment in the shadow of the Queen's house. Then, when their breath came easily again, they rose and ran swiftly to a side-door, which they knew well enough, and so into the ante-room, without meeting anyone.

There, in the dark, the straw crackled beneath their feet and, as they moved, one of them knocked over a bench. They stood frozen for a while, hardly daring to breathe, their hearts hammering at their sides. Then, as their eyes became accustomed to the blackness, they saw a faint line of light before them, coming from below a door, and as they felt for each other before they went on, a peevish, high-pitched voiced called out from the inner room, "Who is there? Is it Glanaff? Who is it? Come in; don't stand there in the darkness like a fool! Come in, I say, and let me see you!"

The others heard Gwyndoc's vicious chuckles and the sound his sword made as it came out of its hard leather sheath. They felt him begin to move, and they pulled out their own swords and moved with him towards the line of light. And when they reached the door they kicked it open, suddenly, and stood staring into the low; dimly-lit room.

Not one of them had ever seen Cartismandua like this before. In their minds was an impressive, almost montrous effigy of power, a fierce woman whose word was law from the broad river in the south to the great hills in the north; someone infinitely strong, infinitely treacherous, infinitely deserving to die. . . . Yet, as their wild eyes searched the room, they saw no royal personage such as they had pictured in their dreams above Viroconium. The only being in the place was a hunched and shrivelled old woman who crouched on a heap of skins before the smouldering fire, a small creature, hardly bigger than a child, whose yellow lined face was turned towards them, framed by the folds of a dull-coloured cloak. And as the tribesmen looked at her, open-mouthed, the hag stretched out a quivering bony hand towards them. They saw the silver bracelets on her wrists and the gold threads woven into her tartan glittering in the firelight. This was their quarry, the old Queen Cartismandua.

The old creature's eyes were hooded, and her voice was thin and snarling. "Well," she said, "what is your business? I see that you are strangers. I even see that you are Caradoc's people. That much is in your faces! Speak up, you dolts! Tell me your message!"

She chuckled to herself for a moment, poking about in the ashes with the toe of her little shoe. Then she looked up at them again, from under the shadow of her hood, and her eyes stayed on Gwyndoc. "I seem to know you, my friend. Are you not a scullion from Caradoc's hall? And were you not in my own kitchens, on some business or other, once?"

For a while Gwyndoc smiled back at her, and his face began to work. But she went on, "Are you afraid to tell me why you are here, then? Well, shall I tell you? Yes, I will tell you, since I have long expected a visit from you. You are here to avenge the Badger and perhaps the wounds which my old friend Jagoth so rightly inflicted on you! Is it not so?" She grinned wickedly at them, and Gwyndoc stepped forward a pace and raised his sword to strike.

But the Queen held up her withered hand, and her voice was commanding. She said, "Stay! This is no occasion for haste. You have no need to fear that your mission will be interrupted. As you see, my guards have deserted me to drink in the village, or you would not be here now. They no longer obey me, but live in my house as my masters. My body-servants have left me. Even my slaves have been taken to other houses."

Her face formed itself into a ghastly grimace of irony, and she slowly uncovered her arm to the shoulder. In the firelight the men saw that the limb was half-eaten away by disease. Even Graig shuddered.

"You see now, my lords," she said, "why I do not fear your swords! Why, you are small things, tiny snapping field-mice, the wind-blown creatures of the moment. I, who move each second in death's dark shadow, cannot even force myself to fear you. What does it matter? By next sowing-time, or at the latest by snowfall, I shall have passed into freedom from this outworn, stinking body!"

Graig's eyes turned away from the grinning toothless mouth,

and Arddog began to look towards Gwyndoc, appealingly, like a dog asking to be let outside.

"Seat yourselves, gentlemen," she went on, "and warm your hands by the fire. Even I can see that you are cold — or why should you be shivering so?" She laughed slily as she spoke, and the men shuffled their feet where they stood.

Then Gwyndoc said simply, "Madam, we care not to sit by your fire. We are here to put an end to you." And he walked to her, his sword in his hand, while the others took their positions, one on either side of the door.

The old woman smiled again, more than ever like a vulture, her thin neck thrust forward from its wrappings. "Come here, my boy," she said, tired and almost gentle. "Let me see your sword, that fine instrument which will set me free for ever from this foolish and perhaps cruel old body of mine. Do not be shy now; come and let me examine your sword!"

She reached out to take the sword, and Gwyndoc sprang back, his teeth bared, the hair of his face bristling. And Cartismandua laughed, this time as loud as her dying body would let her, the tears standing in her eyes from the effort. And when she could speak again, she said, "The gods bless you, man, but I never thought to see a grown warrior afraid of what I'd do if he let me hold his sword!" Then Gwyndoc's muscles slackened, and at last he went forward sheepishly and gave his sword to the Queen, who examined it carefully and expertly. She looked first at the rough-cast bronze hilt, then ran her thumb along the notches in the scarred blade. And when she looked up again at Gwyndoc she was smiling ruefully and shaking her head. "Young man," she said, "this is a poor thing, a mere hedging tool, a rough mouth to kiss a queen's throat!" And she flung the sword at Gwyndoc's feet. As he stopped to retrive it, his face flushed with anger. "What is wrong with it, old woman?" he said. "It has killed vermin before. It is not a weapon I keep for warriors!"

For a second the old queen glared back at him, two sudden patches of colour coming into her wizened cheeks. Then her face relaxed once more, and she smiled cynically, her hands falling helplessly at her sides. "Forgive me, my lords," she said. "Sometimes, even now, I forget that I am a woman, and an old woman. I always wanted to be born a warrior, you understand. But we will let that pass. . . . The talk is of swords, and I repeat that yours is a poor one for the present purpose. Go you to that chest in the corner and bring me what you find there." And she turned painfully and pointed towards a great iron-bound box at the end of the room.

Gwyndoc looked at her in wonder, then he did as she said, and came back carrying a long bundle wrapped in calf-skin. "Unwrap it," ordered Cartismandua, and Gwyndoc obeyed her. Then he gasped with wonder and envy at what he saw: the fine, slightly curved blade was almost as long as a man might span with his arms wide-apart, and from end to end it was delicately engraved with gold-inlaid figures of running animals and huntsmen and signs, most of wh Gwyndoc did not understand. The long silver hilt was carved into the shape of an eagle, its wings outspread to form the guards. Its opal eyes flashed as Gwyndoc tried the balance of the weapon. It made his own sword feel like a piece of unshaped iron, and the old woman smiled a little ironically as she watched his face working.

"You like it," she said. "You like it as a child likes a new toy! Men are like children, yes, all of them, however remote and austere they may seem on the surface! Well, you like the sword — then use it! Use it cleanly and then keep it as a gift from Cartismandua, until such time as she meets you again — and she will, never fear! And when we meet, I will claim it from you again."

And the men looked at her in astonishment. But she went on, "I have long kept this sword for tonight's purpose. It belonged to one whom I loved many, many years ago. . . . Ah, it seems many centuries ago, when the seas were as narrow as trout streams and the great oaks sheltered from the unkind summer breezes behind blades of meadow-grass. . . . He used it well, who came to me from the rising sun, and, I promise you, it did him no dishonour! He was a true warrior, one of the greatest of them!"

As she spoke those last words her eyes ran over the travel-worn figure of the man before her, taking in his wild eyes and strained face, his tattered cloak and torn breeches. And under her gaze Gwyndoc felt nettled, as though the Queen had spoken disparagingly of him in praising her long-dead Scythian lover, and he was about to protest, but the old woman waved his words aside, shaking her head. "This is no occasion for childish quarrelling," she said. "You have work to do which is no doubt hardly to your taste. And you must return before dawn the way you came. As for me, I am a tired old woman who seldom has any company now. . . . You will remember Jagoth? He often used to come in here and sit by my fire and tell me what the slaves had been doing that day in the kitchens. . . . A kind-hearted

man, he was, though a little over-zealous when it came to prose-
cuting my orders. . . . Ah, a madman killed him one night when
he was drunk. . . . Poor Jagoth, I often told him that the mead
would kill him. . . ." And she chuckled to herself in the firelight
for a moment.

Then she said, "You have a long journey to make, so I will
not keep you. I have an even longer one. Do not forget that,
though you hate me, I am a queen."

Almost against his will, Gwyndoc gave her the royal salute
with the new sword in his hand. She acknowledged the gesture,
inclining her head. Then she said, "Please help me to rise."
Gwyndoc nodded to Arddog, who came forward and took the
Queen as gently as he could by the arms, and steadied her as she
knelt before Gwyndoc.

As she bowed her head the rick cloth fell away from her, and
the men saw that her hair had gone, leaving the skull as bare as
that of an old man, and they shuddered at the wrinkled neck.

Then Gwyndoc breathed deeply, and taking a grip on the
sword with both hands, swung it high above his head. And, as
he did so, Cartismandua spoke again, this time addressing Graig,
who stared fascinated through the rising smoke. "You with the
broken nose, entertain me! Set me off on this voyage with a
merry tale! I would die smiling!"

And Graig tried to tell a story he only half-remembered, his
tongue stumbling over the words, his voice pausing here and
there in uncertainty. Then the Queen spoke sharply again.
"Strike!" she said. "This fool wearies me! He has no manners!"
And Graig looked down, ashamed of himself, as the blow fell.

Her neck was so thin that one stroke severed the head easily,
and Gwyndoc bent swiftly to prevent the kneeling body from
falling into the fire. For a moment the three men bowed their
heads, then Gwyndoc suddenly said, "Caradoc!" and they all
smiled again.

As they walked to the door Gwyndoc turned back and laid
the long sword by the dead queen's side. "I am not allowed to
wear one, madam," he said. "Take it with you. I have no wish
to meet you again where you might come to claim it!"

And as he spoke to her he felt so weary that it seemed to him
she had suddenly become young and beautiful again. She lay
with a quiet smile on her flushed face, long black hair tumbling,
it seemed, about her white shoulders. . . . Then it seemed to
Gwyndoc that a bird broke out of her slightly parted lips, a
linnet, which wheeled about the room for a moment and then

flew up through the smoke to the chimney-hole and out into the night.

And when he had seen this, he turned, and the three went through the door, two of them carrying swords in their hands. And in the ante-room many guards stood, staring past them, through the open door, at the body of their queen. And as the three walked forward the warriors fell back, their eyes averted, and let them pass unmolested.

Then, as they untethered their horses in the wood outside the town, they looked back and saw the great flames rising from the Queen's house and glowing in the sky. And from the clustered huts round about the palace there seemed to come the sound of joyful singing and cries of merriment. So they rode away to the west.

Then on the afternoon of the second day they came to more open country, where the rock struck through the soil and few trees grew, and as the sun sank before them Gwyndoc reined in his horse. "My friends," he said, "this is where you must leave me. I can offer you no more than a herdsman's life from now on. A cow's life among the beasts of the byre. But you are men, young men still, and your swords are still your own. Go to the south, both of you, and take service with Rome. There lies your only hope, now that the tribes are broken."

And the men began to argue, saying that they loved Gwyndoc's children and were content to be herdsmen and have him as their overlord. But he replied, "Go and get children of your own again and watch them grow. As for me, I wish to be no man's overlord again. I wish to think for no man, and to pay no man, and to love no man. Go, my friends, I say, and leave me in peace."

Then they saw that his mind was made up, and they dismounted and kissed his hand and said that they would come at his call, wherever they might be, whoever they might be serving, while there was breath in their bodies. But he only smiled at them and waved again and again as he watched them riding south along the valley. And they looked back and saw him sitting there on his white horse, with his greying hair blown back in the evening breeze. And Graig said to his companion, "There is a man who should have been a king."

And Arddog answered, "Yes, but he lacks one thing — resolution. He would have been a king for but a short while, then others would have dragged him down. Perhaps he is happier as a follower, not as a leader of men."

And when they were out of sight Gwyndoc turned his horse towards the west again. And as he did so, a strange thing happened; it seemed that, out of the corner of his eye, a long shadow thrown by the setting sun had come to his side, and it was the shadow of a big dog or a wolf. But when he turned his head to see, there was nothing there, and he rode on into the sunlight.

Then as the darkness fell he came to a small inn set on a hillside, and pushing open the swinging door he went in. At the long table in the middle of the room, his eyes shaded from the light by his black hood, sat Morag. When Gwyndoc entered, the thin lips smiled in recognition, as though he had expected his enemy to come. For a moment Gwyndoc stood in the doorway. Then he spoke. "Are you alone, Morag?" he said. And the other nodded his head, and then indicated a place at the table so that, for very pride, Gwyndoc was forced to sit beside him. Then Morag called to the kitchens and a young girl brought them both drink in long bull's horns. Gwyndoc noticed that she was pretty, but rather heavy in the jaw for beauty. "She must bring much trade to the place," he said, trying to appear unconcerned. But Morag merely looked at him steadily and smiled. "Why do you not wear a sword?" he said.

CHAPTER TWENTY-EIGHT

IT WAS SEVEN days since Gwyndoc and the herdsmen had left the farm. In the bower of Hall i' the Forest, Gaius looked seriously across the table at Ygerne. "We shall have to go through some form of trial," he said. "The Queen was murdered and Gwyndoc was identified with the others as he came from the room."

And Gylfa said, "But don't be so solemn, Gaius; you know that you can arrange these things. After all, you are the commander here."

"This is something different," said Gaius. "The murder was committed outside my territory and cannot be hushed up. It is a queen this time, and one who was at least theoretically on the side of Rome. This is not a simple matter of a slave-master, killed in a fit of anger. The Senate will have heard by now, and since Gwyndoc was under my immediate care I shall be asked why I allowed him to go."

Gylfa smiled. "But how silly you are," she said. "He is a grown man. How could you have stopped him!"

In spite of himself, Gaius had to laugh too. "Really, Gylfa," he said, "you don't seem to understand that I am a Roman soldier, under immediate orders from Rome, many hundreds of miles away. And you, all of you — yes, even you my dear — are the conquered people who must obey Rome, through me! Had I been a little older, a little less foolish, I should have placed Gwyndoc under arrest, or at least have set guards on his door and forbidden him to leave the farm."

"But that would have been most unreasonable," said Gylfa. "Sometimes I think you Romans have got stones where your hearts should be!"

"Do you?" said Gaius, taking her by the arm.

"No," she said. "But it is all so stupid. What has he done? Killed an old queen who had betrayed his overlord. Yes, an old woman whose people wanted her out of the way. And Rome, too!"

Gaius nodded. "The position is actually more fantastic than you make it out to be. You see, the Senate decided weeks ago that if the unrest in Brigantia did not die down soon they would take her away and — well, dispose of her, unless natural death saved them the trouble of getting a herdsman!"

"Well, can't that be argued on Gwyndoc's behalf?" said Ygerne.

Gaius shook his head. "No," he said. "That is a military secret, and when you go out of this room, you must forget it."

"How can she do that, you silly boy," said Gylfa. "Come on, now, and begin to make a plan for Gwyndoc. Ygerne and I will be extremely cross with you and your foolish garrison if you can't do something about it. Go and search for him, or something, then bring him back here and let him lie low till the fuss has died down" She saw the refusal in the Roman's face. "All right," she went on, "let him come home and we'll disguise him and give him a fresh name, and he can pretend to be a groom at Hall i' the Forest, and go home to sleep at nights."

"But I would know that he was not a groom," said Gaius. "We must find him, yes, but then I must arrest him, and he must take his chance. I will get him good advocates, and perhaps he may escape with a comparatively slight punishment. But I am afraid the best we can hope for is five years in the galleys."

Ygerne began to sob. "I could not bear him to be away as long as that. It would be terrible; he has already been away so long and suffered so much. The children would almost be grown up by the time he got back."

Gaius came across to her and put his hand on her shoulder. "You must be quite logical about this, Ygerne," he said. "Gwyndoc has done something very serious. By rights he should himself be killed for it. But I believe we can save him from that — although I am not sure whether I shall be left to see him through his troubles; it is likely that I may myself be punished for letting him go. They may even put me in the galleys. One never knows with the Senate these days. But we must be logical and, above all, brave. I pledge my word to do the best for both of us in this matter. I cannot say more."

And Gylfa said, "Stay the night here. You are in an overwrought state. We could give each other comfort if you stayed."

But Ygerne said, "No, I cannot stay. The children will be waiting for me. And I want to be in my own home to think about this thing tonight. I must leave you. Perhaps I shall come back in the morning to see if Gaius has anything more to say."

Then Gaius buckled on his cloak and escorted her to the edge of the wood and kissed her tenderly before she left him. "Have courage," he said. "I feel that there is a special god who looks over Gwyndoc. I feel sure that you will see him again before very long, and somehow I think that he will stay with you this time."

And his words comforted Ygerne by their strange power, and she went indoors, unreasonably hopeful in view of all that had been said.

In the kitchen the serving-woman met her and said, "We have guests tonight, lady. Two of them; an old man and a young boy. They are singers, I think, on their way to Ireland and the halls of the chieftains."

Ygerne heard little Caradoc crying out in his sleep from the other room and knew that she must go to him. She hardly heard what the woman had said. "I must go to the boy," she said. Then a thought struck her. "Is the old man — Roddhu?" she asked. The woman looked back at her in fear. "May the gods protect us, lady! But I do not think so. This one is quieter, almost gentle, and walks with his head down, nearly helpless."

Ygerne asked, "What is the boy like?" And the woman answered, "A foolish dark-haired young thing — more like a girl than a lad! Not one to rob the nests in the night, I feel sure."

So Ygerne went into the sleeping-room to quieten Caradoc, but the child seemed strangely feverish and troubled in his mind.

It was hard for Ygerne herself to sleep that night. As she lay on her tumbled bed of heather and sheepskins, the moon seemed to shine directly on to her face. She tried to bury her head under the coverlet, but the night was so warm that she gasped for want of breath before long and had to throw back the covers. And all the time her brain echoed and re-echoed with the words, "Caradoc is avenged, but Gwyndoc must go to the galleys! The Badger is free, but the Otter is a prisoner!" Try as she might, she could not control this insane message as it rolled back and forth in her mind, like a log of rotting wood caught in the swirling backwaters of a stream.

And, as though sensing her uneasiness, the children began to mutter in their sleep, tossing and turning in their bed at the other side of the room. Then suddenly Bryn whimpered and cried out in fear, "Mother, oh, Mother, the wolves have red eyes!" Ygerne left her bed and went to the child, soothing him and tucking him again under the sheepskins. "Lie still," she said. "Lie quiet, little Bryn, or you will waken Caradoc now!" And when the child had fallen back into sleep, she left him and clambered wearily back into her own bed. And after an eternity she almost relaxed into sleep, for the moon's mad light was overcast now by a cloud of strange beast-like shape — the shape of a black dog or a wolf. . . .

Then all at once Ygerne was startled back into a full awareness by a dog's howling. It started somewhere among the huts, by the riverside, and then moved slowly up the wooded paths until it seemed right outside the door of the house. Then it was silent for a while and Ygerne almost settled down to sleep again, until the howl started again. And then it did not seem to leave the house.

The clouds had moved from the moon now; and the bright silver light flooded the room. When Ygerne could bear the howling no longer, she rose and looked out of the little window, to see whether she could drive the creature away. The stockyard was as clear as day, every stick and stone stood out brightly. Even the bee-hives at the far end of the meadow were visible through a break in the trees, white in the white light. But there was no dog.

And, as the noise continued, the girl went back to her bed, the skin at the nape of her neck prickling with fear. Then the howling stopped again, and soon there was an urgent snuffling at the door. But this time Ygerne was afraid to stir from her bed, and when she heard the claws scraping at the doorsteps she

pulled the clothes over her head again and lay shuddering.

Then, half-stifled, she fell into a troubled sleep of sorts, dreaming painfully of Gwyndoc and the wolves and the bright moonlight. From time to time she came back to consciousness and listened, almost exhausted now with anxiety. And every time she heard the sound she expected to hear; nor did the whining and the scratching cease until the dawn broke over the grey hills. Then Ygerne fell off into a deep sleep, and although the children woke and cried for her, she did not hear them.

When she woke at last, the sun was standing high in the blue sky, and Bryn had carried his little brother out into the garden to play among the flowers. Ygerne fed them quickly, hardly noticing whether they ate or not. Then she went out, towards the guest house, fearful but curious, wondering whether the two wanderers of last night might still be there, wondering whether either of them had any news of Gwyndoc.

But as she approached she saw with misgiving that the door of the wooden hut was swinging wide open. At first she told herself that the guests had tired of waiting for her to greet them and had perhaps gone walking among the farm-buildings until she came. But when she entered the hut she saw that her guess had been a mistaken one. The room was empty and the table left almost as it had been the night before. The beds were un-ruffled, as though they had not been slept in after all.

For a moment Ygerne wondered whether she had dreamed it all, whether she had spoken to the serving-woman in her night-mare, and not in reality, when she came back from Hall i' the Forest. But, as she looked round, something on the table caught her eye, and she knew then that she had not been dreaming.

It was a bundle, a bag of some sort, made of a rough, home-spun tartan, and it was a Belgic tartan. It lay in the middle of the great wooden meat-dish, as though the travellers had been anxious that she should not miss it. Ygerne went to the table and took up the bundle. It was quite heavy, a present, perhaps, for her hospitality. The girl felt all round it, but could not make up her mind what it was; yet, as her hands explored it through the thick cloth, there was something familiar in its shape that seemed to strike a nameless chord in her memory. Something she almost knew by instinct but which she dared not give a name to.

Then, with the strange fear on her, she carried the bundle to and door and sat down on a stone to open it. And when her trembling fingers had stripped off the cloth and the wrappings of sheepskin she saw that the bundle contained only a head, severed just below the jaw-bone. The hair was filthy with mud and blood and was quite white; many of the teeth had gone from the grinning mouth, and the eyelids were black.

It was many minutes before Ygerne could make herself say that this was Gwyndoc's head, for there was hardly anything about it that she had known, except the long shallow cut across the cheek where she had struck him, many centuries ago, with a stone she had plucked from the stream.

So she sat, wordless, her eyes dry of tears; and her cold fingers stroked the furrowed cheek again and again, and she swayed gently beside the swinging door. And she heard nothing until the sun had become red again and was sinking once more behind the hills at the back of the house. Then Bryn came, hobbling along the stony path in his bare feet towards her, staring like a bright-eyed bird, his head on one side, at what she held in her lap.

And when he could speak, he said falteringly, "Mother, it has been a terrible day! All the bees have been swarming!" And he had to say his words many times before his mother seemed to hear him. And when she looked up at him he could hardly recognise her face. But her voice was calm again now, and she even smiled at him when she spoke. "Yes, little Bryn," she said. "Yes, they always do. That is because no one told them that the master of the house was dead."

And as the little boy backed away from her, she said the same words over and over and over again, smiling all the time.

ACKNOWLEDGEMENTS

For Gwyndoc's verse in Chapter Three, describing Ygerne, I am deeply indebted to the Chapter, *Culhwch and Olwen,* in the translation of *The Mabinogion,* by Gwyn Jones and Thomas Jones (Dent). I have adapted their words only slightly in this passage.

For the incident of the head, in Chapter Twenty-eight, I went back to the Scots story which tells how the forester, Drummond of Drummondernoch, suffered a similar fate at the hands of the Macdonalds, who left his head on a dish in the house of the dead man's sister, Mrs. Stewart of Ardvorlich.

I have often taken liberties with those names which have a Roman version, usually by omitting the Latin termination, which gives these names a less musical, more barbaric sound — an effect which I felt justified in trying to obtain in view of the nature of this story.

H.T.

SAVOY BOOKS LTD

279 Deansgate,
Manchester M3 4EW
England

All prices subject to alteration

Other Henry Treece Titles
from Savoy Books

THE GOLDEN STRANGERS
(125mm x 193mm)

Set at a vital cross-roads in history, this is the story of a young prince of the dawn world — Garroch — who tries to repel the invasion of Britain by the Golden Strangers. It shows the triumph of the fair-haired nomads of the north with their savage sun-worship, over the small dark Neolithic men of the South — the Iberians.

224pp. £1.25 Paperback
ISBN 0 86130 018 1

THE DARK ISLAND
(125mm x 193mm)

A further novel of Britain set during the
Roman invasion before Christianity has
asserted itself, and when the island is
torn and divided by successive raiders
from abroad. The time is ripe for
warriors and kings to prove their
heroism, and, as usual, this book is
written as though by an eye-witness of
the times, vividly evoking bye-gone
characters and settings, and told with a
narrative force and a language that is
both typically rich and masterful.

240pp £1.25 Paperback
ISBN 0 86130 021 1

RED QUEEN, WHITE QUEEN
(125mm x 193mm)

RED QUEEN, WHITE QUEEN is set
before the collapse of Rome: Queen
Boadicea rises against the might of the
Imperial Legions to become the true,
if brief Queen of the British people. It
is a rebellion so bloody and brutal that
Rome itself is shaken, fearing the
complete overthrow of its empire by a
rash of uprisings.

£1.25 Paperback
ISBN 0 86130 020 3

Harlan Ellison from Savoy Books

THE GLASS TEAT
(210mm x 148mm)

THE GLASS TEAT is the first volume of Harlan Ellison's powerful television criticism. First published as a series of outspoken columns for the Los Angeles Free Press this book and its companion volume THE OTHER GLASS TEAT form a record of three years of fiery tv monitoring. But Ellison isn't content to remain *inside* the tube: tv is about the world we live in, and so is THE GLASS TEAT. His intimacy with every aspect of tv production, his strong personal response to subjects which concern him and his encompassing vision make this book entertainment and criticism of the highest order.

224pp. £1.25. Paperback.   ISBN 0 86130 004 1.

PHOENIX WITHOUT ASHES
(With Edward Bryant)
A novel of the Starlost
(210mm x 148mm)

Eight centuries in mankind's future a great ark has been constructed to ferry earth's cultures to a distant star system. After several generations have elapsed an accident occurs which causes the colossal ship to alter course — and plunge towards destruction. This fine and compelling adaptation of Ellison's award-winning television script — with its optimistic ending — is treated to Savoy's arresting new "laser light" cover design.

128pp. £1.25. Videoback.   ISBN 0 86130 003 3.

Jack Trevor Story from Savoy Books

LIVE NOW, PAY LATER
(193mm x 125mm)

In the first book of the famous Albert Argyle trilogy the ace conman of the sixties and prince Tally-boy of Jack Trevor Story's provincial town catches the housewives and the reader fast in the grip of Hire Purchase, devious politics and easy payments.   144pp

£1.25 Paperback ISBN 0 86130 029 7
£4.95 Hard Case ISBN 0 86130 030 0

SOMETHING FOR NOTHING
(193mm x 125mm)

The market seems to be dropping out of Hire Purchase and so Albert Argyle switches to Trading Stamps. Never without a woman, superbly, raffishly, entertainingly ruthless. But you can't get something for nothing.   176pp

£1.25 Paperback ISBN 0 86130 031 9
£4.95 Hard Case ISBN 0 86130 032 7

THE URBAN DISTRICT LOVER
(193mm x 125mm)

Jack Trevor Story takes his character to meet his maker in a hilarious, incisive last book written with superb observation, sympathy and wit.   192pp

£1.25 Paperback ISBN 0 86130 033 5
£4.95 Hard Case ISBN 0 86130 034 3

THE TROUBLE WITH HARRY
The classic novel filmed by Alfred Hitchcock
(125mm x 193mm)

Who's Harry?
Harry's a menace from the moment he
turns up on the Heath. For one long
hot, maddening day he invades the lives
of the inhabitants of the Sparrowswick
Bungalow Estate, terrifying young Abie,
puzzling the Captain, menacing Miss
Gravely the spinster . . .
No-one knows what to do with him.
THE TROUBLE WITH HARRY is he's
an embarrassment. The trouble with
Harry is he's dead.

£1.25 Paperback
ISBN 0 86130 035 1

JACK ON THE BOX
(125mm x 193mm)

Jack Trevor Story, writer, eccentric and
star of his own television series, JACK
ON THE BOX, is renowned for his
idiosyncratic approach to life, his hatred
of bureaucracy and his unflagging
rejection of the obvious. In this volume
of short pieces he lures the reader into
his own eclectic and highly personal
universe, centred somewhere on the
edge of Hampstead Heath, some time in
the 1970's, and presided over by the
lovely Maggie (and her ghost). Why is
Jack falling into the river, fully clothed?
Who is Kaiser Konrad and why did he
announce his own death by telegram?
Will Maggie ever return from Belgium?
JACK ON THE BOX is fully illustrated
with photographs from the ATV series,
and is the first in Savoy's ten-book-
package-launch of Jack Trevor Story's
most famous and best-loved novels.
160pp plus 4pp art inserts. £1.25 Paperback., ISBN 0 86130 025 4

Other Titles from SAVOY BOOKS

KISS
by Robert Duncan.
(125mm x 193mm)

Rock's arcane heavies give the low down
on the band who rose out of Brooklyn
to stamp a new style of heavy rock'n'roll
on a world gone soft at the poles.
Illustrated.

£1.25 Paperback
ISBN 0 86130 040 8

SCREWRAPE LETTUCE
by Jack Trevor Story.
(125mm x 193mm)

Number seven in Savoy's series of Jack
Trevor Story novels. "The book is
volatile, grotesque, brilliantly messy —
like watching a diamond burst in the
hands" — The Sunday Times. Illustrated.

£1.50 Paperback
ISBN 0 86130 038 6

Michael Moorcock from Savoy Books

THE RUSSIAN INTELLIGENCE
(193mm x 125mm)

Michael Moorcock's hilarious comic detective thriller sequel to *The Chinese Agent* continues with the further half-cocked investigations of super sleuth Jerry Cornell. Cornell follows the mysterious clue given to him by "The Devil Rider", a vengeful character from one of Wayflete's comic strips, and quickly finds himself in the thick of espionage at a quiet Soviet ambassadorial residence in Notting Hill Gate. But he is more concerned about the "Tail" that has been put on him — by his wife. A new novel from the pen of Britain's best imaginative writer, introduced by novelist Jack Trevor Story.

160pp £1.25. Paperback. ISBN 0 86130 027 0

THE GOLDEN BARGE
(210mm x 148mm)

Pursuing an impossible goal and hounded by dark dreams which drive him to cold-hearted murder, Jephraim Tallow seeks the meaning of life in a wild and intense world. Moorcock's first anti-hero predates the creation of the world-famous Elric of Melniboné by 12 months in a classic novel that combines the elements of symbolism and fantasy as masterfully as Peake or T. H. White. The high quality, 3-D "Video-back" packaging of this very first Michael Moorcock novel follows Savoy's trendsetting design for PHOENIX WITHOUT ASHES by Harlan Ellison.

224pp. £1.25 Videoback. ISBN 0 86130 002 5

SOJAN
(125mm x 193mm)

Moorcock's first Sword & Sorcery
hero now in print for the first time in
20 years, with superb new illustrations
by leading fantasy artist James
Cawthorn.

160pp. £0.80 Paperback.
SBN 0 86130 000 9.

STORMBRINGER
Adapted by James Cawthorn
(427mm x 305mm)

Brilliantly drawn in powerful black
and white, this very large format
illustrated version of Moorcock's
famous fantasy novel tells how Elric,
last Emperor of Melniboné, battled
with the hordes of Chaos, summoning
the Lords of Law to fight for Earth.

80pp. £1.00 Paperback.
SBN 0 7045 0226 7.

JEWEL IN THE SKULL
Adapted by James Cawthorn
(335mm x 244mm)

Containing Cawthorn's finest artwork,
this is the first story in the famous
Dorian Hawkmoon series, and tells of
the warrior-duke's fight to save himself
from the power of the Black Jewel.

80pp. £2.95. Paperback
SBN 0 86130 0068.

Mike Harding from Savoy Books

UP THE BOO AYE, SHOOTING POOKAKIES
(125mm x 193mm)

Illustrated in colour and black and white by Roger McPhail.

Paperback £1.95.
ISBN 0 86130 039 4